LEARNING
COULDN'T BE
MORE FUN.

The PERFECT LESSONS

BETH GELMAN

The Perfect Lessons

Summary: Trudie is attending a psychology conference when she walks into a wall of hard pecs and abs named Dr. Alexander Pierce. The nationally acclaimed psychologist specializing in childhood trauma, who looks like a Grecian god, will be her lecturer all week.

Too bad he's not half as humble as he is smart.

His superiority complex inadvertently puts Trudie on the defensive. When he challenges her, she pushes something he certainly didn't plan on happening this week—or ever.

They both leave the conference happy that they'll never see each other again...that is, until Dr. Pierce walks into Trudie's middle school on his first day as a consultant. Not only will they be coworkers, but they will work together intimately every day.

Trudie needs a teacher to heal her past emotional wounds. Alex needs a reason to get off his high horse. They'd better find a way to work out their differences, or the consequences could be devastating.

THE PERFECT LESSONS

The Perfect Lessons explores life's more colorful intimacies—their steamy romance will leave you panting with pleasure—all while getting to the heart and soul of what makes us happy.

This is the second book in The Perfect Series by Beth Gelman. They are written as stand-alone novels and can be read in any order. This is a cliffhanger.

[1. Romance 2. Contemporary romance 3. Romantic comedy 4. Teacher love story 5. Healing love story]

First Edition

Contents

Dedication

Nothing comes from nothing.
Nothing ever could.
So, somewhere in my youth,
or childhood,
I must have done something,
Something good.
The Sound of Music, *Richard Rodgers & Oscar Hammerstein*

Chapter 1
TRUDIE

WHEN I CLICKED *ACCEPT* on my registration in January and committed myself to another psychology conference, I never dreamed it would start out this way. Kissing strange, beautiful men years younger than me didn't exactly fit my school's approved teacher behavior profile. But, boy, was it fun.

This was the fifth conference I'd attended since I became a middle school teacher five years ago. This niggle that I had to get to the heart of my issues kept me returning each year. I hadn't been physically abused or neglected (nothing like that, thank God). Yet, some of the emotional trauma I sustained as a child lingered in my psyche, and I was determined to do whatever it took to eradicate it from my life.

My trauma was due to proximity, or lack thereof, as it related to my father. He was a CAT adjuster. Yeah, no one knew what that was. I didn't until I was twelve. He was the guy insurance companies hired to assess the damage from hurricanes, tornadoes, forest fires, and the like. One ring of the phone and he was gone—sometimes a week, sometimes longer. The longer he was gone, the greater the disaster at home when he returned. Thus, therapy and psychology conferences. Lots and lots and lots of them.

This year, the conference was in San Francisco, and I was hyped to spend a few extra days afterward seeing the sights. I booked a day trip to Yosemite, leaving at the buttcrack of dawn to see the giant sequoias, and I considered a sunset cruise on San Francisco Bay but thought it might be awkward to go alone. I hated looking desperate. Most of the time, I found like-minded people at the conferences who would hang around after the workshops were finished to check out the sights. However, being back in the dating world. I was out of practice, and honestly, I wasn't even sure what I was looking for.

Had men changed much in the six years I was dating Sam? Social media was rife with ways to attract people to be with. But did I really want to "be" with someone or hook up? It was just too confusing. Ruby, my friend from college, always said, "Have no expectations, have no broken heart." How does one date or hook up without expectations? I wasn't opening my vajayjay to some pervert or rando to get off. I had standards! I wanted to know their name first and maybe see current STD test results.

The fact remained that I wanted to walk away from a tryst and feel good about it, not dirty—unless, of course, I discovered I liked being a dirty girl. But seriously, that guy would have to be a god. In the meantime, I took Ruby's suggestion and kept my expectations low, hoping to be pleasantly surprised when that guy found my G-spot in the first ten minutes—not six years.

Registration for conferences always happened six months before the event, so when it was time to leave for San Francisco, I had almost forgotten about it and scrambled to find everything I needed for the trip.

My apartment was tiny—like tiny house tiny. Four hundred square feet didn't even feel big when nothing was in the place. It was a temporary situation for now, but it was much better than living at home like I had to after college, and it was mine. I hung the flowy canary yellow drapes well below the windows to make the room look taller. That's what the home shows said to do. There wasn't much in the way of furniture—did I mention I was a poor middle school teacher—but my decor was on point. I had managed to fit in a couch that faced the window overlooking a pond stocked with lily pads, a side table sporting a green glass vintage lamp with a floral shade, and a nearly matching oversized ottoman for my aching feet. I had passed on a dining set since I landed in front of the TV most evenings when I wasn't with Sam. My sweet, kind, generally dull in the bedroom, and now ex-boyfriend, Sam. Sadly, I didn't miss spending time with him.

Sam and I had dated for six years. We started in college, and like most first loves, he swept me off my feet, feeding me slices of pizza while we snuggled on the couch watching scary movies. We did a lot of hiking in the Upper Peninsula of Michigan and had a blast on a Spanish club spring break trip to Cancun. I probably partied on the beach more than immersing myself in the culture. (And yes, it was my own culture since my family was Mexican, but we were very "Americanized.") The class was an easy A, and I knew enough to find a bathroom, ask for dessert, or swear at someone.

From what I knew of kissing, Sam was a good kisser and an attentive lover. He was new and fun, and we had many things in common. Still, it turned into the most predictable, boring, and vanilla love life I could imagine over the years. Thinking he was "the one" was laughable, yet I kept dating him long after college. The dealbreaker had come two months earlier when he announced he was taking a new position in Colorado and wanted me to join him. Honestly, it was an easy decision—the saddest part was throwing away a six-year investment. Romance novels would have to pick up the slack in the bedroom department, along with my trusty vibrator, Big Ben. I could always count on him—unless his batteries died.

I needed to keep the past in the past. I focused all my energy on packing, grabbing my toiletries, shoving them into my big purple suitcase, and then picking out a few practical outfits to wear during the professional workshops. I also chose a long black and red fitted dress that showcased a sexy kick-pleat along the back hem and a low-cut back that bordered on risqué to wow the crowd at the evening gala and a few flirtier casual outfits for tootling around the city at night, and I was good to go.

My rental car was waiting outside my chic apartment building. This place was a massive upgrade from the one I had out of college and was only a few miles from the busy expressway I traveled daily to get to work. The apartment itself was a standard two-bedroom arrangement. The second bedroom was too small for a bed but a great place to set up a yoga mat, a desk for writing lesson plans, and a comfy overstuffed chair for reading that I had found at a secondhand store in a quaint city a few miles away. But the best part of this place was the courtyard with a meditation fountain and a cherry blossom tree that took your breath away each springtime. A couple of wood-slatted benches and plastic Adirondack chairs sat in a circle around a firepit on the opposite side of the space. I took every opportunity to go there to clear my head, grounding myself as I maneuvered through life's obstacle course.

The ride to the airport was uneventful. However, when I arrived, gorgeous men kept appearing before my eyes while I checked my bags. My imagination jumped into high gear looking at these ripped young men with bulging arms, high cheekbones, full lips, and tight asses. I thought I was hallucinating when one of the hotties locked eyes with me and gave me a sexy smile, making me blush. I was about to say something when I heard a loud "Next," so I gave a little one-finger wave and walked up to the ticket counter.

When I finally reached my seat on the plane, I let out a deep sigh. I thought back to those guys at the ticket counter and chastised myself for even thinking about hooking up with one of them. I mean, I could have—I was young enough, and I had some nice assets, but let's face it, I was almost ten years older than most of them, and it just seemed like a male-bait situation. Regardless, I was headed out to find some answers about myself at this conference, and I needed to stay focused.

The overhead speaker called passengers to attention and to buckle up. As I snapped my belt into place, a large body plopped down next to me.

"Hello, again." A deep voice melted over me. *Mmm.*

I looked up to see the source of that yummy greeting and was paralyzed when I recognized the hottie from the ticket counter. His sexy smile gleamed as he drove his large hands through his tousled, dirty-blond hair.

Oh, shit!

"Uh, hi," I said, squishing my face into an awkward smile. A very attractive look, I'm sure.

He chuckled. "I guess we're traveling to the same place. This four-hour trip is looking better and better every minute." He used his foot to push his backpack under the seat before him and tucked a neck roll behind his head. It looked comfortable—why did I always forget to buy one of those?

My head nodded like one of those drinking bird toys, only not controlled by gravity but by the awkwardness I felt.

"Yeah, it's a long one." Silence. Awkward silence. *Come on, Trudie, you need to practice your game before you meet someone who really interests you.*

I brushed my auburn hair behind my ear and started again.

"So, what do you have planned in San Francisco?" Better.

He pivoted in his chair to get a better look at me. The flight attendant sashayed down the aisle behind him, asking him to sit facing forward for takeoff. He shifted back with a slight huff.

"Soccer training camp. I play for my university, and they send us to one of these international training camps for a week each year to prepare us for higher-level play. We used to play in the fall, but the NCCA voted to move our season to spring, so now we have an extended training schedule. No rest for the weary," he added.

I would be pissed if I didn't have three months off during the summer, but he seemed easygoing about it. As a teacher, summers were sacred. We worked our asses off during the school year, and when the bell rang in June, it was a race to our cars.

Years ago, during a takeoff, I had created a ritual of praying to the Almighty in case she was listening. Just a few prayers—to send wisdom for the pilot to land the plane safely and to send a mental blanket of white light all over me and the other passengers to bring us peace and safety while in the air. I know it sounded a little bonkers, but it has worked every time so far, so it has stayed a part of my travel routine.

I may have said some of it out loud instead of in my head since my flight buddy was eyeing me suspiciously. Thinking out loud had maybe gotten me in trouble once before. Maybe.

"You doing okay?"

"Uh, yeah. Did I say something out loud?" I asked, paranoid.

"Yeah. You did. Not a fan of flying, huh?" He helped me out.

"Did the white knuckles tip you off? Takeoffs are the worst. I'll be fine in a few minutes." I closed my eyes and tried to calm myself down. I added "mortified" to my list of issues this trip.

I was going through my prayers again, inside my head, and engaging in a breathing technique to settle myself when I felt a large, warm hand wrap around my white-knuckled one, choking the seat rest. I'm not going to lie. It felt good. Safe. Protected. All those elusive things I wanted in my life. I opened my eyes slowly, tilting my head, then back up toward our entwined hands and then back to his face.

He smiled nervously. "Is this okay?"

If I hadn't been such a head case then, I'd have considered this a violation of my personal space, but his strong reassurance left me taking my first full breath since I had walked onto this bird, so I nodded my head appreciatively.

He continued. "Good. What's your name? I'm Jared." He squeezed my hand gently.

Why was I coming up with reasons not to engage with this guy? He could know my name. I doubt he was a stalker who would hunt me down after this flight. *Just give him your fucking name!*

"Trudie," I blurted out. "It's Trudie," I whispered a second time.

I stared at his lips a little too long, I think, because he leaned his head forward, almost touching our foreheads together, and whispered, "Don't worry, I've got you. Whatever you need, I'll take care of it for you." His tone insinuated a lot more than he was saying. As his breath warmed my face, his eyes twinkled, presumably hoping to alleviate *any* discomfort I might have on this flight. I blushed at his innuendo and then looked out the window for a moment of relief.

What do you say to a guy who was that forward? I mean, it wasn't that I wouldn't want him to kiss me, touch me, or ask me to visit him in the restroom, but I didn't know who this guy was or what diseases he was walking around with. And maybe it was ridiculous to think that was what he intended to do, even if my deranged mind wanted him to.

Chapter 2

ALEXANDER

EVERY SUMMER, MY FAMILY traveled to a family beach house in the Hamptons, which had been handed down from patriarch to patriarch for the past eighty years. The house was a one-hundred-and-twenty-year-old Victorian mansion originally owned by some railroad tycoon and then purchased for a song before WWI by my family. From there, it has been handed down from patriarch to patriarch over the past one hundred years. Suffice it to say, I came from money. Stupid money. And all the prestige and pompous bullshit that comes with it. Which was why I would have done anything not to have to attend my parents' annual summer gala to raise scholarship money for underprivileged inner-city children. The cause was great, but it reeked of absolution for their obscene amount of money and the conveniently significant tax deduction they got for helping those "less fortunate souls."

I stood by year after year with my two sisters, acting like the perfect children from the perfect family, while I resented being used as a puppet to make my family's foundation look good. Trust me, I'm no saint, and quite frankly, if my parents knew half of what I did, they would disown me. This was why I jumped at the opportunity when I was asked to be the keynote speaker at the West Coast Psychology Specialists Conference in San Francisco the weekend of the gala.

I didn't follow in my father's footsteps, much to his chagrin. I was an intellectual—more interested in what drove my parents to do the shit they did than perpetuating it in another generation. I wanted to know why they turned out the way they did and how their marriage stood the test of time, given that they hated each other. We had that in common: I hated them, too. Well, it wasn't actually *hate* hate—it was an obsessive wish not to be around them. They didn't exactly exploit us in the way so many billionaire parents did. Still, the passive-aggressive way they got what they wanted from me and my sisters made me very wary of anyone else's personal agenda. I learned from a young age that unless someone walked the walk and talked the talk about what they believed, they were fakes and phonies. At my ripe old age of forty-two, I could spot those fakes a mile away, and I loved nothing more than exposing them for who they were.

I was attending this conference as *the* expert in my field of study. I had a doctorate in psychology emphasizing childhood trauma, and I would be celebrated when I got there.

A diverse array of people were coming together to hear the truth, from my perspective, about the impact of childhood trauma on adults and how the manifestation of these issues could be eliminated from their lives.

It's not that I was full of myself (at least I didn't think I was). It's just that I learned it firsthand, and in the aftermath of my youth, I still had to deal with the fallout. It was part of my tapestry and my audience's tapestry, too. Every fiber of who I had become directly resulted from what I had experienced, both positively and negatively. I could compartmentalize certain people or situations to protect my emotions—to build a wall if you will. I had tried coping mechanisms for a long time, but they only increased my anxieties, and it was a fruitless endeavor. Confronting my parents eventually, once I felt strong enough, proved to be liberating but useless. The hard-won lesson of "You can't change people; you can only change how you react to them" became my mantra, and that one idea changed my life. Resistance was futile. *Said the guru who struggled to practice what he preached.*

"Hello, Mother," I said stoically as I paced my living room floor. "I'm sorry to report that I will not be joining the family at your summer gala in the Hamptons, but I will be the keynote speaker at a conference in San Francisco." I paused and waited for the tirade.

"WHAT?!" She bellowed. *Yeah, here it comes.* "That's unacceptable. You have an obligation to be at the summer house. The governor is scheduled to join us, and your father and I must have you standing strong with your sisters as we receive a commendation for our work with the foundation. Cancel your plans immediately!" You could hear the spit hitting the receiver as she delivered her usual monologue.

There was never any discussion or congratulations for the honor of being chosen to speak. There was no "I'm proud of you, Son." It has always been about my parents' narcissism or their precious foundation. *Fuck that!*

It was time to use my well-practiced psychobabble to end this conversation. I closed my eyes and inhaled softly and deeply, steadying myself for a calm delivery. "I'm sorry this news upsets you, Mother. I'm sure the governor would be most happy to hear that your beloved son is honored in California and sends his best regards. My sisters will do their part, and you and Dad won't lose face with my absence." *There! Nailed it!*

If the Academy could only hear the intense dramatic sigh and what was surely a gentle dabbing at the corners of her eyes, they would have presented her with an honorary Oscar on the spot.

"Alexander, you have no idea what your father and I sacrificed to make this foundation successful. Having the governor there validates everything we doing to give back to our community. You're not being there will be unforgivable." *The crowd applauded wildly.*

Time to drive the final nail in the coffin.

"No, Mother, I will not be attending, and this conversation is over. Do not have father call me or my sisters. Have a wonderful time and send me some pictures when it's over. Goodbye, Mother." I ended the conversation and gently set my phone on my desk, even though I wanted to chuck it across the room. I was finished feeling like a child with my parents.

Chapter 3

TRUDIE

J ARED PROVED TO BE the most attentive seatmate for the rest of our trip. It was easy to see he was just a flirt, but I played up the attention like a starved animal released to a room full of prey. I pounced on the opportunity and let things play out.

"Thanks for looking out for me today," I whispered sweetly. Just as I hoped to have some honest conversation, the captain announced that we would experience some turbulence and needed to stay seated with our seat belts fastened. Jared took the opportunity to take my hand again.

"I've got an idea. Why don't we make out until the plane settles down?" His eyebrows waggled, and I couldn't keep from laughing.

Not wanting to crush his ego, I instead offered, "You're funny, but I don't know you well enough to stick my tongue in your mouth." I squeezed his hand and smiled coyly.

His smile grew, and his turquoise eyes pierced mine. "What do you want to know about me?"

Cornered. "Well, for starters, you could tell me how you got into soccer. And then what you're planning after college." I nodded my head quickly, hoping he'd take the bait.

The airplane shook, and my teeth almost chattered in fear. With another bump, I fell to my left, brushing along Jared's shoulder and chest. My mind was torn between the peril of a plane crash and the peril of his hand moving anywhere else on me. Zings of heat traveled down my body, but he held me tightly, whispering calm words to settle me down. He let go of my hand and swung his arm around me to draw circles in the middle of my back. I'd be damned if that didn't distract me until we were out of that patch of bad weather.

Several minutes later, his hand stopped, and his eyes locked on mine again. The tiny creases along his forehead softened, and his lips twitched upward.

"You know, Trudie, if we weren't on this plane, I'd have you on your back in my bed, calming you the fuck down with my face between your legs."

I gulped. *Christ!*

I sensed the flight attendant coming down the aisle with the drink cart and pushed myself back into a straight sitting position before she warned us this was a family flight, not an X-rated sex club in the air. *Now that's a great idea!*

We both agreed that we needed to take a breather and calm down for the rest of the flight since there wasn't a satisfactory outcome for either of us without attracting attention. Jared kept me under his arm as we watched a movie, and my left hand sat on his thigh. It wasn't my fault my hand had a mind of its own and that my thumb strummed up and down his long, thick muscles.

By the time the movie ended, our flight was half over. My eyes were too heavy to stay open, and I rested my head on his shoulder. He pulled me closer to rest his head on mine, and we drifted off to sleep. It wasn't until Jared gently moved me off his shoulder that I woke up. Panic started to rise into my throat. I hated landing, too. And what would I say to this guy when we exited the plane? Would he want to have a quickie in the bathroom? Would he pressure me for my number? Did I want either of those things? Hell, they both sounded great to my heart, but my head was too practical. "No" was the most prudent answer. He was too young, and we were in very different places in our lives. Nothing would come of this but a good memory. Or a fantastic, sexy, steamy memory.

"You better stop moving your thumb, or you're not leaving this airport without me having my way with you," he growled in my ear.

"Oh! S-sorry. I didn't even know I was doing that," I stuttered, blushing a deep red.

"You do things to me, Trudie. I'd like to see you again in Michigan," he pressed.

A loud ping notified us that we were descending, which gave me a moment of reprieve. Then, a flight attendant instructed us to stow our personal items and return our tray tables and seats to their upright positions. It gave me another minute to think about how I wanted to respond. *Be strong, Trudie. You already made up your mind. There is nothing to think about. The fun is over.*

He gently lifted my chin, making me stare into his turquoise eyes, which begged me to give him this gift. He expertly kissed me—just the tip of his tongue dragging across my upper lip, leaving me to pull on his lower one. I was a goner.

"Yes," I replied. *Wait? What did I just say?*

"That's awesome, Trudie. Let's swap numbers." And without thinking, I handed over my phone to a large, almost-man. When he gave me my phone back, I placed my hand over his.

"Jared. How old are you anyway?" I pasted on a hopeful smile, and prayed he was over eighteen.

He chuckled, placing his other hand on top of mine. "I'm twenty-one. Safe enough?"

I nodded to myself and spoke with optimism, "Yeah."

We held hands until the plane landed, and my apprehension subsided once we had taxied to our gate. Jared's phone pinged with texts as he took it off airplane mode. He looked down at my face as he pointed to his screen.

"My teammates. We're meeting up immediately after we deplane. I won't be able to hang with you, so we should say goodbye now. I'll call you when I get back home. Shit, I didn't even ask why you were traveling. I'm an idiot."

I laughed nervously and attempted to put his mind at ease. "It's a psychology conference, and you're not an idiot. We got...distracted." I patted his chest. His drool-worthy, broad, muscled, tight, T-shirted chest.

I licked my lips as he smirked at me, gawking at his pecs, and nodded his agreement.

"It's been amazing meeting you, Trudie. Have a terrific conference and get home safely. I want to see you again soon." He pulled me into one last hug against that delicious chest.

One of his teammates cleared his throat, and we broke apart, looking guilty. We both smiled as we reached under our seats to grab our things and stood, waiting for our turn to exit our row. He was a real gentleman and offered to pull my bag down from the overhead bin, giving me a wink as he pulled me in front of him tightly for one last hug.

If there was one thing I learned on this trip, I desperately wanted to find love. Jared, although young, made me feel desirable and sexy, but I deserved to have it all and then some. I sent prayers to the universe to bring me a man worthy of me—one that not only adored me but truly valued me as a partner. Now...where to find him?

Chapter 4

ALEXANDER

I'D HAD MY PHONE off for three days. I wasn't going to entertain any more pushback from my parents, siblings, or anyone else who decided I was a pawn in their life. The only correspondence I had during that time was with the conference operations staff, letting them know I was boarding my plane. With any luck, I would arrive at the San Francisco Airport at noon and ask to have a driver waiting at the baggage claim for me.

I'd planned to sleep the entire trip since I had been preparing for my sessions nonstop for the past two weeks. I'd earned some downtime to rebuild my energy to deliver three exemplary workshops. It had been a last-minute booking, so I could only find a flight that had a quick stop in Detroit. The good news was that I didn't have to deplane—the bad news was that I was stuck on a flight with a bunch of athletes who thought they owned the plane. If not for the stacked brunette who came on ahead of them, I would have pulled my baseball cap over my eyes and crashed immediately.

She couldn't have been much more than five foot three, yet she carried herself with the grace of a queen. Confident, but not standoffish. She seemed sweet, yet I sensed a mooniness in her eyes, making me wonder what she was thinking. She sat toward the front of the plane, so I couldn't get a better read on her, but I knew there was something interesting that caught my eye, and I wanted to know more. *No time for that big boy. You're working.*

I pulled my murder mystery out of my computer bag, cued up a downloaded playlist on my phone, which I had finally turned on, swiped on airplane mode, put in my AirPods, and got ready to relax for the long flight. I noticed the seat next to the tiny brunette was still empty, and I wondered who the lucky person was who'd get to sit next to her. I thought about changing seats before we took off to get to know her better.

I hadn't been in a relationship for almost three years. I had dodged a bullet when I caught my fiancée with a high school friend of mine who attended the foundation's golf outing a month before our wedding. Apparently, she thought his putter was better than my driver.

I would never consider the tiny beauty sitting ahead of me as my type, though I would have been open to exploring her curvy assets. Sadly, at the last minute, some young dude dropped into the seat next to my wet dream and all thoughts of making my move were over. Since I couldn't keep an eye on her, I made a mental note to investigate when we landed.

Flying wasn't my preferred mode of transportation—but it was the easiest way for me to travel to many of the prestigious clients who kept my bank account full. It wasn't that I was afraid to fly—my own therapist had ruled that out almost immediately when I was fifteen.

"My dear boy, you take more risks than most young men I see in my practice. Your anxiety comes from 'allowing' things to happen out of your control," she explained. In short, you're a control freak. This belief that you can and will control everything in your world will only add to your troubles. You'll need to find ways to let go and be okay without it. That will be a lifelong exercise."

It had been almost twenty-five years and the only thing I had let go of was the belief that my family would be happy with my career choice, that they'd appreciate my helping people in the flesh instead of writing a check. Ha! What a laugh. But I'd done well enough being the captain of my boat, the general of my emotions, and the master of my domain. I was doing fine without factoring in anyone else's opinion of me, and I planned on keeping it that way.

After an interminably long deplaning process, I finally reached the baggage claim area. I arrived in time to catch a hilarious revival of *I Love Lucy*, except it was that little bodacious brunette I noticed earlier riding the baggage carrier while trying to get her luggage carrier. I was two seconds away from walking over to assist when one of those young athletes hopped up to dislodge her bag and help her off the conveyor. Priceless.

With a little luck, I got to my hotel without mishap and was ready for my keynote address on time and looking good.

Chapter 5
TRUDIE

Nothing made me feel more like a princess than when I stayed in a posh hotel room, which was...never! Until now, with my freebie suite. The room was nothing short of spectacular! I hit the lottery big time with this place. Literally hit the lottery. Every attendee who booked during early registration was put into a lottery for an executive suite to enjoy while at the conference, and I won. *#ILoveMyLife...sometimes.*

Standing in my twentieth-floor penthouse not far from San Francisco Bay, I imagined dozens of sailboats and people lounging around, probably enjoying fruity cocktails. This convinced me that I had to take that sunset cruise regardless of my relationship status. I deserved it, and since I didn't have to pay for a hotel room for five days, this girl was going to party.

Before I lost my nerve, I grabbed my phone and the notes app I kept all my plans in, clicked on the boat excursion I had drooled over yet hesitated to pay for, and booked myself on a Thursday night once-in-a-lifetime experience. *Yay, me!*

I continued my self-guided tour around the spacious and chic penthouse suite. Soft creamy carpet covered a good portion of the sunken living room off the marble foyer, which had direct access to the private elevator. Matching cream leather lounge chairs faced a gas fireplace with gold sparkling granite bricks playing backdrop to a stunning oil painting of the famed sequoias that I would see on Friday. The floor-to-ceiling glass wall allowed me to see the sparkle of the cerulean water, dotted with hundreds of boats and it had me sighing in appreciation for this perfect moment. *I made it. I'm here.* I'd never been able to afford a room like this. Goodness knows, my family could never afford this when I was growing up, either. But this view was the perfect frosting on my delicious cake of a day, which started with Jared on my flight to California, and I wasn't going to take it for granted. I just wished I could have lingered in the room for the rest of the night. But alas, the conference kickoff event was starting at seven o'clock, and I needed to wash off the grime from the plane's recirculated air.

The short walk down the marble-floored hallway in my bare feet felt so good after being in shoes all day. Honestly, if I never had to wear shoes again, I wouldn't. I felt so closed in at my apartment in Michigan and my small, simple life, and I needed to stretch out while I could. I longed to have my feet in the sand on a wide-open beach with a gentle breeze blowing through my hair and filling my soul. I could hardly wait.

"Holy shit!" I gasped. "I think I've died and gone to heaven."

I entered the bedroom suite and bolted to the king-size bed, literally jumping on the fluffy cream and gold duvet. I counted ten pillows of all sizes, threaded with gold, purple, and black. I looked up toward the heavenly angels who protected me and knew that if they could be in human form, they would be envious of this glorious bed. Later that night, I planned to make snow angels on the down comforter and pretend I was going to live like this forever.

I pinched myself while looking around the bedroom. So, this is what living the good life looked like. What I presumed was the bathroom door was gilded and molded to look like a piece of art. I gaped when I noticed the big claw-foot tub, which I was positive was glowing with a halo above it, beckoning me to jump in. Strike that—humongous claw-foot tub. I let out a shriek of ecstasy as I climbed inside the empty vessel, envisioning millions of bubbles taking me away. There was a pull-around curtain, candles on little stands all around the room, waiting to be lit, and two big, fresh floral arrangements that sat opposite each other on mirrored pedestals, inviting me to smell their glorious blooms. *I may have had a tiny orgasm.*

Without any additional encouragement, I plugged the tub with an intricately flowered pewter stopper that screwed into the threaded drain and then looked around for some bubbles. Spotting a whole array of spa-worthy creams, soaps, and bathroom accouterments, I found some deliciously scented orange and lavender bubble baths. Turning the ornate petal handles to scorching hot, I dropped several dollops of the yummy nectar into the steamy water.

Slowly, I peeled off my wilted blouse and dress pants. I ran out of the bathroom for a hair clip I had left in my purse and twisted my hair into a high bun. I cracked myself up when I looked in the mirror and found a messed-up girl with barely a savings account to her name in basic cotton panties living in a dream room. How ironic was that? To come from nothing and to be so lucky to have won this room had me taking a breath in a moment of gratitude. I slipped my fingers inside my undies to slide them off, then turned from side to side, admiring my figure. I popped my bra off and lifted my breasts just a little, noticing that even though I was twenty-seven, my tits still looked high and proud.

"You'd better let your assets do the talking this week, girl. You need to find a playdate." I made a pistol out of my thumb and forefinger and shot myself some luck in the beveled mirror. *Pew pew!* "This is the week, girl," I said and winked at my reflection before stepping into the balm of the hot water and bubbles and luxuriating as I contemplated a vision of my perfect man.

One of the realities of attending a conference was that I was alone. Very alone—unless I forced myself to connect with people that first evening. That I felt awkward was an understatement, but I consoled myself with the knowledge that most of the people here were in the same boat. Or life raft.

The simple solution was to start drinking a steady flow of alcoholic lubricant to keep at a.06 on the DUI chart. Fun and lighthearted, but not sloppy and morose. I was a lightweight, so two drinks in the first hour would get me where I needed to be, and a steady refresher every hour after that would keep me there. This year, though, I managed to nurse the first of my two free drinks in my conference package. I positioned myself inside the ballroom, to the right of the entry door, so I could scope out everyone without being too obvious.

Sometimes, I'd play a silly game, making up stories about who the attendees were and what they would want to say and do. It would keep my mind occupied while I nursed my rum and Diet Cokes. This year, however, I scoped out the room for a playdate. Or a date to play with, as it were. I needed to get back into the dating game before cobwebs grew between my legs.

"Hey! You look like you could use some company." A very perky girl with tight curls and a heavy southern drawl slid up next to me. "I'm Izzy. I just love these things. So many people to watch and things to learn. My daddy said I would make an amazing detective with all the intel I could collect in an hour." She took a gulp of air and another of her fruity drink.

Not wanting to be rude, I acknowledged her declaration. "Hey. Sure, yeah, please join me. I'm Trudie. My daddy would say that I was putting my nose where it didn't belong, but I guess that's why I'm here," I said, laughing it off. *What the hell, Trudie? Don't be a Debbie Downer.*

"That's very true. We all have a past, and, well...a daddy," she mumbled into her straw.

To pick up the mood, I divulged a little more information while playing with the straw from my drink. Why not? Wasn't that the best way to find common ground with strangers?

"This is my fifth summer conference. I'm a middle school teacher, and I believe that if kids had a way of tapping into their psyches and figuring out their childhood issues early, they could live full and happy lives. Present company included." I smiled shyly.

"Oh my gosh! You, too? Well, I'm not a middle school teacher, but I am a human resource specialist at a large IT company, and you should see some of the mental breakdowns that have happened in my presence over the years. Those poor souls never had a chance with the pain they'd been holding on to for decades. I just want to hug them all to make them feel better." Izzy patted her chest to calm herself down.

"I can't even imagine. Whereabouts are you from?" I asked, shifting the conversation to a lighter note. I didn't want to be depressed right out of the gate.

"Mobile, Alabama. My family goes back over one hundred and fifty years, back to the slave days. My great-great-great granddaddy was emancipated and eventually was able to buy a few acres of land, and his vision turned into a mega-million-dollar company.

"Wow! That's incredible for him and your whole family. Those were despicable times. I firmly believe that cultural traumas carry through each generation, even if we can't identify them clearly. I'm hoping to get more information on that topic this week," I said and then encouraged her to do the same.

Izzy was quite a spirited woman. A little older than me, she filled me in on all the keynote speakers she'd seen in the past five years and who were on her roster of must-sees this year. Two weeks before the conference, we had to request which seminars we wanted to attend in order of preference, but we wouldn't know which ones we actually got until later that evening.

Izzy and I agreed that we absolutely had to be in Alexander Pierce's Release the Grief and Forgive and Live workshops. I'd read about this guy. He sounded like the be-all and end-all in the childhood and educational arenas, and from his profile picture, he was swoon-worthy and and arrogant-looking. A delectable combination. If only I could get some time to ask him the litany of questions that had been percolating in my head for a decade, maybe it would help me feel at peace for the first time in my life. I desperately wanted to resolve my daddy issues—to lessen my disdain for who he had been as a father and separate that from the actual person he was. Whoever that may have been.

I nursed my drink while being thoroughly entertained by my new friend. She had more stories than Mother Goose, all bundled up in a very southern package. She almost convinced me that cows could actually "udder" words.

The conference itinerary led me to believe that our keynote speaker, Alexander Pierce, would be joining us for a meet-and-greet that evening, but it was pushing eight o'clock, and he was nowhere to be found. I excused myself to use the ladies' room.

These conference centers were always massive, and this one was no exception. The giant atrium windows on either side of the long, carpeted hallway were designed to let in the colorful sunset. I wasn't going to get to enjoy it this evening, but it gave me hope that tomorrow night I would. Luscious green plants lined the entryway. Directly over us was a spectacular display of twirling stained glass, each hung at different heights to refract all the colorful rays that came in, sending splashes of rainbow down the walls to the floor.

I should have known better than to walk and look up at the same time because I smashed into a brick wall. It wasn't until my eyes adjusted that I saw it for what it really was: a charcoal-gray pinstripe suit molded perfectly around a white-shirted Grecian god. I clearly wasn't the only one not paying attention since he swore as his phone plummeted to the floor.

"Oh my gosh. I'm so sorry. I wasn't looking where I was going," I hurriedly said, trying to cover the awkwardness of what had just transpired.

"You're damn right you weren't. That phone better not be broken," he barked. He morphed into a demon with black eyes and a furrowed brow. Realizing who I had just slammed into, I stepped backward with a gasp.

"Oh shit. You're Alexander Pierce. I just ran into Dr. Alexander Pierce. I'm so sorry, let me get your ph-phone."

Stuttering and bending forward to grab his phone didn't quite help the situation like I had hoped, especially since he bent forward simultaneously, and our heads collided. Oh boy! I didn't think he could look any madder than before, but I was quickly learning all the angry faces a ridiculously hot Dr. Pierce could make.

"God bless it! Get away from me. I don't need your help—there's a crack on my screen," he growled as he pinned me with a glare that even Satan himself would have run from. I looked around for witnesses to help bail me out of this mess. Finding none, I tried to apologize again, but he wasn't having it.

"I'm sending you the bill for this repair. Give me your information, and I'll have my assistant send you the invoice." He shook his phone in my face and jammed his other hand on his hip, giving me attitude. Little did he know who he was dealing with. I'm a middle school teacher, and I know how to deal with a tantrum from a prepubescent, pimply little prick. Except, of course, this was a grown-ass man with not a pimple or pockmark in sight.

"I don't like your tone. This was a simple accident, and for the record, I wouldn't have bumped into you if you had been paying attention as well." *Take that!* "You can pay for your own repairs since you're too stupid not to have a case on it." Turning on my heel, I marched away to the ladies' room before I peed in my pants.

Chapter 6
ALEXANDER

WHAT THE HELL WAS that? Some whirling dervish, not paying attention, had smacked into me and then given me a lecture. Well, I wasn't having it. I marched after her, right up to the door she walked through—and then a woman walked out. *Jeez, man, you almost walked into the ladies' room.* I could wait. I had to check in with the registration table and I was late as it was. My plane had gotten me to San Francisco in plenty of time, but after shutting my phone down for most of the day, I had a hundred emails and twenty phone calls to respond to.

From my sister Sarah, the angel of the family:

WTF Alex? I can't believe you left us to deal with this bullshit party by ourselves. You're going to pay for this when you come   home. Don't be surprised if all the locks are changed at your condo and dog shit is smeared across your front door.

Lovely, just lovely. And not to be outdone, Tabitha, the real troublemaker of the three of us:

By the powers vested in me by the fiery depths of hell and the wrath of the metaverse, you will be stricken down, torn apart bit by bit, and your head left on a pike for all to see. If you don't get your ass over to this godforsaken party RIGHT NOW, I will drive your Porsche into the Hudson River, torch your hoity-toity condo in your bougie neighborhood, and take out a full-page ad in the New Yorker *of what a dick you really are. I'm serious, Alex! Not funny. Get your ass over here NOW!!"*

This was followed by a string of no less than twenty angry-faced emojis.

Several more pleas for cooperation tainted my screen—eventually, my thumb cramped scrolling through them. Sadly, not sadly, I was on the other side of the country, far away from the insipid party. Anything, even getting smashed into by a hellion, was better than being in the Hamptons that weekend. At that thought, I realized the hellion looked familiar. *I'll figure it out later.* Refocusing, I reached the registration table, announced who I was, and apologized for being late.

The rather large woman with giant round black glasses looked up, her orange lips arranged in a tight smile, and clapped her hands together.

"Oh, hello, Dr. Pierce, we've been expecting you." She rambled on as she gave me a thick packet of information I was sure I'd spend half the night reviewing, two drink tickets, and directions to the conference directors' table where I'd be meeting my hosts.

I nodded my professional "I appreciate you" smile and walked directly to the bar.

I took a moment to orient myself in the extremely large space. Everyone was mixing and mingling as smooth jazz floated through the air. Music was so much better than awkward silence. Many of these conferences missed the boat on creating an inviting mood for their participants, so the decent music here was promising. I loved to people-watch. So many telling characteristics could be stored or analyzed for future reference. Many of these people would be in my workshops, and I wanted a jump on who they were and how they behaved when they weren't aware they were being watched. People were always happy to tell you about themselves and their essence, yet quite often, they were delusional. Their body language, however, belied the message they intended to deliver. In short, the receiver of the message never picked up what the sender was actually putting down. I'd seen it over and over again, leaving me frustrated that they couldn't transmit a complete message.

A sweet, whispered voice came from behind me, placing an order with the bartender: "I'll have a Captain and Diet Coke with a lime, please." *What a beautiful, rich tone to her voice.* I'm not a womanizer, but I'd had a few conference hookups over the years, and I wasn't going to hold back tonight if the vibe was good. Straightening my jacket and feeling suave and debonair, I gracefully turned around to see the mouth that uttered those sexy-sounding words and cringed with disgust. It was her! The bodacious bitch that ran into me and didn't even apologize when she broke my phone.

She was leaning both elbows on the bar, sucking a maraschino cherry between her ripe red lips. If I hadn't been so pissed at her, I'd have plucked that cherry out of her mouth and sucked on it myself. She saw me in her periphery, but her gaze was unperturbed; there wasn't even a twitch of her lip as she shifted her gaze back to the bartender, dismissing me.

Dropping a couple of singles into his tip glass, she smiled appreciatively and said, "Thank you so much," then took a long pull from the straw. "Delicious. See you again soon." Turning away from me, she sashayed back across the room to a high-top cocktail table and an animated, curly-haired woman.

I was apoplectic watching her—no—glaring at her from across the room, hoping my laser vision would explode her gorgeous head off. No such luck. *Better get those laser eyes checked when I get home.*

After she conveyed a story to her friend, they looked at each other and then disdainfully at me before throwing their heads back in convulsive laughter. Like a rabid dog, I foamed at the mouth. Who did she think she was mocking me that way? I was a celebrated psychologist and published author with two PhDs. I'd never been so insulted in my life. I knew if she so much as looked into my classroom, I would have her kicked out immediately.

TRUDIE

Izzy was a blast to hang out with, and the other two ladies who joined us later were a hoot, too. We all shared our stories of what brought us to the conference and what we hoped to get out of it.

I'm pretty sure mine won the Saddest Story award. Needless to say, the distinguished keynote speaker, Dr. Alexander "the Ass" Pierce, droned on and on about how fabulous he was and how his research was the most cutting edge...*blah, blah, blah.* The only thing he said that caught my attention was that he had to bow out of a family obligation this week thanked the committee for getting him out of that situation. I wondered what kind of family he grew up in.

Dr. Pierce put the pompous in pomp and circumstance. Thank God his speech finally ended so we could pick up our seminar assignments and leave. I had to admit, it was a clever ploy to get us all to stay until the end of the evening, even if we were all hammered.

I hurried down the main corridor and found a tufted bench to sit on while I opened my packet. I scanned the welcome letter, and then flipping the page, I saw my itinerary and my jaw dropped to my lap. Three. Three of the five seminars I signed up for were with Dr. Pierce. On any other day, in any other lifetime, this would have sent me to the moon and back, but after today—today I was petrified.

Oh shit, what have I done? I muttered to myself. Grasping my papers to my chest, I looked around, hoping no one had heard me. I shook my head, willing myself to breathe. *No, I must have just read the page wrong.* The registration stated that participants could only attend two workshops with any one speaker, and I got three. *That's like crazy, right? First, winning a beautiful complimentary suite for the week, and now this? Since when did I get so lucky?*

Archangels Metatron and Raphael not only have my back—they must also have my ass, too!

I quickly stuffed the papers back into the yellow envelope and scurried down the hall with it tightly under my armpit. I felt like Gollum sneaking away with his Precious, that bewitched ring in *Lord of the Rings. Mine, mine, mine!*

Chapter 7

TRUDIE

MY HEAD WAS KILLING me the next morning, no doubt thanks to the four drinks I had consumed the night before. I was still on Eastern Time, so I did get to sleep in, which helped. Regardless of how I was feeling, I wasn't going to waste this amazing suite, so I ordered room service, with a side of Excedrin, and ran another bubble bath in the amazing claw-foot tub. I carefully opened the heavy curtains, which brought in a burst of vibrant yellows and oranges that cut through the carpet in my bedroom. What a great way to start the day—too bad the brightness seared my eyeballs and caused temporary blindness.

While waiting for the water to heat up, I selected a professional red dress with tiny cherries, a pleated kick flare that hit just below my ass, and a buttoned-up bodice. I needed a sweater to keep me warm, and my simple black cardigan would do the trick. Whoever adjusted the temperature in those conference rooms must have worked in a meatpacking plant. They were always freezing!

Luxuriating in the tub put me in a calm, grateful mood, where nothing could upset me, and after last night, I needed to start today fresh and unperturbed. I grabbed the fluffy robe that I had put on the stool by the tub and wrapped it around my body. No towel was necessary. I then spent twenty minutes gazing out the window, enjoying the view of sparse clouds, sand, and sailboats. There was a knock on the door as I was slathering hotel-branded eucalyptus and lavender body lotion all over my body. *Thank goodness—I was starving.*

The hospitality staff member displayed my breakfast beautifully on the glass dining table by the window facing the bay. As he smiled and headed back to the door, I realized I hadn't tipped him.

"Wait for just a second," I called as I shuffled the monogrammed hotel slippers towards my purse and pulled out ten dollars. Since I saved a bundle not having to pay for a room this week, I figured I may as well be a big tipper. He gave me a sweet smile and a small bow and then bowed again as he walked out the door. I'd never been bowed to before, but I sure could have gotten used to it.

As I settled myself at the table to enjoy my breakfast, I took in my surroundings: the crystal cut bud vase with a single pink rose blooming perfectly, the shiny silver domes keeping my food warm, and a view to die for. I relished this moment for what it was—a gift from the heavens. I was reminded of a lyric from *The Sound of Music*: "I must have done something good."

"Good morning," I said, greeting the person at the registration table. "I just wanted to be sure my itinerary is correct. The registration form said only two seminars can be with a single speaker and I have three. Is this right?" I pushed my itinerary across the plastic banquet table that served as their desk.

"Well, aren't you the lucky one!" she exclaimed. "All our seminars are assigned via a computer algorithm, but you got the best glitch ever. Dr. Pierce is an exceptional speaker; you get to hear all three of his lectures. Lucky lady," she gushed, handing my paper back to me. "Have an amazing week!" she called as I walked away, stunned all over again.

Three seminars. What the heck was he going say to me when I walked into the first one, let alone the second and third ones? Did I even want to hear all three of his lectures? No!

Liar! You've wanted to hear this guy for years. This is your chance to suck this guy dry of his psychology and educational knowledge. Although, after getting a good look at his backside at the bar last night and yelling into his fucking godlike face, you might like to suck something else of his, too. Oh, stop!

I ducked behind a potted palm as I took a few deep breaths. I needed a plan. Fast. I had two minutes to get to my first seminar and find a seat. After two more deep breaths, I thought to myself, *Okay. Here's the plan: walk in directly behind someone and sit at the back of the room. He won't notice you're there and even if he does, it won't be until it's too late to say anything. Perfect.* With renewed confidence, I slipped into the room, sliding behind the largest person I could find, and started looking left and right for the perfect seat.

Back row—full.

Next three rows—full.

Next six rows—full, full, full! *Crap!*

The only other seats available were directly in front of the podium or at the end of the second row. Mentally reciting a Hail Mary, I bolted to the second-row seat before the person behind me got it. *Please God, it's me, Trudie. Don't let Dr. Pierce spot me.*

I kept my head down while perusing the course materials, and moments later, Satan's smooth voice announced his arrival and the title of his first lecture.

"Welcome, everyone. It's a pleasure to be here with you this week. Sure beats entertaining the governor of New York." *What a pompous asshole.*

"My seminar, Release the Grief, was designed as a thesis paper for my second doctorate." *Massive arrogant pompous asshole.* "After which, I expanded it into my first book. Today, we will examine the main components of grief and why people choose to hold on to it instead of letting it go. My second seminar tomorrow will focus on forgiveness and how to allow yourself to live happy, healthier lives. Some of you will have the opportunity to hear my third and final lecture, When Forgiveness Isn't an Option. While forgiveness is often the best way to move forward to a happier life, sometimes extenuating circumstances prohibit this path. At any rate, most of what will be covered this week is always available to you in my books. Please contact your preferred book retailer for more information."

Well, if that wasn't the most prepared infomercial I had ever heard, I'd eat my shoe. This guy was so full of himself. "My book this, my book that." I got that he was omnipotent—the best, fan-fucking-tabulous in his field. If he hadn't looked like the porn star in a suit and hadn't sounded like Harry Connick Jr., I'd have walked out of there. I was a sucker for a crooner in a tailor-made suit. I'd take the high road and stay, but only because I paid to be here, no other reason.

I looked up through my bangs as Dr. Pierce turned to walk back to the podium to open his tablet. I hoped that with no sudden movements, he'd have no reason to look in my direction. It would have been so much easier if he hadn't paced back and forth in front of the class. He stopped abruptly two people away from where I sat, and turned to face the rest of the room, leaving me outside his line of sight. *Whew!*

"How many of you have experienced the death of a family member, friend, or pet?" He marched closer to the center of the room with his hand in the air, briefly observing his audience. Obviously, almost all of us had experienced death by the time we were adults. *Off to a great start, doc.*

"No surprise there. You can hardly reach adulthood without at least one person or pet dying. However, are you carrying the pain of that death with you to this day? And, if so, why?" *Now we're getting somewhere.*

"Today we will explore those whys, and establish a new set of expectations to help you move through and past the grief that is holding you back."

"Hallelujah!" I chirped. *Oh shit. Did I just say that out loud?*

I growled to myself, not moving my head but shifting my eyes to see if he heard me. *Of course, he'd heard you, stupid.* Green eyes locked on to mine and I gulped. So much for anonymity. New plan.

I sat up straighter, raised my head proudly, and looked back into those fabulously furious eyes, challenging him to make a scene. Why didn't I feel as confident as I appeared to be. I thought I heard a faint growl leave his throat as he walked over and stopped in front of me—to do what? I was frozen in my seat waiting to find out.

"Agreed, Miss...?" He challenged me to give him my name. Fine. I gave him what he wanted just so that we could get this over with.

Clearing my throat quickly, I blurted, "Gonzales." *Ha! You'll get nothing more out of me.*

He smirked an evil smile at me. Turning abruptly toward the rest of the class, he nodded his head and then gestured to me. "Ms. Gonzales concurs with this morning's lecture, which makes her my star pupil." *No, I'm not.* He came around to the end of my row and motioned for me to stand up. I looked around at the two hundred plus people staring back at me curiously. He intentionally put me on the spot. To embarrass me further? He could have just nodded in my direction and kept walking and talking, but he recognized me and took the first proverbial punch.

I stood slowly, rising to my full height of five feet two inches, and set my things on the not-so-comfortable banquet chair. I was hardly a formidable opponent to him, as he was clearly a foot taller than me and built like a linebacker for the New York

Giants. As I looked farther north, his grin got bigger and more sinister. Undoubtedly, he liked giving orders and having petite females abide by his command. Typical alpha male behavior—yet my stomach had just launched a hundred butterflies throughout my body without my permission.

"Please tell us why 'Hallelujah' was your response to my last point regarding setting new expectations." I knew he was hoping I would fumble and give a dumb reply, but I'd done my homework and showed him I knew a few things myself.

I turned to look at my audience, nodded my appreciation for their attention, and responded clearly and lucidly.

"Without your own change of expectations, the constant cycle of pain, regret, remorse, and self-loathing cannot be halted. Not forgiving yourself of trespasses and those of others who might be a party to your pain will only serve to perpetuate the cycle. It must start with you." And, with that, I bent to pick up my things and parked my carcass back in my seat. And began to breathe again, too.

The class applauded and several of the people around me shared their agreement. I nodded my appreciation and hoped Satan would move on. Sadly, that was not the end of it.

"Well done, Ms. Gonzales. It is Ms., correct?" He chuckled. *Asshole.* "Everything you said was completely true. Rumi said it best, 'Your heart knows the way. Run in that direction.' Except when it can't. Some have said that avoiding forgiveness gave them the power of making the other person feel unsafe. In other words, withholding forgiveness gave them power over the person they sought to forgive. So, what is it, Ms. Gonzales? From whom do you withhold forgiveness to keep your power?"

I could feel the color drain from my face. His statement hit so close to home my throat dried up and I couldn't speak. I just sat there staring at him, his head tilted as if he had just placed the winning chess move—*checkmate*. The room was silent; you could hear the gears turning in everyone's minds as they absorbed his words.

"Okay, everyone. Grab your pens and look up here to the presentation. You already have my slides in your packet, so please jot additional notes beside each slide to refer to later." Dr. Pierce gave me one last look of what, I'm not sure. Appreciation? Smugness? Apology? I was still too stunned to respond.

Chapter 8

ALEXANDER

WHY ME? WHY DID I think lecturing at this conference would be better than a pretentious fundraising event in the Hamptons? I know it sounds arrogant of me to think everyone attending would just be sheep that I could herd around—that they would go willingly wherever I took them. However, some sheep had minds of their own and felt they could chime in whenever they wanted. I should have walked her out of that first session and told her not to come back to any of my others, but the look on her face, when I asked her who she was withholding forgiveness from, turned her from a fiery comet to fallen ash. I, too, froze at her response and then considered my position as an educator: she was there to learn, so I altered my course to help her save face. My personal vendetta against her didn't have to be played out in front of two hundred unsuspecting participants. So, I redirected the class and let her off the hook. Looking out at her peers, it seemed quite a few of them had a similar visceral response to my words and needed redirection, as well. Taking my cue, I learned a lesson in compassion and moved forward.

Everyone in attendance had my PowerPoint slides. Therefore, I could breeze through each concept quickly and concisely without interruption. As luck would have it, I finished fifteen minutes early and eagerly awaited another fully caffeinated dark roast coffee to lift my spirits and my heart rate. But I should have known I wouldn't get out of the lecture early.

Ms. Gonzales's hand was raised for almost three minutes while I answered any question other than hers. Not wanting to look like an ass and dismiss her completely, I reluctantly pointed my hand in her direction and leaned tiredly against the podium. *Maybe she'll fall mute and forget what she was going to say.*

"Dr. Pierce, I'm intrigued by your statement, 'Forgiveness is a form of compassion.' To whom is the compassion directed? The afflicted or the inflictor?"

She sat back confidently in her chair—not smugly, but in a way I couldn't quite put my finger on. Was she challenging me, or did she really want a straight answer? I took the opportunity to assess her body language and saw she was willing herself to keep her eyes locked on mine. It was then that I noticed her small nose, defined eyebrows, and heart-shaped face. I couldn't tell if she was Latina or Indigenous. It didn't matter, really. She was enticing, and I had to shift my feet to adjust myself surreptitiously. I took a few steps closer, giving the class the impression that I was formulating an answer with one hand in my pocket and another clutching the lapel of my suit jacket until I stood no more than six feet away.

I could see more clearly the light dusting of freckles across the bridge of her nose and a dimple on her right cheek. Her chest seemed to heave a little faster as I got closer, and it coaxed mine to speed up as well. Alluring. That's what she was. This sultry siren with a smart-assed, sassy mouth. I would be okay if only I could get my brain to stay connected to my mouth.

I knew I had better come up with the perfect answer to her question, or I was going to hear about it lecture after lecture. Clearing my throat, I proceeded:

"While it seems logical that forgiveness to the offender would be the first course of action, I would argue that forgiveness should begin with oneself. After all, you have control of how and what you feel and no control over anyone else. However, as humans, we suffer from a conscience. We want to do the right thing and be seen as doing the right thing, and therefore, we look outwardly to heal others' wounds as a show of compassion. But I assert that you should not waste time investing in others until you have invested in yourself first. You are the one who cares most about you, or you should anyway, and therefore need to absolve yourself or own your involvement and fix your end of it. Are you following me?" *You had been doing so well at not being patronizing.*

She nodded, and I stupidly thought she agreed with me. But apparently, not all head nods equal agreement. She recrossed her very shapely legs and responded, "While looking inward to re-solve the conflict and absolving oneself is an excellent suggestion, I would assert that not all conflicts are two-way streets. Therefore, rectifying one's actions may not be an alternative, making being compassionate an impossibility." She pulled a smug smile across her sweet little face, but I wasn't done with her yet.

Pulling on both lapels now, I spread my legs wider to show her I was holding my ground and gave her my final word.

"Be that as it may, Ms. Gonzales, as *Merriam-Webster* defines it, compassion is 'the desire to alleviate the suffering of others.' So, I would say to you that by executing one, you deliver the other. Therefore, again, start with yourself, and perhaps there will be a happy outcome. And with that, I bid you all a farewell and hope you have a great conference."

As I turned back to the podium to grab my things, I felt her drilling me in the back with her laser-beam eyes, so I hightailed it out of the classroom in search of a bathroom and some sanctuary. Unfortunately, the siren was positioned just outside the door with her arms crossed, making her already large breasts appear even larger.

She snarled, pushing her chin into the air as she said, "I'm not sure what you hoped to accomplish in there, Dr. Pierce, but my question was sincere, and you turned it into a shaming session, which I didn't appreciate." *To answer or not to answer. That was the question.*

"I'm sorry you feel that way, but my only intention was to break down your question so that it could be sorted out efficiently." I moved past her quickly, hoping to shut down the nonsense of her overreaction.

Alas, in keeping with her bloodhound persistence, she chased after me and continued. "Do you have a problem with me? I paid a lot of money to attend this conference and I deserve to be treated with respect and professionalism, not belittled and rebuked."

Oh shit. I really stepped in it this time. I shook my head and looked up at the ceiling—for what reason, I didn't know. Maybe lightning would strike me dead and I'd get out of answering this pain in my ass.

"Listen," I started, but she put her palm up in front of my face.

"Do not start that way because I'm already turning down the volume on what you're about to say." She shifted her head from side to side with that DFWM attitude (you know—don't fuck with me*). DFWM? I'll tell you who not to DFWM.* I gently grabbed her elbow and led her away from the classroom doors in hopes of avoiding a scene. I spun her around to face me and let her have it.

"My problem *is* with you. Your attitude is off the wall—nuts. Do you think everything revolves around you? You, who wasn't watching where she was going yesterday? You, who spoke out of turn in *my* lecture. *And you,* who challenged me in front of two hundred people just now. So, tell me, Ms. Gonzales, are you my problem or not?"

I stared her down, waiting for her to bolt, and in the process, noticed that the top button of her dress had popped open, giving me a perfect view of her luscious full breasts. How was I supposed to tear her a new one when her tits had me by the balls? *So not fair.*

She pulled her lips into a thin line, slowly sliding her head from side to side as she started to respond. Wisps of silky auburn hair fell from her messy bun, and I had trouble focusing on why we were fighting instead of finding a place to fuck. My hearing came back into focus midway through her tirade—I knew I had missed some vital information, but I didn't care. I let her go on, hoping she would fizzle out while I imagined doing unspeakable things to her upstairs in my room, before I got my second dose of caffeine.

"...I'm attending two more of your lectures, and you'd better not do that again." And with that, she turned in a huff, swaying that JLo bubble butt. *Wait, what? Two more lectures with her? The universe hates me.*

TRUDIE

It was lunchtime, and I was spent after that highly emotional, nerve-racking seminar. I grabbed a few things from the buffet and went up to my room. Thank God I didn't run into anyone I'd met the night before, *especially* Satan.

The only person capable of helping me was Ruby, my best friend from college. She had known me at my worst and still wanted to be my friend, so we went to college together and became inseparable. I put my food in the suite's stainless steel refrigerator, grabbed a bottle of cold water, and threw myself onto the over-stuffed paisley-printed ottoman. *Note to self: when you buy your first house, get an incredible kitchen like this one.*

Reaching into my pocket for my phone, I rolled onto my back and dialed Ruby. Hopefully, she wasn't in a meeting.

"Hello? Trudes? How is San Fran treating you? Getting your psych on?" she blathered into the receiver. Ruby was a bit of a long talker—always so much to say with so little time. I loved it.

"Hey, Rubes. You won't believe it, but because I did the early-bird registration, I was put into a raffle for free accommodation for the five days I'm here. And I won! And, when I say accommodations, I mean a ridiculously posh penthouse suite. Ha! Me, right—penthouse suite—can you see me draped over a chaise longue?" I wasn't trying to put myself down, but I only knew how to struggle, not waltz around on Easy Street.

With an audible huff, she replied, "I hate it when you do that. You deserve everything good in this life. If you didn't win, then someone else would, right? Take the good luck and drop that self-deprecating language from your vocabulary before I reach into the phone and knock you upside the head." When it comes to me, Ruby was not known for holding back.

"Fine. I'm a winner!" I exclaimed, waving my hand in the air, even though she couldn't see it.

I heard her slurping the last remnants of what was probably her favorite latte drink, so I pressed forward with a quick synopsis of what happened last night and this morning. I really needed some guidance for how to deal with tomorrow's lecture.

"Rubes, he's just so arrogant, and he hates me. I didn't do anything to him. We were both at fault—neither of us was looking when we crashed into each other—why is he taking it out on me?" I knew I sounded deflated and whiny, but I didn't want to give up all my power and hope to this idiot. He was the best in the business, and I needed what he offered. What I didn't need was his attitude.

"I only have one more minute before I need to meet with our new client, but it sounds like maybe he has a little crush on you. Before you go getting freaked out about that, you should know that you're little/not-so-little toned booty and those bodacious tatas look really good with that pretty face and sassy mouth of yours. I think you short-circuited his brain. Keep up the good work, I gotta go." And the line went dead.

"Wait!" I spluttered, letting out the rest of the breath I hadn't known I was holding before she bailed on me. Short-circuited his brain? What did she mean by that? I didn't have that kind of power or effect on people. The only power I had was the ability to Jedi mind meld my students into thinking I was an awesome teacher. *Now that's good trickery.*

I abandoned my starfish pose on the ottoman and rolled to the floor with a big sigh. With every ounce of strength I could muster, I stood and walked sluggishly back to the kitchen. I pried the top off my bottle and had a long-deserved slug of water. Feeling like a petulant child who had been mocked, I slumped over the granite countertop to rehash, once again, each of the encounters I'd had with Dr. Pierce. After thoroughly pondering the situation, I assured myself there was only one time he could have checked me out and that was when he embarrassed me during his lecture. I recalled noticing a subtle tick in his jaw when he'd tilted his head down toward my chest later during our conversation after leaving the classroom. Come to think of it, his eyes grew big while he was dressing me down.

Hmm.

I shook my head to clear it, then pulled myself off the counter and walked back to the foyer, checking myself in the mirror. I thought that none of this really meant anything until I looked down and saw the buttons just above my breasts were open. Smacking both hands to my chest, I yelped. *Shit!* He would have seen right to mid-boob and my cream-colored demi cup lace bra. I smacked myself in the head, feeling embarrassed for hanging out of my shirt. It must have happened when he pulled me out of the classroom by the elbow. *Who was the idiot now?* No wonder he made himself scarce after that conversation.

I returned to my bathroom to rustle through my toiletries for a small pin, which I then wove through the back and front seam to keep my giant tits from busting open my dress again. I went back to the kitchen for my water and the salad I had grabbed from the buffet and then sat at the island counter to figure out my next move.

What I really wanted to do was take a nap and bail on the afternoon sessions, but as I said to Dr. Pierce, king of the assholes, I'd paid hard-earned money to be there, and I wasn't going to let him or anyone else get in the way of my plans.

Chapter 9

TRUDIE

T HE AFTERNOON LECTURE WAS so much more fun and uncomplicated. Izzy was in my session, and we giggled as our instructor had us do icebreaker exercises to learn about verbal and nonverbal language. I was pretty good at deciphering most people's body language, but I found some facial expressions to be almost indistinguishable from others and, if misinterpreted, could get you, *me*, into trouble. Example: Dr. Satan Pierce.

Izzy and I decided to hop a cab over to Aquatic Cove to decompress from the day. We still had a few hours before sunset, and it made sense to leave the hotel and enjoy the surrounding area without a lot of people around.

We found a cute smoothie stand steps away from the beach that was too enticing to pass up. I got the Summer Berry Blaster with a shot of protein, and Izzy got the Maui Mango with kale. Turns out both of us were health nuts, and even though we loved a doughnut occasionally, we agreed they didn't look good on our thighs.

I kicked off my sandals and hit the sand first, my toes delighting in the warm grains. "Ahh. I've been waiting for this moment for nine months. Finally, my soul can rest on this sugary white sand,"

I said with a flourish of my right arm while my left steadily kept the straw of my drink in my mouth. I marched a few more steps toward the water. "Can we sit near the water for a few minutes and let all this summer sun soak into our bodies?"

"Of course, darlin'," she drawled. "We've got hours to enjoy ourselves if you want to blow off tonight's buffet. I know I won't miss it, except for the dessert. I heard they were having a baked Alaska parade at about eight o'clock. Can we make it back for that?"

How could I say no to baked Alaska? You don't get to see that every day. It's spectacular and quite a physics lesson, with all that meringue wrapped around ice cream and set on fire. *Hmm. Maybe we could pair up with the science teacher and try that this year. Okay, fine, it's not English, but we could write an essay on how awesome it was, right?*

With our plan in place, we let the wind whip through our hair and the sun pour over our faces, restoring our peace and tranquility. Seagulls dipped and dove into the water, scaring little children and threatening to steal their ice-cream cones when they landed on the sand. We always called them sea chickens because they pecked at anything and ate everything.

The salt air always heightened my senses. I could hear better, see more clearly, and relax my face muscles. And, of course, my taste buds tingled. When I was little, my mom took me and my two brothers to a local beach near our home. We only went when my dad was traveling, so we wouldn't have to hear him complain that sand was traipsing through the house, getting stuck on his socks.

We would bring all our plastic pails, molded pink castle buildings, and tiny umbrellas to make our castles look authentic. Mom would let us sit anywhere we wanted, which was usually five feet from the water, and she would read while we got lost in our medieval castle construction. From time to time, she'd come over and play make-believe, with me being the princess in the tower and my brothers being dragons and knights. It was a blast. We all left warm and golden brown, dreaming about our next beach adventure while rubbing sand out from between our toes. Once our things were back in the car, we'd walk down the boardwalk to get ice cream, and Mom would ask what the best part of the day was. I couldn't say mine out loud because being happy that Dad wasn't there was not a nice thought.

"Izzy? Does your mind go blank while you look out to sea, or do you think about stuff?" I asked because I often wondered what other people thought about while watching the pulses of the waves and the flickering ripples of light on the horizon.

She had pulled her knees up under her chin resting her head on them. She looked at me now, seeming contemplative. "Sometimes both. Today, my mind is open space. The thrum of the bay makes me sleepy and peaceful." To demonstrate, she closed her eyes and took a deep breath.

I let her have some quiet time as I returned to my silent contemplation. I spread my sweater on the sand and lay back, willing myself to just breathe and let go of this morning's seventh circle of hell. I would not let that egotistical asshole doctor make me doubt myself. I was determined to start tomorrow fresh, with a new "open" attitude and enjoy his next lecture. *God, give me strength.*

My breathing slowed and I drifted off to sleep, while visions of cut abs and a deep V flitted through my mind. The next thing I knew, Izzy was shaking my arm.

"Trudie, get up. Trudie." She shook me emphatically, her voice strained.

"What? Where am I? Shit, I must have fallen asleep." I yawned, screwing my fists into my eyes to wake up. "What time is it?" I mumbled.

"It's seven o'clock already. We need to go so we can grab some food and get some dessert." She was pulling my arm, apparently to help me up, which was difficult with my ass buried in the sand.

We made it back to the hotel within fifteen minutes, but we were pretty windblown, so we stopped in the ladies' room to freshen up. Methuselah had nothing on me. My hair was going in five different directions, and the salt on my skin made me feel like a deer's salt lick. A real looker. Thank goodness I had a comb and a hair band. I could whip my hair into a ponytail, and with a quick wash of my face and some lip gloss, I elevated myself to a spunky teenager. Simple but presentable. Izzy somehow fared much better, but she moaned enough for both of us.

Izzy was mesmerized by the flaming meringue of baked Alaska, and I had to admit, when all the lights were turned off, and the servers paraded through the dining area with fire snapping off their large trays, I was smiling like a kid in a candy store. Pure unadulterated wonder.

"It's so magical," Izzy drawled out, her tongue slightly falling out of her mouth and eyes as wide as saucers.

Amused by her enthrallment, I nodded in agreement.

"It really is, and it tastes even better," I said, rubbing my hands together and standing up. "I'm heading to the bar—want any-thing?" She shook her head, and I sauntered over to my now fa-vorite bartender.

Resting my elbows on the bar, I tried my hand at Izzy's South-ern style. I'm sure I sounded stupid, but what the hell, live a little, right?

"Howdy, big guy. How about another of your fabulous rum and Diet Cokes with a lime twist." I batted my eyelashes to give the full effect of a damsel needing assistance.

Now, I could have been dehydrated from being at the beach or perhaps malnourished since I'd missed most of the dinner, but when that big bartender turned fully around, he sure looked a lot like Dr. Alexander Pierce. *Nah, couldn't be.* I shook my head, scrunched my eyes, and tucked my chin down for a moment of clarity. When I lifted my head, his dark eyes held my stare. This wasn't my favorite bartender.

"I'll have..." *Gulp.* I tried again to speak but nothing would come out. I stared back, helpless.

He shifted his stance and leaned forward over the top of the bar, observing my confused face.

"You'll have what, Ms. Gonzales?"

"Uh, um, a Di...et Coke and rum, please. Uh, and why are you playing bartender?" I stuttered, probably sounding like an idiot. Why the hell was he there instead of anywhere else?

The real bartender from yesterday stepped back behind the bar and thanked Dr. Pierce for keeping an eye on things while he ran for more napkins.

Dr. Pierce looked back at me with a raised eyebrow and a slight nod to the other guy, indicating that was why he was behind the bar. Grabbing two glasses, he took the opportunity to make himself a cocktail as well as my drink, before stepping back around the counter to my side. He handed my drink to me, holding on just long enough to graze my hand, sending shivers down my spine.

"Here's your drink, ma'am. Happy to assist such a spirited young woman," he snickered.

I kept in character because he wasn't going to ruin my fun. "Much obliged, sir," I drawled, and dipped a small curtsy before turning around to leave. I did love a good role-play.

Before I could get too far, however, he called after me in a husky southern drawl, "Y'all come back now, ya hear?" I looked at him over my shoulder and watched his devilish smile turn into a full-on grin as he tipped his drink my way. *Clever asshole.*

It had been a long day, and I was hoping tomorrow wouldn't be another cat-and-mouse game. I just wanted to have fun and gather more important information for myself and my students. Today opened up a wellspring of feelings about my dad and why I still can't get rid of the pain he caused me. I hadn't seen him in almost six years, and after the last get-together, I never wanted to see him again.

My college graduation party had turned into a disaster when his car squealed up our driveway, and he drunkenly staggered up the front lawn to throw his arms around me, professing how proud he was. Like he knew what my education meant to me and how many emotional and financial obstacles I'd had to overcome to get my diploma. No thanks to him. His slurred words and disheveled appearance were a huge embarrassment, but the fact that he puked in my mom's rose bushes topped it all. I was mortified. There weren't enough words to make this right or to make the sixty people present develop amnesia about what they'd just witnessed.

Thank God for my mom—my rock and my intermediary. After dragging my dad's plastered ass into the living room, she thanked everyone for attending and gently ushered them out of the house and to their cars. Each whisper was like being swatted with a twig; each one stung a little, but put together, it felt like a wasp attack. Deeply painful and hard to forget.

That was why I attended these psychology conferences. Traveling and making friends was great, but the education was what I was paying for. Arrogant speakers and lush accommodations were just distractions, and I needed to stay focused. Okay, I'll admit I did want a playmate, but that just seemed to be another distraction I couldn't entertain. *Crap!*

Chapter 10

ALEXANDER

IT WAS DAY THREE of this conference, and I felt like I was being set up for a big shoe drop. Yesterday, Ms. Gonzales sat in the back of the room, taking copious notes and barely looking at me while I lectured. I could tell she wanted to raise her hand to ask questions, but she leaned over and asked another person for whatever she needed. Twice, I asked for audience participation, and twice, she physically held her arm to her side so she wouldn't volunteer.

I had to applaud her. Her self-restraint was tremendous, even though I could see pain streaking across her face. The questions were designed to evoke an emotional response, pushing the audience to dig deep and reflect on the issues that continued to weave into their personal tapestry. Regardless of the pain and suffering each of these people had experienced, their dedication to learning how to overcome their issues was the reason they were here.

As it was, I had my own ongoing issues to reconcile, especially those related to my family. It was just past noon, and I already had no less than four emails from my mother and twenty-six text volleys from my sisters. I knew I shouldn't have joined this idiotic sibling group thread.

It was the same ridiculous conversation we'd had every year after the annual gala:

Tabitha: I can't believe we had to stand in 90-degree heat for 30 minutes listening to this overstuffed buffoon go on and on about how he was personally responsible for the minimum wage being raised.

Sarah: I know. First off, he could have said everything in 5 minutes, and we could have been back in the pool enjoying ourselves. Second, he had NOTHING to do with getting the wages raised. Yeah, he signed the bill, but his constituents did all the work. What an ass.

Tabitha: Exactly! If Alex had been there (are you listening, Alex?), he would have stepped in after 10 minutes, clapped the asshole on the back, and thanked him for his good work. See, Alex, I bow to your fabulousness, even when you're not here to see it firsthand. (clapping and a king emoji)

*Sarah: Hellooo??? Alex??? When the f**k are you coming home? It's not too late to change your condo locks. (wink and key emoji)*

I wasn't going to dive deep into this conversation, but I felt I should answer in solidarity. So I did, dutifully.

Me: So happy to hear you made it through another tedious,

mind-numbing event inflicted on you by our parents. Thank you for missing me—your groveling has not gone unnoticed. I'll be home on Saturday. Let's have brunch. Sarah, stay the fuck away from my condo! (wink, wink)

Using emoji was juvenile, but they really did help drive the message home. I clicked on the main screen and pocketed my phone as I headed over to the coffee barista at the far end of the lobby. A Java jolt would be the only thing that would get me through the day. I had two educational meetings with four other psychology professionals to share the latest and greatest studies on childhood trauma and the effects it had on concept retention in children.

I'd like to say I wasn't annoyed that Ms. Gonzales kept to herself yesterday, not torturing me with her inane, smart-mouthed questions, but I was. She had a way of waking me up and keeping me on my toes, elevating my game. Her sexy mouth and provocative questions had me thinking about her more than was prudent. When I thought back to her accosting me after the first day's lecture, with her dress buttons undone, I was perplexed. Not because I didn't know how things like that happened, but because I'd seen that happen before and I'd never been obsessed with it afterward. I wouldn't call myself a player exactly, but I had gotten around quite a bit in my youth, and it took more than a pair of generous tits to rile me up. This woman had entranced me in a way I'd never experienced before, and I had been engaged to be married no less than three years earlier.

I took the seat closest to the big floor-to-ceiling windows, to the right of the coffee stand, sipped my caramel macchiato—a special treat for my addled head—and looked out onto the infinity pool one level down. It reminded me that I wanted to go sailing on the West Coast while I was here. I'd been told the view of San Francisco from the water was spectacular and shouldn't miss it. Speaking of spectacular views, I turned my head to the left while recrossing my legs when a tiny Latina with a gorgeous ass in a snug shift dress with big colorful flowers caught my eye. She was walking with another woman, and their animated conversation had her smiling from ear to ear. It was quite beautiful to witness. There wasn't a single characteristic about her that defined her beauty—it was the combination of her assets at work that took my breath away. Too bad she had a lot of baggage that I did not want to be a part of. I could deal with sassy and smart, but combative and stubborn—no way. I left that shit just shy of the altar. Of course, it could have been my fiancée's cheating that was the real problem, but still, I drew the line at crazy town.

I took this as a sign to move on to my next meeting, not wanting any more attacks on my character. Standing quickly, I moved with purpose toward the other side of the foyer, forcing my eyes forward, but her siren stare drilled into me, and I had to look up to acknowledge her.

Stifling a smart-ass comment, I lifted my head, raised my brows, nodded politely to both women and said, "Good day, ladies." And kept moving at a good clip.

They nodded back, both smiling and calm until the siren spoke. "Excellent lecture, Dr. Pierce. The lecture, Forgive & Live, was illuminating." She quirked her head toward her friend, leaving me feeling there was some double meaning to her words. *Damn her for making me feel like I was lacking.*

Always wanting the last word, I couldn't leave that clearly snide remark unquestioned, so I stopped, pivoting to speak to her backside. "I'd love to hear more about that later after dinner if you're free." *There, now, she was on the back foot.* Too bad my ego didn't leave room for her next response.

She stopped, straightened to her tallest possible height, and slowly turned toward me, resting her hand on her shapely hip. Resigned to speak with me again, she cocked her head to the side and responded in a deadpan sort of way, "As much as I'd love to chat more about that tonight, I already have plans. Enjoy the rest of your day."

My lips pulled into a line, and I, too, pulled myself up straighter, giving her a nod while mumbling a string of not-so-nice accusations under my breath as I stormed off to my meeting.

As it was, I didn't see Ms. Gonzales the rest of the evening—and I looked. And looked and looked. Even her friend wasn't around to drop any clues as to where she was, so I decided to end the night early and went to my room to catch up with a buddy of mine from high school.

Jacob and I had a long and sordid past. I knew that if I ever really pissed him off beyond repair, he'd have me on wanted posters and paying reparations for a tennis court, a golf cart, and maybe, for public indecency in a fountain. I won't fully own that last one because it was Jacob who dropped the drugs in my beer without my knowledge.

I walked through my suite, yanking off my tie and kicking my Cole Haans across the floor. This room was paid for by the conference committee, so I took full advantage of the minibar and cracked open a Heineken. I'm not a big fan of drinking alone, so opting for a beer instead of hard liquor seemed like a good compromise.

I kept the lights off to take advantage of the glittering skyline outside my window. I should have gotten outside today, but my meetings ran long, and I almost missed the dinner the conference provided. Instead, I dialed my friend's number, put it on speaker, and walked into my bedroom. The king-size bed sat on a four-poster frame and was adorned with crisp white sheets, six pillows, and a down comforter. Of course, that was how I saw it when I checked in—now it looked like a tornado had twisted everything into a giant ball. And yet, still, it looked inviting.

After four rings, the call was answered, and I heard screaming on the other end. I didn't think anything of the screaming and wasn't concerned. However, I couldn't figure out if his kids were killing him or if his wife finally got smart and locked him out of the credit cards.

"Hey, Asshole! What's going on over there?" I screamed back, going with the flow.

"We're in an escape room and my kids are fucking killing me. Again, and again, and again. I'm going to beat their little asses when we're done. They ganged up on me, little shits." He finished his rant with a healthy chuckle.

"You probably had it coming. Call me when you're finished, and we'll catch up," I responded, then ended the call with a chuckle. I shook my head and tried to imagine having a set of twins to deal with every day. *Yeah, no.* It's not that I disliked kids, I loved them a lot, but the shit their tiny brains had to process freaked me out. I knew firsthand how one wrong parenting decision or just one lapse of judgment could emotionally or physically maim them for life. Raising kids was the slipperiest slope a person could choose to maneuver. Running a multi-billion-dollar company couldn't touch the anxiety of raising a dependent child. I'm forty-two years old, and some days I can barely take care of myself—and *I* had an assistant. Definitely not for the faint of heart.

I needed a long, hot, muscle-relaxing shower to empty my brain. This afternoon's meetings had been so heavy. The emotional impact of child abuse, whether by neglect or intention, created a visceral response in our nervous systems. Our bodies take over, and our minds fight or take flight. The discussions we'd had about how to identify abuse early and find meaningful interventions that last were painful. But it was why I got into this field in the first place.

My reality was that even though I had a very privileged childhood surrounded by money and opportunity, it didn't change the outcome at all. Money and opportunity didn't make my parents love me more or give me the attention I craved. In fact, it was the basis for their neglect of me and my sisters. It was a good thing that I had to undergo psychoanalysis before receiving my PhD. That shit was terrifying. And it still didn't take any less out of me every time I revisited it as a professional.

I dropped my clothes on the marble floor and stepped into the shower. The hot water worked wonders for my tight muscles, but my mind was still sore. In my experience, only one thing could alleviate a fraught mind: release—a hard, mind-blowing release—and the one person who came to mind first was the last person I needed to be thinking about.

Chapter 11

TRUDIE

I woke earlier than expected. I was still on East Coast time and feeling it, probably because I hadn't made time to practice my yoga and clear my mind of all the clinical information I came here to learn. It exhausted me when I tried to apply all of it to my own life. Psychology was no joke. This "psychobabble," as Sam used to call it, took a lot out of me because I really used it. Anyone who said therapy was a waste of time and money didn't want to look behind the curtain and deal with who they found. It took courage, and I learned as a child how to be courageous during hardship. My mom was the queen of courage, God bless her.

I threw on my new yoga outfit, a cute summery two-piece, and headed to the pool, collecting a yoga mat on my way as I passed through the workout room. These fancy hotels always seemed to have everything I needed; sure enough, this one was no different. Wall-to-wall mirrors with the cardio equipment facing the pristine lap pool and lounge chairs that baked alone in the sun. My body ached to be able to lie out in the sun all day, lazing by the pool with a piña colada in one hand and a sexy rom-com in the other.

Stop it. You came here for one reason only. I needed to stay focused on healing. As part of that healing process, I would practice yoga while focusing on the said scenario.

I rolled out my mat near a group of pool loungers and set my smartwatch for twenty minutes. I found that peaceful place in my head where thoughts floated away one by one as my muscles relaxed and my jaw unclenched. I nudged my body and mind to enter that familiar black tunnel of complete emptiness connecting one breath to one body movement, surrendering my anxiety and stress. Just as I reached the pinnacle of my nirvana, the screech of a chair next to my mat ripped my focus from my serenity, and a loud exhale marked the end of my practice.

I took several more cleansing breaths to bring me back to my center, then finally gave up just as my watch trilled on my wrist. Rolling from my cross-legged position to a cat-cow pose, I moved through my post-meditation flow without opening my eyes. I wasn't ready to engage with anyone, and my need for calm overrode anything else. Three forward flows later, I stood, circling my arms out from my body, up over my head, and into *samasthiti*. My heart center sent out love and positivity into the world, and I opened my eyes to a new woman. Except there was a set of dark green eyes with crinkles at the corners watching me.

Legs outstretched and relaxed, the rest of Dr. Pierce was the epitome of a sun-kissed Greek boy toy. His slow perusal of my body inspired my nipples to stand at attention, betraying my feigned disinterest. It didn't help that he only wore a sweaty tank top and shorts. I didn't know where to look first, so I settled on his bulging pecs and rippled abs.

"Good morning, Ms. Gonzales. How was your yoga this morning? Ready to take on the day?" he goaded me.

I patted my face with the towel I had grabbed earlier and mimicked his expression since my mouth was parched and my brain sizzled with all the things I'd like to do to a body like his.

"Quite good, Dr. Pierce. I'm always ready for a new challenge. See you in class." *You stalker.* I turned quickly to bend down and grabbed my stuff before sashaying my ass back inside to wipe down my mat. It didn't even occur to me that I put my ass right in front of his face when I picked it up—I had better things to do with my time than worry about what he thought of me. *What does he think of my ass? Don't answer that.*

During the quick elevator trip to my floor, I was preoccupied with a myriad of questions that probably would never be answered. The one that consumed me through my shower and through breakfast was why he chose to sit next to me while I had my eyes closed when he could have sat anywhere else by the pool—or in the whole conference center, for that matter.

I texted my mom quickly to let her know that I'd be home on Saturday and asked if she wanted to have dinner with my brothers on Sunday night. At her house, of course, and she could put it all together, too. Great invitation, right? My mom's cooking was legendary, from Chilean *empanadas de pino* with beef chilies that burned your tongue to *pão de queijo*, Brazilian cheese puff pastry, and Spanish *polvorones*, which most people call Mexican wedding cookies. She did a little catering when we were younger, but now it's too hard for her to stand and work in the kitchen for so long. *That's why you should be making something, brat.*

Ten minutes later, she responded with a thumbs-up emoji, and I responded with a red heart. I couldn't wait until Sunday. It had been too long since we all sat around a table.

I stopped once again at the coffee stand, and when I went to give the barista my money, a presence I was becoming all too acquainted with stepped alongside me.

"Give me what she's having, and I'll take care of the bill." His air of authority was electrifying, even though I didn't need his charity; I paid my own way.

"That's not necessary, Dr. Pierce, but thank you anyway." I took that moment to look up to his smug face but found a glimmer of something I couldn't quite put a name to. I cleared my throat and turned to leave when I felt his hand on my elbow. He received his coffee from the sweet lady behind the bar and steered me away from the crowd behind us.

He walked me halfway down the hall as he had three days ago, stopping me by my now-favorite potted plant, and exhaled heavily.

Before he could begin, I snapped out, "That exhale was just like the one you used to interrupt me at the pool this morning. What exactly does that mean?" I crossed my now free arm, along with the one holding my coffee, under my breasts and jutted my hip out. *He exasperated me.*

He took his sweet time, and I changed hips, waiting for the big reveal.

"It means—we did not get off on the right footing from the beginning of this conference, and I don't know how to fix it. It's not that I don't like you, Ms. Gonzales, it's that I don't know you, and you don't know me. I was hoping that I could rectify that last night. However, you had other plans and were nowhere to be found."

His face softened, and it seemed like his whole demeanor was deflating. Could this be his attempt at sincerity? Did the great Dr. Pierce just offer up an olive branch? Perhaps so. *Just take the damn branch, Trudie.*

My inner voice made up its mind and was absconding with my heart, yet my brain wouldn't let it go. I'd been tricked by moments of contrition from my dad all my life, and I almost always regretted believing them.

I knew that by trusting him, I could be free-falling later, but what if he was being sincere? Did I want to take this small risk for a possible long-term payoff? This guy could be the key to so many professional avenues for me. Certainly, I could allow him a reprieve, right? *Sure. Just don't hold your breath.*

I inhaled a long, measured breath before speaking, looking at my cup as if it were an oracle. I smoothed out my face, swallowed, and lifted my eyes to confirm what I already knew. He was sorry.

"You're right, Dr. Pierce. That series of unfortunate events didn't help us get off on the right path. Let's fix that now and let it go." I smiled openly, then extended my hand as colleagues and professionals do.

"Thank you for that, Miss… may I call you Trudie?" His raised eyebrows were a good sign we were entering calmer waters.

"You're welcome. Sure, call me Trudie." I pumped his hand one last time and tried to pull back, but he didn't let mine go. I searched his eyes for some sort of trickery, a sign of smugness that he got me to do something I wouldn't have offered up willingly, but instead, I felt his thumb softly brush over mine, leaving me shivering with anticipation.

His other hand came up to join the two already clasped and squeezed my small hand between his two larger ones, making my knees a little weak.

"You are a class act, Trudie. I'll see you shortly." And without further ado, he walked away smiling. A smile crept up my face, and I enjoyed the walk to my next lecture.

Chapter 12

ALEXANDER

WELL, THANK GOD MY little problem got resolved. I didn't want to go through another lecture with her pouting in the back and not getting the benefit of class participation because she was being stubborn. My experiences alone, aside from my education, were enough to fill a week's worth of lectures, and frankly, that little minx could have benefited from all of them.

I wasn't worried. During the next session, I planned to be jovial, amenable, and professional. The air had been cleared, and it was going to be a great day. I was sure of it—mostly.

Conference volunteers opened the doors to my classroom, and each participant was handed a glossy portfolio of all my books, recorded lectures, and contact information. And because I'm such a great guy, I included all my PowerPoint slides with places to write notes so everyone could focus on the lecture instead of scribbling everything I said into a notebook—or on cocktail napkins, as the case may be.

I stood off to one side, giving the impression I was looking at my phone, but I was actually taking a facial assessment of each attendee. People-watching was one of my favorite activities, although in this case, I watched for one person who wouldn't be happy about being scrutinized. Outward appearances typically don't tell the whole story about someone; however, the entirety of their facial expressions can help you prepare how you want to proceed with them. The studies on this alone could fill a whole lecture series, but that day, I was going to use it as a basis to help my class move past their childhood scripts and personas and become the people they truly wanted to be.

Half the room was filled when Ms. Gonzales, I mean Trudie, walked in confidently and purposefully. She wanted to be there. Her dynamic face was a thing of beauty. She didn't realize that the tilt of her smile and the fierce quality of her eyebrows made her a formidable opponent. Certainly, I'd already been subjected to her fiery demeanor, her face leading the charge. She was a typical beauty by most social constructs, yet her shoulder-length wavy hair, bold jewelry, curvy body—and let's not forget that sassy mouth that was demanding to be kissed—had me swallowing hard and praying for a smooth, uneventful lecture.

Perhaps emboldened by our earlier conversation, she appeared motivated to move to the front of the class but stopped halfway. She looked left, and then right, and then at me, contemplating her most strategic perspective, and settled on a middle seat to her left. I noted she'd never sat in the middle of a row before. Did she think she would be safe from me, hiding among the masses? *Silly girl. I know where you are—you can't hide from me.*

It was two minutes before class was to begin, and I asked everyone to stand up and fill in the front rows, leaving the back for latecomers. Several people rolled their eyes, thinking this was so middle school, but I had my reasons—they just didn't know them yet.

I took my place behind the podium and clicked on the opening slide of my presentation When Forgiveness Isn't an Option. Then I stepped out from behind the podium, hoping to create a more intimate setting, one that didn't include barriers and showed that we are all people with not-so-different issues. Unbuttoning my coat and loosening my tie, I shoved my hands into my pants pockets and took a wide stance.

"Good morning, everyone. I hope you slept well because today will be the first day of the rest of your lives. I hope you will be open to creating something special, if not magical, today." I was met with more rolling eyes than sparkling ones—there was a lot of skepticism.

"Seriously," I assured them. "Today will be the day *you* decide to either accept your past and let it go or continue to look at your childhood relationships through rose-colored glasses; decide to deny the truth or forgive your trespasses and learn from them to do better, knowing you're worth so much more than you believed before this conference." Now, the heads were all working in unison. Up and down, up and down. *Now we're getting somewhere.*

Deciding to be a little more transparent than I'd ever been with my students, I removed my suit jacket, laid it over the empty chair in the front row, and then walked along the outer side of the room. I hadn't planned to stop at Trudie's row. But she deserved the truth about my past and why I could be an asshole. I was no saint, and

I wanted to own it. That's not to say it was a good thing, but if nothing else, I was self-aware. Or that's what I told myself.

"I spent my youth being paraded around by my parents, who wanted to convince the New York elite they had a perfect family. My sisters and I were the proverbial 'dog and pony show' and, therefore, never allowed to step out of line. You can only imagine the childhood traumas I had to endure. I'm not telling you my traumas were more complex or disturbing than yours—I only mean to share with you that no one goes through childhood without a few bumps and bruises to their ego and psyche."

I moved more quickly through my monologue to get to the bottom line: "We all have suffered, some more acutely than others, and we all have to reconcile with ourselves. My question is, when is it the right time to say goodbye to that young child and hello to a life of peace and joy? You are all deserving of both, and I hope you know that this change is purely a decision, an internal switch you can choose to flip. Nothing external can change this for you. Not even a pompous, egotistical guy like me."

I returned to the podium to the sounds of laughter and "amens." Before giving the group what they came for my last selfish act was to peer over at Trudie. Her face was the softest I'd seen it. She sat back in her seat, relaxed and ready to move forward. I gave her a wink, and her beautiful mouth quirked up on one side. *One for the doc.*

Reading the room one more time before I wrapped up today's class, I noticed two people in the back conversing, which set me on edge. Even small conversations are distracting to people around them, and after seeing the annoyed looks from the attendees surrounding them, I found myself having to intervene like a middle school teacher.

"Well, it looks like a hot topic is going on in the back of the room. Would you two care to share with the class?" My lips pulled into a grimace as they looked at me in shock. *Yeah, I'm talking to you loudmouths.*

The bearded man of this dynamic duo dared to feign ignorance with a shocked look on his face and uttered a mild, "Oh, sorry, were we too loud?" *Yes, asshole.*

The woman next to him harrumphed indignantly, her shock aimed not at me but at her friend.

"I can't believe you just apologized. We can have a conversation if we want to." She crossed and uncrossed her legs, adding tightly crossed arms around her midriff to complete the irritating pose.

Why did I find myself in these situations? Had I done something so horrible that the universe stalked me and placed idiots in front of me just for kicks? It was time to shut this daytime drama down.

Moving down the middle aisle, I stopped at the end of the row where my not-so-favorite students were still bickering. Any professional in this situation would call them out to the hallway, but I was ten minutes from finishing this class, and I was feeling feisty, so instead, they got my angry dad to whisper.

"Listen, I'm sure the topic that compelled you to raise your voices and interrupt my lecture was, in fact, important; however, I'm going to have to ask you to cease and desist or please leave the room. Everyone here has paid to be able to hear the lecture, and your behavior is compromising their experience. So, which will it be? Stay and be quiet, or leave?" As I slid both hands back into my pockets to wait for their response, I heard a familiar voice call from the other side of the room.

"Answer him so we can get back on topic. You two are way out of line. You've been talking all morning, and if Dr. Pierce hadn't intervened when he did, I was going to do it for him."

Shocked and annoyed, I shot her an evil look over my shoulder, hoping to get her to sit down and let me handle it my way. She got the look all right, throwing her hands in front of her and then putting them on her hips in a challenge. I turned back around for an answer, politely asking again, "Stay or go?" I fought to keep my expression neutral, but my jaw was ticking, and my molars were being ground down to nubs.

They didn't answer. Instead, they stood up and grabbed their things to leave, muttering about disrespect and threatening that the conference committee was going to hear about this. *Whatever.* Thanks be to all that is holy they left when they did, or my little warrior might have unleashed the Kraken on them. *My little warrior? When did I become so possessive of her?* I didn't realize how inflamed this situation made me feel until I claimed Ms. Gon—Trudie as my little warrior.

I felt the need to corral my students back into line, and as I marched back to my place of authority behind the podium, I cleared my throat to get everyone's attention and considered how best to move forward. Hard ass? No. I didn't want to end their conference, remembering me as the asshole I professed to be earlier. Nonchalant? Trudie would think I was a pushover, and I am definitely not that. Settling instead on a little humor to break the tension, I laughed and then clapped my hands and rubbed them together as if conjuring up a magic spell—or maybe an evil genie.

"Well. That was something, right? Nothing like a little drama to get the blood flowing." Nodding my head up and down seemed like the right way to get everyone else to do the same, and thankfully, most everyone got on board.

This was the moment that would seal the deal on what this lecture was all about. I knew this material well and didn't need my notes to deliver a meaningful ending. I abandoned my PowerPoint by closing my laptop cover and walked from behind the podium to grab a vacant chair. The carpet squeaked as I dragged the chair to the front of the audience, centering it in the aisle between both sides of the room.

My hair itched with impatience, and all I could think of was that this final lesson needed to hit the right note to be the game changer I wanted it to be. I hoped this moment would change their lives forever, so every word needed to be felt at a cellular level. So I spun the chair around, placing its back in front of me as I sat, and let the atoms of energy settle while I pieced together my final thoughts.

"I'll be honest with you. What I'm going to say next should make a difference in your lives. It should have you jumping out of your seats to start living as you've always imagined. But I'm struggling over whether you'll think it's crap or a bunch of propaganda to give you the impression I know what I'm talking about or if you'll truly hear my message, take it to heart, and do something magical with it. Again, let's circle back to the beginning of this lecture. You get to make the choice of how you want to live your life. You're not children anymore. Your parents don't get to dictate who you are today."

My hair still itched, and I ran a hand through it, hoping to wipe away the sweat that trickled down. The urge to stand pulled me out of my seat, and my frustration at this predicament had me pacing. I stopped on the right side of the room. Everyone was looking at me, and their eyes were begging for my message. It would have been a giant ego boost if I hadn't truly felt they needed it.

With an outstretched arm, I panned the room in an inclusive gesture.

"The incident you all experienced moments ago is a microcosm of your childhood trauma. You knew those people were talking, and you did your best to put it out of your consciousness. Knowingly or unknowingly, you dismissed their poor behavior for your own preservation and because of your desire to stay present and focused in the lecture. This is precisely what I've been getting at today. Shit happens all around us, and we make millions of decisions about whether we will engage or whether we will let it go and stay focused. Are you following me?"

My mouth was parched, and my heart was bouncing out of my chest. Their heads were nodding in the affirmative, and I felt like a marathon runner who had just spotted the finish line. Using my forearm, I wiped my shirtsleeve along my brow and pressed on.

"When I called out those two people in the back, I could feel your energy growing along with mine. You were waiting for me to do something, but what? You were aggravated that they interrupted your concentration and now you wanted them exposed. Again, knowingly or unknowingly, you were out for blood. Our animal pack intelligence kicked in because in the end, we are animals. We are at the top of the food chain because we can reason. But that, my friends, is where the similarities of the human race fall apart. Our logic isn't universal—our life experiences vary, and our cultural differences play a crucial role in responding to outside influences."

I was on a roll and now was the time to reel it all in and put a bow on it. My final thoughts came together as I walked back to the other side of the room, stopping in line with Trudie's row. Her face was flushed and her eyes, with their heavy lashes, were wide. She sat up tall in her seat, waiting impatiently for the words that would change her life. I was going to give her more than words if she ever looked at me like that again.

Clasping my hands together, again imploring my class to stay with me, I spoke my final truth barely above a whisper. My microphone picked up my husky tones and shared my words for me.

"At that moment I chose to be fair, professional, and merciful, if you will. I wanted them to own what was theirs and apologize not to me but to you—let go of their egos and show reason—to do the right thing when given a choice. You saw what happened. The man knew immediately he was wrong; he felt contrition and apologized. She did not. She was indignant at being called out. She showed no remorse and no compassion for her friend, or you, her community. Yet he walked out with her feeling small and castigated. He had a choice to stay and let her deal with her indignation on her own, but he didn't. He allowed himself to stay in a role and follow the script of what may have been a childhood trauma. Breaking free of that script took great courage and support. I wish he could have stayed to the end of this lecture because all of you would have been a great support system for him." I smiled and took my place behind the podium.

My message was clear, heartfelt, and passionate. I hoped I'd made a difference in their lives. At least I knew one person heard me. Trudie looked exhausted as she slumped in her seat at the end of my lecture, and I could see the wheels whirring in her head. Or was that my head spinning with adrenaline?

The lecture ended with wild applause, and then I took several questions. Fifteen minutes later, I was shaking hands and wishing people good luck, but the one person I expected to see or confront me had slipped out of the room.

Chapter 13

TRUDIE

M Y ROOM WAS COOL, and my bed was remade—the benefits of staying in a posh hotel room. I stripped out of my dress and haphazardly kicked off my heels. My head was buzzing with everything we had spoken about today in Dr. Pierce's session. He appeared so open and self-actualized. But was he? Or was he just a good actor? The kind who could have you believing anything they had to say because their gorgeousness rendered you stupid. I never thought I was that kind of woman, but sometimes a guy like that left me dumbstruck. I saw his mouth moving as his eyes floated all over my body, yet the words never actually made sense. It was like those Peanuts characters and their teacher who just sounded like a *wa-wa* drone.

Today's lecture started that way, especially since he made a concerted effort to rectify his behavior from a few days ago. Of course, that could have been a manipulation, too. I hated being so cynical. He was so incredibly right, though. Being cynical was a strategy that I needed to let go of, even if it had served me in the past. My father's actions shouldn't have affected me anymore, and that was going to stop there and then. I didn't want to feel trepidation about meeting new people, it should be fun and exciting. How would I ever find someone when I was constantly questioning their motives?

My luxurious bathroom called to me. I turned both nozzles to full throttle to fill the tub with scalding water before reaching for the delicious bath salts on the ledge nearby. I needed to decompress and sort through all the amazing information I'd learned that week. The kids in my classes in the upcoming year were going to get the best version of myself, and hopefully, some of the high-risk kids would be comforted by my words and deeds.

As I stripped down, I took a moment to take in my appearance. My lightly pigmented skin was toned, if not a little disproportionate in the ass. I used a scrunchy to hold up my shoulder-length hair. I was very fortunate to have soft, curly hair that wasn't course or frizzy. I planned to curl and pin some of it up for the awards gala. It wasn't my favorite part of the conference, but I knew how much effort those in psychology gave their field of study, and I knew they should be recognized. Maybe one day, I'd be recognized for my efforts in education.

Letting go of the day, I sank into the calming hot water and closed my eyes, hoping to reach a Zen state of mind. Deep breaths lulled me into a peaceful haze, and the hum of the air conditioner in the bathroom was my sound machine. Time was an illusion as I found the peace I was looking for while the temperature of the water was my clock. I brought myself back to the present with a few more deep breaths. I reached for my robe and only then noticed on my phone that I had missed a call from Ruby.

The gala was in an hour, starting in the main hallway outside the ballrooms with drinks and hors d'oeuvres. I had time to spare, so I unpacked my cosmetic bag and called Ruby. Three rings went by. Just when I was sure she wasn't going to pick up, a gasping, out-of-breath Ruby finally answered.

"Hey, Trudes, how is your conference going? Did you bag the lecturer yet?" The huffing and puffing on her end forced me to put her on speaker.

"Where are you and what are you doing that has you so out of breath? Please tell me you didn't pick up while having sex with someone," I begged. It had happened before.

"Nooo—I'm working out but didn't want to miss your call. Fill me in while I finish my run." I could hear the hydraulics of a treadmill through the receiver, and I was alarmed at how much she pushed herself. I'm a pansy—a gentle flower. I had no high-powered, high-adrenaline workouts: yoga, walking, swimming, and meditation—they were the ticket.

While applying a second coat of mascara, I gave her what she was asking for: "Yeah, I banged him. Handcuffed him to a chair and did a rowdy lap dance all over his cock until he begged to be set free. He ate my pussy for almost an hour before he let me come. It was the best night of my life." I stifled a laugh.

The whirring of the treadmill ceased, and Ruby struggled to get her breathing under control. "Are you trying to kill me? I almost fell over laughing while running. Not a good idea. So, nothing yet, huh?"

I filled her in on my conversation with Satan and his attempt at reconciliation. Like me, she seemed a little leery about how forthcoming his apology was. Highly unusual.

"I know I should take his words at face value, but I know a player when I meet one, and this guy just oozes hidden agenda. He's a psychologist. He knows how to play mind games and read people like a book. If I give him the benefit of the doubt, trusting him not to play me, am I being naïve?" Ruby never steered me wrong and always had my back. I'd follow her blindly, but *only* her.

A deep sigh breezed through the phone as I started to apply my garnet-red lipstick. "I'm not sure what to tell you in this instance. I think you can have the upper hand since it appears as though he is still interested in you. Why would he go to the trouble of stalking you around the hotel if he wasn't sincere? He had to have more important things to deal with than your feelings, especially if he didn't already have any about you. What does your gut say?"

I hated when she did this—making me decide for myself. Sure, I'm a grown woman, but...

"You're right, you're right. Accepting his apology wouldn't be the first time I ignored my past in hopes of a better future. But I'm really scared I'll get burned and never try again. Is this the hill I want to die on?" I had a flair for the dramatic.

"Listen, babe. Nothing ventured, nothing gained. What's the worst that will happen? You'll get on a plane and never see the guy again. Right?"

Maybe.

"Right. But I hate stretching myself. It's so painful, no matter if it's physical or emotional. Thanks for pushing me along, Rubes. I love you, girl."

"Love you back more. Now, tell me what's on for tonight." She was switching directions like she always does so I wouldn't perseverate.

"Awards dinner, schmoozing, and lots of alcohol. I did make a new friend from Alabama—Izzy. She's a firecracker, so we get each other. We've been down to the beach and have hung out a few times. She's terrific."

"Wish I could meet her, but she's not taking my spot as bestie, so don't get too attached," she said, her tone decisive.

I shoved all my makeup back into the bag and carried my phone as I walked out of the bathroom, flicking off the light as I left.

"No one could ever replace you, Ruby. You're one of a kind. I've got to get dressed and get downstairs. I love you, and I'll see you some time next week." I gave her a verbal "mwah" kiss; she returned the love and hung up. She was the sister I never had.

The dress I brought specifically for the event was hanging over the mercury glass armoire door. It had a straight seam at the back that went down to the top of my hip, making me look really thin. Then it kicked out, the fabric lying gently over my curvy hips. When I walked, it accentuated my sway and made me feel very sexy. I looked forward to seeing how Satan liked it. They were his colors: red and black.

Cool jazz wafted through the three-story conference concourse hallway and long shimmery swags of fabric were draped from the ceiling to the floor with dramatic uplighting. As I exited the elevator, I made sure I didn't let my eyes linger too long—I couldn't have another Dr. Pierce mash-up while admiring the decor. *Still wasn't my fault, but I'll be the bigger person and own my piece of that disaster.*

With my black sequined clutch tucked under my arm, I enjoyed a glass of champagne and a canapé with cucumber and smoked salmon while I took in the festive transformation of the hall. I found my favorite plant and spent the next fifteen minutes standing by it and people-watching. I was entertained by the fascinating nonverbal expressions and stone-cold faces until I felt a warm presence behind my back. I really hoped it was Izzy, but her presence felt like sunshine and unicorns, and this didn't.

I kept my back to him, knowing he wanted me to acknowledge his arrival. *Too bad.*

"Hello, Trudie," he murmured over my right shoulder.

I could feel his breath spread over my neck, and my body betrayed me, sending ripples of electricity down to my belly and beyond. If he was anyone else, I would have leaned back into him and fed off his heat, but I didn't want to encourage him. I couldn't trust myself to keep things professional and we'd just found some solid ground, so I slowly brought my glass to my red lips and hummed in reply. I intended it to be more of a harrumph, except he must have interpreted it as a purr.

"You look beautiful tonight. Might you save me a dance?" I watched a devilish smile stretch across his perfectly sculpted face as I turned slightly to respond more clearly.

"Thank you for the compliment, although it won't earn you a dance, I'm afraid." Several stunningly dressed women walked by and I focused on them, as I'm sure he did, too. "Perhaps one of those lovely ladies would be happy to entertain you tonight." I clutched my purse in one hand and my empty glass in another and escaped.

Two steps later, his hand fell gently on my bare shoulder, freezing me where I stood.

"To be clear, Trudie, I don't speak to a woman and watch others at the same time. That's rude. Additionally, I didn't compliment you to get anything from you. You are obviously a beautiful woman, and your care in getting ready for this evening didn't go unnoticed, not by me, and not by the dozen other men I've observed watching you walk to your hiding place."

Damn it! How did he call me out like that and make me feel like a petulant child? No one had ever spoken to me this way, and truthfully, I wasn't sure if I liked it or if it was a turnoff.

"And finally, it would be my honor to dance with such an intelligent, beautiful, and feisty woman. I'm sure you have dance moves that would actually make me look good." His face begged for forgiveness and I couldn't leave him hanging that way. I was just too damn nice for my own good.

"Fine. One dance, and not a slow one, either."

His face beamed and a laugh erupted from his chest. "You're too kind, Ms. Gonzales. Too kind. I'll see you again soon." He left me with a formal bow that had me giggling into my hand.

I walked the opposite way and found a waiter with more champagne and another with those yummy mini egg rolls and plum sauce. Truth be told, I'd rather make a meal out of those and a half dozen pigs in a blanket than a rubbery chicken dinner.

My mouth was full of food when I felt the stampede of a single unicorn coming toward me from across the room and skidding to stop in her glittery pink sky-high sandals. Izzy definitely had the flair for cotton candy, and she made quite a statement with a sparkly pink A-line 1950s-style dress that hung off her shoulders, offering a deep V cut through her bosom. She looked every bit the refined southern belle. Her glittery stilettos were her only tell that she had a naughty side. They were decadent.

"Oh my God, Trudie!" she squealed, fluttering her hands. "I totally love your dress and your hair. Did you do that yourself? You're amazing. What's the name of that lipstick? I couldn't pull it off, but my BFF back home would love it." Her bubbly personality pulled me in, and I found myself vacillating between bashful and proud.

"Thank you, Izzy. You look amazing, too," I said, hugging her. "I did my own hair. YouTube has some great tips on how to get professional-looking hair by yourself. And the lipstick is called 'Get Me Garnet.' Great name, huh?" I laughed and pulled it from my purse so she could take a picture of it.

After we scoped out the hall and all the hot men in it, we made our way into the ballroom to find our table. I really hoped we were sitting together since we had spoken to a conference coordinator earlier in the week to see if they could make it happen. The place card table was next to the bar, so I stood in line for drinks while Izzy grabbed our cards.

"Look, Trudie. We didn't get the same table, but we did get tables next to each other. At least we can pull our seats together for the awards part." Her positive nature was contagious, so I went with the flow and let the disappointment go.

Ten minutes later, lights flashed, alerting us to the beginning of the program. We grabbed our drinks from the bar, found our tables on the other side of the room, and did our best to sit as close as possible. However, a group of four showed up at my table just before I arrived, pushing me to the opposite side with an empty seat next to me. *Please, God, don't put me next to a long talker or a person who missed their shower today.*

Here's the thing about prayers: they need to be crystal clear, with no ambiguities. The results could be devastating, hilarious, or, in my case, ironic. *Please welcome the incredibly egocentric, perfectly styled beauty himself, Dr. Alexander Pierce. Argh!* How was this even possible? He should have been sitting up front with all of the nominees and fancy people, not off to the side with me. Did he piss off someone other than me this week?

I must have looked like a hooked fish because he tapped the underside of my chin to close my mouth.

"A little shocked are we, Trudie?" His smugness was like putting flint to tinder.

"No, doctor. Not a little—rather a lot."

"Not to worry, it won't be as bad as all that. We'll get on just fine." His arrogant laugh sent my good mood out the door. "Drink up. This night is going to be a blast."

As we introduced ourselves to everyone else at the table, I caught Izzy looking at me with wide eyes, pointing to Dr. Pierce. *Seriously? Does she think she is being nonchalant?* Everyone saw her, even Dr. Pierce himself. I could only offer a slow nod as I hid my face behind my water glass and gulped the whole thing down.

Thankfully, we got through dinner without incident. When the food was cleared, I excused myself to hide in the ladies' room before the awards began, but Izzy quickly found me.

"How did you get so lucky to have Dr. Pierce at your table and next to you? He's so dreamy. Seriously, why are you hiding in here and not out there groping the magnificent muscles under that Armani suit?" She had gotten on the "Dr. Pierce train" like every other woman here. She saw him as Mr. Perfect, with his straight white teeth and a shock of black silky hair that drooped over his forehead. I got it. He was gorgeous. But most people hadn't had the unlucky experience of being with him when his arrogance was unleashed. He was rude, demeaning, and insulting. She could have him.

Although Izzy seemed great, I didn't feel like sharing my Dr. Pierce encounters with her. I really didn't know her well and wasn't comfortable exposing myself.

"He's something, all right. I don't have a clue why he's at my table, let alone sitting next to me. Luck?" I forced a laugh. Rather than explain why I was hiding, I excused myself into a stall for more isolation. After a few minutes, she called out that she'd see me back in the ballroom. I tiptoed out of the stall when I heard the door click shut and reapplied my lipstick. Five more minutes, I thought, and I could be safe to return to the table just as the awards began.

Satan studied me as I walked back to the table, scanning my figure again, and then gazing at my face. It may have been a subtle form of eye fucking, but he did it all the same. When I sat, he stretched his arm over the back of my chair. *Really?* His attempts at seduction were laughable—he needed to up his game.

"Everything okay? You've been gone awhile."

I met his mock seriousness with sarcasm. "Yeah, I was out at the pool meditating—alone." I cocked a wicked smile his way.

"Sorry, I missed that. You do a mean meditating flow."

Nice try, asshole. Did he want to fuck with me? Fine. I was ready to do this. "Did you miss me?" I simpered.

Leaning a little closer to my side, he replied, "Maybe a little. You have a habit of heating me up."

"Is that so? You should see a doctor about that. Maybe you have a disease that you're unaware of."

Tipping his head toward my ear as if sharing a secret, he retorted, "What kind of disease were you thinking of? Obsessive love disorder?" He chuckled at his own cleverness.

"Not exactly," I said, dropping my eyes to his lips and catching his quick intake of air. "More like...gonorrhea or syphilis," I whispered, then pulled back to look into his shocked eyes. The flash I saw there could only be interpreted as anger—I'd hit a soft spot in his armor, and he was not happy about it. *I* thought it was hilarious, but it seemed the self-confident doctor didn't get rejected or mocked often.

His retreat back fully onto his seat left my side cold and empty. I liked sparring with him—he was smart and quick-witted—but it wasn't in my nature to be abusive. As he started to leave, I grabbed his sleeve.

"Alex." He stopped. I noticed my red nails juxtaposed with his black suit. Satan with a vixen on his arm. "I'm sorry," I whispered. "I was only playing. I didn't mean to hurt your feelings."

"Not to worry, sweetheart. It takes more than a potshot to get under my skin. However, you will pay for that little comment in the future." As he walked away, my hand slid down his arm and touched his hand, igniting something in me. That minuscule moment of skin-on

skin sent an electric current through my body, leaving me wet and wanting.

Chapter 14

ALEXANDER

Those awards dinners felt so contrived at times. Was I expecting to receive an award that evening? No. Was it appreciative and heartfelt? Possibly. Was this an hour of my life I'd never get back? You betcha. I was now the proud recipient of the Golden Apple Award for my work in childhood trauma resolution. I'd never heard of this award, and I was certain they made it up for me, so every lecturer left with a party favor. Considerate, yet not necessary.

The room took on a new tone as the DJ lit up the stage with gel lights, disco balls, and other things that made me feel nauseous. I had been standing at the back of the room for the presentation, so Ms. Gonzales didn't have to endure my attention, but I wasn't finished with her yet. She owed me a dance, and I was going to get it, but when I returned to our table, she was gone.

I shook a few hands, accepted congratulations from a few other guests, and headed for the bar. I'd find Trudie and collect my dance. I was positive that once I had my hands on her, she would drop this tough-girl facade and give me a chance. A chance for what, I didn't know.

An hour later, I had combed the conference venue and there was no sign of her. Interestingly enough, her friend, Izzy, was nowhere to be found either. It looked like these two birds had flown the coop. I wasn't in the mood to hunt them down, but I was in the mood to walk on a beach for some solace. I exited the building and hailed a cab, asking him to take me to the closest beach.

My phone rang as we arrived. Seeing Jacob's dorky face flash on the screen, I picked it up. I had totally forgotten he'd forwarded me a picture from our childhood, and I added it to his contact profile. In it, we were both trying to climb a tree—each of us on a side, grabbing the bark, scraping our hands, and laughing our heads off.

"Hey, doofus. What are you up to?" Jacob poked at me jovially.

"Just finished the last night of the conference I've been attending. They gave me another doorstop. I feel so special." My self-deprecating tone was a real downer.

"Aw. Are you tired of being at the head of the class? You want to go slumming with the rest of us?" His baby talk was annoying. Time to turn the conversation around. I put my phone on speaker for a moment while I pulled off my shoes and socks and rolled up my pant legs.

"You're a dick. I'm heading down to the beach to enjoy myself finally. How did your vacation finish up?" I considered changing my ticket and staying another day to relax on the beach. I'd turn off my phone again and veg out.

"The biggest dick, to be sure." He cracked himself up. "Vacation was fun. I love watching my kids enjoy life, and Ellen is still smokin' in her bikini."

"Not going to lie, your wife is gorgeous. I don't have a clue why she picked you." I chuckled to myself as I looked down the beach. The sand underneath my feet felt like a massage. It made me feel cool and relaxed, settling me onto the earth. There had been a nonstop frenetic energy that buzzed around the conference center. But now a wash of calm came over me that I couldn't remember feeling. *This must be what Trudie keeps working on. She may be onto something.*

Jacob agreed. "When are you coming by for some drinks and darts? The girls want to hang on to their Uncle Alex, and Ellen wants to introduce you to a colleague of hers." I could hear Ellen yelling from the other room, "Not colleague—friend." "Friend," he corrected.

I truly wished I could drop all my commitments and spend time with him and his family, but I had to tell him the bad news.

"Sorry, Jacob. I have three more gigs coming up and won't be available until the end of August. Let's do Labor Day weekend, though—you'll be my excuse as to why I can't go visit the family in the Hamptons. You'd be a lifesaver."

"Mission accepted, but you better stay the whole weekend. I can't protect you if you leave." He cracked up again. Why did he think he was so funny? *Probably because you laugh at every stupid thing he says.*

"Terrific. I'll add it to my calendar now. Take care, buddy." I smiled into the receiver.

"You too, doofus."

I pocketed my phone and headed toward the water, where I spotted two beautiful women, one in a pink confection and another who would make a toreador fall at her feet. *Trudie.*

My petulant inner child wanted nothing more than to interrupt these women and chastise Trudie for running away from me. Another childhood script, I'm sure, that needed to be removed from her repertoire. But she would have received my intrusion like a Mack truck smashing her car. That was the complete opposite of how I wanted this evening to go, so I left her alone with her friend and walked into the bay, my jacket over my shoulder, and pondered why I had invested so much emotional energy in her. The moonlight reflected off the gentle ripples and soothed my troubled mind. If I knew more about her, perhaps the shine would wear off, but I didn't want to be the stalker she kept implying I was.

The tide was still coming in, and I had to back up before soaking my trousers. Unfortunately, the suction on my foot was too strong and as I tried to release it, I fell onto the surf.

Feeling embarrassed, I jumped to my feet and felt for my phone to be sure it hadn't gotten submerged. Thankfully, it hadn't. My ass, on the other hand, was soaked like a soggy diaper. There was no possible way I would embarrass myself in front of all the conference attendees gliding through the lobby looking like I did, so I opted for a walk on the beach. The warm summer night would take care of my little problem, and as long as I didn't get too close to anyone, I'd live to face another day.

I had almost made it back to where I had entered the beach thirty minutes earlier when Izzy recognized me. I felt my ass one more time, sending thanks to the heavens that it was mostly dry. She rushed over to me, her curls bouncing around her deep bronze shoulders. In another circumstance, I might have been tempted by her attention, but a certain Latina's creamy light-brown skin mesmerized me.

"I thought that was you, Dr. Pierce. Fancy meeting you out here. Why aren't you mixing and mingling at the after-party." Izzy tilted her head to the left, dropping her hands behind her back, acting demure and flirty.

Not wanting to be rude, I placated her with a cordial response. "Yes, ironic, isn't it? I was going to stay and dance a bit, but it seems my dance partner had other plans." I pinned my stare on the beauty catching up to her friend. My ego was still stinging.

Izzy's expression was a little crestfallen, but I wasn't going to lead her on. That wasn't my style. She looked to her right as Trudie fell in line with her and gave her friend's shoulder a sweet nudge.

"You took off so fast, I thought something was wrong," Trudie panted.

"Nothing wrong. I just noticed Dr. Pierce and didn't want him to leave the beach without saying hello." She turned back to me with bright eyes. "I really loved your lecture this week. I have a lot to process about letting go of my past." Her sincerity was charming and appreciated. I loved it when my students were making progress.

"I'm sure with some hard work, you'll get your desired outcome. Thank you for the appreciation." A slight bow toward her had her smiling. "And you, Ms. Gonzales, were you able to distill any information this week that will help you on your journey to peace and serenity?" Time for me to provoke her.

She seemed to take my bait. She put a single finger to her chin, rolled her eyes upward, then crossed her left arm across her waist, tucking it under her right elbow.

"Perhaps a few things. I'll have to review my notes when I go home to really make that determination, but I do recall meeting a pompous, egotistical asshole who felt his shit didn't stink—so, yeah, I learned some stuff." I noticed her shoulders were shaking with suppressed laughter, which got me going, too. Full-on laughter was the perfect ending to our evening.

I flagged a cab and escorted the girls back to the hotel, and said good night. My irritation at missing out on tracing Trudie's curves on the dance floor was temporarily forgotten. The conference was over, and so was our time together. I bid them a fond farewell, wished them success in their quest to put their pasts in the past, and stopped at the front desk. I settled my bill, and when I exited the elevator on my floor, I was surprised to see Trudie entering her room. Why the hell hadn't I known she was two doors down from me the whole week?

"Trudie, wait." I walked quickly down the hall, hoping to catch her before the door closed in my face.

She stepped back out her door, and her eyebrows shot up when she realized it was me.

"Are you following me? I knew you were a stalker." There was no laughter, only irritation.

"Of course, I'm not. What is with you thinking I'm a stalker? My room is two doors down from yours. I can't believe we never saw each other until now."

"So now that you know where I'm staying, we can conveniently hook up without calling attention to ourselves?" she asked.

Not a bad idea, I thought.

"No!" I said indignantly. "Unless you twist my arm, and then, of course, we can hook up. I'm really a nice guy with a very creative mind."

I may have pushed it with the humor because Trudie's would have been on fire if smoke could come out of people's ears like the cartoon characters. Her hands smacked her hips so hard I'm sure she left a bruise.

"Dream on, asshole. Goodnight, and get lost." Turning on her heel, she barged back into her room and slammed the door.

That had not gone well. But she was right about one thing—maybe two: I *am* an asshole, and I would dream about her tonight, repeatedly.

Chapter 15

TRUDIE

I DISCOVERED A LITTLE bakery across the street that made amazing Spanish *torrijas*. It was hard to find this deliciously sweet bread, which is like French toast covered in cinnamon and sugar. I was on my second one when Izzy showed up to join me for brunch. She was leaving at noon, and I'd already checked out of the hotel to take my day trip to the Sequoias. I usually skipped the morning mixer at the end of a conference to get out and see the sights, and this trip was no different.

The sun was shining, and so was Izzy's face. She had something she was dying to tell me. Sliding into my booth, she dropped her purse and pulled off her periwinkle cardigan that coordinated with her flowery blouse.

"You will never believe what just happened? It's just too amazing to even digest." She sipped from her coffee cup too quickly, and it burned her tongue.

"Calm down. What? What just happened? Did you meet Mr. Wonderful? Or his equally hot friend?" I chuckled.

"Ugh," she threw her head back dramatically, "I wish. No, but my brother's high school friend, whom I ogled and loved from afar for four years, just moved back to our hometown and Elias, my brother, invited him over to hang out." She was giddy, making tiny clapping motions with her hands.

"Wow! That sounds promising. Does he know you liked him? Does this mean you'll be hanging out with them, too?" I wanted to be encouraging, but this sounded like a long shot.

She frowned, slumping in her seat. "Well, now that you say it out loud, I have no idea. I mean, he used to be nice to me, but maybe he was just being polite. Come to think of it, I didn't get invited to hang out tonight," she said, annoyed. "How am I supposed to remind him I'm alive if Elias doesn't invite me over?"

I didn't want to be a wet blanket about her hopes of a marvelous future with this guy, but we weren't in high school anymore. She needed a more sophisticated approach to catch his eye. Let him know how fabulous she was now that she'd grown up without looking so needy.

"I have a thought if you're interested." I leaned across the table conspiratorially. "What if Elias had a barbeque at his house on Sunday and invited you? You know, a casual surprise attack? Tell Elias not to mention you'll be there and then show up looking hot. Nothing too over the top, just a wake-up call that you're on the market. What do you think?" I gave her my most animated head nod.

She started nodding her head slowly and then picked up speed. "You're a genius, Trudie. I'm really going to miss hanging out with you. Please stay in touch." She got up and slid into my side of the booth to give me a big hug.

"I'm going to miss you, too." Another hug and then we swapped contact information and said goodbye. She was probably the nicest person I'd ever met at a conference. I hoped we really would stay in touch.

I had never been under such majestic trees in my life, and I never wanted to leave. There were people lying on the ground like leaves, looking up at them. I almost stepped on a lady's hand. It was fascinating that these trees stood alive, given the number of forest fires they'd been exposed to. Our guide was very informative, though just staring at them had been fascinating enough for me. My only experience with trees was climbing apple trees as a kid. Not that you could compare a giant sequoia to an apple tree, though when I stepped into the hollow of either one, I felt safe and protected. The energy in a tree hummed within me and reminded me of the universal *ohm* sound. I'd used it a lot in yoga, and it grounded me to the earth. This had been a magnificent day and I was so happy I had the opportunity to squeeze in the side trip. Now for the four-hour bus ride back to San Francisco.

I checked into a budget motel near the marina and double-checked my sailing excursion scheduled for that night. I had an hour to shower, put myself back together, and walk four blocks down to the pier for my sunset cruise. I hadn't given up on the thought of meeting someone that had broad shoulders, a tight ass, and naughty sexy eyes.

Speaking of sexy, the crewman holding his hand out for me to board the vessel winked at me, making me blush, and he directed me to the upper deck for the best views. In my mind's eye, I thought there would be seating, a sleek build to the boat, with a tailored crew, and a sophisticated bar stocked with a bevy of seaworthy drinks. Instead, what I got were sails with masts as big as telephone poles, heavily painted equipment, coiled ropes, and oxidized hooks, which gave me a sinking feeling. *Pun intended.* If it weren't for the smooth brass fittings, polished wood handrails, and decking, I'd swear I was in a locker room from the 1950s. I couldn't believe I had picked the wrong boat. The thrill of having met Jared on the plane, the free posh room, and jet lag must have left me bleary-eyed, and I had clicked the wrong button. Nothing could be done about it now, so I shuffled up to the makeshift bar with plastic cups and all, and chose to make the best of it. Water was water, alcohol in any form took the edge off, and the description of the excursion guaranteed me a gorgeous sunset. I tucked myself between the edge of the boat and the helm, took a few deep breaths, and readied myself for another amazing adventure.

The ship's wheel looked like any picture I'd seen in books and film, and the captain channeled Johnny Depp in those pirate movies—sexy, wiry, and very charismatic. His lanky frame was wrapped in an antique velvet waistcoat featuring brass buttons to match the ship's bell and a gold chain that hung across his tight belly. The incongruous straw hat and a cup of soft-serve ice cream he was holding left me chuckling. I couldn't wait to hear what stories he would share.

About a dozen people surrounded his "sacred space," as he put it, and we were firmly instructed to steer clear of various thickly coiled ropes and pulleys lest we wanted a quick ride to the top of the mainsail. Our captain, Captain Jesse Rockford, twirled his long, waxed mustache, which pinched at the ends of each side of his angular face, and informed us, "Yes, it's real and fabulous." There was a story there, too, and I wanted to collect them all. My eyes strayed from the top of his sandy blond hair blowing in the wind to his burnished, tanned skin to his thin-toned legs, and I hoped to see pirate boots to finish the look. His tan Velcroed Keens dissolved my romantic illusions.

"Ladies and Gentlemen, may I have your attention, please." He cleared his throat and began again. "It seems we have more partygoers this evening since their boat is having some mechanical difficulties. Our passenger manifest was about a dozen shy of our capacity, so several of those passengers agreed to join our tall ship cruise instead. Please put your hands together for our new poop deck crew." Captain Rockford cracked himself up, slapping his knee and enjoying the terrified looks of our new shipmates. The rest of us laughed at his wry sense of humor and hoped he wasn't serious.

"Don't worry, there's no poop deck duty on this ship because there isn't a bathroom, so keep those legs crossed." His mouth turned up in a slow smile, more devious this time. *Damn! Now I had to pee.*

After the sails were raised, we were off to tour the bay for the next two hours. The captain regaled us with countless stories. I listened passively for a while, then tuned back in to hear him spout, "Courts do not accept pictures of cartoon sharks as evidence!" Our captain may not have been amused, but the rest of us thought that story was hilarious.

The sun began its descent over the horizon, bathing the skyline with radiant hues of oranges, yellows, and fuchsias. My soul was soaking up the beauty of the diffused rays and the gentle lolling of the craft under my feet. The two glasses of chardonnay didn't hurt either. I decided to take a stroll down to the lower deck to get a different perspective. Everyone was super friendly, presumably because they were imbibing too.

I found a railing at the stern and rested my forearms on it with my drink between my hands. My shoulders dropped another inch as the activities of the week fell away. I felt such gratitude for having won that hotel room. Otherwise, this boat trip wouldn't have happened. My simple sundress of periwinkle blue with a deep V-neckline was perfect for the gentle breeze that whispered across my chest. I had brought a light sweater, not being sure what the weather conditions on the water would be like, but finding it unnecessary, I had wrapped it around my waist. The sweater slipped off my hips as I shifted my weight to my other foot. My first instinct was to pick it up, but instead, I chose to remain present in my peaceful Zen moment.

I felt a shift in the energy around me, and my spine tingled. The last time this happened was two days ago, caused by a certain godlike creature who tormented me daily this week. *Please, God, please let it be some other gorgeous guy. Okay, he doesn't even have to be good-looking. Maybe just straight teeth and no comb-over. Anyone other than Satan himself.*

"Ma'am, I think you drop..."

I turned my head slightly to my left and was seized momentarily by his laser-like emerald-green eyes. That devilish grin taunted me whenever he had me cornered and now was no exception. I turned slowly, appreciating his high cheekbones, olive skin, and the rakish dark hair whipping around his face.

"Well, look who we have here. What odds would the gods put us both in one spot?"

Not me!

He slid his elbows onto the rail beside me and handed me my sweater. Not wanting it to fly into the bay next time, I pulled back, shoved my almost empty glass into one of his hands, and double-knotted the sleeves around my waist. Finished, I made to grab my wine back, but he held on to the glass just a moment longer so that our fingers brushed. I realized how amazing the many nerve endings in a hand were because, just from that touch, a zing danced its way up my arms, spine, and lower belly.

Perhaps playing the damsel in distress would minimize our interaction, so I pulled my lips into a tight smile and bowed my head.

"Thank you kindly, sir. Very gallant of you," I said and polished off my drink, eyeing him over my glass.

He pursed his insanely beautiful lips and replied, "The pleasure was all mine. Can't leave a lady in distress, especially out at sea." In spite of my irritation, I kind of loved that he played along.

I didn't want to miss a moment of the view, so I turned back to face the bay as I composed myself. I wanted to avoid confrontation tonight—just relax and unwind, maybe scope out some beautiful bodies to ogle and add to my rub hub. Tonight was mine, and I wanted to end my vacation by having fun, making memories on a sunset cruise, and meeting interesting people all on a peaceful summer night. We learned this week to let go of what was truly insignificant in our lives so that we had more room for joy, peace, and new beginnings, and what better time was there to practice that than now?

I turned back to my companion. "Listen, Dr. Pierce—"

He bumped my shoulder gently and said, "Alex, please." His voice was low and throaty.

"Uh, okay, Alex. As you put it, the gods may have brought us together to put our differences aside, and I would like nothing more than to do that. Would that be okay with you? I'm too tired to fight." I leaned into the rail once again, fiddling with my cup. But then I looked down at his rather large hands and imagined them on my body. *Stop, girl!*

The ship turned into the wake, and everyone bumped into the person next to them. I was glad my drink was gone; otherwise, I would have been wearing it by now. Alex's large hand draped itself around my hip, steadying me, while he wrapped his other one around my shoulder, keeping me from falling overboard. My hand reached for something to hold onto and found his shirt balled into my hand.

"Steady there, little one. I would hate you to become shark food," he jested, pulling me even closer.

Little one? To whom did he think he was talking, and why did I like it?

Chapter 16

ALEXANDER

Little one? What the hell was I thinking?

Of course, Trudie was smaller than me, by almost a foot. A grown woman with a big personality, she was hardly a meek girl needing protection. Yet I still felt protective of her at that moment. I was concerned for her safety and would have felt horrible if she'd literally slipped through my fingers off a moving ship. That didn't mean she meant something to me, right? Just some woman who aggravated me, challenged me in front of my students, called me out on everything, and snubbed me when I tried to fix our communication issues. Although that was probably my bad, rushing things like that.

Loose curls blew across her face as I stared into her hazel eyes. Until now, I had not had the time to study the amber rimming the outside of her irises. They mesmerized me. She looked up at me as though she wanted to say something, yet nothing came out. Her small hand was still pressed to my chest and seemed to burn through my button-down shirt. I kept my hand on her curvy hip and pressed her closer as I tucked a wild curl behind her ear. The electricity between us could have lighted a small city, and my pants got tighter every moment we stayed like this.

We didn't breathe. We didn't move. We didn't speak until some drunk stopped in front of us.

"Whoa, dude. That was intense. Don't let that beauty out of your hands, she's hot." He eye-fucked her for a few seconds, then staggered away.

Her hand went to her mouth, and she snorted.

I needed to make this moment right. I also needed to know that if I gave her my attention, she wouldn't mock me again. I wanted her to look at me seriously—not as her teacher or as a professional in the field of psychology, but as a man.

I leaned into the shell of her ear and whispered, "He's right, you know."

Her deep exhale spread onto my neck. "Right about what?" she whispered back and brushed the palm of her hand over my right peck. *Fuck.*

It encouraged me to continue. "You're hot, and I don't want to let you out of my hands." I moved my hand from her hip to the base of her back, adding more pressure and keeping her close to my body. The audible gulp in her throat drew a guttural sound from mine. I didn't want to think past this moment. I wanted to remember how she felt in my arms, on this packed boat, on this beautiful summer evening with the sun setting over the skyline of San Francisco.

"You do things to me," I said into her ear. "You make me want to do naughty things to you." She gasped. Her whole body went liquid, and I took that moment to lick the corner of her mouth and then traced her full lips to the other corner. She shuddered, and so did I. I couldn't remember kissing someone like this—ever.

She shifted in my arms, turning her back to my chest. I tightened my arms possessively around her midsection, and I could no longer hide what was growing inside my shorts. I pressed into her as my nose inhaled the vanilla and cinnamon scent of the shampoo she used. She was like a caramel sundae, and all I wanted to do was devour her cherry.

The humming sounds that came from her throat made my heart sing, knowing she enjoyed my protective attention. We held this pose for several minutes before she tilted her head up to speak to me.

"Alex. I didn't expect this from you. I thought you hated me. Why are you being so nice to me now?" The vulnerability in her eyes told me she was exposing herself to me in body and soul. How could I make her understand that I just realized she was more to me than that annoying woman who had smashed into me?

She was piercing my façade and I was experiencing something I had never wanted to feel again. The reawakening of my emotional self was intense, creating an unbalance that alarmed me. I wanted to put those emotions into words, but they were still elusive and still forming. It was also clear to me that this was a moment where I could shatter her already fragile ego, or I could help repair a childhood trauma. Who knew if we were going to have a future together...could we? Nah, this had just been a steam valve opened to release life's pressures. Just some fun. *Please let it just be some fun.*

My moment of contemplation was over. She needed an answer, but I still didn't have one. I dragged my nose through her hair again and settled my cheek along hers.

"You are an enigma, Trudie. I thought I had you figured out that first night, but then you persisted in showing me otherwise. Starting, but not ending, with that red dress of yours. Your confidence showed through that delicate fabric and your sassy mouth made mine water." I let my hands lay flat along her hips, inching my way down her legs. "Should I go on?" I drawled out.

Her chest heaved as her heart rate picked up. *Fuck.* "Oh, yes, please," she breathed out.

"The way you made me raise my game by calling me out when I came across as arrogant and by sharing unconditionally in front of almost two hundred people made you a formidable opponent, and I wanted to spar with you every time I saw you. So smart, so wise, so—real." I nuzzled her cheek and dropped my lips to her neck, licking her. *Jesus, I just licked this woman in front of a whole ship of people. What the hell was I doing?*

Before she could respond, I spun her around and set her back a foot from me. Her eyes widened, and she looked confused.

"What's going on, Alex? What just happened?" she asked, a plea in her voice. I felt her pain. Tearing myself from her was akin to pulling a Band-Aid off a hairy chest. Painful.

I reached for the side of her face and rubbed her cheek in apology. Her pupils were blown out—I needed to make another important decision.

"I, I forgot where we were. Look around. People were staring at us, and I would never compromise you that way. We needed a breather. It changes nothing of what I said." I stepped closer again. "Do you believe me?"

She took that moment to turn her head and see what I had seen. The men were licking their lips and so were the women. We might as well call this the Sunset Porn Cruise, the way we were so hot and heavy. *Now that is something to consider.*

I noticed the sun had dropped behind a few more buildings. Our cruise would end soon, and I could see the captain and crew adjusting sails and booms and packing up the makeshift bar. Fifteen more minutes and these moments would be a tiny bubble of one of the best memories of my life. I felt my hand being taken as Trudie turned and walked us across the lower deck, up the stairs to the upper deck, and right up to where the captain was manning the ship. Abruptly, she turned around and grabbed my shirt forcibly, getting my attention and the attention of everyone near us.

"You are *the* most infuriating man I've ever met. You also get me doing things I never would have done before this week. You go and say these amazing things and then break the moment with chivalry. What guy does that? You can't be from this decade or even this quarter century. I'm not sure whether to be grateful or humiliated. So, which is it, Alex? How am I supposed to feel about all of this?" She slumped against the rail and let out the rest of her air, exhausted.

Wow. If you had told me twenty years ago I would be having such a straightforward conversation with a woman without innuendo or subterfuge, I would have poked my eye with a fork. PhD or not, I was a man first, an asshole second, and a spoiled brat third. I hadn't needed to speak to women like Trudie. I just seduced them and let them think whatever they wanted. But this siren tore through all my pretenses and got to the heart of the matter. Both of my hands went into my hair in hopes of pulling out some reasonable line of defense. Did I want to stop the decadent path we'd started because I was terrified of where it would take me, or was I finally respecting myself and the woman I was with? What value did I place on her? I had just met her, for God's sake. She affected my mind and my body like a volcano erupting. It was rare, but the world was never the same when it happened.

TRUDIE

The crew had moored the ship at the gangway, and the passengers were laughing and saying their goodbyes. The evening had brought on a whirlwind of emotions, and I wasn't sure if I wanted it to go on or run away before I created a problem I couldn't resolve. Alex had said so many things I wanted to hear, and the way he whispered in my ear was absolutely intoxicating, which is why I almost made a spectacle of myself in front of the whole ship. *Well, maybe not the whole ship, but it might as well have been.* He hadn't answered me and I felt hollow, gutted. Wasn't I even worthy of an answer? Our time was up, and my fairy tale of a perfect night had evaporated.

I took my cue from the people around me and made to leave the ship when a strong hand on my wrist stopped me.

"Wait, Trudie. Please," he implored. I took one last look at the gangway and then toward the front of the ship, where the captain gave me a wink. Was that supposed to be encouraging or was he hitting on me, too?

"Listen, Alex. This was fun and all, but maybe we should cut our losses and bid each other adieu." *Practical. Yes, that was the way to go.*

His eyes clouded over. "I'm not leaving, and neither are you until I give you a proper answer to your question. I feel incredibly grateful to have had this time with you, met you this week, and even sparred with you."

My throat tightened as I thought about what I was going to say next. But he beat me to it. "You have done what no other person, man or woman, has done in my whole life, and it scares the shit out of me."

I yanked my wrist out of his hand, placed it on my hip, and gave him my best stink eye. "And what would that be, Alex? I'm dying to hear this," I snarled.

He must have thought I was intimidating because he kept me at arm's length. If he had been a soldier, you could have seen the red flags flashing behind his eyes as he worried that he was walking into a minefield but hoped he wasn't.

He took a full breath and proceeded cautiously. "When I was in high school, I was encouraged to take life by the horns and tame it. My father didn't have patience for half-measures and insisted I was all in or all out. I was groomed to make decisions and not look back, especially if it involved people. He felt they were expendable—collateral damage to his aspirations. I learned to bury my empathy and became an egotistical asshole," he admitted.

"And you did a fine job. Congratulations. So what's changed? How did I become the key to your inner humanity?" I gibed.

He returned the stink eye and proceeded.

"You, Key Master," he pointed at me, "found the right door to unlock me and walked on in. It's entirely your fault I'm having to stop and think about someone other than myself. Congratulations, Trudie, you found my empathy door." He put his hands together as if holding a sword and stabbed his chest, feigning death.

I rolled my eyes. "Me? I slayed the dragon? Is that right? And how, pray tell, did I do that?"

"Promise you won't laugh?" he pleaded.

"Fine." She smirked, lying to me.

"It's two things, actually. First, it's your sass. You said things that provoked me to evaluate what I've said and how I've acted. I'm not sure how you did it, probably because you're a siren meant to distract me beyond reason, but you made me care." He looked pained to admit it.

He pointed a finger at me and shifted his weight, preparing to make his next point.

"And it's your ass. And your smile. And those witchy eyes of yours that should make me run for the hills, except I keep finding myself running to you." I was afraid he was going to pass out from his disclosure.

The captain walked over to us and gestured for us to get off his boat. "Thanks for coming, folks. Maybe get some coffee or a room and continue this conversation somewhere else."

He was right. It was time to go, and the way Alex was looking at me, it clearly wasn't coffee he wanted.

We walked in silence up the pier and stopped in the park in front of the marina. He sat down on a bench and pulled me onto his lap. To say I was surprised was an understatement. Our enemies-to-whatever plotline seemed to be moving rather quickly, and I hoped I wouldn't regret a few minutes of his close proximity. He smelled fresh, with a tangy citrus cologne that electrified my senses. I wanted to lick him just like he licked me on the boat, except I wasn't going to stop. My years with Sam had dulled my desire long enough. I wanted more, but was Alex the man worthy of my wantonness? I knew that as soon as the lid of my desire was lifted, it wasn't going back on.

Chapter 17
TRUDIE

Diffused light glowed across the park; streaks of color washed away under the moonlit sky. Several couples walked hand in hand, and parents corralled their kids. Another Zen-like moment draped over me, and I was here for it, present and peaceful. Gulls overhead, the slapping of water against nearby boats, and Alex's arms tight around my waist gave me a sense of serenity and safety. I couldn't recall ever feeling like this in my youth. There had been too much turmoil. My father was always rushing out of the house to get to his next job or crashing in the front door like a comet destined to explode. Which was what usually happened. Thank goodness my mother had magical arms that took away all the pain, or as much as possible. There was so much uncertainty from my formative years, it's a wonder I was secure in myself at all.

"Hey, where'd you go?" he whispered in my ear.

Realizing how much my mind had wandered, I replied, "Sorry. I was really enjoying this moment. It's been a while since I've been able to appreciate being like this."

Turning slightly, I saw his sultry, deep, emerald eyes darken, and it made my heart speed up. When this happened earlier in the week, I wasn't sure what it implied. Now, it was clear as day what his eyes were saying, and my belly fluttered in anticipation.

His hand rested on my knee—his forefinger drawing circles around it. We both watched, measuring each other's breaths, as he deftly grazed his fingers up my inner thigh. I gasped, and his eyes snapped to mine.

"Trudie," he moaned. "I need to know where you want this to go because my patience is coming to an end."

That was the question of the night. What did I want from him? This was what I'd wanted all along, right? I could enjoy a wild, romantic moment for months or years with my electronic friend. Alex was everything I wanted physically from a man. Dark and sultry. Muscles that bulged under expensive shirts. Strong, long fingers that made my lady bits tingle. Broad shoulders that cut deep down into a sexy set of abs. I'd been looking at his ass for days, and I can honestly say I had never seen a man wear a pair of trousers like this guy. So why was I hesitating?

Probably because he'd been an ass most of the time. If his attitude hadn't preceded his gorgeous body, there wouldn't be anything to decide.

I was conflicted. I didn't know if this night was over or not, but my fingers wanted to travel through his dark, silky locks. "You are so fucking sexy, Alex, and I'm sure we would have an amazing night together, but I don't want to mislead you." Putting it on me seemed like the best strategy.

"Mislead me how, exactly?" He nibbled my earlobe.

His distraction was working. "I-I," my chest heaved with pleasure, "I don't normally do this kind of thing." I felt light-headed as he drew a small circle with his tongue behind my ear. "What kind of thing?" he asked, and he did it three more times. Fuck, he was good. I made a list of what else he could do with that tongue.

He wanted me to say exactly what was on my mind, which frustrated me to no end. Saying that my heart couldn't handle him potentially breaking it? All my deep-down dirty thoughts about what I wanted him to do to me...and everything in between? No. We were too new to have those thoughts aired. Instead, I cupped his jawline with my hands and savored his soft skin and evening stubble, his full lips inches from mine, and offered him specific thoughts.

"Letting a stranger touch me the way you are. Letting a man with an ego like yours makes me feel protected and adored. Having this electricity run through me for the first time in my life. It's daunting." I breathed out what was left in my lungs and hoped he wouldn't jump up and dump me on the ground, running as fast as he could away from the mess that I was.

But instead, he brushed his beautiful lips over mine, then licked the bottom one slowly.

"I know I seem like a paradox to you, Trudie. I'm not easy to define, and you, sweet girl, are so strong and yet so vulnerable. If we had more time, we could explore all these facets completely; however, our real lives start again tomorrow. You don't need to fear me. I won't make you promises, and you won't make any, either.

The only question is, do you want this moment to end now or in the morning?" His thumb traced my bottom lip again as his eyes drank me in, leaving me helpless to his charms. This was what I wanted. Now was my moment to live.

I dove at his lips. His tongue plunged into my mouth, taking my last doubt with it. Holding my face firmly, he pulled back, "Say it, Trudie. What do you want?"

A small moan emanated from my throat. "I want you, Alex. My motel is four blocks away."

His face lit up, relieved I didn't say no. He set me back on my feet, and his fingers threaded through mine as we quickly walked from the park to my motel.

ALEXANDER

She led me up the outside staircase of her rather sketchy motel. This place was a far cry from the hotel we stayed in this week, yet so convenient for us tonight. But my sexy minx was giving me mixed signals—at the park, she was all in; now, she seemed tentative. The alpha in me wanted to take charge, but for once, the psychologist stepped forward and demanded I give her control and the space to express herself. I knew she wanted me, and, fuck, I wanted her, too. But I saw that while those big hazel eyes were alight with arousal, there was also uncertainty there. Of course, I would not push myself on anyone who didn't want me, but she wanted something from me, and I was confident I could help her express it.

Her keys hit the floor and waves of her silky hair fell across her face as she shook her head in frustration.

"What is my problem tonight? I can't get anything right."

I bent to retrieve her keys and offered, "Can I be of assistance?" with my eyebrows raised in hope. She nodded, resigned to accept my help. I inserted the key into the door and pressed her lower back, guiding her into her room.

The space had an unlikely charm, especially given its outside appearance. The decor was simple and nautical. Trudie made a beeline for the bathroom and closed the door. When she reemerged, her eyes were swollen, and her cheeks were stained with tears. Even with two sisters, for the life of me, I still couldn't handle the emotions of a crying woman.

I disregarded the shaky sensation in my chest and took her hand to lead her over to the side of the bed. We needed to talk, or this night would go up in smoke. I pulled the desk chair over and sat facing her. Her gorgeous curls were hiding her face, and I tucked a silky strand behind her ear. I knew my girl needed some TLC to feel better. *My girl, what? When did she become mine?*

"Come here, baby, let me hold you." I gently tried to coax her to stand, but her head fell backward, like a child who wanted to have a tantrum or shut down completely. I gave her a stern look, hoping it would incite some other response.

"Why are you crying, sweetheart?" I wanted her to share with me, but she stiffened instead.

If she wanted to act like a petulant child, then I would treat her as such. Unceremoniously, I picked her up and dropped her onto my lap, and she was flabbergasted by the look on her face. The inside of my mouth smarted from biting back my laughter as she tried to pull away. Big Bad Trudie Gonzales, who wasn't afraid to speak her mind and take life by the horns, hated losing control. I wanted to be the one who would hold her as she unraveled. She had a story to tell, and I couldn't wait to get to the crux of it.

"Don't fight me, Trudie. Let me hold you. Cry if you need to. But you will tell me what has you upset." She raised her chin at that, and I brushed another curl behind her other ear. Choosing my words with care, I offered, "Let me help you let go."

Her voice wavering, she asked, "Why are you here, Alex? Wouldn't you rather be with some vapid bitch who would do anything you asked her to do?" She tried to push herself from my hold, but I increased the pressure.

"You intrigue me, Ms. Gonzales. You're a paradox, too. Can't I be your rock tonight?" I cocked my head and hoped to get a good read by watching her mesmerizing eyes.

"Am I your puzzle to solve? I'm not a Rubik's Cube, Alex. I'm a person with too many layers to figure out in one night. Maybe you should go?" She tried yet again to jump up, but I wouldn't allow it.

Words were useless now. Action would have to do the talking. My lips tucked into the nape of her neck, loosening her resolve. That was all I needed to keep my forward momentum. Her body became pliant, and I loosened my hold enough to insert my thigh between her legs. Her back was to me, and I couldn't see her face anymore, but I knew she could feel my erection pressing into her ass. She moaned, arching her spine. I squeezed her breasts through the thin material of her sundress, which elicited another sexy moan. It was quickly becoming my favorite sound in the world.

"Rest your head on my shoulder, baby girl, let me take care of everything you need," I whispered as I licked a path down her delicate neck to her clavicle. Salty, sweet, and smelling of vanilla—she had my mouth watering.

"You are delicious, Trudie. I want to taste all of you." I sucked on her neck, leaving a mark, and felt my cock grow even harder. I wasn't letting her go. She'd have to be mine now.

"Alex," she pleaded. "Please, Alex."

My hands found her full breasts again, and I grasped each firmly. "Is this what you want, baby girl?" Her nipples were thick and protruding, and my filthy mind was making plans of what I wanted to do to them.

"Oh, God, yes. It's been so long," she half screamed.

My fingers went to work as I twisted and pulled on her tits, and each time I got it right, she arched her back more, giving me what I wanted.

"Tell me what you want, sweetheart. Tell me exactly what you want." The devil in me taunted her, but I wanted to hear from her lips what she was willing to give.

"I...I don't know, exactly. I just know I want you to fuck me." She deflated a little in my arms. My heart squeezed in sympathy for her. *She isn't a virgin, is she?*

Trying to keep it light, I asked, "You've been with a man before, right? Like in the biblical sense?"

"Of course, Alex. Except, my last boyfriend wasn't very good at variety or experimentation, and that was one reason, one of the big reasons, I left him."

Her head dropped to my shoulder again in disgust. I'd never done so much talking to seduce a woman in my life. "Well, what if I could be your teacher tonight? You could be my perfect student, and I would school your body." I tipped her head up so I could see her eyes. Her pouty lips begged me to kiss them, but instead, I sucked on her bottom lip and tweaked her tits again.

Her reply was timid and maybe a little embarrassed, too. "Teacher, like a role-play, or clinically?" This woman and her crazy, intense mind would be the end of me.

"How about we just roll with it, and if you need clarification on what I'm asking you to do, you can just ask?" I brushed my lips over hers again, and she sighed her consent.

This wasn't going to be a freshman college lecture with a few exercises to complete. Oh, no—this was going to be a lab that required proofs, diagrams, and a full-on presentation. If she wanted a teacher, she would get the very best.

Chapter 18

TRUDIE

ALEX WANTED TO BE my teacher, to role-play. I couldn't have asked for anything more. This was what I had hoped for, right? All the boxes were checked, all I had to do was let go. *Ha!* When had Trudie Gonzales ever just let go? And there were repercussions for these types of decisions, too, including the obvious risk of getting pregnant. *I did take my birth control pill today, right?*

He'd asked me to trust him, lean on him, and let me take my frustrations out on him. When would I ever get an opportunity like that again? I was hungry for what he was offering me, but was I hungry enough that it needed to be from him?

My wandering thoughts were brought back to attention when Alex reached under my dress and palmed my pussy. It was more powerful than anything I'd had done to me before.

"Listen," he demanded, "Dr. Pierce will only ask you once, and if you don't comply, you'll be put in a time-out."

Does he think I'm a child?

"You will address me as Dr. Pierce when you want a teacher. Do you understand?" He squeezed my tits firmly.

Tuning out the practicalities running through my mind, I answered with a shaky voice, "Yes, Dr. Pierce."

"Good girl. Stand up, but don't look at me. Take off your dress and sit back to straddle my thighs."

"Yes, Dr. Pierce." With shaky hands, I slowly pulled my dress up, shifting to get it over my breasts, and dropped it in a puddle on the floor.

When I was seated again, he pulled my thighs open with his powerful legs. The feel of his hands pressing down my abdomen toward each thigh ignited my whole body. He was kissing and sucking the nape of my neck, and it gave me the most glorious goosebumps. I wanted more but didn't know how to verbalize it.

"Dr. Pierce, I-I'm, please, sir." I'd never begged for sex. Sam was only too happy to pounce on me and didn't have a clue about how to seduce me.

"Let's play a game," he growled. "I'll do something, and you tell me how it feels. Together, we'll find the words to describe what you want for next time."

Next time? How many times was he planning?

His strong adept fingers pulled my labia back, and the air from the overhead fan wafted across my pussy, leaving me gasping. He cleverly dragged each digit over my clit so slowly, teasing me, taunting me, that I could have orgasmed with that alone. I was a live wire ready to burst into flames.

"Alex," I gasped.

"Dr. Pierce, you mean?" He scolded me again.

"Yes, Dr. Pierce. That was—is—feels so good," I hummed, enjoying the varying pressure he was applying to my clit.

"Good girl. What am I doing that turns you on?" he encouraged, licking my neck.

"You're playing…with my…pussy." I was breathless. Heaving every word out was agonizing.

"Yeah, baby. I'm playing with your clit, and it's making you feel so good," he clarified.

"Oh, yes."

His left hand came back to my breast and flicked the tip over and over again while he pressed into my pussy with one finger. The unexpected timing had me bucking my hips toward his hand in unabashed want.

"Looks like my student is learning how sweet a finger fuck feels when it's not her own." I could feel his lips turning upward as he sucked my neck. "Look at me, Trudie."

I angled my mouth toward him, feeling his hot breath millimeters from my desperate lips.

"This is what foreplay looks and feels like. Wine, dancing, and a few kisses are for the public to see, but what we're doing now is for hungry, sweet girls who want a strong, take-charge man. Do you understand?" He pulled my head demandingly toward his, and our lips crashed. His tongue penetrated my mouth relentlessly, the same as his finger—now two fingers—penetrated my pussy.

"Dr. Pierce, I'm going to come. Please let me come." I couldn't believe what was coming out of my mouth. I had never felt this way, and I was near to bursting, emotionally and physically.

He pressed his palm into my clit and pumped his fingers over and over, making me wetter than I had ever been. His cock ground against the top of my ass, and he moaned into my mouth, making me lose control. My hands lifted into his hair, pulling on his neck to gain traction. I was so close.

"You'll come when I tell you to and not before, or there will be consequences." His chiding made me more wanton, and I wasn't sure I could comply.

I pressed my ass as hard as I could into his trunk of a cock in hopes of making him come sooner. I couldn't hold on any longer. I was strung out so tightly my ass was beginning to cramp, and my legs shook from fatigue.

"Please, Dr. Pierce," I whimpered. "Please."

His cock bucked up two times in rapid succession, and he ordered me to come. "Fuck, baby girl, come. Come all over teacher's fingers."

That was all I needed to squeeze his fingers with the most volatile orgasm I had ever had.

The aftershocks were intense and went on and on. I felt Alex's strong hands reach under my thighs, and keeping me tucked close to his chest, he stood up as if I didn't weigh a thing and carried me to the bed. He pulled the covers back and lowered me gently. The rasp of a zipper and the clank of a belt buckle alerted me that class wasn't over yet. My euphoric haze wasn't enough to keep me from feeling desperate for his closeness again. He got in behind me. He nestled me into his back, his strong arm making a pillow for my head. His fingertips traveled along my right side down to my knee and back up again to rest on my ass. Gentle squeezes helped to relax me, but the more he did, the more my pussy wanted his attention again.

"You were a very good student, sweetheart, and I'd like to reward you for your desire to learn. Would that be okay?"

"If it feels anything like the last lesson, I'm all in," I giggled, and that was all the encouragement he needed.

He pulled my hips roughly toward the end of the bed, and I fell to my back. He sat up on his knees between my legs, licking his lips as if to devour me. Towering over my body and taking me in, he made me feel like I was under a microscope. His hands traced every contour of my breasts and massaged my abdominal muscles in sensual circles, pulling sounds from my throat I didn't know were possible. I ached for him to move his hands down to my pussy, but instead of rubbing me, he started rubbing himself. Three pulls to his engorged cock extended its length another whole inch.

My eyes widened in surprise, and he let out a devilish chuckle. "You like what you see, baby?" I dismissed his cockiness as I licked my lips.

"Your reward comes with a contingency, though. Would you like to know what that is?" His eyes gleamed, and his jaw ticked, revealing what kind of lesson he wanted to teach. I nodded my head quickly.

"I'm going to fuck you so hard and so deep; you'll remember me for days. The contingency is your sight. You'll wear a blindfold. You'll feel my length and my width vividly, but you'll only have your imagination of what I looked like when you remember this."

I gulped. I wanted him deep inside me, but I also wanted to see how his body strained during sex. I nodded my consent anyway.

"Good girl. Close your eyes." I felt the loss of his weight on the bed, and then I heard him rummaging through my suitcase. "Excellent," he drawled as he found something to use as a blindfold. I wondered what it was.

He tied a wound band of material around my head, removing all light from my vision. He also took my wrists and placed them gently over my head.

"Move them, and I'll have to tie them up." His dominant tone sent shivers to the apex of my thighs.

"Christ, Alex, I mean Dr. Pierce. You're killing me with your demands."

"You asked for a teacher, not a playdate. Deal with it." He wasn't wrong.

"How long has it been since you've been with a man? Let me rephrase that. How long has it been since you were thoroughly fucked?" Oh, his dirty mouth had me reeling with desire.

"Three, maybe four years ago. I had sex two months ago, although you could hardly call it being fucked." I mumbled the last part.

"I'll ease in then. Stay relaxed and welcome every sensation," he coaxed.

"Yes, Dr. Pierce."

My sight was gone, but my anticipation was clear as day. I lifted my ass as he dragged the head of his throbbing cock along my slit. I could hear the hum of the fan, along with Alex's heavy breathing.

The pressure of his long muscular legs on my tender inner thighs made me groan as the tiny hairs of his thighs gave me gooseflesh. The pressure increased, and all I could see was the tightening of his cut abs as he plunged his dick deep inside me. My hips bucked up of their own volition, allowing him to sink deeper and deeper, giving me the kind of pleasure I could only dream about. He felt so good. I never knew a man could have this kind of control over me and still allow me to let go and fly so freely.

"Patience, little one. I've got you." Those soothing words pulled another buck from my hips. *But what did he just call me? How much older is he?*

Like he was reading my mind, he answered my question.

"I may not be old enough to be your father, but I am forty-two. Do you like being with an older man? Do they bother you...my terms of endearment?"

His thumb circled my clit as he pressed the last of his cock into me. I could feel every throbbing vein in his shaft and heard a moan from his throat.

"I've never been with an older man. The benefits, though, are thoroughly appreciated." My sex clenched down around him, inducing a roar that shook the mirror.

"Fuck, Trudie. I'm barely holding on as it is. Don't do that again."

"What...this?" I held the contraction a little longer. I could be a devil, too.

"You're going to pay for that," he said, pulling out his cock and leaving me shouting indignantly.

"Put that back in!"

"Don't fuck with me, Trudie. I'll wait all night until you apologize for not listening to your teacher."

Well, fuck me. Really, fuck me now.

"Fine. I'm sorry I didn't listen. It won't happen again. Please put your cock back in me." Tears leaked from the corners of my eyes—he had to take pity on my lady blue balls.

Without compassion, he drove his cock in until his sack slapped my ass, then kept sliding in hard and out slowly until he was on his precipice. His thumb rubbed hard and fast around my clit, bringing me back to my edge.

"Please, Dr. Pierce, please. I'm going to come." He pinched my engorged button, and an explosion of stars burst behind my eyelids.

"Fuck, Alex! Oh my god, fuck, yeah." I screamed out my pleasure in pure abandon. Alex was a genius in bed; I couldn't have asked for a better teacher. His understanding of my body was better than my own, and I was so grateful.

By the time I came down from my euphoria, there was a stillness in the room. My stomach fell, and a wash of dread filled my veins. Wasn't he enjoying this as much as I was? Did I piss him off when I called him Alex instead of Dr. Pierce? Without warning, he flipped my legs over my head and slapped my ass hard, and then continued his mission to destroy my pussy. The rumble from his chest sounded like Vesuvius ready to explode, and it created kinetic energy that reverberated in my own chest as he roared his climax. I would never have thought I could come with only the sound of a voice, but my pussy quaked again, and I evaporated into the ether.

He pumped several more times, emptying his load into my already dripping pussy. Lust blazed in his eyes, and it gave me pause. This guy was an animal in bed, so different from Sam, and it would take me some time to get used to the intensity of it all.

"You will be the death of me, vixen. Don't you ever leave class before I dismiss you. Do you hear me?" He pulled out abruptly, and the dip and creak of the mattress moaned as he departed from the bed.

He was mad at me for not calling him Dr. Pierce? Like, for real, mad?

I wanted his arms around me, not his condemnation. Especially since those words were the last thing I thought I'd hear after life-changing sex. I ached not receiving his approval, and the whiplash left me emotionally paralyzed.

I couldn't stay like this anymore. I tore at the blindfold and ran to the bathroom, locking the door behind me. This incredibly thrilling night was ruined by his assholery. We were having fun. It was a game. He taught I learned, and it shattered my conception of what sex was and now could be. But then he went and ruined it. Another fucking man who made everything about himself. I knew he wasn't my dismissive father, but I had played the game right down to acting like an obstinate student. Why was he making me feel so small? I must have been delusional to think I was an equal in this—this scenario. That only happens to other people. Fuck this.

With a towel wrapped around my body, I went back out to grab my clothes, zipped up my luggage, and stormed back into the bathroom to wash off what was supposed to be the best time of my life. I was holding on by a thread and needed to get myself together. How could one moment be so heavenly and the next a living hell?

"Trudie...Trudie!" he yelled, banging on the door. "Tell me what's going on. What just happened? Talk to me."

I had no words for him. No emotion to spare. "Get dressed and get out!"

Five minutes later, I was dressed and ready to evict him from my room if he hadn't already left. I flung open the door to find a very angry Greek god. But he wasn't going to stop me. All I wanted to do was run away, just like when my dad came home from a work trip. But this was my room, and I wasn't leaving. Even if I theoretically understood what was happening—emotionally, I was a scared rabbit, and I needed space. Lots of space to work through this whole evening.

"Get out of my way, Alex." I elbowed him in the abs, and he grimaced.

If looks could kill, we'd both be dead. He'd managed to get his pants back on and stood there with both hands on his hips, fumes metaphorically emanating off his stupidly gorgeous head.

"Stop. Please. Let's talk this through. What happened?" He captured my shoulders in his large hands and stared at me, willing me to give him the answers that I couldn't provide.

All the dirty talk and intensely intimate things I just let him do to me. Did he deserve an answer? Maybe. Did I want to share any more of myself with this pompous piece of shit? Hell no. Whatever connection I thought—he thought—we had was fleeting. Our time was up, and so was this conversation. This misguided adventure had come to an end.

"Alex—Dr. Pierce. Thank you for your tutelage. It was quite illuminating. Where I go and what I do are none of your concern. Consider class dismissed for good. Fuck you, and good night."

I pulled away from his grip, stifling the tears I so desperately needed to shed, and watched as he slung his shirt back on, grabbed his socks and shoes, and shook his head in dismay. If he thought his teacher persona could steamroll through my erratic emotional state, then he wasn't the professional I thought he was.

Chapter 19

TRUDIE

"Y ou're an idiot!" my older brother, Paolo, screeched at my younger brother, Zander.

"I'm the idiot? I wasn't the one who got on a ladder three beers in and decided this was the best time to clean the gutters. What the hell is wrong with you?" Zander roared back.

I loved Sunday dinners at my mom's. Her smorgasbord of Spanish rice, chicken fajitas, Caesar salad, and Waldorf salad required two stomachs and a two-mile walk before I could even consider attempting my favorite dessert, sopapillas and vanilla bean ice cream. The other best part, hands down, was our family's version of *Survivor*.

No, there wasn't a tribunal unless you counted my mother's frantic attempts to get my brothers to calm down and go to their respective corners. And, no, no one was voted off our family island. However, the emotional—and sometimes physical—obstacle course consisted of intellectual verbal sparring, varying levels of vitriol, leaps of logic, and long-distance running if all hell broke loose.

Wanting a turn myself, I threw my buck and a half into the ring. "For what it's worth, I think you're both idiots." *That ought to do it.*

As expected, they replied in unison, "Shut up!" See? Now, they were on the same team, working for the same result.

I pulled bowls and trays of food from the table, wrapped them up, and found room for them in the refrigerator while my brothers cleaned the dishes. From a young age, we were assigned jobs, which have generally not changed. Mom cooked and therefore got to enjoy watching her children work in tandem cleaning up. It's the one time we all felt each other and knew that we were a part of a team—appreciated and loved.

Our Sunday dinners became more sporadic as we got older. Paolo had landed an amazing civil engineer position in Detroit, and Zander had just graduated with a nursing degree and worked per diem in Downriver, with his ever-changing schedule often interfering with our tradition. It was better that he worked than eat with us, but we missed his presence and wicked smart-ass mouth.

Mom stood to pour herself another cup of coffee from the French press. We were Latino through and through, save for the coffee.

"*Niños*, will I see you next week?" she asked, sipping from the *No Habla Stupido* mug I gave her a few years ago.

"No, Momma, I have to work over the weekend. I'll swing by during the week, though, and pick up dinner for us," Zander said quickly, kissing her forehead and making his way to the front door.

"*Te amo, Hermana.*" He blew me a kiss, his charm warming my heart.

"*Te amo, Bro.*" Zander rapped his chest two times with his fist and finished with a peace sign aimed at Paolo.

"*Estar seguro,*" we all sang out. Wishing safety to each other became another family tradition, originating when Dad would leave for work and because he once came back from one of his insurance trips with a broken leg and two broken ribs. Our " traditions " seemed to come from a place of protection or love.

Paolo offered to stay with our mom for a while, and I appreciated the gesture. I was wiped. Teacher Return Day was only a week away, and I had a myriad of tasks to accomplish, starting with transcribing all my notes from the conference.

My phone rang as I drove home, and Ruby's ridiculous drunk face popped up on my heads-up display.

"*Hola, Chica! Que Pasa*?" My Latina homegirl ringtone rang throughout the car, and a video call flashed on my phone. Since I was driving, I accepted the call as audio-only, and managed to do it without running a red light.

"*Hola, Chica! Teniendo sexo esta noche!*" Ruby blurted out. "And how was dinner?" She could oscillate from one topic to another in two seconds flat.

"Girl, so much to tell you and so little time." I regaled her with the highlights of my evening cruise and what happened afterward during my twenty-minute ride home. I was too tired to go through all the gory details, though, and quite frankly, I was still mortified and shocked at how it started and ended. I clearly needed to process further what happened before I shared.

"Dinner was good. Did you hear my brother graduated at the top of his nursing program? He has a terrific per diem job in Downriver. I'm so happy for him and my mom. She needs to stop worrying about all of us so much." I sighed as much with exhaustion as worry about her health.

"That's amazing, I'll have to send him a gift when I have two nickels to rub together. I kind of lost my job this week," she said sheepishly.

"You're kidding, right? What the hell happened? Did that limp dick you called a boss make a pass at you again? I was this close to marching into that asshole's office and kicking his dick."

She sighed, resigned. "No. He just decided that he couldn't come up with any new sales ideas and that mine were stellar. Of course, to pay for those new programs and stay in budget, something, someone, i.e. me, got cut. I was spitting nails, Trudie. Every fucking time a misogynist male passes himself off as a genius off the back of a smart woman is another day toward the revolt of women across the globe!"

Yeah, she was super pissed, and rightfully so. "I'm sorry, sweetheart. Do you need me to bring Oreos and wine tonight?" These items were our survival kit while we figured out life.

She bellowed out a "No!" And my heart broke at her pain.

"I had to move home again. My mom was moments away from tearing my room apart so she could have her coveted sewing room. I found a stash of pictures and quotes of how she wanted to redecorate my room and now she'll have to wait again. I feel like such a disappointment sometimes."

"Are you sure you don't need me to bring the makings for a sugar coma? It might knock you out, at least for tonight." I was too pooped to make the effort, but my girl needed her friends' support.

"Normally, I would have loved that, Trudes, but I'm going to take a hot bath and call it a night. Next week is going to be another whirlwind of looking for new opportunities, and I want to jump on my plans first thing in the morning. By the way, I'm going to give you a pass on spilling those details tonight, but you owe me a thorough accounting of your trip next week.

"Of course. Let's catch up soon. Love you, *amor*," I cooed.

"Love you more."

ALEXANDER

My next two conferences went smoothly. Thankfully, each was only a two-day appearance. I needed a break, and with Labor Day coming up, I was going to take advantage of the long weekend. Now I was exhausted and also annoyed that my mother was calling me. The incessant knocking on my front door wasn't helping, either. I just wanted to collapse on my couch with a beer, scratch my balls, and watch football. The Giants were looking good in preseason, and I was hoping for a few good conversions before the official season began.

"Yeah, Mother. What's going on?" I deadpanned, an improvement from some of the other intonations I've sent her way.

"Are you home? I've been knocking for a millennium." So dramatic. *Is that her at my door?*

I whipped open the door without using the peephole, not caring who was on the other side, and barked, "What?" And there, lo and behold, stood my perfectly coiffed, Chanel-ed mother with a phone to her ear.

"There you are, darling. I'll need some ice for my hand. I think I bruised my knuckles with all that knocking." Her distress was palpable as she waltzed through my front door. To my dismay—chin to my chest, my hand still wrapped tightly around the door handle—she air kissed me twice, then promptly forgot the ice and walked to the bar to pour herself a scotch.

I didn't have the energy to ask her why she thought both calling me and banging on my door was necessary. Everything she did was so overly dramatic that I was desensitized to her theatrics. After shutting the door like I was swinging a golf club, I took her lead and went to the refrigerator to get a cold beer. I stared at the puff of condensation from the opened bottle and wished she would leave the same way—quickly and in a puff of smoke. Time to review my tactics on how to best navigate through this visit:

What the hell, Mom? Can't you just text what you need like a normal person? Provoking.

Hey, Mom. Everything okay? Fake empathy. Not my style.

Bitch! Are you crazy? What the fuck is so important you had to call and beat my door down at the same time? Tempting and to the point, but too harsh.

I checked myself and stole one of Trudie's life hacks, breathing in and out several times to gain some control.

"So, Mom." I cleared my throat. "Bring me up to speed on what is going on in your life." *Caring and deflecting her attention off me. Well done.*

"I'm so glad you asked, sweetheart. My life is a shamble, and only you can fix it."

I'd heard this one before. It usually starts and ends with a broken fingernail.

"Go on," I urged her.

"Your father is cheating on me again. Tabitha is dating, of all people, a florist, and Sarah ignores me." Her chin fell to her chest as she dramatically placed the back of her hand on her forehead in despair. *Oh, hell.*

I couldn't help that my father was a philanderer. Being married to my mother, the spoiled brat drama queen, couldn't have been pleasant. The fact that they stayed committed to each other, even through the worst of times, was admirable. There were too many assets to dissolve and affiliations to divvy up to consider divorce. Discretion was our family motto.

Regarding Tabitha, she was a hippie, a free spirit who couldn't be tamed. Good luck to the florist was all I had to say about that. On the other hand, Sarah needed a mother more than a shopping buddy. Ignoring my mother wasn't kind, nor was it helpful to her situation, but I understood it as a survival tactic.

I attempted a tone of sincerity and replied, "Sounds like a full plate, Mom. Dad is Dad. Is he not being discreet?" That was an easy fix.

"Yes, it's just...why doesn't he want to be with me?" she whined.

"Sounds like a conversation to have with your therapist, Mom. Maybe up your visits to weekly instead of yearly?" Loving advice from a son who didn't want to touch that with a ten-foot pole.

"Perhaps." Her index finger circled the top of her glass, making it hum. She sounded so deflated, imagining she'd have to work at something other than her figure.

"Is Tabitha happy with her florist friend? I bet she could get you a great deal for your weekly arrangements." Again, I offered loving and helpful advice.

Her finger came up to her lips, "I never thought of it that way."

Of course, it wasn't about Tabitha, but what she could get out of the situation. Par for the course, again.

"But what about Sarah, my baby? She must love me, right? I'm her mother, for God's sake."

Another land mine to avoid.

"Mom, children inherently love their parents. Even bad parents have children who love them. I'm not saying you're a bad parent—actually, I am. " It's just that children grow up and want to be their own person. Learn to embrace her individuality and love her unconditionally, and she'll come around. You'll see." There is not a chance in hell that Sarah will ever have a mother like that. I tried, *though.*

"That's so much work, darling. Can't I just send her to Hawaii for a month and have her return home, happy to see me? Grateful for all my sacrifices?" *Okay. I'm done with this.*

"Mom, you know I love you, but this woe-is-me attitude needs to stop. If you're asking your son, the psychologist, for professional advice, here it is: Your children are grown. Love them and let them be. Next, go find out who Eleanor Pierce is. Do the work. Move out of your home if you feel you need to and start a new life starring yourself. And, last, learn to be grateful for all you have and think about how it can help others. You have too much. Learn how to share your resources, personally and professionally. Find a simpler life. When you do, Dad will stop looking around. It's totally up to you."

I chugged the rest of my beer and got up for another one. I hadn't planned on getting plastered that evening. *Hmmm, why not?*

My poor, overwhelmed, highly sophisticated mother flopped—yes, flopped—onto my sofa, with dread in her eyes.

"Starting over sounds unbearable. I've worked so hard to achieve our status and reputation—what will people say?" she said, wringing her hands.

"Maybe stop caring so much about what others think and focus on yourself and what you think, Mom. Yours is the only opinion that matters in the end." *I really am a good son.*

With a deep sigh, she launched herself off the couch and strolled to the front door. With one last harrumph, she bowed her head in thanks. "You're a good son, Alex. I'm proud of you, but really, that psychobabble stuff couldn't possibly help my situation. Thanks anyway for trying." Two more air kisses, and she was off.

Why do I waste my breath on her? Oh, yeah, she's my mom.

Now that she was gone, I needed to get my act together. My maid was coming tomorrow, and the pile of laundry alone would keep her busy for three days. That would give me just enough time to repack and fly to Austin, Texas. There is nothing like heat on top of more heat in August.

However, Labor Day in the Hamptons sounded peaceful as long as I didn't have to see my family. Going with my gut, I emailed Emilio, the groundskeeper at the family beach property, and had him speak with the head housekeeper to see if they would tidy up the old carriage house above the garage and stock it for me. If I could quietly stay there for a few days, I'm sure I could clear my head of a certain vixen that had bailed on me without an explanation. She was history to me; except I couldn't understand the vehemence of her retreat after the most intimate sex I'd ever had.

Chapter 20

TRUDIE

I LOVED MY CLASSROOM. The sun blasted through the window every morning, easing me into my day, and by the time lunch was over, the room was cooler, so my kids could still pay attention. An ideal setting for learning. Speaking of which, I saw a video on YouTube about self-awareness and regulation in children and immediately wanted to set up a spot in the back of my room by the window for a "Rest and Return" space where kids could take a break when they were feeling out of control. No lie, I was going to model how to use this space every time I felt myself needing a time-out. It's true that meeting achievement markers was important for the school, but what price had to be paid to get there? I couldn't fix a kid's IQ—I could only provide diligent and consistent teaching—but I could fix their EQ. My father had the emotional quotient of an old shoe; he was lifeless unless moved by external forces. Most kids, however, had low EQ when they lacked love, attention, and even nutrition. They needed to feel settled and have some confidence to learn. *Enter me!*

As I finished my contemplations, Robin, one of my favorite teacher friends, breezed through my door and planted herself on the corner of my desk.

"Welcome back, my brainiac friend. How was your summer?" Robin was a music and drama teacher, and her lyrical voice filled my classroom. "You won't believe what happened to me."

She was kind of glowing. "Let me guess—you got laid!" I squealed in hushed tones.

She doubled over, slapping her hands on her knees. "Oh my god, you are so right. It turns out that I needed a plumber for a legit problem in my basement, and not only was he able to fix that, but he also knew how to fix my "downstairs" issue even better. I know it sounds cliché, but when it happens to you, it's orgasmic."

We both laughed uncontrollably. Robin was exuberant, to say the least. Straightforward and a real riotous bitch. Lunches with her were never dull, and whenever I needed a hand with school matters or kid problems, she was always there with her wisdom and support.

"That's so exciting, Robs. I'm so happy for you. Are you dating now or just getting it on? Oh, and does Jody know yet?" I loved it when I got the scoop first.

My besties were my school rocks. We were like the Chicks without Dicks in the way we banded together each year. They were almost a decade older than me, but ironically, they kept coming to me for my advice. Sometimes I was like Lucy from the Peanuts cartoon with her "The Doctor Is In" sign. My work was never finished—with my students, my colleagues, my administration, and my family.

"Nah. I love her to death, but I don't want her making it out to be something it's not. Besides, I saw you first." She smiled angelically. "Listen, I've got to check into the office. I'll catch up with you at lunch?" She didn't wait for an answer as she waved while walking out the door.

It wasn't long before I had my new area set up with a soft yellow carpet and a small multicolored rocking chair that I picked up at a thrift shop. It was the perfect little spot to chill out in. With the addition of a few specific books to help guide them through the restoration process and a few succulent plants on the windowsill, I was overjoyed with the aesthetic. I snapped a picture and sent it to Ruby, who "woot, wooted" me with several appreciation emojis.

Two loud knocks on my door alerted me to an overly excited Jody waving her arms overhead in joy.

"Tru-day! Girl, how are you?" Her thick arms wrapped around my shoulders. "I want every detail about your summer, but first, love the plants in your Zen area. I might have to steal this idea for my art room. Those whack-a-doodle kids need a spot that doesn't involve scissors, glue, and confetti. I'm still cleaning up last year's mess. Listen, just wanted to say hey. See you at lunch? Are we still on for yoga Thursdays? I'm already desperate for a mental stretch." I nodded as she blew out of my room as fast as she blew in.

I sat at a desk in the back of the room and perused my space. What did the kids see from back here? Every year I ask, "How can the kids in the back feel as integral as the kids in the front?"

Perspective was everything. This year would be no different, except I had learned a strategy from a middle school teacher's social media page and was pretty sure it would be a game-changer for a few of my kids. I couldn't wait to try it when school started.

The countertops were laden with potluck goodies ranging from Cooper's carefully engineered seven-layer dip to Robin's latest Barefoot Contessa creation of flourless chocolate cake with raspberry coulis. It looked amazing. The leftover sopapillas I stole from my mom's the previous night were my contribution this year. Not very creative, but quite tasty.

I made my way through the line with everyone else hugging and asking about each other's families. Too many people asked about Sam and what we were up to, and I was paralyzed when I tried to produce a neutral response. I hadn't even told my best friends yet, and I didn't want to blurt out some lies.

"Oh, yeah, Sam is doing good. He moved to Colorado for an amazing position, and he's, uh, doing terrific." A perma smile was pasted on my face as I scooped way too much food on my plate and then darted out of the line of fire. I needed some fresh air and found Jody and Robin at our favorite picnic table. We were fortunate to have a principal who was all about aesthetics: comfortable places to sit, soothing colors to encourage relaxation, and lots of perks to keep us from leaving our jobs.

"Eloise did a great job painting these picnic tables. I kept getting splinters in my ass last year. I heard she did them herself," Jody exclaimed.

"Eloise did *not* paint these herself. What's wrong with you?" Robin retorted. "She's the principal, not the facilities staff. She lured several Junior Honor Society kids to do it as part of their community service. In other words, she blackmailed them with their acceptance into the program this year." Robin always had dirt on what was going on behind the scenes.

Not me, though. I did everything I could to be deaf, blind, and stupid about the inner workings of our school. It wasn't that I wasn't concerned or able to contribute, it was that when I did get involved, I overcommitted myself. I had a "Go big or go home" attitude that usually consumed me.

Last year, Paula, the other English teacher, asked me to help her update our curriculum to exceed the state's required testing benchmarks, and, in my zeal to improve it, I kind of rewrote the whole curriculum, including diagrams, exercises, contingencies, and, well, everything. Our eight-hour collaboration ended with me spending sixty additional hours on my own. Paula loved that I took the lead, but she questioned my sanity. This year, I was going to stay in my lane and only do what was required under my contract. I had plans for those sixty hours this year, which didn't include unnecessary projects.

Skipping the main course on my plate, I stuffed a ridiculous amount of Robin's cake in my mouth and made moaning noises, most definitely suggestive in nature.

"Slow down, girl. I'll make you another one if you love it so much," Robin chided.

"I can't help it," I mumbled, her cake sticking to the roof of my mouth. "Ish sho good." I rolled my eyes back in my head for further dramatic effect.

"Yeah, that's what she said." Jody glared at Robin. I guess she heard Robin's good news about her new plumber. "If I didn't have the man I have, I'd be asking for his friend's phone number." Her fork paused in midair. "Maybe you should ask for me anyway, just in case." We all cracked up at her. Jody's mind was a hamster wheel on steroids, always moving at high speed.

"So, Ms. Trudie. What did you do on your summer vacation? And don't leave out the dirt about Sam. I know something went down by the way you avoided responding to the staff's questions about him."

My moment of truth. I kept my emotions in check when I shared that Sam asked me to move to Colorado with him, and I said no. I told them about flirting on the plane, without any details, and about the amazing lectures I attended at the psychology conference. However, by the time I finished my conference story, my face had crumbled.

Robin didn't miss a beat and went in for the kill. "Hold up. What's with the face? There's more to this story and you need to spill it right now." With her eyes boring into mine, I couldn't escape her interrogation.

"Yeah, what she said. Give it up," Jody implored. Curiosity was embedded in her every pore.

I decided to tell them everything and get it over with. *Well, almost everything.*

"One of the lecturers was not only the best in the biz, but he was also quite a looker, and, well, we smashed into each other the first day, and, and he kept goading me all week long. He was a pompous asshole, so arrogant in the way he spoke to me that I wanted to smack him in the face." I damn near picked my cuticles to the quick getting this stupid story out. I wished I didn't care, but for some ridiculous reason, every time I thought about Alex Pierce, my panties got wet.

"Sounds like a real piece of work. Is there more to this story you're leaving out?" Jody's spidey senses were never wrong.

I steeled myself for the big conclusion, grinding my back teeth down to nubs. *Breathe.*

"It just seemed like he was everywhere I went. The pool, the beach, the sunset cruise. It was like the cosmos kept shoving us together like magnets. It was freaky." Letting out the rest of my breath, I focused on settling my heart rate. Even speaking about him turned me inside out.

"More like freaking hot, I'd say." *Thanks, Robin.* "How good-looking are we talking?" she asked, pushing at my shoulder. Thank God the lunch bell sounded at that moment, giving me an excuse to bolt. I stumbled over the picnic bench seat before righting myself and heading back to the building.

"Hey! How good?" Jody yelled behind me.

"Greek-freaking-god good-looking," I tossed back, irritated to have to admit it. The conversation wreaked havoc on my mind and body. It's a good thing I had a panty liner on, too, because I would have slipped off my seat and embarrassed myself even more if I had tried to describe him.

The rest of the week was filled with lesson plan updates, department meetings, logistics for the spring field trip to the Cranbrook Gardens, and general tidying up. My mom had been in the area and wanted to have lunch on Thursday, and since I had my act together in the classroom, we met at a cute diner to split a salad. One of the best things about Michigan was the cherry season. They were in everything from cookies to salads and when they were paired with pecans, goat cheese, and balsamic vinegar, it was divine.

We ate quietly, enjoying each other's company, until my mom brought up a sore topic: dating.

"Baby, I know you hate when I bring it up, but it's been two months since you broke up with Sam. When are you going to start dating again? How am I supposed to become an *abuela* when you don't even have a man in your life? You're not getting any younger, *niña*." Her bottom lip slipped past the upper one in a pout fit for a five-year-old.

The clatter of my fork falling on my plate startled the people around me, so not only was I agonizing over being single again, I was also mortified about having my failures called out.

"Momma, please. Women no longer need a man in their lives to be happy. I don't miss having to think about someone other than myself. Why can't you let it go for a while?" And for good measure, I assert, "And I have two brothers who can just as easily find a woman and make babies for you." Why do women have to do all the heavy lifting in a family? Let the guys take this one thing for a while.

"Trudie, sweetie," she cajoled. "You know your brothers aren't capable of finding, let alone keeping, a good woman. Paolo may be good-looking, but he can't even tie his shoes. And Zander is too busy working and sowing his wild oats to be tied down. You, sweetheart, are in your prime. Seize the day, *amor*."

Throwing my napkin on my plate, I pushed back, defeated. This conversation was a broken record for me, and I needed to throw away the phonograph.

"Thanks for lunch, Mom. I've got to get back to school." My arms wrapped around her ever-thinning frame. Time had been difficult for her, and I wanted to ease her heart, just not at my expense. We said goodbye and promised to see each other Sunday.

I couldn't tell her I found a man who checked every physical box I wanted, though not the important emotional ones, like trustworthiness and compassion. Besides, we lived hundreds of miles away, and our paths would not cross again.

The school bell chimed at the end of the day, and the PA squealed, getting our attention for final announcements.

"Don't forget tomorrow is Field Day, and everyone is expected to participate. We have a special guest joining us, and I'm sure you will make them feel comfortable. Have a good night and prepare yourselves for your last weekend of peaceful sleep for the next nine months." Chortling and squealing buzzed through the speakers before the hum of the PA ceased.

Dear God, it's me, Trudie. If I survive tomorrow's Field Day, please let me sleep for forty-eight hours. As adept as I was with my yoga practice, I still had a hard time settling my brain for a full night's sleep. I'm pretty sure it was a remnant of my youth, and it was very annoying, especially since I had to get up by six every morning. I needed every hour of sleep I could get.

I heard an array of conversations and door closings that, in combination, sounded like a disjointed machine until only the fading clacks of heels and squeaks of tennis shoes signaled that I was alone. Unlocking my desk drawer to retrieve my purse, I heard a small knocking on my door and looked up to see Principal Eloise poking her head inside.

"Hey, Trudie." She smiled sincerely. "I'm so sorry I haven't made time to catch up with you yet this week. So many new things are happening this year, and I can't even find time to eat." She walked tiredly up to a student desk in the front row and plopped down unceremoniously.

"Eloise. It's good to see you too, although you do look the worse for wear." I laughed and pulled a desk up near hers.

Her eyes closed, her face contemplative, and her deep breaths slowed her heaving chest. Minutes went by, and I wondered if she had, in fact, fallen asleep.

"What can I do to help, Eloise?" So much for my promise to keep my head down this year.

Her long black lashes fluttered up, and a deep, knowing smile split her face. "Now that's what I needed to hear, Trudie. Someone who has my back when I need it the most." Her relief was palpable.

"We've been friends a long time, El. If I can be of service, you know I'll do what I can."

She grasped both my hands, which were resting on my desk. "Thank you. We'll talk more tomorrow. Thanks for sharing my load." She pumped my hands again, slid her curvy body out from the tiny desk, and headed for my door.

On a whim, I asked, "Uh, El, what load am I going to help you carry?"

A slow smile curved up her face again, making her look like the Grinch Who Stole Christmas.

"It's right up your alley, girlfriend."

Oh shit! That didn't sound good.

Chapter 21
TRUDIE

BLESSED SLEEP WRAPPED ITS cuddly arms around me, refilling my soul and forcing tremors through my body as it convulsed, stretching my muscles like an electric arc. Snaking my arms over my head and twisting my limbs from side to side to open up pockets of locked energy had me exhausted after fifteen seconds. Staring at the popcorn ceiling and feeling like a corpse in *Shavasana*, my first coherent thought was that the last time I was this still in bed had been when Alex had been between my legs staring me down like a predator. Remembering the thrill of having such a magnificent, powerful body right there, ready to teach me things I couldn't put into words, gave my nether regions tingles. That moment changed my life in such a significant way, one I wouldn't completely understand for a long time.

My heart rate ramped up when I realized I had time for a little morning self-care. My hands slid to each of my nipples, which were already hard at the idea of getting myself off. They'd always been so sensitive, and as I've gotten older, they seemed to have become even more so. Thoughts of Alex speaking to me in his teacher's voice, firm and commanding, made my body quake in anticipation. My right finger slid down inside my pajama shorts, circling my clit slowly, with just enough pressure to have me sighing my relief. Just thinking about the sheer size of Alex, the bulges of muscles along his shoulders and upper arms, and his strong hands had me coming almost immediately. Fuck, he was so hot. I slid my fingers further into my pussy, bucking my hips upward at the memory of him hovering over me. *Please, Dr. Pierce!* I moaned his name repeatedly until I flew over the edge, my body shaking violently with the aftershocks of the best hand job I'd ever given myself.

Big, sinister red numbers flashed on my alarm clock, which insisted I get up. My euphoric state of bliss was obliterated and I remembered that my principal had a secret message she needed to disclose today.

I turned on the shower, brushed my teeth, and looked at my phone to see if I had missed any texts overnight. Ricky, the building secretary, insisted I check in with him by eight. Robin sent me her regular morning emoji, wishing me a good day, and my mom begged me to stop by after school to help her with some chores around her house. It was just another day in paradise.

The shower still wasn't hot. I prayed I didn't need to get a new water heater. I hated talking to my leasing company—they were so condescending and slow to resolve any issue I brought up. Later—I'd call later. Lukewarm water would have to do. I felt nervous about El's cryptic response from the previous day. I hoped her project was something fun and not onerous. I was not in the mood for onerous.

It was Field Day, and by the end of it I would be filthy, sweaty, and elated. It was one of my favorite days of Teacher Welcome Back Week. Last year the English Department slayed the Performing & Fine Arts Department in lawn bowling. You've never seen the ridiculousness of this sport until you see a bunch of uncoordinated and non-team-oriented people pretending to be accomplished bowlers. Our blooper reel alone was priceless.

Suited up in shorts, a Hart Middle School V-neck tee-shirt from three Field Days prior, and a tracksuit, I was ready to go. I grabbed my purse and school bag and headed out the door. As usual, I was one flight of stairs down before I realized I had forgotten my water bottle and hoofed it back up to grab it. I hustled back down the stairs, held my breath as I went under the cherry blossoms (a little superstition of mine), and got in my car just as Ruby called.

"Hey, Ruby. What's happening? Are you feeling any better being home?" I gasped out. *I really need to work on my cardio.*

"Good morning, sunshine. Yeah. It's not that I don't like it here, it's just that I feel like I lost six years of independence. When can we meet so we can catch up?"

"I'm free later tonight, say seven-thirty?" I was pulling into my school's parking lot, and I had four minutes to get to Ricky.

"Perfect. Text me and we'll figure out where to meet." Her voice sang the last part. "I was thinking that I'd use my voice for my next career move—a voice-over artist. What do you think?"

I laughed, slamming my car door. "You have more talent in your pinky finger than I have in my whole body. That sounds like an awesome plan. Look, I've gotta go, babe. Field day is calling me."

"Oh shit, no. That's today? Please do not get a black eye like you did last year," she chided.

"Hey! That was so not my fault. If Paula hadn't twirled around so emphatically after she got a strike, that wouldn't have happened," I explained indignantly.

"Well, maybe you should keep your distance while people are bowling. Give them a wide berth this year, Trudie." She was infuriating sometimes.

"Love you too, Rubes. Have a great day and don't forget to clean your room like a good girl." *That's what you get when you mess with me.*

"You're just jealous that my breakfast is being made for me every day. Have a great one."

The line went dead as I got ready to lambaste her with another witty comment. I'd get her next time. Not that I was keeping score or anything.

Hart Middle School was the epitome of upper-crust Middle America. The newer building, with straight lines, pristine concrete driveways, tidy landscaping, and colorful carpets, housed a bunch of entitled children of entitled parents.

I jogged through the main doors and crossed the wide lobby to the main office, where not only Ricky was stationed front and center, but also the attendance secretary, Mona. Behind her, the administrative assistant, Roxanne, protected her two main charges,

Eloise and the assistant principal, Charlie Schultz. As much as I loved shooting the breeze with Ricky, I may as well have broadcast anything I had to say over the PA. There was no privacy in the main office, and little more in the teachers' lounge. The only way you could assure privacy was in the counselors' office, and that was where Ricky headed when he saw me walking in. He signaled for me to follow him, which put me on high alert that whatever he had to say would be big.

He motioned me into the tiny room and closed the blinds.

"Girl, we've got trouble. Did you know we have a guest in our building today? A guest who will be participating in Field Day? A guest who looks like the star of my most private wet dream?" Ricky was so flamboyant that he reminded me of my favorite TikToker, Greg. Hilarious in his seriousness, and poignant in his outlandish delivery.

Not wanting to offend dear Ricky after his over-the-top speech, I answered in feigned concerned confusion. *Okay, not so feigned. What the hell was he talking about?* "Oh my god, no! Who are you talking about? And, who in the hell would want to participate in a Midwestern middle school's Field Day event?"

Ricky placed one hand over his sculpted chest and one over his mouth. "I probably shouldn't say their name, but girl, there are some changes happening this year and you are going to freak out when you hear about them. I had to give you a heads-up before Eloise dropped the bomb on you and all the other teachers. The school board hired a consultant to raise our school's status to "exemplary." They are hoping there will be more state funding and more opportunities for our teachers and students in STEM-related areas." His body seemed to deflate now that he had revealed his secret.

"Are you shitting me! Like we don't have enough standardized testing to prep for, now we have to perform like monkeys to get prestige? Fuck that, Ricky. Thanks for the heads up and for ruining my favorite day of the year." I whipped open the door and stormed down the hallway to Eloise's office.

Was this the project Eloise had been hinting at yesterday? The project she needed me to help carry the load on? Don't I do enough for this stupid school?

I stopped abruptly at El's door and forced myself to pull my shit together. Two breaths later, and back in a calmer place, I knocked not so lightly on her door. A moment later, it opened, not by El, but by Satan, resplendent in a blue pinstripe suit that hugged his body better than any Spanx ever could. Why was this happening to me again? Wasn't it enough that he slammed into me in San Francisco? Why had he opened another door and slammed into my professional life? Why was I being punished this way?

"Trudie." His voice oozed sensuality, which was definitely not appropriate for daytime, let alone in my principal's office, with her five feet away.

"Ahh, hi?" I looked to El, pleading for an explanation and feeling faint.

Asking Alex to take a seat in one of her comfortable leather swivel chairs, she walked around her desk and, without preamble, pushed me out of her office and back down the hall to the counselors' office. *Apparently, this was my new time-out room.* We both stepped into the tiny office, and El insisted I take a seat.

"So. You forced me to jump the gun on the introduction of Dr. Alexander Pierce, the consultant hired by the school board to raise our game and meet the criteria for an exemplary school designation. This assignment was the extra load I mentioned to you yesterday. I really appreciated your offering to help me get him situated and to act as the liaison between him and the teachers this year."

Shock. Panic. Lust. More Panic. More shock.

Had someone picked up my life and started spinning it precariously around on the top of a stick, like in a juggler's act? Nothing in my life was stable now. It was all quicksand and I was about to get sucked into an emotional void. Alex was more than a fling in California, he was the guy who opened my Aladdin's lamp. He had too much power over me when he looked at me, and when he touched me, I ignited. How would I make it through a whole year with him? El didn't know what she was asking of me. Alex and I were connected on a level I couldn't even define. It scared me and made me wet at the same time.

"Trudie." She snapped her fingers in front of my face. "Did you hear me? You're scaring me." Scaring her? *Ha!* If she only knew, and—my god, she couldn't find out about us.

I closed my eyes and braced myself for my acting debut.

"Yes, I heard you. That sounds…like…a big task. Are you sure you don't want a more tenured teacher to handle this?" I needed a way out.

El jammed both her hands on her curvaceous hips. "Of course you're the right person for the job. You have been training for this opportunity your whole professional life and I'll be damned if I'll give it to some idiot teacher who only wants the money."

Well, that got my attention. "Money?" I asked. "What kind of money are we talking about?" Now my hands were on my curvaceous hips.

El chuckled. "I knew that would get your attention. How does $10,000 sound?" Her Grinch smile grew, and grew, and grew.

Pressing my lips together and rolling my eyes skyward, I sighed frustrated. "Fine. Fine. What exactly do I need to do to earn this blood money?"

El pulled me into a big momma bear hug. "Let's go back to my office and make your introduction. Then we can cover all the details later this afternoon after all the games. We'll be done by four as usual." She hooked her arm through mine as we exited the office and walked down the hall, bumping hips back and forth.

Pasting a smile on my face, I reentered El's office and extended my hand to the good doctor. My acting career was taking flight. Robin would be so proud.

"Hi. I'm Trudie Gonzales. I'm the English Department head and I've just learned that I'll be your liaison for this designation project going on this year." *Whew. I'm glad that's over. I hope that was convincing enough to both Alex and El.*

"Hello, Ms. Gonzales," he crooned, shaking my now electrified hand. I don't know if I'll ever be able to hear my name said that way without a Pavlovian response. "Thank you for working with me on what I hope will be a fruitful and exciting year." He winked. Too bad El only saw his back. He turned in his seat and straightened his body and his face as I sat down in the other swivel chair.

El went on to list all of Dr. Pierce's accomplishments and why he was the right man for the job. She surprised me by listing all of my accomplishments and credentials to him as well. I sounded pretty good on paper.

"Dr. Pierce, you might have attended the conference Ms. Gonzales went to this summer in San Francisco—does she look familiar?" What was she doing? Since most people ask questions that they already know the answer to, why was she poking the proverbial bear?

Alex stroked his tanned hand over his mouth in reflection.

"Now that you mention it, she does. I think she may have been in one of my lectures. Come to think of it, she did ask some very provoking questions. If she's as good a teacher as she is a student, you've got a tremendous asset on your hands, principal." He nodded in the affirmative, his eyes darkening the way they had the night he stroked every part of me until I convulsed under his relentless hands.

Eloise nodded her agreement as well. "The best this school has." She rose and came around her desk to stand by the door.

"Thank you for coming in today, Dr. Pierce. It's a big day here at Hart Middle School, and I'm sure Ms. Gonzales needs to meet up with her team before the games begin at ten. Why don't I take you on a tour of the building and then let you get changed, since you want to get to know the teachers while they compete? Ms.

Gonzales, why don't you add Dr. Pierce to your roster today?" *This sounded more like a directive than a question.*

Hitching myself to a standing position, I pasted another smile on my face.

"I'd be delighted. Have you played Hungry, Hungry, Hippos before?" I smirked, knowing how ridiculous he'd feel playing this highly competitive children's game.

The crease in his brow said it all.

"Oh, you're going to love this. It's a real crowd-pleaser." I slapped my hand over my forehead, just thinking about how much fun this was going to be, and walked out of the main office in the direction of my classroom.

ALEXANDER

That was the best surprise I'd ever had. Never in a million years would I have thought this long-term consulting job would have the lovely, sexy, and highly annoying Trudie Gonzales tied to it. When she shoved me out of that motel room, leaving me hard and my gut in turmoil, I never thought I'd see her again. Mind you, I searched for her on every social platform I could find, and only found her listed as an attendee at several previous conferences. She had a lockdown on her social media that was second only to the FBI. Not even a sniff in the white pages and everyone was listed there.

I followed Principal Jackson up and down the halls of the very modern school. The white cement block walls were covered with graphics that inspired, directed, and reminded these kids of what they could be and where they could go if they only believed in themselves. That alone would be a major focus of my stay here. I truly believed that when kids believed in their abilities or their potential abilities, they'd test better, and they'd create a better social environment for all around them. Multiply that by the five hundred-something kids attending this school, and every 1 percent improvement each kid, teacher, and staff made changed the outcome. It was limitless.

I should have probably paid more attention to where I was going so that I could find my way around more easily, but my feet became glued to the floor when I saw Trudie in her classroom sliding her track pants off her toned legs. Images of her bucking up underneath me made my pants very tight and very uncomfortable. I forced myself to keep moving, although I fell a few steps behind Principal Jackson.

In the midst of her canned speech about extracurricular offerings at the school, I cleared my throat and interrupted. "Principal Jackson?"

She stopped and turned toward me with a small polite smile that reminded me of my Aunt Lorraine. She was nothing like my mother. Absolutely nothing like her. "Are there any programs offered to high-risk students at your school? Academic or social-emotional programs?"

Bemusement washed over her face, her eyes rolling back slightly. She crossed an arm under her breasts and her other hand cupped her chin between her thumb and forefinger. "If you're referring to student support programs, we currently utilize paras who support specific children who have been identified as needing special assistance. And, we do have ESL-focused classrooms to get those children to understand, write, and speak English better. However, if it's what I think you're suggesting, we'd need to rob a bank or find a renewable endowment to cover anything over and above what we are currently able to afford. So, Dr. Pierce, what exactly are you getting at?"

"It wasn't my intention to alienate you or your school's practices; I just wanted to find out how invested you might be in identifying other factors that make a kid high-risk." I motioned for her to keep walking so that she would have a moment to think and not feel like she was under a microscope.

Principal Jackson stopped outside the office and cocked her head to the side, waiting for me to continue. I mirrored her stance, spreading my legs wide. Probably more intimidating than necessary, but I wanted to drive my point home.

"Principal, it is my professional and personal belief that if we provide support to children who can be identified as high risk when they're young, we can save our society millions of dollars by helping them become contributing members, rather than eventually paying the costs of their incarceration or public assistance. Now, I haven't compounded the math on this theory, but let's say conservatively that if we could find an investment of twelve thousand dollars in a dozen kids each year, say over four years, wouldn't you agree that those kids had a greater chance of becoming productive citizens when they were older? Can you imagine the realized value of that investment? Staggering, isn't it?"

She nodded slowly. "Dr. Pierce, the way you put that was astounding. What I wouldn't give to make that theory a reality." She turned on her heel and pushed through the office doors, waving a hand above her head. When she spun around abruptly, I almost ran into her.

"But by any chance, do you know where we'd get the money for that? Do you have a Money Fairy you could call on?" She chuckled.

I couldn't help laughing too. "As a matter of fact, I do. I have a Money Fairy so big, that if we can demonstrate how a simple program with the right people could change the trajectory of those dozen kids, they would expand this program to your whole school district. What do you think?"

"You are a godsend, Dr. Pierce. Not only will you be able to make privileged students focused on raising their standards of success, but you'll also help less privileged students see an equally bright future. That's more than a win-win in my book."

Elated and overwhelmed by her response, I extended both my arms in what I hoped would be a welcomed hug. Principal Eloise didn't disappoint, and she squeezed me so hard I almost fell over.

"Well, that's enough for now. Go ahead and get in your exercise clothes, and we'll continue our conversation at three. You can use the men's bathroom in the office for your convenience. Head down that hall and out that door by nine-fifty, and we'll get started shortly thereafter." She pointed toward the hallway on the right and left me standing by the secretaries.

TRUDIE

This was either going to be the best day of my life or the worst. Or maybe both. I needed to alert my team that an alien would descend upon us in twenty minutes. My gut ached and I felt lightheaded—probably because I had been holding my breath the whole way out to the playground. The shock of seeing Alex standing in Eloise's door, and then hearing his smooth sexy voice utter my name, had me reeling. I needed to stop thinking about what it meant to have him back in my life and my new role as teacher liaison for this initiative. To be honest, I wanted some closure to whatever you'd call this relationship between us. He couldn't possibly want more than to teach me some magical sex maneuvers, could he?

I gave a halfhearted wave and a small smile to the English, social studies, and gym teachers, and motioned for them to huddle up.

"Today is our day, friends! Before Eloise's little surprise arrives, I wanted to give you a heads up about it." I explained why Alex was here and how I met him as simply as possible, leaving out all the annoying comments he had made, or how he had strummed me like a guitar. I really needed to stop thinking about that part.

Paula interjected first: "You can't be serious! I can't have someone watching over my shoulder every damn day. It will be nerve-racking."

"Can't we ever have one year where we just teach and help our kids become industrious human beings? I've got nothing against improving ourselves, but we never have time to improve on what we just started. It just seems like the school board doesn't follow through with the programs we already have in place," added Chip, a social studies teacher who seemed ready to lose it. The bulbous nose and beer belly that gave him the appearance of an up-and-coming Macy's Santa Claus only made him look more apoplectic. "We need time to make something stick. Am I right, or am I right?"

"You are right, Chip. So right. Except the school board made the call on this one and we don't get a say. And—we also don't get a say about having him on our team today," I muttered.

"Helll no!" Jensen, the gym teacher, drawled his disapproval. "I'm not pulling this asswipe's ass all over the field. I want to win. We have a reputation to uphold, and we're going to reign supreme in this year's new game, Hungry Hungry Hippo. I bet he's a scrawny asshole too, right?" He crossed his arms, widened his stance, and put on his best stink face.

Electricity sparked in the air, and my stomach fell. He had arrived.

He cleared his throat, and he planted himself right next to me—arms flexing, shoulders bulging underneath his black tank top, and that devilish smirk he always wore tugging at the sides of his gorgeous face.

"Yeah, I hope I don't weigh the team down. I know how important it is to set the right tone at the beginning of the school year and being a winner hits the right mark." He shifted, bumping into my hip. "Oh, sorry." Jensen was right: asshole.

Jenson gulped and had the decency to look embarrassed by his earlier comments. I may not have wanted Alex on our team, but I knew having him at odds with Jensen could be a disaster.

"Sure," I responded, moving away and glaring at him. "Listen up, this is Dr. Alexander Pierce. He will be on our team today and will also be here through the school year doing something that will elevate our school to exemplary status, whatever that will be. I have been appointed by our illustrious leader to be his teacher liaison," I explained, and then mumbled, "Whatever the hell that means," under my breath.

"Anyhoo, let's focus on our strategy for today's games. I'm sure there will be a formal announcement regarding Dr. Pierce later today, and all the gory details will be explained." I glared at Alex as I finished that last remark.

Chip extended his hand to Alex in contrition for his callous remarks. The rest of the team made similar attempts at welcoming him, with Alan, our sixth-grade English teacher, concluding the greetings with a thunderous clap to Alex's scapula. Chip called our team to order, and we huddled up again for one of his infamous pep talks.

"As most of you know, we only participate in two events. We have been assigned the three-legged race, same as last year, and a new event called Hungry Hungry Hippo." He looked left and right to be sure everyone was paying attention and then continued animatedly.

"We will act as a 3D version of the board game. We'll have wheeled sliders as our bases, laundry baskets as our gathering devices and the rider will be propelled by a teammate. You'll lay down on your stomach, and, like in the wheelbarrow event, you'll be pushed out to a pile of foam balls, and you'll use your laundry basket to scoop up as many as you can before being pulled back to your starting position. There will be four rotations of different teams of people to complete the task. The team with the most pieces collected wins. We'll only have three minutes, so efficiency will be key. Everyone with me?" We all nodded giddily. This was going to be hilarious, and I couldn't wait to post the videos on Facebook.

"Since we have eight people on our team, let's pair up one male and one female. I would suggest the guys be the propellers and the gals are the gatherers. Just figure out who can push the fastest. We'll be playing math and science and they are going to be tough to beat, but I believe in you. We're agile and lighter to propel." Chip was interrupted by the squawking of a bullhorn coming from the top of the building. Our pep talk was over.

Eloise did her usual welcome back speech all about positivity, encouragement, and fair play. There was more nonsense, and then she reminded us that there would be a mandatory twenty-minute meeting at two-thirty in the cafeteria for awards and announcements. All the while, Alex had been not so nonchalantly checking me out as I fist-bumped Chip and a few other male teachers I hadn't had a chance to say hello to yet. That snarky grin he always wore became predatory, and his darkening brown eyes and twitching jaw clued me in that he wasn't thrilled about my interactions with my male colleagues. *Too bad, dickweed.*

The starting whistle sounded and we all walked to our first activity.

"Hey, Alan, do you want to team up?" I asked. We had partnered in the past, so I assumed we would again.

"Uh, sorry Trudie, Paula tagged me," he said, clearly chagrined.

"Chip, ready to team up?" I chirped out, hoping for a positive response.

"Wish I could. Gina asked me during the meeting. Try Alex. He looks a little lost."

Shit! "Okay. Thanks for nothing." I moped off and met up with Alex.

"Guess it's just you and me, gorgeous," he snarked.

"Listen, Alex. At school, comments like that are called sexual harassment, so knock it off before I get you fired before you even start. If I must be your partner, you'll treat me with respect and play hard. I've never lost at Field Day and this year will not be any different."

Having reached our event, I spent the next few minutes stretching and preparing myself for the competition. Everyone else did the same, including Alex. His deltoids stretched his skin when he reached one hand behind his neck. My nether regions grew damp and my focus turned to mush. It became very apparent that any move he made had me salivating. Of course, the black tank top shirt and black track shorts accentuating every curve of his pecs and tight ass didn't help. I couldn't be the only one checking him out, and looking around, I saw that my speculation was correct. At least six other teachers, plus Ricky, were licking their lips, but Alex wasn't looking at anyone else but me. If another whistle hadn't screeched through the air, I would have started licking my lips too.

Turning my attention to the other team, I sized up our competition. Their steely eyes bore down on us in an effort to intimidate, but with Alex flexing repeatedly, every woman on their team was swooning and completely distracted.

"Way to go, muscles. Very impressive the way you eliminated the women on their team," I chortled.

"Just working my assets, Ms. Gonzales. Smoke'm if you gott'm." He smirked confidently.

Just when I thought he couldn't get more self-absorbed. Obviously, his ego was ready to go, but if he wanted to be my partner, he would have to put his money where his mouth was.

"I'll tell you what, Dr. Pierce, if you are so sure your brawn will make a difference for our team today, I'll buy your first round of drinks at Teddy's tonight."

"You're on," he said with a wink and strutted over to Chip to get the lineup.

Chip explained that our team's name (GESS) represented each of our departments, and he had arranged each team in order of strategic attack. His words, not mine. Jensen hopped from foot to foot, building up a head of steam, while the rest of our team got into place: Chip and Gina, Jensen and Marni, Alan and Paula, and me with Satan—I mean Alex.

Having Alex and me as anchors was actually a good decision. We were both very competitive and quite frankly, I was very bendy since I practiced yoga frequently. Hopefully, my strong core and my agility would give me an advantage.

Another whistle sounded and the squelch of the bullhorn tore through my eardrums.

Atop her perch on the roof of the school, Eloise gave a two-minute warning and read off the rotation for the second event, which would follow thirty minutes later. Her final singsong message of encouragement and good sportsmanship floated through the air, and we were off.

ALEXANDER

I felt like I was back at summer camp, except I was a scrawny kid back then, and the girls didn't look like Trudie. I couldn't tear my eyes away from the voluptuous globes stretching her tank top, her tight abs, and that bubble butt that called to me to grab hold and not let go. She was right, this was a school setting and suggestive comments were just asking for trouble, especially when the person you wanted to flirt with wasn't having it. So instead, I flaunted my guns, successfully distracting her—and several other men and women as well.

Chip gathered us together and asked if anyone had any questions or comments. There was a moment of silence, and it seemed like a good opportunity to offer my thoughts.

Clearing my throat, I raised my hand and looked to Chip for his consent. "I just wanted to thank everyone for including me in today's events. I know I was thrown into your community without notice, but I wanted you to know that I'm committed to helping our team win. Everyone's efforts matter and I'll do my best to help bring us to victory."

I didn't win an Emmy for that performance, but my teammates responded with "Cool man" and "Sounds good." Even Trudie looked at me for a minute without venom in her expression. I called that progress. Chip had us put our hands in the middle of our group to shout, "Go, team!"

The event began and we were off to a good start. Ricky, the head of my fan club, had been appointed referee. The women were on their bellies wielding laundry baskets destined for the hunt while their partners held their legs and propelled them forward. Our first team won their heat, while our second team wobbled the slider and lost speed, giving Team Science and Math the advantage. The third team crashed into Team Performing Arts, which I'm sure was going to result in a bevy of scrapes and bruises. Our pile of foam balls was almost equal to that of Team S&M—*how ironic*. It was up to me and Trudie to carry us to victory in the final leg.

I yelled down to her, "Are you ready to kick some ass?" Her face lit up, and her eyes gleamed as she watched the team before us racing back to the starting line.

"Let's kill the bastards!" she bellowed. My little firecracker wasn't taking any prisoners, and my dick twitched in appreciation.

When Paula returned with the slider, Trudie dove onto it just as Paula jumped off and shoved her basket into Trudie's arms. And just like in the final scene of *Braveheart*, we charged the center pile of foam, screaming our heads off, the laundry basket held high like a weapon.

"Get in my basket, you little fuckers!" Trudie hollered as she scooped up a huge amount of foam. "Turn me around, now!" she commanded, and I drove her legs forward with as much speed as I could. We finished before any other team.

Trudie leaped to her feet, waving her arms above her head in glee. She spun around and jumped onto me, wrapping her legs around my waist and kissing my cheek.

"You were amazing, Alex. What a blast!" she roared over my shoulder.

I hadn't anticipated this reaction and I didn't know how to respond. If this hadn't been her school, and I hadn't been hired as a consultant, I would have planted a hot tongue-filled kiss on her pouty mouth while squeezing her ass in gratitude. Sadly, I could only give her a quick squeeze of her ample hips and whisper, "You were fucking amazing yourself. Seems like a good competition gets you hot and bothered."

To my surprise, she blushed. "I guess so."

Ricky spent the next five minutes counting each team's foam balls while we high-fived the other teams and rehashed the hilarious event. The school librarian, Marsha, assembled each team for a picture to document the event. I hoped there would be a slideshow or at least a collage of the day's most priceless moments.

A whistle went off and everyone gathered around Ricky.

"Ladies and gentlemen and all of those in between, today's Hungry Hungry Hippo contest winner is—it's a tie!" I heard gasps and objections all around me.

We chanted, "Recount!" and Ricky agreed. A team of two other staff members retallied the balls, and Ricky declared a winner. "The recount shows we have a single winner: the GESS team! Congratulations, let's move to the three-legged race on the other side of the playground. Competition starts again in ten minutes."

TRUDIE

When Alex's large hands slid along my legs as we finished our race, tingles rippled through my whole body, leaving me heaving for breath. It wasn't the race that had me amped up, it was remembering the last time he had touched me like that—when I was on my back in a motel room, and he had yanked me down the bed to eat me out like a starved man. *I wonder if he remembers, too?*

Chip, Alan, and Jensen buddied up to Alex after that performance as they walked several steps ahead of us girls. Since we were semi-alone, my friends took the opportunity to interrogate me about my overzealous display of affection when we won.

"I don't know what you're talking about. I've jumped on just about every guy in this school." I shook my head and rolled my eyes upward. "Okay, that didn't come out right, but you know what I mean."

"Uh, we may have believed that, if you hadn't kissed him on the cheek and then blushed when he said something to you." Gina nudged my shoulder. "By the way, what did he say to make you blush?"

Marni jumped in front of me, while the other girls boxed me in. "Come on, Trudie. Fess up. What's the deal with you two?"

Trapped, ugh.

I suppose if I had said, "This is so middle school," I would have been spot on since we were literally at a middle school. If I thought I could walk away from this challenge unscathed, I would. My first thought was, *Screw you*. And then, *Okay fine, just a morsel*. But I knew if I didn't give them something to sink their teeth into, I'd never hear the end of it.

In my most exasperated voice, I snapped back.

"Fine. You want to know what the deal is? Here it is. He was the featured lecturer at the conference I attended this summer and bought me a drink. That's all. Nothing more." It wasn't even close to the whole truth, but I thought it should be enough to let them create whatever story they wanted so they could think they understood.

Chapter 22

TRUDIE

THE THREE-LEGGED RACE HAD its own challenges. Only one pairing on our team was close to the same height, but as luck would have it, everyone wanted to keep their partner from the previous game. The whistle blew again, and Alex slid next to me, sending tiny sparks of electricity throughout my body. When was that going to stop?

Sixteen teams lined up at the starting line, with each struggling to strap Velcro bands on two places around their legs.

You could hear cries of, "Come on! My thigh is at your waist. This is never going to work," across the field, as well as, "Ouch! It's too tight, you're killing me." It was inevitable when banding adults together this way. At least when we were kids, we were closer in size, so it wasn't so complicated. Alex and I were exceptionally mismatched.

"Hey, little pixie, why don't I just carry you across the field and back since I obviously look like a gorilla carrying its young," he gibed. He was not wrong. It was a ludicrous pairing and everyone around us knew it, though they didn't have it any better.

"Does that mean I have to call you Tarzan now?" I asked coyly. *Stop poking the bear!*

He slipped his arm around my side with his hand landing just under my breast and I gasped. Stark memories of his alpha tendencies had me fighting for control. This was my school, my friends, and my reputation; his playfulness could jeopardize all of it.

"I'll be your Tarzan, Trudie if you'll be my Jane," he whispered in my ear. "We could swing around together, and I could protect you from all those filthy male animals out there." He growled quietly. I turned to meet his deep emerald eyes, which were turning darker. I knew what it meant when his eyes looked that way. Trust me, I didn't need any reminding.

I swallowed hard, struggling to regain my composure, and snuck a sidelong glance at my teammates, hoping they weren't watching us.

In an exasperated whisper, I replied, "Alex, stop it! Swinging through the trees? You're incorrigible." I tried to walk away and almost landed on my back. I felt like an idiot forgetting that we were bound together, as his big hands scooped me up tightly against his ridiculously muscled chest.

"Looks like we're bound together, sweetheart. You're not going anywhere." He waggled his eyebrows, stoking my temper.

"You're loving this, aren't you?" I grunted back.

"You know it. Now, let's go win a race so I can have you wrap those gorgeous legs around my waist again," he taunted devilishly.

I hated him! He always had to have the last word. And he knew that I wanted his hands all over me, but that couldn't happen again. We were working together—all year. This was going to be impossible. I was going to need an army supply truck of batteries to keep me sated, knowing that he wouldn't be able to give me any lessons in the bedroom. *What's the word for female blue balls?*

The race started and again. One hundred yards down and one hundred yards back. It was going to be a long race but hopefully no one would get injured. Paula screamed some not-so-gentle comments at Marni and Jensen's team, and Chip heard nothing as he hyperfocused on the turnaround marker. Last year, Jody ran with Robin, and the two of them looked like a tumbleweed for most of the race. Robin ended up with a separated shoulder—not good for conducting—and Jody was on crutches for two weeks. But if these casualties were necessary to bring our teaching team together, then these were the sacrifices that had to be made. Just as long as I wasn't one of them.

Alex and I were next, and the pressure was on. We were neck and neck with Team Science and Math, and we needed this win for today's victory. Alex squeezed me tightly and whispered one more time in my ear, "Do you trust me?"

Well now, that was a loaded question, but I didn't have time for reflection, so I nodded.

"Good," he growled, "because I have another lesson to teach you." My core tightened and my eyes blew wide. I was like a fucking Pavlovian dog with him. That was another word—I wouldn't be able to hear *teach* again without seeing his dark eyes and his sculpted body hovering over me.

We tagged up and the next thing I knew, Alex had lifted me up and only my outside foot could touch the ground. We were going so fast that I barely had time to register that we were cheating. Okay, not exactly cheating, but the only reason my tied leg felt the ground was because it was, well, tied to his. Twenty-three seconds later, we were crossing the finish line and collapsing into exhaustion. Our teammates jumped around us, presumably cheering the win, but the only thing I heard was Alex's breath on my face and the pounding of his heart as he pulled me over him for a very strong, very inappropriate hug.

"Thanks for trusting me," he gasped. "We're a better team that way." His arms flopped to his sides, his eyes closed, and he looked absolutely edible.

The sound of ripping Velcro all around us underscored the bullhorn screech as Eloise congratulated us on another successful Field Day. She directed us to the catered lunch and the afternoon's Trivia Pentathlon like she was giving orders, and we all cheered our acceptance. I liked the trivia event almost as much as the physical events. We had some wicked smart teachers on our team, and contrary to appearances, Chip was no jughead. He had even auditioned for *Jeopardy's* Teen Tournament when he was in high school and had almost made it on as a contestant.

Everyone ran into the building for lunch while Alex and I stayed back to debrief.

My fingers were twisted together as I began, "That was some smart thinking back there. Very clever."

He chuckled, swinging the looped Velcro band around his long fingers. "Thanks for trusting me. I had to pull that trick back in college and though legal, it is a bit questionable."

We needed some clarity in our relationship immediately and now seemed as good a time as any to discuss it and to get our stories straight.

"Alex." I stopped walking and turned to him. "I—I know we have chemistry, and, quite frankly, it scares me a little bit. You've been hired to improve our school—the school where I have been working for five years and where I have a reputation as being diligent, effective, and above reproach. I'm too committed to my students and my colleagues to jeopardize that, and us, together, just spells disaster. I hope you understand."

The way he flexed his shoulders and grimaced spoke loudly—he was hurt. He had to know that what I said was true and that his reputation would also be scrutinized. Another time, in another place, maybe we could have had something. Just not here and now.

He nodded his head slowly, pursing his lips in what I hoped was agreement.

"Trudie, I want you to know that I've heard every word you said, and I would never take advantage of your position at your school. It's not my intention to make you uncomfortable, but you were assigned to me as a liaison, and we will be working closely together. Our feelings for one another, whatever they may be, will be tested. I'm only human, Trudie. The only promise I can offer you is that I would never intentionally hurt you or endanger your reputation. I hope that will be enough."

Was it? We were only human.

In the six years I dated Sam, we had never had this kind of lust and electricity. When Sam wasn't around, I rarely thought about him or missed his touch. All I had to do was conjure up Alex's face, and it made my panties wet. Certainly, this kind of lust, or desire, or whatever you want to call it, couldn't possibly last for a lifetime. My parents weren't exactly role models in the love department. Maybe I saw some passionate kisses or hugs when I was younger, but there was nothing like that by the time I was ten years old. Pain and anguish had been the more common fare at my house. I wished I could understand more about what I was feeling.

He was still staring at me, presumably for a reply. How was I supposed to answer him? Another minute ticked by, and he threw his arm over my shoulder like I was his long-lost buddy.

"It's okay not to have an answer right now. I'm usually a patient man, though you have found a way to push all my buttons. And I don't have all the answers when it comes to you either, Trudie. I'll give you some breathing room. Go eat with your friends, I have a few calls to make."

Clasping my hands together in appreciation I gave him a small smile and went to make myself a plate. By the time I sat down, all the eyes at my table were aimed at me.

"What?" I asked with a roll stuffed in my mouth.

"What, *what*? What the hell is going on with you two? There is no way you only had one drink with that guy. He was on you like white on rice." Marni shook her finger in my face, and it wasn't helping me keep my composure. I didn't want to share my backstory with Alex anymore. I didn't poke into their personal lives unless they offered. I highly doubted someone who looked like Alex popped up in their lives very often—if ever.

"Listen, please don't make more of this than it is. We had a drink in San Francisco. I attended three of his lectures the week that I was there, and for some reason," *us smacking into each other,* "he's attracted to me. I had no idea the school board hired him and that I was to be his liaison this year."

"Wait, you're what?" they all exclaimed. Maybe they hadn't heard that last part already. I cringed. Damn that Eloise for not explaining my role in this plan.

"Maybe I jumped the gun on the announcement, but Eloise will be explaining all the details after trivia. Would you mind waiting until then? It seems she left a lot out of Alex's introduction." Not waiting for a reply, I shoved my apple between my teeth and bolted from the table.

Needing some alone time, I made a beeline to my classroom, shut and locked the door, and called Ruby. I was on a ledge only she could help me navigate.

Three rings later, she picked up.

"Hey, babe. Are you killing it at Field Day, or are you calling me from the ER? Do I need to get you a coffee and a scone while the doctors do an MRI?" And now you know why she was a voice actor. Way over the top but deliciously sweet.

Putting her on speaker so I could stretch out, I detailed the morning. "Can you believe that guy is now working in *my* school with *my* friends, and *I'm* responsible for being his sidekick? I want my mommy." I pouted and sighed in disgust.

"Geez Louise, Trudie. When your shit hits the fan, it sprays all the way across the room. Your year of calm and bliss seems to be out the door. Is it too early to drink? I could be there in thirty minutes, and we can get loaded. It won't change your situation, except three out of four drunks insist that there is better living through alcohol." God bless her for cheering me up. This was why she was my BFF.

I took a deep swan dive so I could hang inverted for a few minutes. It calmed the nervous system, disengaging my fight-or-flight reflex and putting me into a rest and digest mindset, which was something I really needed at that moment.

"Drinking sounds perfect, except I can't start until after four o'clock. I'm going to be at Teddy's with the gang when we're done. Want to join me there?" Bending my knees, I pressed my feet into the ground and rolled back up. Yes, that was exactly what I needed. Well, that and alcohol.

"Oh, babe, I'll try. My parents have been looking forward to Friday movie night all week, and I feel like I owe them quality time with Moi. It's hard being me," she whined. "Let me text you about six-thirty, and I'll let you know if I can find a way to bail on them."

"You're a good daughter! Any luck with job leads in your new voice-over field?"

"Oh, my gosh, I almost forgot to tell you. I have an audition next week! It's a long shot, but seriously, what do I have to lose? Bye!"

And she was gone. I felt better already for having called her and for stretching out. Sometimes, I got so caught up in my own head I couldn't see the forest for the trees. But for now, my ponderings would have to wait, so I fixed my ponytail, added some lip gloss, and marched down the hall to the cafeteria to press my luck again.

ALEXANDER

As I strolled into the cafeteria, I knew I would find Trudie surrounded by several people wanting the details on why we were so familiar with each other. I didn't want to be around to witness it, so I grabbed a sandwich and an apple and kept going out the other door to deal with the messages on my phone.

Thirty-seven emails and ten phone calls, all mostly from my family, which could wait. But while scanning my emails, a message from my past halted me outside the main office doors. Sheila. When was the last time I had heard from her? Oh, yeah, it was two days before our wedding, and she was begging me to understand that marriage made her claustrophobic. That was probably why she needed to bang my friend, so she didn't have to settle for just one man. It took three years to let go of my anger at her, and then I was just bereft of feeling. That kind of limbo lingers and is undoubtedly the reason I couldn't figure out how to be in a committed relationship.

I was a masochist to open the message, but I still hoped she would explain the real reason she left me.

Dear Alex,

I know it has been a long time since I contacted you. I know the way I left you was terrible and regrettable.

I've wanted to write numerous times, yet, obviously, I didn't. I wasn't ready. But I'm ready now. Would you please consider meeting me so that I can give you a proper explanation and apology?

My therapist encouraged me to reach out to share my journey and how I have changed. I know I do not deserve your forgiveness, but it would help both of us put some closure on the past and perhaps open a door to a future, even if it's just as friends.

—Sheila

She gave me her new phone number and left it all in my hands. The new number explained why I couldn't reach her all these years. The bigger question was should I meet her now? Did her explanation matter to me anymore? I was tired of taking the high road; when did anyone ever do that for me? Maybe, Jacob, my best friend from college, but that was it. Certainly, not my family. That was laughable.

"Is everything all right, Dr. Pierce?" Ricky asked kindly.

"Uh, yeah. Just a weird email."

"Okay—I just noticed you from my desk and saw your face go pale. I didn't want you to faint on the concrete floor without help nearby." Ricky batted his long lashes at me. Wouldn't he have loved to give me mouth-to-mouth resuscitation?

"Much appreciated, Ricky, but I think it would take more than an email to knock me to the floor. Thanks for caring, though." I said appreciatively.

"Terrific. Well, we better get back to *le café* for trivia," he quipped over his shoulder as he sashayed down the hall. He did have great glutes, not that I was looking.

I loved trivia almost as much as sports. The more obscure, the better. For me, it showed what was housed in a person's mind. What did they think was funny, weird, or unique? Some of my favorite bits of trivia were from my youth. I remembered every commercial, every nuance of the sitcoms I used to watch, and all the great one-liners from classic movies. Science questions were logical and easy for me to remember, but social studies and historical facts were not my strengths. I hoped the rest of my team would be able to fill in the gaps.

The cafeteria was abuzz with tables being moved and Staples "Easy" buttons being set out as buzzers, one for each team. The competition bracket was set up on a giant chalkboard, and Eloise had opted for a microphone instead of a bullhorn for the afternoon's activities. Thank God.

I found my team in a huddle. I'd have noticed that curvy ass of Trudie's anywhere. It took all my decency not to smack it and claim it as my own.

"Hey, Doc. Glad you made it back for round two. Any other secret skills you possess before we begin?" Chip thought he was so clever. Fine. I'd bite.

"Besides holding a BA in trivia, no. No other secrets to share." I laughed, as did everyone else except Chip, who apparently missed the joke.

The preliminary rounds went smoothly, with everyone having the opportunity to answer. As it was, we prevailed, which brought us to the next round. That meant we needed to pare down our team.

"Let's try to do this democratically. Would anyone like to step down from further play?" My little Vixen was an amazing leader. She was very gracious about giving people the opportunity not to embarrass themselves any further. Thankfully, Marni and Jensen backed out.

"Great. Thanks, guys, for doing that. Your cheering is still valuable to our team, though, so don't get lost. Now, we still need to eliminate two more. I can pick, or we can draw straws, so to speak."

"Draw straws," Paula demanded.

Trudie took the same pack of cards she had used earlier and fanned out six cards.

"Okay. I have six cards and two are jokers. The jokers mean you are out. Ready? Alex, pick first."

I gave Trudie a sly look and slid my hands over the fanned cards, stopping by the one next to her thumb. I ran my finger along it as I slipped a card out and watched her shiver.

"Looks like I dodged a bullet." I winked, showing three of the clubs.

She rolled her hips from side to side, making my mouth water.

"Great. Who is next?" she asked. The rest of the team picked cards one by one. They all flipped their cards over at the same time to reveal Chip had the other joker. They collectively sighed in despair.

"Come on, guys. We can still win this. Stay positive," I coached. I was the new guy here, so I needed them to see me as a leader who was working for their benefit.

Encouragingly, Trudie agreed. "Exactly, Alex. Thank you. Now, let's decide on a strategy and stay strong." I loved it when she took charge. Her amber eyes went steely, and her hands turned upward with fingers spread as if saying, "Come on, everyone, get on board with me."

Semifinal rules were slightly different from the rules in the first rounds. With the first set of questions, anyone from the team could hit their buzzer if they knew the answer, but in the second round, the team would have to come to a consensus before one of them hit the buzzer. Speed and precision were crucial. Thankfully, I was assigned as the dedicated buzzer-smacker. I was agile, and I loved smacking things. *Especially the ass sitting next to me.* I had to stop thinking like that, or everyone would get an eyeful of the tent that was starting to form under the table.

Ricky called for attention and asked the teams to quiet down.

"We are down to the semifinal questions, and the score is twenty-three, Red, and twenty-five, Blue. Remember, only one person can hit the buzzer and answer. If that answer is incorrect, the other team will have five seconds to respond with their answer. Judge's decisions are final, so good luck."

Ricky read the first question. Our team buzzed in first with the correct answer and proceeded this way for the next four questions. Unfortunately for us, question number five was a stumper.

"What is a family of bears called?" Everyone started humming the *Jeopardy* theme song when Jody smacked the red button, yelling, "A huddle!" Her team was so annoyed that she didn't confer with them that she almost literally slid off her chair and under the table in shame.

"Sorry, that is incorrect. Red Team?"

We looked like one of those families on Family Feud huddling and shouting our answers. Everyone's eyes locked onto mine and the pressure was on. We were at a standoff between *family* and *sleuth*. Neither one seemed correct, but I was not willing to be the final decision-maker. If I botched the answer, I was sure it would follow me through the whole school year and that wasn't happening.

"Trudie. What does your gut say?" I asked. I knew with every fiber of my being that for all the bravado she exuded, she was lacking self-worth. Trusting her gut and winning would be crucial for her self-confidence.

Ricky announced, "Answer, please."

She mouthed, "Sleuth," and I mouthed back, "Yeah, baby."

"Our answer is *sleuth*." I confidently stated, knowing it was correct.

Ricky jumped up and down, screaming, "Yes! That's right." Wiping his brow, he continued, "Whew, that was a tough one. Excellent job."

Our team was bouncing all over the place, and we all hugged it out, feeling victorious. My hands landed on Trudie's hips, and I mouthed, "Good job, baby." She blushed, biting her lip.

The squeal from the microphone stopped us all in our tracks and our hands flew to our ears.

"Oops. Sorry about that," Ricky said, looking sheepish. "Here are the rules for the final trivia round. Only two people per team can play. Correct answers get a point, and incorrect answers lose a point, so get your ducks in a row before presenting your answer. This round could go either way. Oh, and there will only be three questions asked, so...there's that. Isn't this the most fun?" he bellowed. The group responded with a combination of yips and moans that lingered in the institutionalized air we were forced to breathe.

Five minutes later, Trudie and I mounted the stage. We sat with one buzzer between us, our legs a hair's breadth apart, and my heart pumped like I was a sprinter. I wanted to touch her, to hold her, and to encourage her, but every move we made was on stage for everyone to see. Instead, I leaned over to her ear still, looking straight ahead out the cafeteria window, and whispered, "We've got this, and I've got you." Her audible gulp made my dick twitch; I knew she understood exactly what I meant.

"I know. Let's do this," she replied under her breath as she slowly eyed me in her periphery. A rumble started slowly and began to accelerate throughout the room.

I yelled over the caws and hisses to Trudie, "What the hell is that?"

She was laughing and taking bows. "We're the Hart Middle School Hawks. It's the sounds a hawk makes."

I understood but thought it sounded more like desperate souls descending into hell.

TRUDIE

I had known we would make it to the finals, but I didn't expect Alex would be such a team player. He picked and chose where and when he'd be effective and lay low otherwise. I wasn't sure Whether he was calculating or genuine. Either way, my fellow teachers seemed to like him, and I supposed that would help us in our efforts to bring the school to exemplary status. What I couldn't seem to get my head around was how the littlest comment, whisper, or touch from Alex distracted me to the point of amnesia. At times I couldn't even remember my name, it was so bad. His hands were like weapons of destruction when they grazed mine, and his voice was like that of the devil himself, getting me to ignore all levels of decency in public. He wasn't even the alpha dude he had been in California, and still, I fell at his feet.

I couldn't wait to speak with Ruby about it today. A good venting was in order, along with a few margaritas to wash it all down. One more round to go and I was out of there.

Ricky was back with a boa and a tiara, explaining he wanted to mark the occasion with festival attire. I loved this guy; everyone did. He had a heart of gold and the sass of a drag queen—an amazing combination in my book.

Clearing his throat, Ricky used his best game show announcer voice to introduce the final contenders.

"Lad-ies and Gen-tle-men, let me present to you your finalists. On the Red Team, we have the power couple, Alex and Trudie, and on the Blue Team, we have the illustrious two-something, Marsha, our librarian, and Consuela, our international languages specialist. Welcome, all.

"Here are the final rules for this round. As mentioned before, there are only three questions. Right answers get you points, wrong answers are deducted from your total. And just for shits and giggles, correct answers get you two points and wrong ones get you minus three." The crowd responded with groans and snippy comments.

"Are my contestants ready?" Ricky addressed both teams, getting four nods in return. "Awesome, let's do this!" he cheered. "Don't buzz in until I've read the whole question. Question number one: when geese walk across the street, are they a gaggle or a skein?"

You could hear a pin drop as Alex and I literally put our heads together to decide on an answer.

"Aren't they called a flock?" He asked.

"Yes, if they are flying. What is a skein?" I wondered.

"No idea. Why walking? Is there a difference?"

I had a light-bulb moment: "Let's go with a gaggle—at least we know what it is."

His big, veiny hand smacked the buzzer, but the Blue Team hit theirs a nanosecond sooner.

"A gaggle," Marni announced confidently.

"Yes!" Ricky gleefully shouted.

"Question number two: where does the word didactic originate?" Ricky winked when he finished. Was he implying something about us?

"I know this, one hundred percent," I insisted.

"Do it, baby." *Why did that sound sexual?*

"It's Greek," I stated. "It comes from the word that means 'to teach.' Because we are teachers. Ha! Good one." I was smug, I know, but I was right.

Ricky announced dramatically, "So here is the updated score: Red Team with twenty-eight points and Blue Team with twenty-seven. If the Red Team gets the next question they will win, if they don't, they will lose. Quite a predicament. Let's ask the last question and see what happens. Question number three: why do they sometimes call a mushroom a toadstool?"

The Blue Team buzzed in and Marni squealed her answer.

"Wrong! So sorry Blue Team, there is no difference between the two. Heartier mushrooms could certainly hold up a small toad. We have a winner, people!"

Alex and I hopped up from our seats and he lifted me into his arms for a massive hug and another sexy whisper for my ears only.

"You're so fucking hot and smart, and I want to throw you on this table and show you what you do to me." He smiled politely and let me slide down his massive body. I bumped into the bulge that filled his pants on the way down.

I wobbled on my legs, not sure if I could stand properly. Alex kept his hands on my hips while I found my balance. *Do not look at him. Do not look at him.*

"You, okay?" he purred. And then I looked at him. *I'm so weak.* His sculpted jaw twitched as his eyes studied my face. Why did there need to be so many people in the damn room? My resolve to keep my distance had been shredded, and all I wanted to do was climb him like a tree and devour his face.

I shook my head and said, "No, I mean, yes. I'm good. Having you on our team made an enormous difference. Thanks."

I pulled away quickly and turned to my other teammates, who enveloped me in hugs. I popped back into my classroom to peel out of my clothes and put on my tracksuit. Then, I grabbed my satchel, purse, and water bottle and reentered the cafeteria just as Eloise assumed the mic again.

She walked through the highlights of Alex's program, just as she had explained to me earlier in the day, while I looked at my phone, swiping away meaningless emails.

She caught my attention when she mentioned my new "voluntold" position as liaison between the teachers and the consultant, a.k.a. the Devil. Although my feelings toward him may have changed, he still made me feel like Ariel was selling her soul to Ursula, the sea witch in *The Little Mermaid*. He was captivating but also dangerous.

"If you have any ideas, complaints, concerns, or requests, please direct them to Ms. Gonzales. She and I will review them and bring them to Dr. Pierce's attention. We are a team first. No doubt there will be a misunderstanding or misdirection here or there, but nothing that we can't work out with a little patience and an open heart."

Eloise was articulate, if nothing else. The teachers and staff sat dutifully with pasted smiles on their faces, knowing there wasn't a way out of this project. I, however, felt trapped. There was more to this story, and per my instructions earlier, I grabbed my things, hugged my team and praised them for the great win, and walked to the principal's office like a naughty child. No one knew the truth of the relationship Alex and I had begun in California. It wasn't like two people who just met. We had history, and I was in trouble. My only question was how much trouble I was truly in.

Chapter 23

TRUDIE

"I'M SORRY TO HEAR that this arrangement is going to be uncomfortable for you, Trudie. But we all are required to step up our game, and I wish I had someone else half as qualified as you, but I don't. You have special certifications that make you not only the perfect liaison but the perfect ambassador for what we have been trying to achieve at our school for the past five years. Dr. Pierce needs your talent and your skills to make this program work."

Eloise tried to pacify and flatter her way into my resolve not to accept the position of liaison. I couldn't disclose the details of what had transpired, but I could try and rally to get out of my assignment. I followed her back to her office and like a petulant child, I jammed my hands onto my hips and conceded.

"Fine, Eloise. Only because I said I'd help you before you told me what was involved. For the record, I will require a detailed outline for any future 'help' you request of me." I pointed my finger at her and frowned for emphasis. All she did was smile and walk back to her desk.

Today had been a trying and emotionally exhausting day balancing my personal feelings for the devil incarnate and focusing on the task at hand. Every time his fiery emerald lasers locked on to me, my anatomical operating system threatened to shut down. There wasn't even the "blue screen of death" to warn me that my systems were overloaded, it just happened instantaneously. How could I possibly survive a daily pummeling like this all year long?

I was planning to storm out of her office when there was a knock on the door.

"Hey there, sorry I'm late, but I wanted to change." Alex smelled like a dream. Clean and fresh like newly laundered clothes and sweet minty breath. I smelled like week-old laundry with hour-old, iced coffee breath.

He took the seat next to me and rearranged the angle to see me better. Eloise smiled slyly, seeing what he was doing. When he looked up and saw her mouth lifting at the corners, he pulled a quick smile himself in acknowledgment. *Where these two up to something?*

Without further ado, Eloise pressed into my hands two copies of the school board's proposal and the criteria to elevate our school, along with a few dos and don'ts regarding student involvement in the process. In addition, she pointed out that although Dr. Pierce will be on retainer for the entire school year, he would not be at the school the entire time, so I would lead the charge in his absence.

"So, as you can see Ms. Gonzales, not only will you be working alongside Dr. Pierce when he is in the building, you will oversee certain aspects of keeping our efforts on track when he is gone. Good news for you—as I mentioned earlier today, I insisted that the school board should offer you a stipend during this process. Your credentials certainly demand it, and the amount of time you'll be involved in this project would necessitate a substantial financial supplement. Starting on Monday and continuing through May 1 of next year, that stipend will be prorated weekly and added to your paycheck. At the conclusion, if it's a successful project and Hart Middle School gets its exemplary designation, you will get an additional spiff of two-thousand dollars. Any papers or recommendations that are generated will have your name attached and can be added to your resume. You can thank me later." Eloise's smug attitude was not only annoying but calculated. She knew she was dragging me into this, and if I hadn't mistaken her earlier looks, she may have been plotting to get me and the good doctor more acquainted.

I shut my mouth and exhaled rather loudly in shock, looking, I'm sure, like a deer in the headlights.

"Wow, Principal Jackson. Your generous efforts to make sure I'm well compensated for this project are very much appreciated, yet not necessary," I professed.

"Sure. Right. You'd do it for free? I don't believe that for a minute. Go and buy that new hybrid car you wanted," she chided. That's right! I completely forgot about the new car I wanted.

"I'm not looking a gift horse in the mouth, but..." I was reaching for a snarky remark. Eloise and I had a long-standing shtick dating back to my first year at Hart Middle School. She would give me her high and mighty edict, and I would comedically bow in front of her and say, "Thank you, ma'am." Then she would hold out her hand so I could kiss her majestic ring, and then we'd both break into laughter. Things had evolved over the years, with our banter growing and expanding to sarcastic interjections and condescending retorts on days we were feeling especially salty. That day was one of them.

Giving her attention back to the great doctor, Eloise continued her monologue.

"Now, Dr. Pierce, the expectation is that you will be in the building for approximately twenty to twenty-five hours a week for the next three months to get this program up and running. After that, your participation will drop down to ten hours per week. You'll be expected to communicate via email, text, and phone as required to effectively do your job. As much as I'd like to say all work needs to be done in the building, I'd be lying. Since Ms. Gonzales teaches full-time, obviously, she won't be able to meet often during school hours. I'll leave it to you both to figure out when you can meet. Please use planning periods whenever possible so her evenings aren't disrupted. Any questions?" She looked first at Alex and then at me. I bit my lip and shook my head from side to side. I was exhausted just thinking about all this extra time and energy I would be spending.

"As for you, Ms. Gonzales, you will be expected to add six to eight hours per week through the end of the year, and then we will reevaluate your workload depending on our progress. I should add that an ancillary program is being formulated in conjunction with the project as we speak. I will reply with those details in a week or two."

Eloise drummed her desk. Trepidation wasn't something she was known for. She made a decision and that was that. The last time I saw her this leery was when Mary Lou, our female gym teacher, entered the girls' locker room and found over fifty jockstraps hanging from the light fixtures. Hilarious, but not in a good way. Did she think I would jump ship without even starting the program?

"Is there anything you'd like to add, Dr. Pierce?" Eloise asked.

Of course, he had to have seen his contract before agreeing to come here, so what was the hold-up? His jaw ticked while he read the paperwork he was given; he was calculating something, and I wanted to know what it was. I fought the urge to drool over his pecs as he tightened and relaxed them under his golf shirt and slid my eyes to the right. I smirked when I found Eloise's gaze in the same place. Naughty principal. I signed her damn contract and left unceremoniously.

Teddy's on a Friday night was better than beer pong night at any college campus, especially because you could lift your foot off the floor without feeling like your shoe would be stuck to it. They also had the best burgers, and if you got there before five o'clock, you got a beer and a burger for five bucks. As a penny-pinching teacher, that was my jam: food and drink for a fraction of the regular price.

After placing my order, I went to the bathroom to freshen up. I am not one of those people who gets all sweaty and smelly after a workout, though I did have a certain musk that followed me. I splashed off the grime, haloing my face, and used a few body cleansing wipes on my underarms. I'm not new to doing a traveling bath. My father made sure we all had go bags as well as miscellaneous hygiene products stuffed into our backpacks in case there was some apocalyptic event that kept us from making it home from school. The habit never died; hence body wipes for a grown-ass woman. And a toothbrush, toothpaste, toilet seat cover, tissues, and whatever else we could stuff in our bags.

After I added a few swipes of pale shimmering lip gloss, it was time to eat. I found a few of my teacher friends already at a table and joined them.

"Did you see Eloise gawking at Dr. Pierce all day? I think she has a little crush on him," Marni teased.

"I'm not so sure Mrs. Jackson would be too happy about that, yet I must say Dr. Pierce sure is pretty. And that ass!" Paula pretended to swoon and fall off her seat.

"You never say that about my ass, and you two are always looking at it," Skip whined before chugging his beer.

"You know who must really like him, though?" Gina swiveled her head and pierced me with her eyes. Everyone at the table followed her stare, and for the second time today, I felt like I was under a microscope.

"Come on," I cried. "Not again." I covered my head to hide from their accusations.

"Uh, I think I missed something. What are you talking about?" You could always count on Jensen to be a day late and a dollar short of knowing the 411 around the school.

Gina helpfully filled Jensen and the rest of the guys in about what we girls were supposedly not going to repeat to anyone. This was why I had censored myself and didn't give them too many details.

"Well, now, that makes more sense. Seriously, what does that guy Pierce have that I don't?" Chip blustered. Unfortunately, that was also the moment Alex approached our table, and again, Chip had his foot in his mouth.

Alex planted his hands on his hips and spread his legs wide with a "don't fuck with me" stare directed at Chip.

"I may be wrong, but how about a doctoral degree, a Porsche, a New York City penthouse, and a home in the Hamptons," he deadpanned.

A collective gasp had Chip looking around the room for an escape. He found it and gave a quick wave as he rounded the table, making a beeline for the bathrooms. "Gotta piss," he grunted.

"Yeah, that was definitely a pissing contest," the ever-quiet Alan added. "I had a blast today. Anyone else?" He chuckled and downed the last of his beer.

Left mute at that show of testosterone, I swallowed a few gulps of beer myself, thankful that that line of questioning was over for tonight. Alan grabbed a stool for Alex from a neighboring table. and then Alex helpfully pulled me closer to his right side.

When the server came back for refills, Alex whispered in my ear.

"Fine," I replied without looking at his smug face. I didn't forget our wager. "Miley, get this guy whatever he wants, the first one is on me."

"You bet, Trudie," she replied. This fifty-something-year-old had been a fixture at this bar for as long as I'd been coming. Always a loose bun on the top of her head, a tight muscle shirt, and jeans that were painted on. To have a figure like that at her age would be a dream come true. Sadly, not for this curvy girl.

I was relieved when no one noticed Alex whispering again in my direction.

"Can the second one be on me?" His double entendre wasn't lost on me, and I raised my eyebrows in challenge.

"You wish," I hissed back.

"Mmm. A challenge. Accepted," he growled, reaching under the table. The whisper of a touch floated across my knee to the inside of my thigh, and I smacked his hand away. He taunted me with a short laugh, knowing it would be game on if we weren't sitting before my coworkers.

Our burgers arrived, and five minutes later, the jukebox started playing a bunch of '80s tunes. The conversation moving forward was light as we rehashed the day and established new inside jokes that would last the year. A few more teachers arrived, and our table expanded to two and later to three.

I checked my phone under the table, and there was a message from Ruby telling me she couldn't make it. I couldn't deny that I was disappointed, but I would call her in the morning. Since I returned from my conference, we'd only gotten together twice, both times just for coffee. Sadly, we didn't make time to hang out much between losing her job and spending all her time either lamenting living at her parent's home again or filling out job applications. She was so talented—if only those narcissistic, misogynistic assholes hadn't stolen her work and called it their own. Today, she had an interview, and I couldn't wait to hear how it all went down.

Sighing, I put my phone away and ordered a shot of Fireball.

"What's up? Who pissed in your beer?" Chip asked sarcastically.

Without hesitation, I fired back. "Same guy who pissed in yours." I saluted him with my now empty beer.

Alex chimed in, "Something wrong?"

I let out a long sigh. "Yeah, my best friend was supposed to meet me at seven and won't be able to make it. I'm not mad, just disappointed."

He put his arm around me and pulled me in. "That's okay, Trudie. I will be your best friend tonight," he jested.

"Sure. That...would be fan-fucking-tastic," I retorted, rolling my eyes.

By seven-thirty, the married teachers had peeled away from the table, blaming their spouses for forcing them home, and the band began their first set. The rest of the singletons opted for dancing, and we all headed for the dance floor. I was feeling very fluid and needed to burn some alcohol so as not to have a hangover.

Somewhere between the Sprinkler and the Cha Cha Slide, I realized our group of eight on the dance floor had turned into a duet of me and Alex getting closer and closer. The guy was like a dog with a bone. One minute, we're doing our own thing, and the next, his hands are on my hips, and he's pulling me to his groin. *Geez. It's hot in here.*

In retrospect, this would have been a suitable time to cool off, yet his eyes burned my skin, and his hands locked me in place. I tried to push back from his sculpted chest, panicking that my friends would be watching. Except they weren't—they had all left the dance floor, leaving me in the hands of the Devil.

He looked over at our table and then pulled me even tighter. "Your safety net is gone, Trudes. You're mine now."

My mind was racing, trying to figure a way out of this maze that I had helped create. Why the hell did my good sense have to make an appearance when all I wanted to do was climb up his fucking body and suck the life out of his mouth? This situation was all wrong, and I knew it. This was going to bite me in the ass, yet I couldn't stop. Charles Barkley said it best, "Sometimes, that light at the end of the tunnel is a train." *Woo. Woo.*

I'm sure I slurred it, but I needed to tell Alex to back up. However, when I said it, it sounded more like, "I want you to teach me something new, Dr. Pierce," and his mouth crashed onto mine.

Our PG personas on the dance floor became an R-rated movie and we were headed for some backroom erotica. We came up for air before the groping began and took the walk of shame back to our table. Alex waved over to Miley and shoved his black Amex card into her hand, all the while staring into my blown pupils.

"Fuck, Trudie, I've got to get you out of here. Are you ready to go?"

"Yeah," I gulped out. I downed the glass of water still on the table, and we left the moment Alex signed the receipt.

He steered me over to his rental car and opened my door. By the gentle way he pressed me back to my seat and buckled my seat belt, I thought he'd had a change of heart. But as he pulled himself from across my body, he pressed his lips hard on mine and then pulled on my lower lip as he retreated. "Mine," he growled.

"Where do you live? Give me an address, now," he commanded, and I complied. Fifteen minutes later, he pulled into my complex. "Don't move," he commanded again, and I waited for him to round the hood of the car and open my door. Again, he insisted on unbuckling my seat belt—I assumed he wanted to demonstrate his gentlemanly manners. Nothing Alex did was uncalculated. He had to have known that his alpha ways lit me up. Never in my life had I given myself so freely to a man and it scared me. I needed control—insisted on it—except every time he looked at me with those deep emerald eyes, shaded by long thick lashes any woman would covet, I was lost. It was inexplicable and undeniable.

We silently walked to my apartment, hand in hand. My mind was spinning with thoughts of what was to come, and my core was wet and wanting.

ALEXANDER

So much for control and discretion. Why did I think I could suppress my feelings for this woman? She obviously wanted me, but we, *she*, already stated all the reasons that we should keep our distance. Maybe we could fuck the desire out of ourselves and then stay focused on the project? *I'm delirious.*

She fumbled the keys once, then managed to pick them up—with the help of my hand on her ass—and opened the door. Her purse thumped on the floor as I kicked the door shut. Her clothes never stood a chance as I ripped both her tracksuit jacket and shirt off in one jerk. Her warm brown skin pebbled, right down to her perfect tits. I cupped the round globes that fit my hands so perfectly, eliciting moans and pleas for more. I lifted her small frame onto her counter and sucked her left breast into my mouth. I memorized her every response as my tongue flicked and sucked her delicious nubs. I pushed her limits harder and harder until she screamed.

"Alex! Oh, my god, that hurts," she cried, and I moved on to the other waiting breast.

This one was even more responsive, and I was dying to bite her, but not tonight. I needed her trust completely. She wanted to learn, and I was more than happy to help her find that gray area between pleasure and pain. She needed someone she trusted to unleash her hidden desires, and I'd gladly sign up for that position if she wanted me to.

"You taste so good, T. I want to taste all of you." I laid her back on the smooth surface and pulled up a kitchen chair so I could eat my favorite meal. When she realized what I was doing her body shuddered in response.

"What, what...?" she mumbled.

I kissed past her soft belly, licking the sweet swirl of her navel. Darting in and out with my tongue had her humming her approval. When I reached the top of her track pants, I looked up to see the perfect arch of her back and her tongue licking her deep red lips. She was gorgeous.

"Sweetheart, look at me. Look what I'm going to do to you," I purred. My words pulled a long moan from her wet lips, and I pulled the rest of her clothes from her body with both hands, flinging them across the room.

She smelled like vanilla, and after one broad-tongued lick up her pussy, I now knew she tasted like tangy honey. I aimed my tongue at her clit and slowly dragged it up her center, watching her watch me. So. Fucking. Hot. Seeing her wide-eyed and wanton made my cock screaming for release. I reached down and unbuttoned my jeans for some relief to find it already creeping out of my boxers.

My focus returned to my vixen's pussy. I found her pink throbbing pearl pulsing and begging for relief, and I obliged. Her hums of gratitude and pleas for more filled the air and fueled my desire to make this woman ache for me when I wasn't around. As I pulled her thighs off the end of the counter, her legs wrapped tightly around my neck, and I plunged my tongue into her pussy as far as I could get it.

"Alex!" she screamed. "Again."

I pulled back to respond, "My pleasure," and doubled my efforts to please my woman.

"I'm going to come. Keep going!" Her screams spurred me on. I not-so-gently shoved two thick fingers into her pussy and went back to her delicious clit, where my efforts paid off in spades. Her arched back and flushed face marked her point of no return.

"I'm coming. I'm coming," she panted. Two more thrusts of my fingers and a long pull on her clit, and delicious come spilled into my mouth. I ate like a man starved. Her whole body shuddered and twisted repeatedly until she was left relaxed and pliant.

I kissed my way back up her body, stopping to suck on each tit in appreciation until I reached her gorgeous mouth. I used my tongue to paint her lips and shared her taste with her. I was positive she hummed a "yum" when our kiss ended.

"You are so fucking beautiful, baby. Bedroom?" I picked her up, threw her over my shoulder, and walked to where she pointed. I didn't have time to notice anything about her apartment, only that it was small. Like *tiny* small—I bumped into the side table, almost knocking over a lamp.

Her bedroom wasn't what I expected from her sassy personality. It was earthy and calm—everything she wasn't. The queen-size bed wasn't made, and it revealed that she only slept on one side of it. The sheets were turned down in a crisp fold, and the pillows were fluffed and stacked neatly on top of one another. It appeared there were many more layers of Trudie Gonzales that I needed to drill down to.

For now, the only thing that needed drilling was my woman's pussy. She wanted a teacher of all things sexual, and I was the man for the job. If my instincts were correct, she did not want the standard repertoire of oral and vaginal sex. She wanted to explore next-level kinky. I'd done my fair share of off-the-rails kink, but I didn't want to go too fast and scare her or push her to a place that would trigger her in any way.

I dropped her gently on the edge of her bed and told her not to move before going back down the hallway to the bathroom to get a towel. Tonight was going to get messy, and I didn't want to leave in the middle of what I was about to start. Returning, I found my naked little minx right where I left her, wringing her hands and looking lost and desperate.

"Hey there, sweetheart. Ready for another lesson?" I purred.

She stared at me with those amber eyes, the corners of which squinted a fraction in concern. "Yes, but..." Her body language communicated insecurity, and as her teacher, it was my duty to ease her mind so she could participate fully in the curriculum I had planned for her.

"No buts. You wanted a lesson, and you are going to get one. Just know that you have a voice in our games. You always have an out." The tension in her shoulders released, and her mouth relaxed into a perfect *O*.

I pressed my hands to the side of her face, pushing her hair back behind her ears. The tilt of her head was perfect for kissing, and I couldn't resist leaning into those pink pillows. She parted her lips and slid her tongue out to meet mine in the hottest and most tender kiss I'd ever had. She trusted me. She opened it for me. She scared the shit out of me. I knew I could get lost in her face and mouth forever. The feelings that her kiss elicited came from the very depths of my soul, which not even my ex-fiancée could come close to. I shuddered at the possibilities—as I did at the risk of what would happen if this whole convoluted project we were working on went south. Yet because I'm a bastard, I didn't let it stop me from doing all the dirty things I promised I would teach her.

I ran my thumb over her bottom lip as my legs pushed her knees open. I stepped between them, putting my cock inches from her face.

"You are gorgeous, Trudie, and the only thing more gorgeous will be your lips wrapped around my cock. Today's lesson is about your mouth and what it does to me every time you open it." She smiled, acknowledging my reference to the smart-ass comments and gibes that have been part of our repartee since we met.

"I haven't forgotten how we left things in California, and we will have a conversation about that soon. However, I need to know if you're in an emotionally safe place to play. Can you stay a student, or should we just fuck?"

Her eyes went big and she nodded her consent to play. I unbuckled my belt and slipped it from my pants. The buckle thumping to the floor was the only sound I could hear alongside my rapidly beating heart. I could see that the sound of my slowly opening zipper heightened her awareness, and she licked her lips in want.

"Open your mouth—wide." She complied immediately. Such a good little girl.

"Tap the back of my leg if it's too much." Her breasts heaved and she squirmed on her bottom as she waited patiently for my cock.

"Suck me, beautiful."

She wasted no time getting me wet and ready. The sounds her mouth made sliding up and down my dick were an aphrodisiac like no other. She wrapped a firm hand around my root and tugged me toward the point of delirium.

"Fuck, Trudie. You are so good at that. Umm," I moaned as she got comfortable with my large thick dick. She seemed proficient enough, but then she grabbed my balls not so lightly in her other hand.

"God dammit, woman. You've been holding out on me." I looked down at her insatiable mouth and saw that she had a wide smile. *Please tell me I'm the first to unleash this sex goddess.*

She pulled off with a pop. "You taste so good."

And that was when I fell even deeper under her spell—this woman who hated me one minute and loved sucking me the next. It's like she had two personalities: one outside the bedroom and one inside. I couldn't lie—I loved them both.

Wait, did I just think the word that should never be said? I needed to put an end to that train of thought. I'd been badly burned once and would not be tricked by love again.

"You can suck my dick any time you want, sweetheart, but you might want to brace yourself for your next lesson," I teased. "Relax your throat and breathe through your nose. Do your best to stay calm. Your yoga breathing will be an asset to you right now," I said, encouragingly.

She nodded her consent and licked the end of my dripping cock. Trudie had no idea what all her little hums and moans did to me. I didn't plan to have a woman in my life, but it seemed that the universe had other plans, and who was I to contradict the universe?

"Stick your tongue out and don't forget to tap my leg if it's too intense."

Our eyes locked, and I felt a jolt of electricity as she kept her focus on my face while I slid my engorged cock back into her wet mouth. My fogged head fell backward, loving the sensations she sparked in my body. Tingles traveled down my spine to my balls, and the tension in my back contracted and released as I pressed my cock deeper. When I looked back down, saliva dripped from the sides of her mouth. My breath hitched every time she managed to take more of me. Not even when I hit the back of her throat did she stop. *Fuck! Where was this woman's gag reflex?*

I'm a big man and my sex goddess had sucked all eight inches of me into her sexy, stretched mouth. The sucking sounds and hums she continued to make were the most fucking beautiful music I had ever heard. I was so goddamned proud of this tiny woman for giving me the best blow job of my tightly wound life.

"Baby, I'm going to come," I howled, pushing her head back. My lesson wasn't supposed to include swallowing. That was a very personal decision, and I would not presume she was cool with that.

Her glassy-eyed grin with my cock deep inside her was clearly happy to stay that way until I came. I could feel my balls tightening and pulling up as I thrust two more times into her appreciative mouth. She grabbed both of my ass cheeks and pulled me hard against her face, which sent me so far over the edge that my legs threatened to collapse. I was out of my mind with gratitude for having this moment with her. I had always been more of a giver in the bedroom, and to find a person so unabashedly open to giving me so much pleasure was humbling.

As she pulled her swollen red lips from my cock, she flicked my slit with her tongue, making sure I was empty. *Fuck she's amazing.* She looked up at me, her doe-eyed expression melting my heart, and I cupped her jaw to memorize this beautiful picture.

"So good," she replied, sounding like a little girl getting to the end of a bowl of ice cream. I imagined some future role-play that involved Trudie wearing her hair in pigtails. *I really am the worst.*

I pulled her up to my full length and pressed our foreheads together lovingly. The soft curves of her body danced under my capable hands, especially when I dragged my thumb down her spine. So responsive.

Time stood still as I relished what she had given me. Her desire to please me was intoxicating, and I was going to remember this moment until I died.

I heard a whisper from her lips, but I couldn't make out what she said.

"Tell me again, sweetheart. I couldn't hear you clearly," I gently encouraged.

The silence that followed my request was palpable. Was she feeling awkward or embarrassed? Did I make her feel bad about something? Then she murmured a little louder.

"I've never done that before."

Carefully, I responded. "Given head?" That couldn't have possibly been the case—she was too good at it.

"No. I mean, not like that. I've never had a man so deep in my throat before. Sam wasn't endowed like you are." I could only imagine how boring this guy was in the bedroom. No wonder she needed a new partner, one who would let her explore her sexuality completely. A strong teacher like me.

"Baby, if you mention that worm's name again, I'm going to beat your ass red. He's history. Dead to you, and most definitely to me."

She pulled her bottom lip into her mouth and bit down like a child with her hand caught in a cookie jar. She didn't laugh in response; she just looked regretful. Sex wasn't the only lesson this powerful yet fragile woman needed to learn. She had implied that her dad was an ass and that Sam was clueless, but there had to be more to this story. I hoped one day she would share it with me.

"Alex?" Her eyelashes fluttered as she looked at me head-on. "Do you think there is something wrong with me for loving what we just did? I have never even considered doing that or anything we've done before. It's as if you have this weird spell over me. It's freaking me out." She pulled into herself, her eyes watering.

I wrapped my arms around her and hugged her tightly to my chest so she could hide her tears in my shoulder, away from my watchful eyes.

"No, baby. You were perfect. There's nothing you did—we did—that you should ever consider wrong. Clinically, I think you have a lot of repressed feelings. Which feeling those are, I don't know yet. Tell me, though, have you enjoyed what we've done?" Her breathing hitched between her sobs, and I stroked her hair and whispered soft affirmations, giving her the time she needed to regain her composure.

She pushed back off my chest and placed a delicate hand on my face.

"You're so patient with me—I mean in the bedroom, not anywhere else, though." She chuckled, her thumbs rubbing my evening stubble. "I feel alive, almost reborn, when you do all those magical things to me with your hands and tongue, and, well, that massive serpent between your legs." Now we both laughed.

She continued, "I feel giddy after you make me come. Something I've never felt before. I just don't know if I should expect that from anyone else. I can't presume you would stick around after this project is done, and I'm concerned that I will have to sample a lot of guys before I find that feeling again. It scares me."

The hell she was going to sample other guys' dicks! I abruptly picked her up, carried her to the top of the bed, and placed her under the covers. I turned off the light, and as the room went black, I joined her in bed, tucking myself snugly against her ass as I wrapped my arms around her tightly.

"Please don't be scared, Trudie. Let yourself be in the moment and live that moment thoroughly, and for fuck's sake, you will *not* be sampling other dicks as long as I'm around." And that could be a long time.

Chapter 24

TRUDIE

IT HAD BEEN A long holiday weekend and I'd had a lot to think about, starting with my over-the-top wantonness on Friday night. It felt like my brain had short-circuited and my mouth promised to repair the world, starting with Alex's crazy huge cock. Where had that girl been hiding? And more importantly, would she make another appearance soon?

After what Alex had called "a life-changing experience," I was afraid he'd never look at me the same way. I thought it wouldn't be so bad, except he now worked at my school. Thank God that after Alex had transported me to another solar system, he had made excuses to leave. Something about appeasing his family in the Hamptons. The poor little rich boy was still at his parent's beck and call.

I guess I wasn't one to talk. I was on my way to my brother's apartment for a barbeque. Being a nurse didn't leave Zander a lot of time to host gatherings, so when he offered to host, my mom was thrilled not to have to cook another family meal this month. Instead, we all brought a dish, and Zander cooked up chicken and ribs. Zander brought his new girlfriend; even Paolo invited a work friend he liked to hang out with. That made me my mom's date. It looked like chicken and ribs weren't the only thing getting grilled today.

Things were tenuous at best with Alex. We had plans to meet at the end of the first week of school since every teacher needed a minute to settle in with their new classes and sort through the trials and tribulations they were going to bring this year. He would likely be too busy with administration and learning school policies and procedures to sniff around my classroom.

I shuffled out of the patio door and was bent over the cooler, deciding on which alcoholic beverage would best numb my mind when I heard a loud smack and then felt my ass stinging.

"Ha, ha, ha, Sis. Shouldn't leave your ass in the wind like that." The flat line of my lips and the rolling of my eyes should have been enough for Zander to know he'd better get out of my way, but, no, he just kept coming with his caustic sarcasm. "Next time, you might get a two-by-four," he said, cocking his head to one side. His girlfriend was aghast at his behavior.

"Listen, dickweed, I'm going to let that go since I don't want to humiliate you more than you just did in front of your girlfriend, but suffice it to say, you do that again and it will be you getting that two-by-four. And you can kiss your dick goodbye." I pointed two fingers from my eyes to his and then hers. "And, by the way, I'm Trudie, this idiot's older sister. You are?" I waited impatiently while cracking open my lite beer.

"Uh, I—I'm Olivia," she said shyly.

"Terrific. Great to meet you. Have fun!" I fired off quickly, spun on my heel, and walked to the far side of the backyard to park my thick ass on a swing. My head ached with all the potential problems I'd be facing this year, not the least of which was Alex. I had finally gotten my finalized student list and saw that I had a kid from my class last year returning for a do-over. I was praying that he wouldn't become a problem for everyone else in the class since I was going to have twenty-seven proverbial cats running all over the place. My new "Rest and Return" area would give kids a positive way to take charge of their emotions—they needed to learn to self-soothe just like infants who needed to learn to sleep through the night. I'd have to ask Alex if he had any suggestions to fortify my efforts. I truly wanted to make a difference in these kids' lives.

I drank half my beer as I considered how to share what was happening in my life with my mom. The key was to be nonchalant yet give enough detail to satisfy her curiosity. If Spain ever had another Inquisition, my mother would lead the charge. I'd never had anyone parse a comment as succinctly and thoroughly as my mother and no one was exempt. Speak of the devil: she glided over the stiff grass with lemonade in hand, smiling knowingly. My mother could glide over broken glass and not get cut. It probably came from years of hiding her true feelings from her toxic husband.

"*Hola, mia solar*. You look sad." She swung her arms around me and gave me a big kiss.

"Hey, Ma. I can't be sunny all the time. It's just that there have been a few changes at school I hadn't planned on, and now I had to pivot." I pouted into my beer.

"Tell me, sweetheart, what changed?" She looked at me like I was being overly dramatic, which incensed me. I had real problems with real consequences now. I was an adult, not a kid who could be placated.

"Some good things like my 'Rest and Recovery' area, and some not-so-good things. Although, it will be good for the whole school, just not until next year." *Could I be any vaguer?* I proceeded to describe each change, hitting the highlights to avoid being interrogated throughout the rest of the evening. Thank goodness my brother called us over for dinner before she gave me her laser-like "There's more to this story" stare. Fortunately, she didn't bring it up again.

By seven o'clock I begged off, knowing that my morning alarm would start its daily annoyance at six a.m. The only things that cheered me up were a brief text from Ruby wishing me a great new school year that I got while I brushed my teeth, and a surprising text from Alex with the same sentiment.

Alex: Sleep tight, Trudie, and be sure to start your school year off with clean sheets.

This was followed by a winking emoji. Seriously? Sure, I worked at a middle school, but did he have to text like a kid? *Though he is thinking of me.*

Me: You are hilarious. Go to bed.

I climbed into my sheets, wearing only a tank top and panties. Now that he mentioned it, my sheets did smell musky, with a hint of citrus. *Hmm. I may never wash them again.*

Alex: I am in bed. I just got back into town, and I'm distracted.

Me: Distracted, huh? Try taking your hand off your appendage.

Alex: That didn't help. That wasn't why I was distracted.

Me: Oh?

Alex: Get your mind out of the gutter. Have a great day tomorrow. Maybe I'll see you around.

I waited a minute, hoping for an explanation about why he was distracted, but the three dots stopped.

Me: Good night

ALEXANDER

Screaming, screeching, and charging children of all makes and models banged into me as I tried to get through the front door of Hart Middle School. I lifted my satchel so my computer wouldn't be smashed and it was a good thing I did. Two girls side checked me against the glass door while squeezing their way to another girl to give her hugs—apparently because they missed each other all summer.

It occurred to me that I was old. Maybe too old to remember the fuel-packed excitement of kids on the first day back from summer vacation. The only analogy I could muster was that of a head-on collision, with their energy matching that of an airbag bursting at you head-on. Shocking and quite often painful.

I don't remember the first days of school quite like this. I went to a private school, and decorum was essential. No public displays of affection and certainly no screaming. Sly looks and jerked-up chins were more my classmates' speed. We all quietly took each other in to see who had filled out or who got braces on or off, and made snarky comments in our minds, while filing away all the details to share with our buddies at football or rowing practice. The occasional high-five had been acceptable out of the classroom, but never in. The biggest faux pas that I remember making was not trying on my uniform blazer before school started and having to wear that incredibly shrinking coat for a week before I could be fitted for a new one. More emotional damage and a life lesson about being prepared.

Instead of rushing to check into the office, I found a bench in an alcove off the main lobby where I could spend a few minutes observing some of the kids, as well as the teachers who monitored the halls. No matter how annoyed these teachers sounded at Field Day, today they showed genuine happiness seeing all their students growing up and shuttling all the incoming sixth graders to their homerooms. It became very clear which students knew their way around and which were lost sheep. The girls' clothes looked like my shrunken coat—too short and pulling at the seams. The boys, however, either looked like they had stolen their big brothers' clothes, which hung off them, or like they were vying for a role in *Glee*: metrosexual and fitted tightly.

The warning bell rang, and I took that as my cue to check in and get this project underway.

"Good morning, everyone...Ricky." I gave a warm smile in greeting and a nod, especially for Ricky, who was kind enough to blush back. We were going to have a wonderful year lobbing looks and gibes back and forth, even though he knew I wasn't playing for his team.

I knocked on the principal's door, and she waved me in with one hand. Eloise was decked out in Hart Middle School regalia: polo shirt with a fleece zip-up. I loved that she kept things fun and school-oriented instead of wearing a suit and being too formal. Middle school kids didn't want to be patronized and, quite frankly, neither did I. *Note to self, ask for school gear.*

"Good morning, Dr. Pierce. I hope your weekend was pleasant and restful because starting today, it's going to be full throttle to the end of the school year." She smirked as she shook my hand and rounded her desk, taking a long pull from her thermos.

"Thank you, Mrs. Jackson. Please call me Alex when we aren't near the students. I'd prefer things to be as casual as possible." I crossed my ankle over my knee and pulled my computer out from my leather satchel to open a few documents I had prepared for this meeting.

I stood slightly to set my laptop on her desk and pulled my chair closer so that I could share my screen with her. I was pleased that she stood up and came to sit on the same side, making it so much easier to collaborate with her.

"I've put together a few documents based on what the school board requires to achieve exemplary status, as well as two other documents that explain in greater detail our hidden agenda of identifying at-risk kids and creating an infrastructure to minimize their growing educational and emotional deficits."

Eloise took her time reading my initial recommendations, rolling her eyes at some and nodding at others. "At least you had the forethought to bullet point the not-so-obvious issues our school needs to overcome, especially our need to focus on the total child. And that while our school has strong teachers and leadership, we lack the family and community involvement we need to be successful. Although those things seem obvious from a distance, they are points of contention up close. Teachers can't be effective if parents—all parents—don't invest in the time it takes at home to prepare their children academically and emotionally.

"I understand that even in our entitled area, we have a diverse group of people and home environments. I really hope that our 'hidden agenda,' as you put it, can significantly impact these families. Tell me more about your timeline." I noted her empathy and concern and knew if I could relieve her concern one iota, my time here would be validated.

Flipping documents, I showed her my timeline for data collection, analysis, establishing best practices, and implementation. Trudie would be essential in all aspects of this process, and I hoped she could get some time out of her classes to work with me, observing students in other classes. I knew her psychology background would be invaluable, even if she did not have a specific degree in it. Her own life experiences and her accumulated knowledge of children, pedagogy, and emotional instability would make this school an even better place for any kid who attended.

Eloise stood from her seat and returned to her side of the desk, sighing. She wrung her hands, effectively telling me she wasn't getting her hopes up.

"Alex, we have a lot to accomplish." She sat down again, slurping her coffee off the rim of her thermos. "Take today and tomorrow to walk around and listen to my teachers, department by department. Submit your notes, with your initial observations of each teacher and their possible areas of improvement, on a daily basis. Identify any teacher using methods that would undermine what we want to achieve, and we will work with those teachers first. I expect you to organize a plan of attack to help these teachers improve and a way to track this. Ms. Gonzales needs to be a part of this phase of our plan; her opinions on how our teaching staff could improve would be more valuable at this early stage. It could be helpful for you to see their daily planners," she suggested.

"Exactly. I'm happy we're on the same page already. And yes, I would like the opportunity to sit down with each teacher next week after reviewing their daily planners. Would one of your office admins be able to organize a sign-up page?" I closed my computer and slid back in my seat, awaiting her reply.

"Absolutely. I'll get right on it," she said encouragingly and shooed me out the door.

As I made my way through the halls, spending a cursory ten minutes outside each classroom, I noticed an encouraging pattern.

Every teacher spoke to their students like adults; no patronizing tone and no holier-than-thou attitude. As with Field Day, I expected both Chip and Alan to have a commanding classroom style, though Alan seemed more collaborative with his students. It was a cool vibe—they were being playful, yet respectful, during dialogue.

My knowledge of the other teachers in that part of the building also came from our team competition, so I had a lot of work to understand their approach to teaching better. The bell sang throughout the hallways, and like the running of the bulls in Spain, the children came out of their classrooms desperate to eat and socialize. A second bell rang five minutes later, and just as quickly, the halls emptied, leaving a few stragglers behind. I'm not sure why I lingered watching them, but something about their posture troubled me. Their feet shuffled without purpose or direction, and their heads hung low like someone had killed their pet. The squeeze in my chest was palpable, and the overwhelming desire to give them a reassuring hug pinned me to the floor. I made some notes about their physical attributes and what rooms they eventually entered so I could follow up with their teachers. One student in particular tentatively turned the knob on Trudie's room, and as he did, he looked up and down the hallway as if he was being watched. (And, of course, he was, by me.) I smiled and nodded my assurance that everything was okay, and without emotion, he opened her door and walked in.

Feeling my belly grumble, I turned back to the main office to drop off my notepad and snagged my protein bar and an apple from my satchel. Not exactly the finest lunch I'd ever had, but it would have to do.

"Hello, Dr. Pierce." Ricky beamed. "How is your first day going? Are you finding everything?" His body language insisted I needed help.

With raised eyebrows, I looked over at him. "Doing great, Ricky. Thanks for asking." I started to walk away but remembered I did have a question. "Could you tell me where the teachers have their meals?" I waited patiently as Ricky got up from his desk and offered to escort me down to the teacher's lounge. If I wasn't mistaken, he put a little swish into his tush in hopes I might notice. When would this guy learn I was not interested in what he offered?

"Here you go, Dr. Pierce. Let me know if there's anything else I can help you find." He used both hands to gesture toward the teachers' lounge door.

I nodded my head in appreciation and let myself in. Sadly, the person I'd most liked to have seen wasn't there, but I saw Jensen and sat across from him.

"Hey, man." I nodded with my chin. From a young age, all men are programmed with specialized mannerisms that were universally accepted as "manspeak." This encompassed everything from greetings, farewells, and comments about girls, parents, and sports communicated in guttural responses and slaps on backs. Nothing more needed to be said or done. It was like our "bro code," but that was more about policies and procedures.

Jensen replied in kind, and I sat quietly like a fly on the wall, immersing myself in the *teaching staff's daily banter. Note to self: Change lunch times daily to get the full picture.*

Ten silent minutes passed before Jensen finished what he had been reading and engaged me in conversation.

"So. Have you cracked the code on us teachers yet? Found out our secrets and planning to out us to the school board?" He cracked himself up. "Just kidding, man. Really, how is your first day going?" He stood up as if he was in complete control of the situation.

I leaned in on my forearms, clasping my hands together, and locked eyes with him as if in a standoff.

"Actually, Jensen, every teacher seems to be doing a great job managing their classrooms and sincerely wanting to understand their students...except you," I deadpanned, trying to keep from bursting out laughing.

"What?" he yelped. Several other teachers stopped what they had been doing to look over at him. He sat down, looking around to see who was still eyeballing him. "What do you mean everyone but me?" His paranoid demeanor almost had me on the floor.

"Jensen, relax, I'm just joshing you." I waited until my explanation sunk in.

Visible sweat had appeared on his brow and I thought he might pass out. "Really? Dude, you just broke my left nut. You can't do that to a gym teacher. Rapport with our students is all we've got." He grabbed a napkin from the table and wiped his perspiration away.

"Sorry, man. Just having a little first-day fun. Actually, I haven't even been to the gym to watch you teach yet. Your nuts are safe—for now." I put out my hand in peace, and he shook it hard. We both got up and headed for the door, and just in case he was still too serious, I added while holding the door. "After you, sweetheart."

"Fuck you, man." He smirked and flattened his hand on my shoulder with a smack.

"Fuck you, too," I smirked back. It looked like I had made a new friend on my first day of school. If my mother gave a shit, she might have been proud of me.

Chatper 25

TRUDIE

I WAS IN THE middle of attendance when Delano walked sheepishly into my room. I nodded with a smile, and he found an empty desk closest to my R&R space. *Perfect for him.* I kept to my plan for the day and walked around the room explaining where to find supplies, where to place their homework on my desk, what the R&R space was designed for, and that we would take a deeper dive into why they should use it later. I handed out textbooks and workbooks and did a mock scenario of how I wanted the kids to respond when I called for their attention. We all had a good laugh when Jack knocked his book to the floor in his exuberance.

So far, the day had been going well. This was my second period out of six, and only two of my students had been no-shows. I was still baffled about how a kid misses their first day of school for anything less than a terrible disease or the death of a family member. However, given that last year's mysterious virus disrupted everyone's schedule, it wasn't out of the ordinary to assume these kids could be experiencing that as well. I made a mental note to contact those parents this afternoon.

Whoever thought teaching was an eight-hour day was never a teacher. It was more like a sixty-hour-a-week job that stuck with you 24-7. Delano was constantly on my mind. He had struggled last year, especially with reading. He wasn't unintelligent—it was his family life. Parents' involvement in their kids' academic success was way underrated. I could guarantee you 100 percent that if my mom hadn't hidden the remote and forced us to pull out our homework while she made dinner every night, we would never have turned out the way we did.

I remember on more than a few occasions, she read our essays in bed and marked them up so we could fix them before school the next day. The best thing about my dad was his paychecks since it meant my mom didn't have to work full-time, especially since he was never at home for long stretches of time. She worked remotely as a copyeditor for a local newspaper and rarely had to go into an office to do her work. My decision to become a teacher was in part due to her dedication to our schoolwork.

Sadly, Delano, like so many other kids in our school, didn't have that kind of situation. I knew I couldn't fix my students' homelives, but I could fix how they felt about themselves as they worked through their circumstances.

"Okay, class. I know you've been looking forward to your first assignment this year, so keep your enthusiasm down." Their response to my attempt at humor was like a field of crickets at dusk.

"I'd like you to take out your imaginary magic wands and think about what would make you the proudest of yourself." Some kids smiled, and others looked completely lost. "For instance, if you got higher than a B on every vocabulary test this semester, or perhaps you found a new hobby that you were good at, or maybe you overcame an obstacle in your life. Make sense?" The sea of nodding heads made me smile.

"Please take out your writing notebooks and spend the next fifteen minutes writing out any or all of those things that would make you proud of yourself. I'm not interested in grammar or punctuation at this time—just in you getting your thoughts on paper. Go ahead and get started."

My summer research taught me how transformative and productive writing prompts could be, especially if students were stuck. I'm not a novel writer, though I like to journal my thoughts, aspirations, and the like. Months later, when I read back through them, I can see if I have been progressing forward or reverting to old ways that I knew would only tear me down. I took out my own journal when my students did, and I wrote down my thoughts and feelings about this past weekend and what it meant to me to have a family who loved me and was comfortable enough to let me be myself, no matter how ridiculous or distraught I was. My feelings about Alex were much more difficult to put to paper—it was a reality I was still coming to grips with. If I had been feeling stronger and more positive about myself, I'm I would have been luxuriating in thoughts of how our relationship—if you could call it that—began and escalated to what it had become.

The first lunch bell jerked me out of my thoughts and reminded me that we needed to wrap up the writing exercise.

"Great job today, everyone. Although I have no idea what you wrote, I love that you all put on your thinking caps and made an honest effort to dig deep." I saw that my praise hit the mark on most of my students' faces. I also noticed a few who looked pained and knew they needed to dive deeper into the writing.

"We have twenty minutes before your lunchtime, so let's use that time to discuss your writing process and any difficulties you found during those fifteen minutes."

Angela shoved one hand into the air like a rocket, with her other holding it up even taller. I would have pointed out the hole in her armpit if I didn't love these kids. *I'm a terrible person.*

"Angela. What are your thoughts?"

Preening like a peacock, she listed three things that whirled through her seventh-grade mind.

"The assignment was super easy because I'm really good at lots of things." Humility not being one of them. "But when I thought about an obstacle, I had trouble picking one." She sat back in her seat, concern written all over her face.

"Thank you so much for sharing, Angela. That was very brave of you. By choosing an obstacle you'd have to admit that there are obstacles in your life, and that can be painful. Would it help you all if I shared with you an obstacle that I want to overcome this year?" Angela beamed and nodded.

I moved my glass apple aside and slid myself on top of the desk, weighing whether to make up an obstacle or share a real one. *So many obstacles, so little energy to attack them all.* Decision made,

I straightened my expression, crossed my legs, and leaned toward my class.

"One of my obstacles is forgiveness." *True, yet vague.*

"Sometimes I withhold it to punish the person who hurt me, and sometimes I refuse to give it because if I do forgive them, it feels like I lost a battle. Does that make sense?" I tilted my head and gave what I called a "thinking nod" in hopes the kids would stop for a second and marinate on what I had just said.

"Whoa, Ms. Gonzales, that was deep," Jack interjected with a consummate California-Valley-guy accent. His long blond hair was tucked behind his ears and his doe eyes expressed his concern for me. That kid was going to be a panty-melter when he grew up.

I nodded in agreement. "That was pretty deep, wasn't it? Those realizations were crystalized this summer when I went to a conference in California. Understanding why I withheld forgiveness was illuminating to me—it opened my mind and my heart in ways I never thought it could. It was only a few carefully organized words that made the difference. Imagine what you could do with a few carefully placed words. We'll explore that after lunch today." And at that moment, the second bell rang, signaling their escape.

ALEXANDER

I wasn't sure if what I overheard from Trudie's classroom made me proud or if it made my dick hard. The fact that my trousers were becoming uncomfortable would indicate that it was a major turn-on. She had used my theory of forgiveness that we had discussed in my lecture during the summer. And not just any class—in the first class of the year. I heard loud and clear that someone from her past still held power over her, and I was going to find out who and why and obliterate them from her mind. Why did she feel she needed to carry that crap with her like a yoke around her neck. Whatever was going on, this teacher was going to educate her and free her from it.

Of course, my other head, the one who could actually make a decision, felt enormously proud that she could synthesize that forgiveness concept and explain it seamlessly to her students. She assumed these thirteen-year-olds were capable of deeply convoluted concepts and would comprehend the pros and cons of giving or withholding absolution. I knew dozens of adults who couldn't possibly fathom those concepts, and she trusted that they would just get it. Trust. Interesting. She was willing to trust her students more than she would an adult. I'd need to marinate on that one for a while.

After such a heavy conversation with her students, I didn't want to interrupt her thoughts, so I kept walking down to the next classroom, which turned out to belong to Robin, the music and drama teacher. From the sound of things, her lecture was way more structured than Trudie's. Instead of calm discourse, Robin was entertaining her students with a monologue from the musical *Shrek*, quoting the donkey character. Something about parfaits and layers. The kids giggled, loving her vocal affectations. After ten minutes outside her door, I concluded that she was a "no shit" kind of teacher. She would give tough love to help her students reach excellence while offering compassion for those who worked hard and played fairly in her classroom. She had all my respect for trying to corral all those cats into an organized production. Better her than me.

As I was flipping through my list of classrooms still to review, I heard a faint voice to my right. The vision I saw of a smoking hot teacher in a pencil skirt with a sexy, flowy top designed to drape her full bosom had me choking. I cleared my throat, trying to get my words out, but it appeared I'd forgotten how to phonate.

I cleared my throat once again, and my vocal cords managed to come together cleanly.

"Hey, Ms. Gonzales." *Achem.* "How is your first day going?" *Achem.*

"You okay?" She scrunched up her nose and tilted her head almost to her shoulder.

"Ah, yeah. Something just caught in my throat. So, a good day?" I deflected.

She nodded her head slowly. I hoped she would share some of the interesting parts of her day, but all she said was, "Pretty good." She pointed to the cafeteria. "Did you eat already?" she asked, keeping her momentum as she moved toward the lunch line.

"Yeah, a little something. Would you like some company?" I asked with my best boy-next-door smile.

She chuckled. "Sure, but let's get one thing straight, Dr. Pierce. You will never be the boy next door to me." It was unbelievable how she saw right through me. The amber in her eyes deepened and became more sparkly as she teased me. "You will always be the devil in a Tom Ford suit. Dangerous and dashing." *Get me the fuck out of this school! Twelve words, and I'm ready to go down on her.*

Struggling to keep a professional distance, I responded, "Well, thank you for that, princess." I licked my lips for effect. "I accept your assessment and want you to know that you will never be off limits to me. And if you keep wearing blouses that direct my attention to those God-inspired tits, I will find a way to teach you everything I know, and then I'll learn a few more tricks just so we can both master them together."

Trudie stumbled backward, and I wasted no time in grabbing her arms to keep her from falling. A few teachers ran over, alarmed by her movements, as did I. The realization that my words caused this gave me pause. I knew I could be intense sometimes—okay, a lot of times—but I'd never made anyone fall over.

"Are you okay?" both Cooper and Mary Lou asked with concern.

Trudie looked down at my hands, which were still on her arms, keeping her steady. When our eyes met, she let out an audible sigh.

"Ah, yeah, wow. I didn't realize my blood sugar dropped so quickly. I'd better eat immediately." Her breathy tone sold them on her story, and we all walked her to a nearby table to sit.

"I'll go and get you something. What would you like?" My soft-spoken words seemed to calm her, and the other teachers said they'd stay with her while I fetched her meal.

"Just a tuna sandwich and some water will be good for now." Her smile widened and I went on my way.

Five minutes later, I was back at the table, and the other teachers were giving her a hard time about working too hard, especially on the first day. They stood up to go when I took a seat.

I gave her a couple of minutes to take a few bites and watched her eyes flit up to my face in wonderment. She trusted me, I knew, since she gave herself to me more than once. My words had promised her a third night of pleasure and potentially an eternity to explore everything about each other. *An eternity? I need to slow my roll.* I understood her trepidation because this was going to require me to expose everything about myself, and I wasn't sure if I was ready to do that. But time was up, and she needed to know exactly what I had planned for her.

"Feeling better, princess?" I teased as she gulped down her last bite.

Her jaw flexed and her eyes narrowed into lasers. This was going to be good.

In a biting whisper, she said, pointing to me, "I'm going to fucking kill you. How dare you speak to me like that in my school? I told you nothing is going to happen anymore. We have to stay professional and I can't do that when you make those, those..." Her lips pressed into a line and her words drifted into the ether.

Being the gentleman that I was, I supplied, "Dangerous comments? When I look dashing and desirable in my Tom Ford suit?" *I'm still an ass.*

"Stop it! You keep doing that. And, to be fair, I never said desirable. More like a disaster waiting to happen."

"Doing what, exactly? You're an English teacher, use your words," I pushed.

My little minx looked like the angry emoji.

"You. Are. The. Most. Frustrating. Man...*EVER!*"

I smiled in agreement. And with as much control as I had ever seen her show, she walked out of the cafeteria in a huff. I was truly enjoying this new hobby of mine, especially when it included her lovely, sexy ass storming away from me. I needed to get my hands on those cheeks again soon.

For my safety and hers, I stayed far away from her classroom and finished my rotation of first impressions by the last bell of the day. Exhausted from all the standing, I dropped into a seat in the main office. Mona, the attendance secretary, greeted me kindly. The sixty-something stylish woman looked at me like she knew a secret, but I was too tired to care. She got up from her desk, walked down the hall, and returned with an apple.

"Here, Dr. Pierce. You've earned an apple on your first day at Hart Middle School. Good job." I didn't know her well enough to think she was patronizing me, so I took the apple, polished it on my Khaki pants, and took a giant crunchy bite.

"Thanks, Mona. That really hit the spot," I mumbled, chewing loudly for her benefit. "The day has been illuminating but exhausting. Your school has some amazing talent and some that still haven't been tapped. I'm looking forward to exploring how to help everyone feel more comfortable with the upcoming changes."

Her face quirked. "Changes? Like what? How?"

I may have been thinking out loud when I said that, but I went with it anyway.

"Change happens every time a different decision is made. It doesn't have to be noticeable, yet even one degree of change can be a catalyst for another. Imagine, if everyone here at Hart Middle School made the effort to exert a 1 percent positive change this year, what greatness could be achieved." Sometimes, I even amazed myself with my little pearls of wisdom.

Mona raised her eyebrows. "I suppose you're right, Dr. Pierce. I never thought about change in those terms. I'll have to remember that when you ask me to choose a different apple variety from the one I just gave you."

We both chuckled at that, and I took my leave to knock on Eloise's door. She was on the phone and motioned me back to my regular seat. Moments later, she hung up, and I stopped flipping through my notes.

"So, Dr. Pierce, what did you learn about my staff today?" She noticed the core of the apple I had finished eating and added, "Any bad apples in the bunch?"

Tossing the core into the basket alongside her desk, I responded. "I have to say, you have a remarkable team of professionals on your staff. I'm surprised you haven't already been made an exemplary school." She beamed and pressed her hands together on her desk.

"So why then does the school board think we need to change anything at all? This little project must be expensive; why spend the money on a machine already working?"

She made a good point. "I'm not sure what they are seeing, and I can assure you none of them has taken the time to see what you are actually doing here. But perhaps we need to change the optics for their benefit," I proposed.

"Change the optics?" Even with a look of confusion, she was formidable.

"Ah, well, it's what I just shared with Mona. Change is a frightening proposition for most people, though if presented for what it really means, it can be more palatable. For instance, where Alan is very collaborative with his students, Chip is more regimented. Neither is right or wrong. However, Alan might need to be more assertive at times, and Chip needs to hand control over to his students so they have more opportunities to try and fail, thus learning along the way. Does that make sense?"

She smiled like a parent whose child was starting to understand the lesson they gave earlier.

"Precisely. Great observation, Dr. Pierce. What else did you learn?" She pulled a protein bar from her drawer, offered me one, and then peeled the foil back on her own.

"I noticed a young man dawdling in the hallway after he was supposed to be back in class. He looked like his dog died this morning. He was going into Trud—Ms. Gonzales's classroom when he looked at me as if he was wondering if I was going to narc on him. I hoped my smile and nod were reassuring, but I'd really like to know what was going on with that kid. He might be a perfect fit for our little project."

She hummed her approval. Or was she just enjoying her protein bar? I wasn't sure.

"For lack of a better description, was he an African American kid? Short hair, kind of big for his age?" Seeing that Eloise was African American herself, I understood how being racially sensitive was taken seriously at her school.

"So you know this kid?" I confirmed

"Yeah, he's a good kid with a kind heart, but his home life doesn't support good study habits. His mom is a nurse—a terrific lady, though not home enough to watch her kids and help when they need it. It's a typical story. We probably have a couple of dozen kids like that, and I can assure you they all aren't underprivileged if you know what I mean." She rolled her eyes.

"Principal Jackson, these are exactly the kind of kids who need to be nudged back on track and made to feel worthy. I'd like to put together a survey for your teachers. Can you encourage your team to get them back to me by the end of next week? It will be important to start our program immediately so we can collect data and change lives by the end of the school year."

"Agreed. I will look to you to create the list of mentors that you mentioned so we can devise a plan of attack once we have identified the kids we'll be working with."

"I'm one step ahead of you." I grinned and got up from my seat, sliding my notes into my satchel. "Oh, and thanks again for your transparency with your staff. It will make doing what I was hired for so much easier." I waved goodbye and said good night to the secretaries out front.

I reprimanded myself for looking around in hopes of catching Trudie leaving the building. I wasn't done with her. We had started something, and neither this project nor any in the future would keep me from getting to the bottom of who Trudie Gonzales was. Millions of opportunities to be with her rolled through my mind, this survey being the first one.

I jumped into my rental car and headed to the grocery store, so I wouldn't be starved for the rest of the week. With any luck, Trudie would be doing the same thing.

Chapter 26
TRUDIE

Me: Ruby! We have to talk...NOW! (freaking out emoji, bomb emoji)

Ruby: Holy hell, girl. What is going on?

Me: Proving Grounds. Tomorrow 7 am. Be there! (exploding head emoji)

Ruby: Ah, that's pretty early, but okay. Are you okay?

Me: Barely hanging on. See you tomorrow.

I wasn't supposed to see him that day, and I hadn't planned on my immune system shutting down when he spoke those very suggestive words to me in the cafeteria. He damn near fucked me with his mouth in public, even if, sadly, it never touched me. The real problem was that he was starting to dominate my thoughts, and my concentration was for shit.

I thought I was hallucinating because just as I thought his name, he appeared, holding a cantaloupe and smiling as I walked into the Pick 'n Save. I shook my head and stepped back outside the sliding glass doors. The woman walking through with two hysterical children looked at me like I was a predator wanting to snatch her children. *Hell no, lady. After three o'clock, I don't want anyone's kids.*

I came up with a plan. First, I'd get my cereal, then I'd stay a couple of aisles in front of him, and then I'd circle back the opposite way of traffic to get my produce. I wished I had a hat to disguise myself and hoped I looked generic from my backside. This was just like when I'd had to hide from a parent last spring because I gave her kid a D for plagiarizing half of his term paper. It wasn't my fault the kid had to take summer school to make it up, yet I had felt that I somehow cheated the kid out of his summer of fun. After three emails and five voicemails after that incident, Eloise insisted I block their number and report the parent to the school board for harassment. I *never* wanted to deal with that again. (I could hear the *Mission Impossible* theme song playing in my head for the next ten minutes.)

Looking at my cart next to the meat counter, I calculated approximately how much I had left in my budget for heartier meals. Fifty bucks. The counter lady called out my number, and I ordered hamburger meat, chicken breasts, and lunch meat. As I waited, scrolling through my emails, I smelled him. *Damn it!* His clean citrus scent overtook me, and I closed my eyes and leaned in.

"Hello, princess. Fancy meeting you here." His smug, perfect face raised my hackles.

"Yeah, hi." He took his hands off the shopping cart and shoved them into the pockets of his perfectly hot suit. He had a smug expression on his face—probably because he was now a part of my neighborhood. My core clenched, and my throat went dry with all the possibilities of this scenario, though what I should have been doing was ignoring him and getting the hell out of the store. But this was my turf, my life, and I'd be damned if he was going to run me off like a scared little girl.

"Are you cooking tonight? Maybe I could come by with dessert?" *Oh, oh, oh...no, he didn't.*

"Alex, do you think I'm the kind of woman who would respond to such a base pickup line? Didn't we discuss ad nauseam that this thing between us was over?" I passed my upturned hand between us, hoping he understood we weren't a thing.

He shifted his hips left and right and proceeded to remind me of our previous conversations and that our hookup this past weekend was an entrée into more sexually desirable activities.

"None of which I agreed to," I flung back at him.

I collected my meat order, threw it into my cart, and took off. I was done with this conversation. Historically, if I spent more than five minutes speaking with him, I would do anything sexual he had to offer, and time was up.

The checkout lines were long, and my patience to get out of the store was shrinking, so I quickly grabbed a *People Magazine* to peruse until it was my turn.

"You can run, but you cannot hide, sweetheart. Tomorrow is but twelve hours away, and you may not have received an email about us working on a teacher survey after school, but you will before you go to bed tonight."

My blood boiled, and I rolled my shoulders to keep myself calm.

"Later, Dr. Pierce." I plastered a fake smile on my irritated face and pushed my cart forward to the cashier.

I made it back to my car without being accosted, only to have my door pulled out of my hand by a bigger, stronger, familiar one.

"Listen, Trudie. I'm not saying this to sound arrogant, but you and I have ridiculous chemistry. I haven't come anywhere close to this since..." He stopped short and shook his head. "What I'm trying to say is you and I have potential, but how can we explore that if you keep running away from me?"

Stunned, I realized that I had run away from him. And on more than one occasion. His energy engulfed me and ignited something in me I never knew existed. He scrambled my brain like eggs on Sunday morning; the most ironic thing was that I liked it. I didn't feel like I had to be in control when I was with him. Of course, I had to make an effort to, because that was how I was programmed. Being in control of everything in my life made up for the chaotic and traumatizing way my father lived his life. One minute, he was there at dinner, and the next, he was gone for six months, or worse, a year. Whiplash. That's what it felt like, and so did this thing with Alex. I was so confused.

I was too weak to stand any longer, so I sat down in my car, throwing my purse into the passenger seat. When I looked back Alex was squatting in front of me.

"Trudie, please give me a chance to prove to you I'm not a jerk. We have so much in common, and I want to talk with you about, well, about everything. If that leads to more, that's fine. Just stop running." He took my hands in his and kissed them. He seemed so sincere. If I trusted him at his word, would he pull the rug out from underneath me? I was broken in that regard. I didn't know if it was Alex or myself whom I didn't trust.

His smile was soft. Without thought, I pulled my hand from his and laid it on his stubbled jaw, hoping he understood my concern. A minute passed with my thumb strumming his face, and I couldn't resist placing a kiss on his ruddy lips. He was exquisite, and I was weak. I stared at him, looking for answers in his darkening eyes. I knew what that color meant and needed to escape the moment.

I slid my hand off his face and stared a bit longer before pulling my feet into my car.

"I'll see you at school tomorrow," I whispered, and he stepped back from the door, clearly as confused as I was.

"Have a good night, and think about what I said." He took two more steps backward, looking like I had taken his ball, and left the playground. I bit my bottom lip knowing that whatever walls I wanted to erect against him would never stand. I needed a good yoga workout and a hot shower to purge my kinetic energy.

"I knew you'd have the best advice." I hugged Ruby tightly.

"It's a gift. Besides, I haven't given you the opportunity to get *my* shit straightened out yet." She eyeballed me and then took a giant bite of her blueberry scone. Scones were a whole food group on its own for Ruby, and she was clear about how essential they were to her health and well-being.

"Did you get the job? Is it awesome? When did you start? I got your text but no details."

"No. It was crappy pay, and the idiot who interviewed me spent more time ogling my tits than listening to my reels. Seriously, Trudie, what does a girl need to do besides the obvious to get a good-paying job?"

I felt for her. Truly I did. Finding a position as a teacher was a no-brainer. Every school was hiring and there were strict policies about acceptable behavior. While Ruby was trying to break into a new career that was male driven leaving her suseptible to Machiavellian tactics.

"I'll find something, I just needed to vent. I have two more interviews set up for next week, hopefully one of those will work out for me." I stared at her telepathically, sending my good juju her way.

I reached across the small bistro table and took both her hands in mine. "Good things are coming your way, sweetie. Hang in there." I released her hands and slugged the rest of my coffee before pressing myself away from the table and grabbing my purse.

"Rubes, thirty minutes to catch up isn't enough. We need a girl's night, stat. Friday night?" I winked at her as I made my way to the door.

She grabbed her things and followed close behind. "I'm really happy you have a new daddy in your life. Having a guy almost twice your age chasing you around sounds hot."

I had my hand on the door and almost choked on my coffee. I glared at her. "Not. A. Daddy. Though maybe a personal trainer? And not twice my age. He's forty-two." I cracked myself up and waved her off. My school was twenty minutes away, and if I was lucky, I'd slide in just before the bell, avoiding my new daddy—ugh, teacher—mmm, trainer.

Jody was the hall monitor that morning, and she winked and waved as I entered my classroom as the bell sounded. She knew I was up to no good, but we'd have to wait until lunch to debrief.

I let the kids continue their shenanigans until I stowed my purse in my desk and locked it, pulled out today's lesson plans, and reviewed them.

Clapping my hands in a rhythmic pattern, I got their attention. We began by reviewing yesterday's assignments and then built on them. Once everyone was back to working in groups, I motioned for Delano to come to my desk. Of course, he must have felt singled out, but I wanted to offer him an incentive program. He had a lot of troubles, and I hoped that a few perks for effort might bring him out of his funk.

"Yes, Ms. Gonzales," he mumbled.

"Hey, Delano. I'm sorry you have to take this class again. It must be pretty boring to do the same stuff all over again, so I'd like to offer you some alternate assignments if you're up to it." I smiled, hoping he would stay open to our conversation. Instead, he gave me a shoulder shrug and a blank stare.

"Like what kind of assignments?" he asked with a wrinkled brow.

"I won't be offering this to anyone else in class, so this has to stay between us. I hope you know I only want what's best for you and for you to advance in your education. No tricks. No gimmicks. No shame. Just you and me figuring out a way to make that big brain of yours work for you in a positive way. Are you in?" I nodded in hopes he'd mirror me.

"Like I said before, what kind of assignments?" The kid was shrewd. He wasn't going to negotiate until he knew the stakes. Good for him. I could have learned a thing or two from this guy.

"Right. Every time I give an assignment, you can either choose to do that or write one hundred words on anything you want." I sat back and waited for the great negotiator to give his verdict.

"Anything I want?" he clarified.

"Yep. Of course, it has to be grammatically correct, with proper punctuation, and you must use two of the vocabulary words of the week." It was my turn to smile. *See? I'm not a pushover.*

"But I don't know how to do all that stuff." He pouted in distress.

"Sure you do. You just don't feel confident in it yet. I'll even let you do two drafts of each essay so you can fix your mistakes. That's how you learn. Fall forward, not backward. Deal?" I thrust out my hand, hoping he'd grab the lifeline I was offering.

You could see the wheels turning in his head. He looked behind him to see if anyone was watching and turned back to stare me down. My brothers and I had played a lot of poker growing up, so I had no trouble meeting his stare. Two minutes later, he finally conceded.

"You drive a hard bargain, Ms. Gonzales. If this gets me a C to pass this class, I'm all in." He took my outstretched hand and gave me an upturned chin. He looked victorious and in control. I suspected that was all this kid wanted, and I was happy to give it to him as long as he complied.

"Excellent choice, Delano. I'm really proud of you. Since our discussion took up most of our work time, please use the next ten minutes to write down some topics you might like to write on." His rolled eyes said it all, and he walked back to his seat, dragging his feet.

The teacher's lounge was packed today, and our Chicks without Dicks group decided that the courtyard would be more conducive for a girls' chat.

Now that I had filled my refrigerator, I could bring my own lunches. Jody had her ritual bagel and peanut butter, and Robin had an all-protein lunch. That poor woman ate more eggs than a chicken could lay in a week.

"What you need to understand is that they're inexpensive, easy to transport, have over six grams of protein, and I eat two a day.

And they fill you up quickly," Robin said as she confidently inserted an egg into her mouth.

If there was one thing I'd learned about this woman in five years, it was that she did everything with a purpose. She knew she was right, and quite frankly, I'd only caught her being wrong on the rarest of occasions. And then she owned it without argument. She was one righteous babe.

Jody replied, "You do you, babe. I can't look at an egg. Give me a bagel and some peanut butter, and I'm a happy camper."

"I don't know how you two survive the way you do. Have you ever heard of a balanced diet?" I asked with disdain.

Robin rolled a piece of cheese between her fingers and slid it into her mouth.

"Nope. Doesn't work for me. I've taken three specific blood tests with a homeopathic doctor, and they all point to a high-protein, low-to-no-carb diet for my blood type."

A sound resembling choking came out of Jody's throat. "Can we talk about something else? Like, tell me what's going on with that hot babe consultant?"

I stifled a choke and stalled for time as I prepared a short, effective response in my head.

"Dr. Pierce is a nationally acclaimed psychologist with a specialization in childhood trauma, and..."

Jody pushed her hand toward my face. "Stop. I don't need his pedigree. I want to know why he looks like he wants to eat you?"

Oh shit. I knew having him here was trouble. Maybe because he does—and has.

"See!" She shouted to Robin. "Look at her, she's all flushed and embarrassed. She's done something. Spill it." Her brows tightened and she pointed an accusatory finger at me. This was my come-to-Jesus moment with my school friends. I just hoped they'd keep their big mouths shut.

"I didn't want to make a big thing about this, because it happened before school started and before I knew he was coming here to work." I should have taken a picture of both their faces as I told them the story. Two fish with mouths gaping open, just waiting for the final hook.

"And, so, when Eloise offered me up as his liaison, I damn near shit the bed." I crossed my arms in what I hoped would be the final word on the subject. Alas, that was not the case.

Robin looked at her smartwatch, then at me. "You have one minute to explain how you plan on working side by side with a man that looks like him, smells like him, and from what I've seen, he'd follow you around like a lost puppy if he didn't have a job to do."

Jody jumped up in solidarity and pointed another finger at me. "Yeah, what she said."

"I'm gonna have to get back to you on that since I'm still trying to figure that one out myself. He's like a weed. I solve one problem and two more pop up." That was my cue to get up. I shrugged my shoulders, and we all walked back into the school.

"Good luck, Trudie. You're going to need it," Robin asserted.

"Better you than me, honey. Let us know if you need anything," Jody said, chortling.

We each held up our right hands in a peace sign and bumped fists. Jody came up with our name and club "handshake." The Chicks without Dicks was back together and God only knew what trouble we'd get into this year.

Chapter 27

ALEXANDER

THE PREVIOUS NIGHT HAD been a pain in my ass. Between my mother whining at me about my father and my familial duty to fix their problems, my sister Tabitha wallowing in the loss of yet another flakey boyfriend, and me, semi-hard all night thinking of Trudie sitting inches from my dick when she sat down in her car, I was so frustrated that I couldn't think straight.

I did manage to complete the survey I promised Eloise. The draft was reasonable, objective, and easy to score, and it left room for each teacher to write in any thoughts they could offer for improvement. Now, if I was able to lock down Trudie, we would be able to get the survey out the next day and have it back by the end of the following week.

I emailed her before I left home, asking her to meet with me after school or after dinner. My preference was to have *her* for dinner and then work, but she was still conflicted about what we should be. My phone buzzed almost immediately, but it was my dad, not Trudie.

Dad: Please call me, son.

This could go so many ways.

I packed my lunch and my satchel and headed to my car. After a quick stop at the Proving Grounds, I got a coffee and a pastry, then called my dad back while I waited for my order.

"Hey, Dad," I said when he answered. "Is everything okay? I haven't heard from you in a while."

"Good to hear your voice, Alexander. I've been busy with some new venture capital opportunities and wanted to know if you'd like to get together to discuss how you can get in on this deal."

"Sounds interesting, but my schedule is jammed for the next few months," I explained. "Don't you usually just send me a portfolio, or is there something else you want to discuss?"

My probing was usually a sound strategy to get him to get to the point. He never calls unless he needs me to do something for him, and his small talk game with family is nonexistent. But he was silent for a while, and my concern grew.

"Dad? Are you still there?"

"Uh. Listen, Alex. There are two things we need to discuss, the most pressing is that I need you to attend a partner's meeting with me at the NYC Conservancy Gala event next weekend. You can bring a date if you'd like, but there have been some rumors that I might be replaced on the board of trustees, and I need to show that our family is strong and that I am still relevant to the organization."

I knew it. Another dog and pony show to prove to the world that my parents are upstanding individuals. Since I blew off the Memorial Day Gala in the Hamptons, I took pity on him and agreed to be there, but I wasn't going to do it without some shaming.

"You know how I hate these things, Dad. Do you have any idea how old I am and that my presence is strictly for show? Everyone will know that, and it's demeaning to all your children when you do this. I will come, and I will bring a date to help you save face, though this will be the last time. Am I clear?"

"Do not get all high and mighty with me, son. You have benefited greatly from our position with the New York City elite, and do not forget it. Your mother and I have sacrificed for our children, and they can stand with their parents a couple of times a year as repayment."

Ah, there it was. Apparently, there was a log of sacrifices versus repayment, and we hadn't balanced the books yet. Not love, gratitude, not even kindness. We had to do this for more than a familial obligation—we had to do it for a tally sheet. Fine. I was sure my scorecard looked very different from theirs, but one day, I'd spell mine out for them and see if they could step off their pedestals to review it.

"Send me the invitation and order me two chicken dinners. I've got to go."

I didn't wait for a goodbye. I just hung up and shoved my gearshift into parked my car. *Fuck!* I slammed my hand onto the steering wheel, screaming at myself for allowing this to happen again. Who the fuck was I going to drag to this thing who wouldn't be a pain in my other ass cheek? There was only one person I wanted to take if she'd consent to go. My favorite sports phrase came to mind as I exited my car, and I mumbled under my breath, "If you don't shoot, you can't score."

Locking my car, I shifted my satchel, which caused me to spill some of my coffee on my pants. An audible sigh of disgust whooshed out of me. "God damn this day. Could it get any worse?" I bit my lip, knowing it could get worse. A lot worse.

"I'm concerned about you." A scratchy voice drifted over my shoulder.

"Hey, Mona. It's been a rocky morning. I'm hoping for a one-eighty by the time I walk through those doors. Wish me luck, hey?"

Her motherly smile warmed my heart and released a pound of cortisol. She was like a warm blanket on a fall day, like today. If only I'd had a mother like her, how much better would my life have been?

"I hope so, too. I'm not going to pray for you, though I'm sure it wouldn't hurt. Let go of whatever has your britches in a bunch and deal with it later. Those teachers and kids need you to focus and do your job to your full potential. Don't let them down with crap that won't matter tomorrow." She bumped my shoulder and hustled through the front door, which was held open by Vice Principal Schultz.

He gave me a big smile as he held the door for me as well. "Good morning, Dr. Pierce. I'm sorry I haven't made time to get to know you better. Could you join me at lunch for a little meet and greet in my office today?

Still feeling a little apprehensive about a possible hidden agenda, I agreed with a handshake and found the counseling room Eloise had assigned me on my way out the previous day. Now that I had a place where I could spread out and lock my research up at night, I had outfitted it with a coffee mug, a desk game for when I needed to think, and a stacking tray. I was a pretty simple guy, though my home desk was littered with photos of trips with friends and one picture of a golden retriever puppy that was too cute to remove from the frame. One day, when I settled down, I planned to have a dog like that. *When will that "one day" happen?*

I finished making my rounds outside each teacher's classroom and returned to type up my notes and organize them into modules that needed analysis. Before I knew it, I looked at my Shinola watch, a gift from Sarah on my fortieth birthday, and realized I was due in Schultz's office in five minutes. Running down to the teachers' lounge, I grabbed my lunch and another coffee, then dumped them all on Mona's desk with a raised finger, indicating that I'd be right back. Nature called.

"Welcome, Dr. Pierce." Schultz stood to shake my hand enthusiastically when I made it back to his office. He was a big guy with a small dad belly. A full head of auburn hair and a chiseled jaw gave glimpses of his former youth.

"Alex, please," I insisted with a smile.

"Alex, I noticed your athletic prowess on Field Day last week and was happy to hear you were an asset to your team. Excellent camaraderie is necessary for a cohesive workplace, and Hart Middle School is no exception." Why did I feel there was a big "but" coming down the line?

"Thank you. I used to play some football and rowed at my university many years ago. It was a lot easier to keep that workout regime than to stop and find a new one." I cleared my throat and continued, "Your team here is quite remarkable. I'm not sure if you've had a chance to speak with Eloise, but we don't have a lot of work to do here on a macro level. Where we will find success will be on the micro level, and that is where I'll be spending most of my time."

I wasn't exactly looking for his validation of my plan, though I felt it was important to have all senior staff onboard.

"I wanted you to know that I'm a little bit protective of my staff. They all work well together, and I'd hate to see any of them feel threatened by this project. With that said, do you see any glaring issues with our teachers?" This felt like a test, and any answer would have consequences, so I played midfield for this round of interrogation.

"No threats I assure you. That would never be my intention—I'm here strictly to offer my opinions and suggest paths to elevate everyone's game. Your administration gets the final call, though my reports will obviously be shared with my employer, the school board." He shifted in his chair, his face blank. *What's up his ass?*

"Terrific. Thanks for speaking candidly with me about your intentions, and don't be afraid to reach out to me with any assistance or concerns. Festering never has a happy ending." Why did I feel like I was being warned?

Charlie stood and rounded his desk. I stood, shook his firm grip again, and collected my trash. I supposed it was my turn to speak, so I smiled, maintaining strong eye contact, and bid him adieu.

The rest of the day included a meeting with Eloise to finalize the teacher survey and send it out before the teachers left for the day. The only unanswered question was whether Trudie would meet me after school or this evening. Since we only had ten minutes left on the clock, I casually walked down the hall toward her classroom, admiring the inspirational posters and display boxes.

I listened again as she gave her students their final instructions for the day and a reminder of tonight's homework until the bell rang. I watched as the kids bolted from their seats and ran to their lockers to make their buses in time. However, one student did not have the opportunity to follow his classmates.

Trudie stopped him as he skulked out the door.

"Delano, a word, please." He swiveled on his heels and marched back to her desk.

"Yes, Ms. Gonzales." His shoulders rounded as if he was in trouble. *Was he?*

She stood up from her desk and walked around to sit on the edge, which made her skirt slide up her thighs slightly. He most likely didn't notice, though I'm a man, and these little adjustments caught my eye.

"I didn't want to make a big deal about it in front of the class because I know you don't like attention, but I wanted you to know that I read your essay while you were working on today's work, and I liked what I saw." She placed her palm over the paper and then handed it back to him.

"This was decent work, and I know you'll make even more improvements as we go through the school year. I've circled words that are spelled incorrectly, so look them up and fix them. Also, make a list of these words, as they will become your personal vocabulary test along with the regular class words. You, Mr. Delano, are destined to be a great author." She stood and patted him on the shoulder for a job well done. He looked a little woozy and confused. Could this have been a turning point in his life? Given what I knew of him, I hoped so.

"Don't forget me when you make it big," she demanded and smiled again. "Run, don't miss your bus." He carefully took his paper and ran from the room, his eyes growing bigger with each step.

She chuckled. "I love it when I have a breakthrough moment with my kids," she said to herself, basking in the glow of success.

I watched her walk around her room, picking up bits of paper and tidying up books and shelves, before settling herself in her relaxation nook. She was at peace, and I didn't have the heart to steal that moment from her, so I waited like a voyeur.

The slant of the sun breaking through the trees to cut across her face was a stunning image. Slowly, I took my phone out of my pocket and captured this moment in time. I once learned that happiness was a continuum. The goal was to have more points of happiness over time, and looking at her made me happy.

The halls were clear, and so was my head. Trudie and I needed to talk and get to work.

"Hey there," I said, strolling toward the window. "Good day?" My smile reached my ears as she sat up in her seat and arched her back.

"Yeah. A good one." She hummed with a knowing smile. "I made headway with one of those high-risk kids you mentioned, and it felt so good. I hope he stays with the new program I put in place for him." She pushed herself to stand and then pushed her skirt down as well. *Too bad.*

Trudie filled me in on the program she put together for Delano, and I couldn't have been more impressed with her ability to pivot and deliver what each kid needed to succeed. If the school board could have cloned her, this school would be the national template for excellence in education.

"That's terrific. He's lucky to have you as a teacher." Being proud of her was easy; broaching my next topic was hard. "So, have you had a chance to look at your emails today?" I dipped my big toe into her shark-infested waters.

"Ugh. I knew I was forgetting to do something this afternoon. Was there something pressing I missed?" Rushing to her desk, she smashed her hip as she rounded the corner to open her laptop. "Ow!" I would have offered to rub it for her, though I liked my nose right where it was.

"I guess I should make a note to look at them more often. Sorry." She frowned.

"No worries. Do you have a preference? Meet now or after dinner?" I pressed. I wasn't leaving without her selecting one of those choices.

If you'd ever seen an animal backed into a corner, snarling and looking for an escape route, you'd understand exactly what Trudie was going through. Her hands pressed down on her skirt, and she licked her lips as if her mouth was the Sahara. The alpha in me loved watching her sweat it out, but I didn't consciously try to be a dick to anyone, so I made the first move.

"We really need to get a game plan together, and this survey needs your attention. It must go out tomorrow, and Eloise asked to see the final draft before she distributes it. Could you throw me a bone?" For her, I pouted and played helpless.

"Neither works. Truly, I'd love to help, but I have several essential errands and a visit to my mother. How about tomorrow? Or maybe just go with your gut?" Her mouth went sideways, and she squirmed in her chair.

"Counteroffer. We work in the car while you run your errands, and we reconvene at seven-thirty. I'm sure that would be enough time for your visit and dinner."

She slammed her computer down and started packing up her things, clicking off her flowery desk lamp, pulling the computer cord from the power strip, and pressing a button that raised the whiteboard back up into the ceiling. She offered me no comment when she pulled her cardigan back into place and shouldered her purse and computer bag. I may, however, have heard some mumblings of "jerk," "pompous," and "never changes" as she stormed to her classroom door and literally left me in the dark.

"Are you coming or not?" she hissed, with more mumbles of "waste of time," "slowing me down," and "hot lips distracting me." I could live with all of those, especially when I could plant my "hot lips" all over her magnificent body.

Chapter 28

TRUDIE

OST OF MY ERRANDS could have waited, except now I was forced to do them with a pompous asshole named Satan. Even when he was pissed off, he looked like he'd eat me for dinner and pound my ass for dessert. Couldn't he put a bag on his gorgeous head so I could think straight?

He looked like a stuffed sausage in my beat-up Honda hatchback. The backseat was filled with my yoga gear and the box of romance books I told my mom I'd drop off this week, so his ginormously long legs were pretzeled around each other in the passenger seat. *#Sorry/not sorry.*

Ignoring him when he asked how long it was to our first stop, I pulled into my regular drug store and threw the car into Park, almost sending his head through the windshield.

"Still working on mastering braking, I see." He smirked. *Fuck you!*

I gathered my purse off the floor by the window and ordered, "Stay, boy. Stay," while putting my hand up in his face like he was a bad dog ready to bolt.

He responded with begging arms and panting. If I was not so annoyed, I might have laughed. Instead, I kept my lips tight and slammed the door before heading into the pharmacy to purchase a few things on my list.

Fifteen minutes later I was back and he was on a phone call. I threw my bag in the back seat and carefully pulled out of the parking space, thinking about my next destination, the dry cleaner. When I arrived ten minutes later, he was still on his call, and with only a brief look, I could tell he wasn't pleased with whomever he was speaking to.

I picked up my winter coat and the awfully expensive brown suede skirt I intended to wear for parents' night, which had cost me a chunk of a month's paycheck last year. Even on sale, it was over three hundred dollars. I had seen a model wearing one months before with a cream blouse and thigh-high boots, (which I had to get too), and a long blue and brown tartan-styled vest. It just screamed, "I belong to you!"

When I returned to the car Alex, was screaming at his phone, "I told you'd I'd be there. Isn't it enough I have to give up a whole weekend to appease you?"

You know those awkward moments when you don't know whether to back away before you're discovered or feign ignorance and jump right into the situation? Being that it was my car, and we were on a tight schedule, I chose the latter. Consequences be damned.

His conversation ended with him roaring into his hands and then shoving them into his dark ruffled hair. This was uncharted territory for me. Usually, I was the overly dramatic one, and I felt a pang of pity for him. The person on the other end of that call seemed to have pushed all of Alex's buttons, and he had responded like a live wire.

I lifted the handle of the back door as softly as I could and hung my cleaning on the hook. By the time I was back in the car, he had relaxed his face back and had transformed back into the calm, cool, collected Dr. Pierce I knew so well.

I started to reach my hand out to him, giving him comfort and support, but then retracted it in fear that I was being presumptuous.

He grunted, "It's okay. I'm—okay." He grunted again and looked through his notepad for something, only to turn back to me with a grim twist to his mouth.

"That was my father." He pulled at his face and continued. "I've been told I need to attend a gala in New York City next weekend and 'no' wasn't an option." He looked like an eight-year-old being told he had to stay home and clean his room before he could go out and play with the rest of the kids.

"I see." I tried to empathize, though I'd never been to a gala and didn't understand why he didn't want to go.

Rearranging his large body to face me, he opened his palms in supplication.

"See, you don't see. You're probably thinking of guys in tuxedos and women in extravagant gowns. Rich food, great music, and dreamy dancing on a star-studded night." His voice dripped with sarcasm.

"In reality, the food will be tasteless and the only sounds I'll hear are a freight train pounding through my head as I say useless and privileged things to make my parents look good to the most entitled pricks that city ever produced. It's a fucking facade, Trudie."

My head buzzed. He had just let me into his inner sanctum and his issues with his family. Did he realize what he just did? My perfect monster was human, with scars and emotional baggage, and knew trauma like I did.

I didn't expect him to shove his door open and head toward the back of my car, but my inner savior took the helm, and I jumped out of the car after him.

"Hey." I touched his forearm gently. There weren't any words that I could speak that could calm him. I didn't know his world or his family or the issues he was facing. My touch was all I could offer. I pulled his arm to my hip and grabbed the other one to join it while I circled my own arms around his waist. I hugged him tightly, bringing him back from wherever his head had gone, re-anchoring him to earth. The pull of his hands on my waist gave me hope that the worst had passed.

I looked up, wanting to see that his black eyes had softened back to the glowing emerald that kept me awake at night. A ragged sigh left his body, and I could feel the outline of his erection pressing against my belly. Proximity was a problem for us, and we both knew it.

"Baby, you need to let go of me before I bend you over the back of your car and do naughty things to you," he said, jump-starting my breathing.

Following his instructions, I released my grip and stepped back, watching his eyes as I did.

"Alex, what just happened in there?" I asked, jerking my head toward the car. I needed to know how such a controlled person could lose his shit, especially with his father. Though I guess I wasn't one to talk about losing shit with a father, given my past. My dad never stopped giving my whole family reasons to lose their shit with him. I realized we may have more in common than I thought.

"Oh. That was me out of control. Pretty, wasn't it?"

"Is there anything I can do to help?" It was a risky move on my part, but I couldn't help him without putting my nose in his business.

"Unless you want to blow off all your plans next weekend and hop a plane to New York when school lets out, uh, no."

And there it was. Be a buffer between him and the debacle he called his family, saving him from a terrible weekend? If I could do it but said no, it would feel like I was leaving him without a safety net. Or I could go and be subjected to his intense stares that turned me into rubble, and his strong hands that had the power to guide me and teach me things my mind couldn't even put into words. Either way, the following Monday we would be back together, working side by side, either angry with each other or glowing from a weekend straight from a steamy romance novel. *Oh, let's face it, you're probably going to be arguing, either way, so live a little.*

As I toed the broken concrete, I said, "I'll do it...but I have rules you'll have to abide by. No exceptions." I pointed at his devilish face.

He was smart enough to give me some space even if his face looked like he wanted to devour me. He knew the potential of what this weekend could mean, and I didn't know whether to run or stick my ground.

With hands in his pockets, he cocked one hip to the side.

"How about you email me your terms, and we can review them later this week? We need to get going, and if I stand here undressing you with my eyes, we will undoubtedly make the evening news." I fumed as he walked back to the car, unrepentant.

ALEXANDER

I could see her through the rearview mirror as she stomped her foot like the brat she could be. This day had so many twists and turns that even Dorothy would have gotten lost if it had been the yellow brick road. But she would be mine the following weekend. She could patch a hole in the dike that was holding back the hemorrhaging of pain and hollowness that came from being manipulated and exploited by my parents for decades. She could deflect and reroute their hideous behavior and give me a reprieve. I knew that, like my parents, I was being selfish and exposing Trudie to the lion's den, but I needed her help and hoped she'd survive—that we'd survive.

I heard the car door open and looked up to see her face flushed and unsettled. The way she was biting her lip threatened to draw blood. Losing control looked delicious on her. I reached out to take her hands. "I promise you'll have a good time and that I'll behave myself," I offered, even if it was a blatant lie.

Her cocked head told me she knew better. She pulled her hand out of mine and started the car. I wanted to give her a minute to breathe, and then we'd get to work. This *had* been the intention initially, even if my subconscious had other plans.

I riffled through a few pages of the survey, picked a few questions I wasn't sure would sit well with her colleagues, and asked her opinions. She gave them and I recorded her answers studiously. Trudie had a keen way of making her point without being overtly pushy. *I could learn something from her.*

On her way back toward the school, Trudie stopped in front of a chocolate shop. I thought this would be a good stop for me, too, so I followed her in without comment.

Trudie instantly warmed up and smiled at the clerk. It was lovely to see the way she engaged people: warm, open, and sincere.

"Hi, Mac." She beamed.

"Hey, Trudie. Things good?" Mac pulled out a small pink box and waited for her order.

"Pretty good," she said, giving me an annoyed look. "I'll take my usual, but leave one coconut haystack out for me...and one for him too."

The shop had a retro feel with black and white checked flooring, frilly wire stands, and a couple of delicate bistro tables and chairs by the windows. The wall behind the clerk was mirrored and lined with jars of all sizes stuffed with myriad delicacies. As I walked the length of the cases, I saw they were piled high with pretty confections for all palates, but what caught my attention wasn't the candy, it was the miniature bumpy cakes at the end. I hadn't seen them in years.

Without preamble, I called out, "Those...please. I'll have four of those." Grown man or not, I licked my lips in anticipation of sinking my tongue into that creamy ridge on the top of the cake. It was the best part. Those cakes connected me to a time that saved me—when my parents forgot I was alive. My grandmother would steal me away and bring me to the bakery down the street from our penthouse and buy four cakes—just for me—and a glass of milk. I'd take my time tunneling my tongue through that white creamy ridge and then eat the rich chocolate cake as an after-thought. Grandmother would wait patiently until I was covered in chocolate with a contented smile on my face. She never berated me for not eating neatly or for being a little pig. She loved me in a way I'd never been loved before. Genuinely. Completely.

I felt the pull on my sleeve before I registered her soft voice. "Alex. Your order is ready." What a time warp. I didn't know how long I stared at those cakes, but obviously long enough that I needed to be pulled back from my reverie.

"Uh, yeah, thanks. I haven't had those since I was a kid. It took me back," I said, feeling sheepish.

"They have been a family favorite of ours as well." She smiled back.

We paid for our treats and went back to the car. During the ride back to the school, Trudie shared that her mother loved everything from Le Chocolate, especially their drinkable chocolate. When we arrived, it was clear she wanted me out of her car, and her lack of enthusiasm to spend more time together was evident in her parting words.

"I'm not sure when I'll be done, but I'll text you when I'm available. Are you sure you need me for this survey? You seem to have things well under control." *Nice try, Trudie.*

Shutting my eyes, I replied sternly, "Let me remind you we are a team. We need to review not just the questions but also the order, syntax, and scoring. You are the connection to your peers, not me."

I collected my things, preparing for an expedited exit, and I fixed her with a parting stare only a father figure could give. "I'll see you at seven-thirty sharp. Text me if we are meeting at your place or mine. Either way, we *will* be meeting this evening." Leaving her no time to argue, I jerked on the door handle, jumped out, and slammed the door just as she opened her mouth into an *O*. I'd be savoring that moment for a long time.

TRUDIE

The sun set so much earlier that it was hard to tell what time it was. I left my mom's sofa to look at the kitchen clock, only to realize it was ten after seven and that I would be late for my forced appointment with Alex. *Too bad, Al.*

The remaining chocolates sat on a plate with a doily. "It is the only way to serve such beautiful creations," my mom always said. We moved the stack of books I brought over to the ever-growing collection on her bookshelf. She had enough reading material to last through the end of the year, which was great because I wouldn't be able to read much for the next few months.

I returned to her modest home's family room to deliver the bad news.

"Sorry to end our playdate, Mom, but I have a meeting in twenty minutes, and I'm going to be late for it." I bent to kiss her cheek and crouched to give her a hug. "Don't eat all the rest of those candies tonight."

She smiled knowingly. "Yes, dear. I'll be good. Oh, and thanks again for dinner and the books. You're a gem, querida. Good luck at your meeting."

I grabbed my purse and dug around for my phone. There were two text messages and one voicemail. The first text was from Ruby, asking if we were still getting together next weekend, and the other was from Alex, asking if we were meeting at his place or mine. So bossy. *My house. Thirty minutes*, I shot back.

I settled back into my car and punched Ruby's number, but it went to voicemail, and I headed for home. I got there before Alex and ran into my bedroom to change into some yoga pants and get out of my boulder holder. Like a timer going off, so did my bra—eight o'clock meant no more bra. If Alex hadn't pushed himself into my evening, that was how it would be. Instead, I put on my comfy bra and figured I'd deal with the consequences.

The front door buzzer sounded, and I let him up. Looking through the peephole, I confirmed it was him. I was intrigued that he wasn't still wearing his suit.

Once through my door, his eyes locked onto my chest. Of course.

"I'm happy you made yourself comfortable. I couldn't get out of my suit fast enough," he quipped. He was dressed in some low-riding jeans with a black untucked T-shirt. I wouldn't have taken him for a Vans kind of guy, but his checked slip-ons knocked ten years off him.

"Take a seat at the table, and we can get started." I turned from getting water, but he wasn't where I directed him.

I set both glasses down on the side table and collected my school bag. Strategically, I sat on the couch as far from him as possible. I didn't trust myself, and I definitely didn't trust him.

Annoyance rolled over his face, and he moved next to me, putting his feet up on my ottoman to create a surface for his computer.

"You'll need to see my screen, so don't run away, little rabbit." I bared my teeth so he knew he had crossed the line. "Sorry, wrong scenario. I'll behave."

He behaved for two hours while we completed the survey and discussed a few ideas about the mentorship program he said he'd been discussing with Eloise.

"This is a fascinating idea. I just don't know which teachers would give more of their time to the school. They already stay for extracurricular activities, and many have their own families to get back home to." I sipped my water with one hand and twirled my hair with the other. Alex looked like he wanted to chuck his computer across the room so he could pounce on me.

ALEXANDER

She shifted in her seat to face me, her right knee making a number four and brushing up against my hip.

"The funding you're offering sounds unbelievable, except my concern is more for the teachers. How do you compensate them for lost personal time?"

Her pouty red lips killed my concentration—I was done.

I shut my computer, placed it on the end table, and shoved all my other paraphernalia into my satchel while speaking as clearly as my tongue would allow.

"You make a valid point. The joy and fulfillment of helping these kids wouldn't be compensation enough. What would you propose, Trudie?"

Her eyes looked off toward the window and the open curtains. It was late, and besides a flood light below us, the only light outside came from the stars. I pulled the elastic tie from her hair and let it fall to her shoulders. The auburn streaks throughout her thick locks were soft and delicate, just like her. Her breath caught in her chest when I tucked a strand behind her ear as she responded.

"Um, maybe additional time off when they need it." She struggled to stay focused, her eyes darting from my hand to my eyes.

"Perhaps. Continue." I was pressing her for answers her brain couldn't provide, and I didn't care. We may have been forced to work together, but I wasn't going to waste the time before and afterward not delving into her soft, curvy flesh.

"Um, Eloise has a cabin up north. Off—offer it to teachers for a weekend escape?" She gasped as I pulled her face to mine and sank my teeth into her bottom lip. Her groan of pleasure gave me encouragement, and I pulled her onto my lap before driving my tongue into her hot, wet mouth.

"Alex," she sighed into my mouth. God. I could hear things, but she seemed to be developing an accent each time I touched her.

It was late, and we both had to be at school early the next morning. I needed that night to last longer, but I couldn't finish what I wanted to start, so I threw her backward onto the cushion and yanked her yoga pants off her sexy body. My prize was finding no underwear, and I wasted no time crawling up her body to devour her mouth again before I planted a long, slow trail of kisses down to her tits. They deserved a few moments of punishment since they taunted me all evening. Tiny moans and gasps of pleasure excited me even further, and I had to calm myself because that night was only going to be about her. My dick would get its relief when I got home, just like all the other nights this past week.

"Please, Alex. I want you." Her throaty plea only served to remind me that her pussy was what I came for. Its sweet taste and the exotic smell drove me crazy, and I needed more now.

I continued kissing down her belly to the apex of her thighs. My nose pushed at her creases while my tongue licked everywhere but her clit.

"Do it! Please eat me," she cried. Her command aroused my sadistic tendencies, and I pulled away to look at her desperate face.

"Take off your bra," I snarled. She looked concerned at my change of tone. "Do it now."

She wasted no time crisscrossing her hands underneath the loose elastic and pulling her bra over her head. It landed across the room somewhere. She pleased me in a way that I couldn't express. It wasn't that she was a submissive; it was more that she let me be myself, to be her teacher and guide her through her sexual awakening, and that turned me on in so many ways.

"Good girl. Are you going to hold still for me?" I asked.

"Shit." She hissed, nodding, giving her consent.

I dipped my head back to her pussy and pushed her legs further apart with my shoulders. I wanted her open wide, and I wanted to see her face.

"Ahh, yes." I hadn't even touched her, and she knew what was coming next. She clenched her belly, and I could tell that, at that moment, she knew she belonged to me. "Please, Alex. Touch me."

"Don't move," I reminded her and flicked her clit with the tip of my tongue, which caused her to buck up against my face. I grimaced, shaking my head.

"I'm sorry. I, I couldn't help myself," she cried.

"You disappointed me. I'll give you one more opportunity to control yourself, or I'm going to leave."

I was being a prick, and I knew it. She needed to understand that I wasn't disappointed about her lack of control; I was disappointed that she was apologizing to me for her visceral response. She was allowed to respond however she needed, even if it went against my direction. I'm not her father and she was not a child.

"You are a grown woman, Trudie. Act like one, and don't apologize for your physical response." The trembling in her lips almost brought me to my knees. I had found a hot button that needed attention. I'd get back to that later. Her obedience was what I was after now.

"Ready?" I stared into the amber eyes glowing back at me. She wanted to please me, but I wanted her to please herself first.

"Yes. I can do this," she promised.

I nodded my approval and bent again to her dripping lips. The slight arch in her back and intense concentration on her face, as she tried to obey me, made me proud. I gathered her sweet bud between my teeth and pulled it into my mouth, where I could suck and lick it until she begged me to stop. I loved her pussy, and everything I did elicited her gratitude right up until she screamed, "I'm going to come! Please, Alex, don't stop. Please."

I did stop. I needed to see her face. She had to be reminded who was doing this to her. I wanted her to want me, to need me, to love me. This moment was deeply intense, and I wanted it to last longer.

"Alex, please, don't stop, I'm begging you!"

I licked my soaking wet mouth and dove back down to claim my prize. I pressed my hands down as hard as I could from this position to hold her in place. She couldn't keep still to save her life, and I loved it. I was the one who wrecked her, and she'd never forget it, even long after I was gone. *What the hell will I do when she's gone?*

I couldn't stop myself from licking her long after her shudders ceased. "You taste so fucking good. Are you sure I can't eat you every day? I'd love to have you on your desk." I winked as I slid up her body to slip my tongue into her mouth, letting her share in her wetness. We tasted so good together.

She blushed and threaded her fingers through my hair, tugging when she got to the back of my neck.

"You're insatiable. I'm sure my friends would love to walk by and see you dining on my crotch on my tiny desk. Your imagination supersedes the logistics." She giggled and pushed me back until I tumbled to the floor.

She grabbed her T-shirt and slid it back into place while I attempted to stand. My cock was banging on my jeans and cutting off the circulation to my feet, making it almost impossible to steady myself.

"Looks as though you have more pressing logistic issues at the moment," she noted with a smirk.

Chapter 29

TRUDIE

"RUBY. I'M DESPERATE. I'VE tried on everything that would be appropriate for a black tie gala, and it's a bust. Nothing. N-A-D-A! I'd ask to borrow something from you, but your ass is way smaller than mine and I'm two inches taller than you." Panic had set in, and I had three days to turn this bus around.

"What about renting one?"

She couldn't be serious. "You're kidding, right? It's not a costume party," I sniped.

"Who would know that you didn't pay a thousand dollars for your dress when you can rent it for a hundred and fifty bucks? I'm taking you after work. No one will be the wiser." Ruby's confidence far outshone mine, and I was going to have to trust her on this one, because what choice did I have? My measly paycheck didn't allow for anything expensive. I could swing the sky-high patent leather stilettos and maybe a simple satin purse. And forget the fancy jewelry. The fake stuff looks fake, and I'd rather go sans jewels than look tacky.

"Okay, fine. Then you're going to buy me dinner," I said, feeling petulant.

"My pleasure. And you won't be broke your whole life, Trudie. The future has big plans for you," she reassured me. "Did I mention I have a casting call tomorrow? I'm out of my mind excited. It's for a spokesperson for a lingerie company. That's all I know, except they wanted a sexy, throaty audition reel. God, please, make this dream come true for me." She clasped her hands in front of her and prayed.

"That's awesome, Ruby!" I must have screamed a little loud, given the look another customer gave me. "I know you'll get it. You're the perfect voice for something like that."

"Thank you, sweetie. I hope so. I'm losing patience living at home. My parents keep dropping the want ads on the breakfast table. Don't they know we use computers for such things?" She rolled her eyes.

I offered a distracted nod. "Doubtful. Listen, maybe now would be the time for me to set up an Only for Your Eyes page while my tits are still high and full? I could build my nest egg in a year or two and finally get an apartment where I don't trip on the couch every time I walk by it."

She laughed and we said our goodbyes. I had some kids to corral.

My lunch time was over, and Alex wanted to meet a couple of my high-risk students during my prep period. It was possible he would include them in this new program. I had to admit, it was pretty fantastic, if not overly optimistic in my opinion. Delano was a must for the program, and so was Ella. Her anxiety and OCD issues had kept her from making friends and trying new things. I'd found her in my R&R area several times since school started, and when I was able to sit with her two days ago, she reluctantly told me not to call her parents because they were out of town, again. Apparently, that was a common theme, and her "Nanbitch," as she referred to her nanny, wasn't keen on dealing with her "petty" issues. Sigh. Without an intervention, this kid was going to be on the fast train to a life of self-harm.

I had asked that Delano and Ella be excused from their fourth-period class today so we could interview them and explain what we intended to offer. I could only hope that they would see this as an opportunity, rather than a punishment.

Alex entered my classroom for the first time since school started, and to my delight, I didn't feel trapped. His smile warmed me, and since he couldn't fuck me on my desk as he fantasized last week, he opted to shake my hand. When his hands enveloped mine, it ignited my core. As we spoke about the kids we'd meet with shortly, he repeatedly stroked his thumb across my wrist and then underneath to my palm. He electrified me. How was a girl to concentrate?

I forced myself to look at where we were. My students were moments from entering the room and we needed a beat to calm down.

"I thought we could have our meeting in my R&R area. How do you feel about sitting on the floor?" I directed him to the comfy sitting area that has already been an asset to my kids.

"Perfect. Do I at least get a pillow for my old bones?" He imitated a wobbly old man as he stopped at the carpeted area.

I laughed in appreciation. "Sure, old man, I wouldn't want to be responsible for your parts breaking off," I mocked.

His closed eyes and pressed lips exuded exasperation. It was a good thing he was settled, because my students had just arrived.

"Hey, kids." I waved them over with a big inviting smile. "I'd like you to meet a colleague of mine, Dr. Alexander Pierce. He's helping to make your school a better place."

Alex was sitting on the floor in a Hart Middle School fleece pullover, which was the perfect touch for getting to the kids' level. Nothing that said, "I'm the one in charge."

"Hey, kids," he said. "Take a seat and let's get to know one another better."

I grabbed several big pillows for all of us and pushed the rocking chair out of the space. *There. Comfortable and safe.*

Alex jumped right in and explained what we had in mind.

"We're here to talk about what you as students can do when the system doesn't give you what you need." He gave them a minute to digest what he said, which also allowed him to assess their responses.

"We want to share another opportunity with you that has become available to the students at Hart. It's only for a select group that needs more of a step-up than other students. Ms. Gonzales and I, along with Principal Jackson, felt that several of our students could reach their potential if they had a helping hand to get there. I'll explain more about the program in just a minute. What I would like to know now is whether this program is acceptable to you. If you would take advantage of an opportunity that could change your future by giving you the tools and confidence to achieve anything you set your mind to? Think about that for a minute."

I looked to Alex hoping my telepathy was working. I wanted him to know that I liked how he had asked for their buy-in, even before they knew what he was talking about.

"Do you have any questions at this point?" Alex asked. They both looked uncertain.

Ella answered first. "I wouldn't mind a little help if it didn't involve my parents knowing."

Delano took his usual combative stance. "Why do you want me in this program? I'm doing just fine."

Alex looked at me then. I had a relationship with these kids, not him, so I picked up the baton and ran with it.

"I like how both of you are using your voice to share your concerns. That takes a lot of courage. I selected you because I've seen that when given the opportunity to grow and learn, you have both taken advantage of it, and you have benefited from your courage. This will be another opportunity to continue that growth in a way that will sustain you throughout your whole life. You won't be at Hart Middle School forever; you'll need more tools like confidence and self-worth to make it in the real world. I needed a leg up myself when I was your age, and I had a teacher who noticed when I struggled and stepped in to better my life. I want to pay it forward to both of you and to several other kids who we'll invite to be a part of this program."

They both nodded and relaxed their shoulders. It was time for Alex to sell them on his proposition.

He smiled again, but this time at me. I had revealed another nugget from my past, and I was sure he'd want to hear all the gory details later.

"Everyone needs a hand at some time—the rich, the poor, and everyone else in between. Let me tell you more about what the program entails, and then you can make your decision. You do not need to include your parents if you choose not to, but I would encourage you to reach out to them as soon as possible and let them know that you are advocating for yourself and that you are worth their time and attention."

Alex went on to explain that they would meet with teacher mentors to work through any academic or personal issues that may be holding them back. They could do this during their lunch period or after school. These four teacher mentors would provide them with alternative ways to handle their stress, such as meditation, exercise, music, and art. Ella loved that part the best.

"I'll be straight with you." Alex had his hands on his pretzeled knees and leaned in. He brought our pitch to a close with his stern face and flair for the dramatic. "This program demands your dedication and tenacity, as well as your determination to make a difference in your lives. The teachers who will be your mentors will be giving up their free time with their friends and family to make a difference in your life, and we expect that you will honor and respect that time and participate in this program 100 percent. We only have room for twelve kids, and I'm sure there are a hundred more who would love to be involved. You can answer now or tell us tomorrow, after you've had some time to think about whether you would like to be a part of this mentorship experiment. The good news is that if the program works, we will be able to offer it to you again next year and bring on another dozen kids. Heck, if things really go well, you might find yourself in a leadership position teaching other classmates what you've learned."

I got chills from his speech. We had never discussed offering these kids a leadership role, but Oh My God—brilliant!

"Dr. Pierce and I are going to step out of the room. Please take one of these packets and take a few minutes to read through it. It has all the information that we just discussed with the exception of the leadership program. I really believe in you kids, and I know this program can make a huge difference in your lives. Please make your decision thoughtfully."

I motioned to Alex with my head and we both left the room. These were the first two kids we'd spoken to, and we hoped that this conversation template would work well for the other ten.

I shut my classroom door and whisper-yelled into his shoulder, "That was amazing, you were amazing. A leadership program? Really? Brilliant, Alex! So inspired." I stepped back to do a little dance, then pulled myself together as I looked around the hallway, hoping no one had seen it. I didn't want to get my hopes up, but we rocked that meeting.

That devil smile crept up to Alex's eyes, which glowed dark green. It wasn't the first time I'd seen them glow like that, but I promised myself to work hard to get them to sparkle more often.

His chuckle was low and throaty, and I knew what that meant: he was pleased and excited.

"We are quite the team, Ms. Gonzales. You hit all the right emotional touch points, allowing me to do the easy part of explaining the program." He crossed his arms and took a wide stance, allowing his confidence to shine through.

We both let out huge sighs and waited. Three minutes later we went back into the classroom to see if they had any questions.

Delano postured himself like Alex had in the hallway, and Alex did so again, challenging the kid to say no. It was gutsy.

"I'm only saying yes, 'cuz Ms. Gonzales is straight with me. I don't know if all that other stuff is for me, but I'm willing try." His tough-guy approach was true to form, and Alex gave him his due.

I nodded quickly and Alex brought his feet together, holding his arms in place. "She told me you were a cool kid, and smart, too. Once you make a decision you stick with it. I respect that. During the process, if you aren't cool with what's going on or it gets too intense, find me and we'll talk it through. No skipping sessions, and most importantly, do not be disrespectful to your mentors."

Alex offered Delano his hand, and Delano did his best to break it. They stared each other down and an understanding was forged. This was a big win for our program, and hopefully one day Delano would see that as well. He left for his next class clutching his packet with his head held high.

Ella, on the other hand, had stress etched across her face. She danced from one foot to the other, not wanting to make eye contact with either of us. But she managed to use her voice and express her concern.

"I want to try the program, but I'm scared I won't be able to finish it. I'm not very good at completing things, and I don't want to disappoint either of you." I knew that took a lot of courage.

Alex took charge again, aware that I was too close to her pain.

"Both Ms. Gonzales and I were in your situation when we were young, and it took a long time—too long of a time—to see how limiting it was to be scared. The best part about this program is that you won't be doing it alone, and that you will have your own village of peers and mentors to shore you up and make sure you finish, and finish strong. You'll have to dig deep and learn to trust your instincts and abilities beyond what the world may tell you. That's what this program is about, and I hope you'll be a part of it. If you join this group, I will personally guarantee that you will not fail."

I was so crushing on this guy.

Ella looked at me like she wanted a hug, so I opened my arms and she stepped in to squeeze me tightly, as if she had already completed the program. There was hope there, and I could work with that alone. She signed her contract with only a single line of stress on her face. Hers would be a long road, maybe even longer than Delano's.

Alex and I met in the teachers' lounge after school to make notes about our conversation and to send emails to the other kids' teachers, arranging to get them in for interviews over the next two days. We wanted to lock down our candidates before the end of the week and before we left for New York.

I stood and stretched my hands over my head, did a forward fold to stretch out my legs and back, and then started packing up my things.

Alex stepped in front of me. "Where are you going?"

"Dress shopping. Some guy invited me to some debutant ball in a faraway land and I need a dress and a mani-pedi before I go." I pushed his chest with a finger, my smug expression challenging him to join in the repartee.

"What a bastard! Is he paying for all this girly shit that you're doing for his benefit, or are you stuck doling out the big bucks?"

"Well, now that you mention it, he is a bastard thinking I could afford nails, hair, and a dress—in less than a week, mind you." I ground my teeth in mock anger.

He bent back laughing in appreciation of my dramatic delivery. Then he perused the room, and seeing it was empty, he pulled the blinds closed and locked the door, trapping me like the predator he was.

"Uh, what do you think you're doing?"

His strong fingers dug into my hips as he pulled me up against him. "I love doing *this* with you. Your fake anger is so much funnier than your real anger. I may never take you seriously again." He laughed devilishly. "Reach around and take my wallet out of my pants." His breath was a whisper on my neck.

"Mmm. Yes, sir," I purred and felt his cock press against his slacks. He liked when I gave him control, and I shared the benefits.

He grabbed both of my ass cheeks and squeezed hard. "Do not tempt me, sweetheart. I'd be more than happy to fuck you on this table, and I'd be smiling every day for the rest of the year knowing what we did on it."

OMG! I would never eat in here again. I pushed back and caught my breath as I gave him his wallet. Five crisp hundred-dollar bills landed in my open purse, and I stared at them in amazement. Who walks around with that much money in their pocket? Alex, apparently.

"I meant to give you this last week, though someone distracted me. You shouldn't have to bear any financial strain to go to this event. I purchased your airfare, and you'll stay with me at my condo. Everything else will be paid for, so please don't stress over this." He kissed my temple and hummed in my ear. "Besides, I will completely enjoy seeing you in whatever you wear." His ass was the last thing I saw of him as he unlocked the door and waltzed out.

Between his lust and his cocky attitude around money, my nerve endings were shot. Dropping five large ones into my purse without so much as a blink didn't enter my realm of possibility. Had I planned this trip myself, it would have taken two years to save for, and that wouldn't have included a formal gown with all necessary accessories. The wealth Alex claimed his parents had seemed to extend to him as well. I hoped I wouldn't embarrass him. It's not that I wasn't cultured or didn't know which fork to use at a fine dining restaurant, it was just like what they say in the romance books I read—it was a long way from where I had started.

Cinderella Wishes was everything a girl could want in a store when going to the ball, and they had it all, including glass slippers, tiaras, and stoles. Ruby wouldn't divulge how she found this place, though I was sure she'd rented a gown here for one of the corporate gigs she had been to in the past.

"You can't keep wearing the same dress over and over again. People will talk," the shop owner insisted.

Ruby sped through the shop like she was a regular, and by the time I picked out two dresses, she already had ten in a changing room.

"Come on, bitch! Let's find a dress that would even fire up Satan a notch or two." There was no denying Ruby would make sure I looked fabulous. I just hoped my tatas didn't have to be halfway out of my dress to get the job done.

"Okay, give me a minute. So pushy," I hissed back at her.

The first dress I put on was bird's-egg blue. Its scalloped sleeves made me look like a small bird trying to fly from the nest. The skirt echoed this theme and was a hard no for me—a little bird, I was not.

The second dress was more promising, though the metallic red accent that ran down the back made it look like my tail was on fire. What was with this owner? Every dress she picked had a bird theme to it.

Finally, I tried on Ruby's first pick, and it was surprisingly stunning: an emerald green sheath that flared slightly at the waist, with a chiffon detail that ran from the right shoulder, down the deep V, through the front seam, and to the floor. It made me look taller, even statuesque, but not overly bodacious. And the light ruffle through my breasts offered a little modesty, though not much. My patent stilettos and the satin clutch I borrowed from my mom would work perfectly.

"Oh, Trudie!" Ruby sighed. "You look incredible in that dress. Turn around. Nice open-back. Satan will love that."

Open back? I looked into the three-way mirror and almost fell off the pedestal.

"Hell, no, Ruby! I could wear a backpack on my back, and you could still see too much skin." The divot in the back sat three inches above my crack, and that would not be the impression I wanted to make in front of his parents. "I'll look like a harlot."

Ruby's derisive snort put me on edge. This was how she went in for the kill, and sadly, today I was her prey.

"Don't be a prude, Trudie. This isn't the 1980s. It's 2022, for God's sake. Show some skin and be proud of that toned body of yours. You may never be able to wear anything like this in ten years. Work it, girl!"

The hell I won't.

Taking a long breath to center myself, I grabbed a pair of shoes, so I could walk around the store to get a feel for how this dress would work in real life—walking, sitting, and possibly bending. I felt like I was kicking the tires of a used car to be sure it wouldn't fall apart at an inopportune time.

"Can you imagine me reaching to shake someone's hand and my breast falling into their palm?" I cracked up, and Ruby fell over, gasping for breath, tears filling her eyes. Having made my point, I walked back to the changing room to try another option.

Forty minutes later, this episode of *Trudie's Runway Disasters* was over.

Ruby held up my best options side by side: the green chiffon that let my breasts and back breathe or the silver metallic longhair eyelash Uragiri lamé (at least that's what the tag said) that would tickle my nose all night, yet keep the girls under control in the halter top.

"I'm torn. The green would match Alex's eyes and is more classically shaped, but the silver is exotic and screams glamour, baby. Which one do you think of when you think of me?"

Of course, this was the moment the owner made her way back and thrust her opinion on me. "Sweetheart, both are spectacular on you. What is the event?" She pursed her lips and flipped her hand upward in front of her. *Maybe her opinion could help me decide?*

"A New York gala," I responded.

"A New York gala? Honey, you need to make a statement. Have you met this crowd before?" I ducked my head down to my chest in answer to her question. "Do you need to impress anyone?" I pursed my lips and kept my eyes on the floor.

"I see. Well, this is a conundrum, isn't it?" she said to herself. She tapped her chin and made to speak, but then shook her head no.

"I've been doing this a long time, sweetie, and my gut is rarely wrong. It sounds like this event has a lot riding on it, and hopefully, you'll come back and try another gown for a different occasion. But I'd stick with the emerald green, especially since you're meeting his parents and other important people. Glitz is for not giving a shit, and by the way you're hesitating, you don't have room for error."

She walked away, leaving Ruby and me to sort through what she had said. In the end, I chose the green dress, and the sweet woman didn't charge me for the extra two days I'd need it while traveling. Two hundred dollars later, I had a stunning dress in a simple black vinyl bag with the company logo, and I walked to my car to stow my package, exhausted.

Ruby hugged me and grabbed my arm, leading me down the street. We had mani-pedi appointments in an hour, and I was starving.

ALEXANDER

Sarah had been on my case all week about who I was bringing to the gala, and I refused to entertain her curiosity. She might be the angel of the family, but given enough time and effort, she would exploit every detail and nuance to her benefit. Trudie didn't need to be her plaything.

I ordered a town car to deliver us to the airport from her apartment and another to take us from JFK to my condo in Manhattan. I discovered that Trudie had never been to New York City before, and I wanted to see the sights through her eyes for the first time. I could help her check off so many things on her bucket list this weekend; however, most would have to wait until we had more time. Our Friday and Saturday nights were spoken for, but we did have time to see a Broadway matinee on Saturday, or we could go to MoMA or Central Park on Sunday before flying home later that evening. Between events, we would be in my bed, which was non-negotiable. I'd had my housekeeper make some breakfasts and load the refrigerator with a variety of beverages and snacks. I didn't want to waste a moment of our time doing domestic things. There would be no brunching with the family or boat rides on anyone's yacht. They got Saturday night, and that was it.

I had the driver pick me up first and then head over to Trudie's. When I went upstairs to collect her, she was in a complete panic.

"Alex! I can't find my sunglasses, my brush, or my purse. Where did I put my purse?" Manic would have been a conservative word to describe her, but bringing that up would stir the pot. Instead, I walked up to her deeply contorted face and kissed her, long and deep. My hands threaded into her hair, and when our kiss ended, I pulled her sunglasses off her head.

"Better, baby?" I asked, squeezing her ass. "Your purse is on the floor by the door." I knew this because I had almost tripped on it when I entered. Her place was way too small.

She rushed to her purse, threw it on the counter, and unloaded everything. Mary Poppins had nothing on this woman. I was surprised she didn't pull out pillows, a hairdryer, and a beanbag chair so she could be comfortable anywhere she went. The good news was that she found her brush, her lip balm, her lost grocery list, and her birth control pills. *Thank God for those.*

"Ready now, sweetheart?"

She spun around and gave me the stink eye. "Listen, Buster, the only thing keeping me from canceling this shindig is that I already rented the dress. Grab my rolling bag, and I'll figure out what else I need to stuff in there that won't pass security."

Like a bona fide husband, I rattled off a parting checklist.

"Keys? Lights? Unplug anything that might burn the place down. Deposit the kids at grandma's house?" That got her attention.

"You're pushing your luck, buster. Yeah, I have it all, and the kids are duct-taped in the closet until we get back, not at my mom's house." I loved her smart wit and her ability to think on her feet. She was going to need it that weekend.

"Good girl! I'll have the neighbor feed and water them twice a day. *Let's go*!" I may have whined a little, or a lot, but time was up.

One minute later we exited the building to our waiting car.

"You did put your ID back in your purse, right?" She loved it when I rode her.

"Yes, Daddy. I did." I gave her a hard swat as she bent over to get in the car. "Ouch!"

"I have all sorts of punishments for bad little girls. Behave yourself," I growled behind her shoulder as I pressed her ass into the town car and slid in next to her. "Starting with my hand right here."

Her mouth fell open in what appeared to be shock. Why? I had no idea. She knew what I was like, and this weekend would be no different. She needed to learn that I was in charge when she was with me. Not that she didn't have a voice, but that I would make sure her pleasure was as great as her devotion to me. The people we would be mingling with were ruthless once they latched onto something noteworthy. Reputations would be made and broken by minuscule fissures in our story. Trudie needed to listen and abide by my instructions to prevent a catastrophe, not only for herself but for my family.

Also, her wraparound sweater dress was the perfect travel apparel for my purposes.

We landed at JFK just after seven-thirty. Our reservation at Chin Chin's was in thirty minutes—thank goodness my driver was out front as soon as we walked through the sliding glass doors. I installed Trudie in the back seat with my right hand palming her ass.

"I'll be there in a minute. Pull your panties off," I growled.

A few moments later, after giving my driver some instructions, he opened my door, and I joined my little vixen for what would surely be the hottest trip back into Manhattan I'd ever taken. As per my instructions, the driver had raised the divider, and soft jazz permeated the backseat.

After removing my suit coat, I dropped to my knees between her already wet thighs.

"Christ, Trudie. You're so wet. Is this all for me?" I wasn't sure to whom I was speaking, but I was three seconds from enjoying that evening's appetizer.

Her head lolled on the headrest as she licked her lips, and her chest heaved in anticipation as she waited for me to eat her pussy.

"Alex. Please. The driver will hear us," she pleaded.

I gave her a devious look as I spread her pink folds. "Be quiet then."

My flattened tongue ran along her pussy, causing her to squirm and moan. I reached under her thighs and locked them with my arms. I didn't have time to play games, and she wasn't slipping away from me. Her red bud throbbed, beckoning me to suck it, and I obeyed. My second pass over her clit had her ass clenching and pressing up as high as I'd let her go. She would come only when I allowed it. We had twenty-five minutes, and I planned to hold off her orgasm until moments before we left the car. Patience would be tonight's lesson, and what better way was there to teach it than for me to maintain complete control?

"Hold still, baby. I'll give you what you want. Be patient." I flicked her clit and pressed kisses all around her labia, tempting her to come. But I wasn't going to allow it.

"Please. I want to come. I-I need to come, Alex. Do it now." Her begging only made me harder and increased my resolve to make her wait.

I pulled back to take all of her in. Perspiration beaded on her forehead; desperation was written all over her face. Her beautiful pouty lips were so like the ones between her thighs, and at that moment, I felt a deep appreciation of womankind. I'd been with several women, mostly those from wealthy and powerful families, and a few who I paid to accompany me on my exploration of my darker side. Trudie was neither of those. She was authentic, powerful, and submissive. Demanding in one breath and pleading in the next. She vexed me, and she challenged me. And now I challenged her.

I ran my hands lightly up the insides of her thighs and firmly on the outside—a combination of teasing and controlling that confused her body and made her more aroused. Her quick breaths and moans confirmed my theory, and I leaned forward to torture her breasts while her pussy dripped even more.

Each of Trudie's breasts had its own personality. The left was responsive, and my touch on it elicited a purring sound from her beautiful mouth. The right was a direct line to her needy core. I rewarded her by rubbing her bud in slow circles with my finger. She arched abruptly, and I pulled back before she could come. She mumbled in delirium, her need escalating, making her desperate to climax.

Ten more minutes. She could wait. She had to wait.

I moved onto the seat and unzipped my pants quickly, pulling them down only enough for my cock to jut out, dripping with my pre-cum. Trudie's eyes went wide and locked onto it, as she wet her lips in hopes of tasting me.

"Hungry, baby?" I purred.

"Oh, yes. Please, can I taste you?" Her submission and desire made my cock even harder.

She drove her face down onto my lap, pulling me into her hot mouth and devouring my crown. She was an animal as she grabbed the back of my legs to give her leverage so she could shove my cock down her tight throat. She bobbed and sucked, and I couldn't hold back any longer. My hot cords of cum shot down her throat, and like the good girl she was, she swallowed every bit. She didn't stop until I pulled her up and shoved my tongue down her throat, battling hers until she relaxed.

Our time was running short, and my woman needed her reward. I stuffed my dick back in my pants and resumed my position between her legs. One last look at her eyes, and I knew she'd do anything I asked.

"Scream for me, sweetheart. Let my driver and all of New York know what I did to you." My tongue flicked her clit several times, and then I pulled and nipped at it until she couldn't breathe.

"Please, Al-ex. Make. Me. Come." Her wish was my command. I inserted two fingers into her and found that spot that drove her wild.

"Jesus Christ, Alex! I'm coming. I'm coming." Her explosive orgasm and shouts of pleasure boosted my already big ego to the extreme. I was a good lover, even described as great by some, but this time I felt proud. Proud, perhaps because she was becoming mine. I gave her all of me, and she gave herself back. This thing we had was foreign to me, even scary at times. It had been three years since I wanted to crack open the door to love, and Trudie had pushed her way through without my even knowing it. What a gift.

We crossed the bridge into Manhattan, and it occurred to me that I had robbed Trudie of the experience of taking in the sights while I selfishly devoured her pussy. I'd make it up to her the next day. I had a few surprises I hoped would make her feel special and help her appreciate the Big Apple.

The two minutes it took to arrive at the restaurant gave us time to straighten ourselves. Fred, my driver, had probably heard every detail of our playtime. I didn't care. It wasn't the first time, and certainly wouldn't be the last.

I brushed a curl behind Trudie's ear. They were so tiny and cute. "You astound me, Ms. Gonzales." Her blush said it all.

Not to be outdone, she replied, "And you, Dr. Alexander Pierce, wreck me every time." She giggled.

"Well, if you didn't always tempt me and challenge my authority, I wouldn't have to take advantage of you in taboo places."

"Well, whatever."

It was my turn to laugh. She was adorable.

We entered the restaurant and were greeted by Tommy, the owner.

"Welcome, Dr. Pierce. Your preferred booth is waiting for you." He smiled and bowed his head in respect.

"Thank you, Tommy. I can always count on you to accommodate me." We shook hands, and I guided Trudie through the throngs of people waiting to be seated. Red vinyl circular booths dotted the restaurant, but the stereotypical Chinese astrological placemats were not part of the decor. Instead, ceramic plates with highly adorned vignettes of Chinese culture in blue and white decorated the white, pressed linens.

A waiter took our drink orders, and I added pot stickers as an appetizer.

Trudie looked around the crowded room, noticing and commenting on everything. I hadn't realized how observant she was. She pointed out details I'd never noticed, and I'd been coming here for twenty years.

I leaned into her shoulder, and she shivered.

"Do you like it here? May I order for you?"

She turned to me, smiling. Her lips were still red from the bruising I had caused them in the car, and her hair was tousled, some of the curls tucked haphazardly behind her ears. She took my breath away.

She softly pressed her lips to mine, licking my lower lip as she pulled back. "You can do anything you want for me." Spoken like a true femme fatale. This could be a very long or very short dinner based on responses like that. I wanted her everywhere, but I needed to be patient.

"Behave yourself. We have plenty of time," I scolded.

The evening was going to be long, and I didn't care if she was rested or not. I would cram as much as possible into every day to have her enjoy this weekend, and if we didn't sleep at all, I was prepared to suffer the consequences.

Chapter 30

ALEXANDER

I'D NEVER TAKEN THE time to slow down and see the world through a child's eyes, but after watching Trudie today frolicking, *yes frolicking*, through the Belvedere Castle, I had a new reason to give it a chance. She was animated and engrossed in reading all the plaques and information placards along every wall and door. When we finally stopped to look at the Belvedere family painting, she all but begged me to sit down and study it. I promised her we'd go back another time since our lunch reservation was imminent and we needed to leave.

The summer sun sliced through the trees, and in the dappled light, Trudie's face morphed from sensual to childlike through every variation in between. Effervescent was the only way I could describe her and the energy she gave off.

My hands never left her body—they were at her back or on her shoulders, or we were swinging our clasped hands like young lovers. I wanted her in a way I had never wanted anyone else, including my ex-fiancée. Sheila hadn't liked public displays of affection. She said it was juvenile and with our social status, we would be mocked. Although I was hardly groping her, a small kiss or my hand on her back would make her uncomfortable, so I all but stopped touching her outside our bedroom.

Trudie didn't ask for or initiate affection, but when I did show it, she melted into me and looked at me with complete trust and wantonness. She loved my lessons, and now she was going to get another.

We arrived on time to Tavern on the Green, and again I took in the familiar surroundings with fresh eyes.

"Wow. This place is posh. Did you see those chandeliers with the flying brass horses? So cool." Her eyes were as big as the charger plates already set on the table. I hadn't looked at anything specific about this place since I was a child when we were dragged here for luncheons with my mom or after tennis camp as a "treat." Quite frankly, a hotdog from a street vendor would have been the real treat.

I chuckled as I watched her do a slow spin, taking in all the classic architecture set with modern nouveau upholstery. The Tavern had undergone several transformations over the years, this last one reflecting haute couture.

"It's very charming, isn't it?" I kissed the top of her head and threaded my large hand through her delicate one to pull her toward our booth. I slid in beside her, not wanting to lose our connection. Touching her calmed me, something I desperately needed that weekend.

We had just placed our order when my phone buzzed. I hoped it had nothing to do with tonight or wasn't more demands from my parents. But it was someone else with a demand—Sheila Lancaster. I cringed.

"What's wrong?" Trudie asked. She placed her hand on my arm for comfort.

Did I want to ruin our day by sharing sad stories of my fucked up almost wedding? I may have alluded to a bad breakup before, but would it affect this weekend if Trudie knew the details? *Maybe.* It would have to wait. This weekend was about us and figuring out if we had more than physical chemistry, even though I had no idea at this point if I even wanted to forge a relationship beyond that. The last one almost killed me.

I cleared my throat. "Nothing. Just something out of my control." *Really out of my control.*

"Can I help?" Her brows knitted with concern.

I took her hands in mine under the table and gave them a gentle squeeze. "You already are."

She smiled and pressed her lips to mine. I returned her gesture and traced her lips with my tongue, desperate to penetrate her mouth with my own.

The clearing of a voice reeled me back to reality.

"I'm sorry, I—I, my timing is terrible. I'll just come back for your order." Our waitress started to scurry away.

Trudie pulled back quickly. "No, wait. It's okay. We can order." Trudie gave the waitress her big smile, which dissolved her wariness.

Knowing the menu well, I took charge and ordered a few things for us to share. The burrata and the lump crab cake were spectacular. and if Trudie agreed, we would split the charred filet mignon salad.

My hands were itching to touch her again. I felt our legs brush each other and saw her creamy thighs crossed prettily under the table. That wouldn't do. I let my fingers trace the inside of her crossed leg, and she pulled it away just as I planned, allowing me access to palm her mound over her linen shorts. Her gasp left me instantly hard and uncomfortable.

Her head whipped to look at me. "What are you doing? We're in a fancy restaurant," she hissed.

"Mmm," I hummed throatily. "I'm having an appetizer." I stared her down and watched her pupils dilate.

I pushed the flimsy fabric of her shorts to the side and then dipped my finger under her lace panties. She was soaked, and my cock grew even more.

"Look at you, little girl. Ready for me already?" I whispered at the shell of her ear, licking it once for effect.

She hummed, enjoying the sensation of my fingers playing with her clit.

I pushed her to use her voice. "Answer me. Tell me what you want." Her head fell back to the booth, and she squirmed on the seat. She'd leave a wet spot to be sure, and I planned to look for it when we left.

"Yes...for you. I can't believe I'm saying this, but make me come, Alex. Please." My resolve to not pull her out of her seat and drag her to the bathroom to fuck her was wearing very thin. Our booth was screened by palms, but it wasn't very secluded. If someone wanted to see us, they could.

It was time to teach her the subtle art of control in public. This skill would serve her well later that night when a room full of idiots said stupid shit to her face.

"Listen carefully, baby. Keep your face relaxed and your head forward. Do not let anything leave your mouth, except to thank me when you come. Understand? Not a word."

I looked around the room to see if anyone was currently looking our way. We only had a few minutes before our food would arrive, and I wanted her languid and amenable to some hard fucking when we got back home.

Her quick pants of pleasure had me concerned this lesson would be too difficult, but I decided to go ahead anyway.

"Yes. Okay," she promised.

I kissed her softly as I pinched her clit, and she moaned into my mouth. Time was running out, but she was close.

"Listen very carefully. You will meet people tonight who will try to get a reaction out of you. You will be impervious to their taunts. You will only think about this lesson, right now. I want to protect you from these vicious self-centered trolls. You can't show any signs of distress. Understand?" I watched her face for any sign of her control cracking

Trudie lifted her head and focused on something across the room while spreading her wet thighs to give me more room. I inserted a second finger and began pumping in and out of her soaking pussy in earnest. She gulped and hummed and kept her mouth tightly closed as instructed. Her hips raised and lowered until she was on the precipice of her orgasm, and then she bucked up against my hand and grabbed my head, planting a deep, long, moaning kiss on my mouth as she came. Fuck, she was incredible.

I pumped slowly into her several more times, letting her enjoy her orgasm fully. When I pulled out of her, I also decided to put on a show. I scooped out her sweet juices onto my fingers and placed both in my mouth, only to do it again two more times. I wasn't letting her cum go to waste. Her mouth dropped open, and the tip of her tongue ran along her bottom lip.

"Did you like that, baby?" I kissed her lips, giving her a small taste of her essence. I dipped my fingers in one last time, swirling them over her swollen bud.

"Christ, Alex. Thank you. That was unbelievable. So hot." She moaned again, running her hand down my thigh. Her delirium was hot.

"Open," I demanded, and she complied, and I slipped my juicy fingers into her mouth so she could suck her own pleasure. A new sound emitted from her throat, and I almost came in my pants.

"Fuck, Trudie. You are as exquisite as you are delicious." And I kissed her again.

Not a minute later, the waitress arrived with our *paid* appetizers (as opposed to the appetizer I had just had, compliments of my delectable vixen). She set our plates down and left immediately. I had no idea if she saw anything, but I didn't give a fuck. She'd be tipped handsomely for her discretion.

We ate our meals, chatting about my undergraduate work and my start in psychology. She seemed mesmerized as I told her about some of the experiments I was assigned and some that I designed.

I paid the bill and headed out of the restaurant to a light breeze and a horse-drawn carriage waiting for us to board.

"Up you go, milady." Like a trained valet, I swept my arm toward the carriage, inviting her to go up the steps. As I took her hand, she blushed.

"You're too kind, sir." She planted a chaste kiss on my cheek.

Our trip around the park was simple and comfortable, and we spent the time sharing stories of our youth. There were a few moments when Trudie's face looked pinched, but I didn't press her. She had made several comments since I'd known her regarding her dad. I wanted to know what kind of number he had pulled on her to make her so mercurial. Maybe it was about why she bolted out of the motel in California.

"Trudie, can I ask you something?" Our hands were together on my lap, resting on my patiently waiting dick.

She tilted her head, and the hazel in her eyes turned amber.

"Sure. What is it?" she asked tentatively.

"I'm not trying to start anything, but I've been confused about something. I thought it would be better to ask once you know me better. I hope you'll help me understand what happened back in California. We—I had just had the most incredible experience of my life, and then you got mad and threw me out of your room. I didn't know whether I hurt you, or if I had said something that pissed you off, or if it was some sort of trigger that made you leave that way." I kissed the back of the hand that I was holding.

"Please tell me what happened," I begged.

Her knee bounced, and she wouldn't look back at me. I knew she wouldn't just blurt it all out, though I hoped she'd feel comfortable enough with me to at least give me a clue. I wasn't exactly forthcoming about my text with Sheila, so that made me even more of an ass to expect the truth from her.

She pulled a deep breath in and exhaled one equally as long out.

"When I was young," she began.

"My dad used to make lots of promises to me and my brothers and almost never kept them. It wasn't that he didn't want to, I suppose, but he wasn't home to fulfill them. It was his job that was the problem. He'd make a promise, and then he'd get the call. He was a CAT adjuster. A catastrophic insurance adjuster. I hated his phone. Every time that freakin' thing went off, so did my dad. Sometimes he would leave for a couple of days, other times a few weeks. Those times weren't the worst of it, though. The trips took him away from our family for months, or even a year. After the planes hit the Twin Towers on 9/11, he was called out to inspect the damage. I found out much later that this was his first catastrophic insurance adjustment job in his new career and my brothers and I didn't see him for almost two years. I was only six years old, but when he finally came home I could tell he was a changed man."

This was not where I thought this story would go. "Trudie, you don't have to continue if you don't want to. I had no idea what you and your family went through." I held her tightly and kissed her hair. I knew there was a reason I felt so protective over her, and now I knew why. She was traumatized by her father leaving so long and so often. If things with us didn't work out, it would just add fuel to the already burning fire within her.

"Alex, you don't understand. He yelled at us like we ruined his life. He emotionally abused my mom, telling her she was a miserable wife and housekeeper. Sometimes he would take a perfectly set table and start smashing dishes just to watch us cower and then have to clean it up to his satisfaction. It was sick and twisted. He wasn't the man who was my daddy before he started that job. My whole family suffered from it, and we still feel the effects of his abuse."

She held on to me like a lifeline and spoke as if giving a confession. "How does a six-year-old remember so vividly the changes in someone's personality, and yet an adult can't pick up a clue when someone's feelings are hurt? I just don't get it." Anger and confusion dripped off her tongue.

She needed answers, and I hoped mine would hit the right chord.

"Sweetheart, young children don't have the developmental skills to sustain long-term memories clearly. After some time, their early memories get mottled and fuzzy. It's the repetitive occurrences that establish our memories, and I'm afraid it caused you some emotional damage."

Her face was ashen and full of despair. I could feel her falling through time, trying to remember the exact moment her life spun out of her control. I was devastated for her.

"Baby. Trudie. None of that was your fault. Honestly, it seems like it wasn't his fault, either. I have a friend in Florida who does the same job, and he lost his family early on in his career. It was too much for all of them to endure."

She sat up abruptly, pain streaking across her face.

"See! That's exactly what I was talking about. I know it wasn't my fault, but punishing us for some reason, was his fault." She screamed into her hands. "Alex, it was shitty he had to leave, I'll give you that, but it was his decision to come home like a wrecking ball and tear into all of us. You have no idea what we had to do to keep him calm and happy when he finally walked back through the door. Imagine a train outside your window, and you watch it coming at your door faster and faster until it smacks into you, leaving you torn to shreds."

She openly wept. She was letting go, and she was trusting me with her pain. And now by articulating it completely and sharing it with a trusted person, she was beginning to heal her inner wounds.

I didn't want to act like her psychologist now. What I should be, wanted to be, was her boyfriend. A lover wouldn't care that much, but a boyfriend? Yeah.

Anything I said at this moment wouldn't be enough. She needed to process what she had told me and what I had explained to her. I kissed her wet cheeks, her eyes, then her red puffy lips, and said, "How frightening for you." I validated her fears and her pain—that's all I could do.

TRUDIE

He cupped my face and looked deeply into my tearful eyes. "I've got you. Let it all go, baby." And I did.

Alex slid me over his lap and held me like a baby while I cried my eyes out over childhood memories that had become a shroud over my life instead of a beautiful tapestry. There was so much more to this story, yet it didn't matter at that moment. Alex gave me space to work out the trauma in my head. He wasn't who I thought he was. His capacity for compassion seemed endless, and I needed every ounce of it. Only when I lifted my head from his shoulder did he speak.

He threaded his fingers through my hair, combing it off my dampened face and tucking the curls behind my ear as a real boyfriend would. That was something to think about another day.

Our foreheads touched, and we breathed in each other's life force, settling our hearts into one rhythm. "Thank you." I cupped his cheeks gently with my thumb brushing against his stubble and enjoyed the intimacy of the moment.

Moments later, our eyes met, and I knew I had to answer his question. He had waited long enough, and after my breakdown, it was even more important for him to understand where my insecurities lay.

He took a breath as if to start speaking, but I cut him off.

"Wait. Please let me finish. I never answered you, and you deserve to know why I left so abruptly." I gulped, steadying myself, knowing that my answer might be too much for him to deal with. I knew I was one card shy of a full deck on most days—on that day, though, I had been missing more like a whole suit.

"That night at the motel, you obliterated any ideas I had about what sex could be. You handled me in a way that no one had ever had. Your command over me was exhilarating but also frightening. You'd have to see that evening through my lens to appreciate how overwhelming what we did was. Think about my past and then think about the last thing you said: 'You will be the death of me, vixen. Don't you ever leave class before I dismiss you. Do you hear me?'

"You sounded just like my father—demanding compliance without hearing my side. You treated me like he did when he wasn't happy with me, and my brain exploded. I didn't want that kind of relationship again. We'd just had mind-altering sex, but suddenly, none of it made sense anymore."

Revisiting that night had me out of breath and, damn it, fragile. I hated feeling fragile.

Alex sat back, deflated, scrubbing his face and shaking his head.

"Jesus Christ, Trudie. It's all starting to make sense. I wasn't even out of you before I opened my big fat mouth. I—I just thought we were still in a role-play—I didn't know you had already left the scene." He made a growling sound that made my heart weep.

He took my shoulders and turned me toward him, his face desperate for something, but I didn't know what.

"I'm a complete asshole. I didn't read the situation properly. Being with you drives me out of my mind. I feel like a man possessed when I'm in you. My ability to reason was for shit. I swear to God, Trudie, I wouldn't never hurt you or leave you like your father did. I respect you too much. Please, forgive me."

I shuddered, thinking about him leaving me. He couldn't. I had given him parts of me I'd never given anyone. I was naive, thinking I could open my soul to him and not become attached. When we've spent time alone—not in bed—I was able to see a future for us. If I only knew whether he wanted one with me, too.

I rubbed my eyes, trying to see things clearly—literally and figuratively.

"I believe you, Alex, and I want to forgive you, but I just need more time with you. We need to learn to trust each other. I know you had a tough breakup we haven't even discussed yet. We've just scraped the top layer of getting to know one another. And I want to be sure that's even what you want. Do you want to be in a relationship with me?"

I needed to get to the core of what we were playing at. The sex was undeniably out of this world. Attraction wasn't our problem. But we worked together. Bottom line: if we didn't agree on what this thing between us was, we would never be able to finish the project, and I wouldn't survive it. If I got fired for cavorting with the consultant, I'd be penniless, while he would just go on to the next job. The only thing that would keep me from ending this whole thing right now was if he could think past his dick and say he wanted more between us.

His forehead wrinkled—you could see his mind flipping through all his options. The fact that he didn't jump at the chance to tell me he wanted me was enough of an answer for me.

"Driver! Stop the carriage!" I bellowed.

"Wait, what are you doing?" Alex asked, finally deciding to engage.

The carriage slowed to a halt, and I grabbed my purse. The driver rushed over to help me down the awkward steps, and Alex followed clumsily. I looked around for a way to leave the park, all but running from another disappointment in my life. I was done with this whole charade. One minute I was on a high, the next I was yesterday's news. I was tired of it.

"Where the hell do you think you're going? You're running again when you should be talking with me." He was out of breath when he caught up with me at a crosswalk.

My gut was on fire, and if provoked once more, I would erupt. I didn't care where I was going. All I wanted to do was be alone and have a quiet, simple life. My constitution wasn't meant for relationships. They made me nauseous, disoriented, and volatile.

When the signal changed, I kept walking, and he kept following.

"You don't know where you're going!" he yelled after me.

I didn't care. I wasn't interested in his games anymore. The proverbial gerbils in my brain were spinning themselves to death. Exhausted after blocks of speed walking, I collapsed onto a bench.

I just wanted to disappear, and what better place to do that than in a monstrous city that didn't care.

I'm not sure how long I sat there. The sounds were deafening and the stale smell of the sewer poisoned my nostrils. I was thirsty and so very tired. It finally occurred to me now why I spent so long with Sam. He didn't overly engage any of my senses or ask to much of me. He just loved the person I wanted to show him and didn't dig any deeper. Very boring, very dependable, very nonthreatening.

Maybe I still needed that. Maybe he would take me back, and I could live that simple, safe life I felt I needed. I closed my tired eyes, and moments later, I felt him. Alex. I could detect his fresh scent and his magnetism. I opened my eyes to his warm ones. He handed me a bottle of water like he had read my mind. I took several sips and capped it off, before dropping my hands to my lap. We both stared at them—a focal point for our fears. We were each waiting for the other to speak.

He broke first. "You scare me," he whispered. "You stir up so many emotions in my head and in my heart, and I'm scared of every one of them." He brushed my hair back from my eyes so he could see me clearly.

I was silent. Empty. My brain hurt.

He put his arms around me and held me tightly. I let him. I was too tired to fight. He kissed me—small drops of affection all over my forehead, ears, and neck. I could sense that he was hurting too, but I had my own shit to deal with, and he could wait.

His fingertips pressed my chin upward, and our sad eyes met inches apart.

"What I want you to know, need you to know, is that I care for you deeply. I don't know what label to put on it yet. You have your childhood trauma to deal with, thanks to your dad, and I have mine, thanks to a woman who cheated on me when I was weeks away from marrying her. We are alike, Trudie. We've both had the carpet pulled from underneath us, and the perpetrators didn't seem to care. We are victims of heartache, but trust will be our salvation."

I hiccuped a sigh, and then another. The continued whiplash of our budding relationship was taking its toll on me. I kissed his cheek and pushed against his chest to stand up.

"I want to go back and lie down. Alone."

Alex stood and took my hand, leading me to the edge of the sidewalk and hailing a cab. We rode back to his condo without speaking, though he held my hand and rubbed his thumb across the back of it to comfort me. Moments before we pulled up to his place, his phone buzzed, making him cringe the same way he had at lunch. As much as I wanted to ask who it was, I didn't have the energy.

I excused myself to lie down in his room, removing only my shorts. My need to rest wasn't an invitation for him to join me. I hoped I had made that clear.

"Let me know if you need anything, like some Advil or Tylenol," he offered while poking his head into the room. I shook my head, and he closed the door quietly.

I pressed my head into the down pillow, ignoring all thoughts that tried to break through. I focused on one thing: sleep. Moments later, it arrived.

ALEXANDER

My phone buzzed again. Sheila was being persistent, and I was getting more aggravated by the minute.

Sheila: Alex, please talk to me. We need to fix this. I can't go on without speaking to you.□
Me: Leave a voice mail and I'll consider what you're saying. If I feel like responding, I will.□
Sheila: I just need a few minutes of your time. At least have the decency to give me that.
Me: Decency? That's how you want to play this? Fuck you, Sheila. You're the one without any decency.□

I slammed my phone down on the counter. Who did she think she was, demanding anything from me? A month before our wedding, the one she desperately had to have with no less than five hundred people at the Ritz-Carlton, she decided to have a fling with one of my high school friends. Trudie thought she had trust issues? Ha! I had a high-rise full of them.

The sun was starting to set, and I needed a nap of my own. It was a good thing we didn't have to be at the Waldorf until seven-thirty. I set my phone alarm, tore off my shirt, and grabbed a blanket. I had chosen my sectional sofa for this exact purpose—a comfortable nap—not to fit the design scheme the decorator had insisted on.

Sadly, sleep didn't come so easily. A collage of Trudie's expressions paraded across my mind. Sexy, exhilarated, coy, sweet, awed, sad, desperate, surrendering. They ran the gamut, each one sincere, honest, and pure. I needed to help her find a way through her pain. I knew I wasn't her therapist—friend would be a better title. Hopefully, a good friend. She needed me, and I needed her. We just had to build a bridge of trust to get there. *Maybe I'll just tie her up until she does trust me.* That was the thought that finally brought on sleep.

Buzz. Buzz.

Shit! I jolted upright. I grabbed my phone and turned off the alarm, noticing it was five o'clock. I needed a shower.

I peeked quietly into my bedroom and admired Trudie from where I stood. Her hair was wild around her head on the pillow, her plump lips ached to be kissed, and her breast spilled gently out of her blouse. My hands itched to touch her. We could still fool around while we were building trust, right?

When her sexy leg moved out from under the covers, I crossed the room and ran my hand down it, but she didn't move. Then I ran my fingers over her breasts, lightly flicking her lace-covered nipple. Still no response. She needed to get up and get ready for the gala, so I tried again. I leaned forward and dragged my tongue across the seam of her sweet lips. That, thankfully, got her to open, allowing me to slip my tongue into her hot mouth. She kissed me back in her sleep, and I savored her taste as we swirled our tongues together. She moaned, and I wanted to rip her top off and have my way with her. Too many hours had passed without her mouth on mine, and my hands couldn't wait to roam over her body.

She rolled to her back, eyes still shut, sleep still blanketing her mind. I unbuttoned her blouse and pulled her tits out to suckle them the way she liked it. Her head lolled to one side, and my name slipped from her mouth like a prayer. I thanked God she was thinking about me.

Her arms circled my neck, and she pulled me closer to her chest. Her warmth and vanilla scent was intoxicating. I moved lower down her abdomen, swirling my tongue in her belly button, and then kissing down to the top of her soft thighs. She was very sensitive there, and I took my time so she'd wake up with desire on her mind.

"Oh my God. That feels so good. Alex?" I hoped she didn't think it was someone else.

I lifted my head and climbed back up to her soft, sleepy face. "Yes, baby. It's me." I cupped her face and kissed her deeply again, and she hummed into my open mouth.

I pulled back, giving her a minute to find her senses. "I tried to wake you up, but you were out cold. The only way I could get you up was to, well, seduce you in your sleep." I smiled mischievously.

"Mmm. Yeah, I'm a deep sleeper after a good cry." She ran her fingers through my wavy hair. "That felt good."

"Yeah?" I perked up. "I need to take a shower. Want to join me?"

Her eyes shifted as she weighed her thoughts. "I'd like that, but I don't want you to get confused, Alex. Sex is one thing. A relationship is different." She pushed at my chest and slid her legs off the side of the bed.

I stared at her. "How could I? You won't let me forget." I pushed myself up on to my elbow as I watched my vixen reach behind her back, unsnapping her bra and letting it fall into the puddle of clothes she was making. Damn, she was beautiful. Every fucking curve.

I was hard like a flash. She was already heading for my bathroom, swinging that gorgeous ass in front of me, when she stopped and turned.

"I'm not okay with you yet. You have a long way to go with me, and I'm not sure you're up for the challenge. But I'm not going to waste your efforts to make my body feel good." She pointed her red polished finger at me, then spun on her heel.

My dick was banging on the zipper of my pants, and I needed to set it free. *Now*. In two seconds, I had pulled both my briefs and my pants off and then pulled each sock off as I hopped down the hall after her. I would give my goddess what she commanded if she felt strong enough to set boundaries.

Watching Trudie through the fogged glass, I thought of all the lessons she had let me teach her and the many more that I had planned. She needed me to teach her mind and body to feel strong. I allowed her let go her control on the situation providing absolution of her angst of the past. I knew she was spiraling out of control, and this was a gift I was happy to give her.

After joining her in the shower, I wrapped my hands around her hips as the hot water dripped off our heads to her breasts and then to the floor. We hadn't spent any time together in a shower, and the thought of taking her there was intoxicating.

"Baby. You're so fucking hot. Tell me what you want. Tell me how I can make this good for you." I sucked on her ear, breathing heavily. I wanted to take her hard and fast, but I had promised myself I'd let her lead.

She dropped her head back to my chest, sighing. I seized her mouth, and then let her guide me with her tongue. She always tasted like cinnamon and vanilla, and I couldn't get enough of it. Her hands reached up to pull my hair, and it drove me wild. When she pressed her ass into my cock, my mind exploded. My resolve to let her have her way was holding on by a thread.

"Alex," she hummed. "Fuck me, hard. I want to feel you deep inside me."

Her hands fell away from my head, and reached for the glass tiles in front of her, her ass pressing harder into me.

"Spread your legs," I commanded hoarsely. My obedient vixen opened her legs wider, letting me see her pink hole and her thick folds. I slid a finger into her pussy, gauging how much preparation I needed to do to make her feel good, and was rewarded with slippery wetness.

I wasted no time and pulled on my rock-hard cock several times before I pressed the tip along her crack, letting the anticipation stoke the flame. She moaned and wagged her ass, begging for more, and I pressed into her, hard and fast, just like she wanted.

"Oh, yes. Alex!" She screamed my name, making me feel like a conqueror. She was mine, no matter what she thought. I would make her see me for who I really was, and I would find a way to get past my own shit. I wanted to do that for her and for myself.

"Yes, baby, you feel so good. I want you, Trudie. I need you," I moaned back.

"Harder, Alex. Please." I stepped slightly closer and laid my hand on her back, pressing her down to get a better angle.

"Yes! That! Yes!" she cried. I found my girl's sweet spot and rammed hard and fast until I felt her inner walls clamp down on my cock and squeeze the life out of me.

"Fuck, Trudie. Yes, baby. I'm coming." I arched my back, spurting my cum deep inside my girl. She gave me the best orgasms I'd had in my life. How could I let her go? I'd be an idiot. We stayed connected while we caught our breath, and I caressed her breasts for my own comfort.

She pulled herself back up the wall, and I helped her stand again. I also took the opportunity to run my hands along her ass and up her abdomen.

"You are out of this world," I whispered. "You're so fucking hot."

"Hmm, you rock my world, baby," she said as if she was drunk.

She called me baby. She hadn't done that before. I spun her around and kissed her softly. "We need to actually clean up now. And I know that if I put my hands on you again, we won't be going to a gala tonight," I growled.

She pushed back and snarled at me. "The hell we won't. Do you have any idea what I had to endure picking the perfect dress? You will see this dress, and you will appreciate every inch of it."

"Well, if you're wearing it, I most certainly will." I gave her one of my devilish grins and smacked her ass before grabbing the soap. I was out of the shower two minutes later, planning for an extended version of this shower the next morning.

We chatted while we got ready, and when she slid that emerald dress over her curvy body, I had to adjust my cock. *Damn!*

I spun her around and slowly zipped up her dress, kissing her back as I went.

"You look incredible." I kissed her shoulder again, not being able to keep my mouth off her.

"You look quite dashing yourself. Your tux is custom-made, I presume?" she teased me.

"But of course, sweetheart. The Pierce family can't be seen with the New York City elite in anything less," I said, sarcasm dripping off every word.

She smiled coyly. "I liked how the color of this dress matched your eyes."

"Very thoughtful. I'll have to thank you with my mouth later." I knew I wouldn't be keeping my hands to myself tonight. I didn't want my family to think she was anything but a colleague, but this dress was a game changer. Open in the back down to her hips, and with the front plunging deep between her voluptuous breasts, I'd be fighting off men all night.

We walked toward the door, her evening purse in her hand, her ass in mine. I pulled the invitation off the front table, and we left for the evening.

The Waldorf, in all its glory, was the height of beauty, class, and elitism. It was the source of the famous Waldorf salad and was once the home of the Duke and Duchess of Windsor. My family had claimed they were associated with the Astor family many decades ago and, therefore, should be considered part of the woodwork. Goodness knows they walked around the place like they owned it, and that night was no different.

We waited at the lobby bar, admiring the turn-of-century crystal chandeliers and old mahogany bar polished to perfection. The only indication we were in the twenty-first century was the striped Chambray upholstered fabric on gently curved furniture snuggled close to beveled glass coffee and end tables. Gorgeous bouquets of lilies and roses dotted the room and gave it a homey yet elegant feel.

"Darling, when did you get in? Why didn't you call? You know we had the Partridges for dinner, and their lovely daughter was with them. I would have sat you with her if you hadn't responded that you were coming with a guest." Her affected voice grated on my ears, and her comments were particularly obnoxious, with my date standing right next to me.

"Good to see you, mother. The last time I allowed you to fix me up, she cheated on me. Stay out of my personal life," I said, grinding my molars.

I pressed my hand into Trudie's back and steered her to the other side of the ballroom toward the bar. I hoped she hadn't heard that particular detail of my past, even if it was the key to why I had cold feet about starting another relationship.

Trudie turned her bright hazel eyes to me, and I noticed the flecks of amber tinting the edges.

"What was all that about? And why didn't you introduce me to your mother? That's rude." She crossed her arms in a huff.

Shit! I knew she'd be pissed off. I should have introduced Trudie, even if my mother would have looked down her nose at her. When she had brought up that other girl, I saw red. How dare she put me and my date in that position, like she was discussing paint color? My mother's filters had dissolved as she had gotten older, and sadly, I looked more and more like a patsy standing beside her. I was sick of it.

"Come with me," I said. She begrudgingly let me take her elbow to lead her to an elevator and then up to the first balcony of the ballroom.

Elegant lights created a diffused haze, making it a very romantic setting if you were looking for that. Plush velvet settees dotted the foyer area, and small tables adorned with vases of small roses lined the hallways that looked over the main ballroom floor. I pulled Trudie behind a marble column for some privacy.

"Do you remember the lesson I taught you at lunch today? The people you will be meeting this evening love nothing more than to grab a piece of information and twist it into gossip. I want you to enjoy this evening, not feel inferior because this isn't where you came from. My mother is incredibly shallow. She doesn't mean to be offensive—she's not smart enough to be that calculating. She is, however, capable of making you feel unworthy, and you, my dear, are worth far more than these ridiculous people."

I kissed her until we were both lightheaded. I wouldn't let her be tricked into believing she didn't deserve to be here. To be with me. She looked amazing and had more depth and class than anyone in the room. It still didn't mean they wouldn't try to take that from her. These were vicious people who thought only of themselves, and my parents were no exception.

Her hands cupped my jaw, and she stared intently into my eyes.

"Alexander Pierce, I will never be a wallflower. I can handle myself. Introduce me to your mother, and be proud of us—and of yourself." She pressed her soft lips against mine, and my stress evaporated.

She was right. I couldn't look at her like she was fragile or broken. She could be tough as nails, and I had the marks to prove it.

"Let me introduce you to my family then. Let's start with my sisters. At least with them, you'll have allies." She smiled and took my hand as we walked to the elevator, energized and ready to stand together in solidarity.

Chapter 31

TRUDIE

MY FEELINGS HAD BEEN hurt when Alex didn't introduce me to his mother, though he did have a point about her shoving the idea of a blind date on him. He had warned me his parents were pushy and obnoxious. Still, I wanted to meet them and develop my own impressions. Most people liked me when they first met me, and there wasn't any reason this situation would be different.

Alex kept me close as he steered me around the incredible gilded ballroom. You could see how the recent renovations amplified its original historic beauty. I loved architecture like this. It took me back in time, and if I closed my eyes, I could see the women in their expensive dresses and rare jewels promenading around the ballroom with their mustached husbands in top hats and tails. *I'm quite the romantic.*

Giant palms filled out the corners of the room, and that was where we found a woman with a face suspiciously similar to Alex's, swatting a gorgeous man with dirty blond hair and broad shoulders.

Alex smiled and hugged his sister tightly, whispering something into her ear.

"Don't be an ass, Alex. I'll be nice to your friend." She frowned at him as though he thought her uncouth.

His hand was at my back, ensuring I didn't run away. "Trudie, this is my lovely and vivacious sister, Tabitha. I'm her older brother and, therefore, get to remind her of her manners," he said mockingly.

"It's wonderful to meet you. Alex was very understated in his description of you. You could be twins with how similar you look." I didn't offer a hand to shake or move to hug her, which I'd normally do when I met someone, but Tabitha's eyes were wary and I wasn't feeling the love.

She did, however, turn to her partner, who introduced himself as Rennie. Alex had mentioned that her boyfriend was a florist. That seemed a little odd for her station in life, but they seemed to fit well together.

"We all have a strong familial look," Alex interjected. "You can thank my father for that. Greek origin. That's why we're all olive-skinned and exotic-looking." He slapped his thigh, humoring himself.

"I certainly will," and then turned to his sister. "It's a shame he thinks so little of himself. He should see a psychologist or something." She and Rennie both doubled over laughing.

"Oooh, I like her, Alex. Keep her around." Tabitha patted her brother on the shoulder, and then she and Rennie excused themselves.

One down. Three to go.

I didn't have to wait long before another woman in a floor-length red satin sheath draped herself over Alex's arm. Her black hair was pulled tightly in a chignon with tiny crystal pins surrounding the knot. I couldn't hold a candle to this girl. What a knockout.

"Hey, Alex," she whined. Not exactly the tone for picking up a guy.

He whined back, "Hey, Sarah. Mommy made you look pretty for the big party tonight." He stuck out his bottom lip and looked pathetic.

She pushed him and then grabbed hold of both his shoulders and pulled him in for a big hug, which he didn't resist. I would have been jealous, but I was pretty sure this was another sister.

"Don't be an ass to me, Alex. I had an opportunity to fly to Paris this weekend with a client, and instead, I'm here looking like a herded sheep." Her forehead dropped to his shoulder. It truly looked like she needed consoling, so I gave them a few minutes while I inspected my manicure for flaws.

"Sweetheart, if you had gone to Paris, then you wouldn't have met my dear friend, Trudie. She is just like you: beautiful, funny, and a pain in my ass sometimes." Alex laughed at his patronizing joke. It was nice to see even incredibly rich people who make fun of each other just like every other family.

Sarah straightened and became herself again.

"I'm sorry, Trudie. I'm not usually such a wreck, though I'm sure Alex has told you about all the super fun we have dressing up and making our mother and father look like 'Parents of the Year.'"

I didn't feel a need to feign ignorance. "It's a pleasure to meet you, Sarah. I've heard many wonderful things about you, and yes, I can appreciate parents who see their children like they see their stock portfolio. One day, you're an asset, and the next, you're a liability." I looked at Alex, and he smiled all the way to his eyes.

Sarah's mouth dropped open, and she reached out to wrap me in a tight hug.

"Oh my God! You get it. You said that so well. Didn't she, Alex?" She stepped back, assessing me again. "Do not fuck this up, Alex. I like her." Without giving him a second look, she walked away, snagging a champagne flute off a silver tray. I grabbed one, too, feeling like I had dodged another bullet and it was time to celebrate.

A strong arm circled around me as Alex pressed his chest into my back. His breath was warm, and his smell was intoxicating. I'd never appreciated fresh clothes before, but now I was a big fan.

His voice was husky, and I knew what that meant. He wanted to play. I wanted to play, too, except we had a long way to go this evening and needed to stay focused. For Alex's sake as well as my own.

"You are either a genius or a witch. Whichever you are, you have ensnared my sisters. Not even my ex-fiancée could do that." *Ugh. Why does he have to mention her?*

I stiffened. Her name came up often, and my curiosity continued to grow. There was much more to this story, and one day soon, I would hear it. Our relationship would never bloom until we came clean about everything. I had told him almost everything about my father, yet he hadn't offered up much of anything about this Sheila woman. As soon as we got back to Michigan, he was going to come clean.

"I choose witch." I smiled up at his angled face. His jaw twitched, and he bent down to capture my upper lip.

"Why witch, baby?" He poked my side, making me laugh, and I swatted his hand away while he ignored my attempts at freedom.

"Because I like to think that I put a spell on you, one that turned you from a pompous asshole to my knight in shining armor. You can save me from myself. I didn't know I needed it."

He abruptly turned me around. His eyes had turned obsidian, and his breath was short. I'd poked the beast, though I didn't know what I'd said.

"I think you have this all wrong, Trudie. I'm not saving you; you're saving me. Tonight only happened because of you. I wouldn't be here if you said you weren't coming."

He pulled me close. His tone seemed desperate. "I'm done dealing with my parents' shit. I'm only here because they agreed to let me bring a date, and you said yes. I knew you'd be great company, as well as a buffer between me and my parents, and you have stood on your own two feet since we got here. I'm so proud of you."

I didn't know what to think. "Really?" I said with raised eyebrows.

He smiled a big toothy smile. "Really. I know we are still figuring out who we are to one another, but nevertheless, we are together. Whether it's boyfriend and girlfriend, or partners, or whatever, I want you to know that you've changed me—for the better. Just give us more time to figure out who we are to each other. Please don't run from me again. It physically hurts me."

Holy shit! What a confession.

I pulled at his lapels and pressed all the black studs that I could see down his crisp white tuxedo shirt before answering shyly. "I'll try. I want to see where this goes. Just keep communicating with me. I don't like to be shut down."

He kissed me again—long and hard—long enough that several guests started looking at us. We came up for air, realizing we looked like we needed a room.

"Deal. Now, let's get out of here for a while." I lurched forward as he pulled me behind him, marching out of the ballroom and back into the elevator. This time, we made it to the third terrace that circled the ballroom.

He didn't look at or speak to me as he dragged me down a hallway to the right of the elevators. He stopped in front of a gallery that had the most gorgeous burl wood piano but then shook his head and walked back the other way. He found another beautifully lit room with a humongous model of the hotel surrounded by several benches. After spinning me into his arms, he kissed me like he would devour me. My hands reached up to his thick, wavy hair, and when he palmed my breast, I moaned his name into his mouth.

"Remember your lesson about being quiet?" His commanding voice sent shockwaves to my core.

"Ye-s. Alex, what are you going to do?" I was out of breath, and my chest heaved.

"What I've wanted to do all afternoon—only you thought having a meltdown was a better use of our time together," he growled, still irritated that he hadn't had the upper hand this afternoon.

"Sit on that bench and open your legs as wide as that slit will allow." Once I did, he pushed me back, laying me down on the freezing-cold marble bench.

I puffed out my air as the cold blanketed my bare back. Talk about not screaming.

He spread me out, admiring me, and I felt my juices pooling in my satin panties. He was a predator, and he had snared me again. When he looked at me like that, all I wanted to do was submit and learn another naughty lesson.

"That dress has had me hard since you let me zip it up. And now I want to rip it to shreds and fuck you hard and fast." He pulled at his belt buckle, savoring the moment.

I pressed up onto my elbows, concerned. "You better not rip this dress. It's rented and has to be returned on Monday!" I gave him my fiercest warrior princess look.

"Calm down, sweetheart. You still have to walk out of here tonight. Lean back," he ordered and then yanked my panties down and flung them somewhere in the huge room.

I waited. Whatever he planned included me being on display for anyone who walked into the gallery. I wasn't sure if that excited me or freaked me out.

He knelt between my legs, nipping at my inner thighs, teasing me right to my apex, and then fading back down to my knees again.

I moaned as quietly as I could. "Alex. Please." He grabbed both my thighs, pulled me to the end of the bench, and smacked my pussy before he flattened his tongue, licking me completely from hole to hood, electrifying my whole body.

"Christ! What the hell? I can't keep quiet when you do shit like that," I hissed.

"Well, then, don't fucking run away from me again. You will learn to stay and talk through your anxieties, or I'll smack your ass red next time." I couldn't respond to him, flicking my clit over and over again.

"God! You taste so good." He came up for air and dove back down on me. I was so close. All he had to do was suck me just a little bit more.

He stood up to take his pocket square out of his tux and wiped his face. Then he grabbed his crotch and stared into my eyes with a lust I couldn't describe. The ratcheting sound of his zipper alerted me to the fact that he was preparing to fuck me on the bench. We'd been going at it for almost ten minutes, and I could feel our time was running out. I wanted him so badly, but he had to be fast.

"What the hell, Alex? I was almost ready to come." My pussy ached for him to finish what he started.

"You turn me into an animal. Bring your knees up and keep them there. This is going to be quick." He pulled out his cock and dragged the velvety head down my pussy and back up again. His pre-cum and my juices mixed, making me very hot and even wetter. When he finally pushed into me, I was delirious. He smothered my mouth with his, capturing every moan and plea coming from my throat. Seeing his body hovering over mine brought me closer to my release, and when he drilled his length into me, I flew over the edge at the same time that he grunted his release. To come at the same time was new to me, and I knew at that moment that we could go all the way in this relationship if only we could find some honesty.

"Fuck, Trudie. I couldn't hold back." His strength waned, and he fell on me to catch his breath.

"My God, Alex. You are a wicked man," I giggled.

"I am your god. Don't forget it." He kissed me again quickly and pressed his hands on either side of the bench, lifting himself like he was doing push-ups.

Voices echoed down the hall, and I shoved Alex off me so I could sit up and straighten myself.

"Where the hell did you throw my panties?" I began running around the room, looking for them, when I spotted the hotel model. My panties were swinging from one of the towers, with a blue uplight highlighting the pale pink satin. "Found them!" I yelled and then whispered, "Oops," fixing my decibel level.

The click of heels was added to the voices, and we knew we only had a few seconds to get our act together. Alex wrapped his arm around my waist and walked me down the hall, past a few milling couples, and over to the restrooms.

"You have three minutes. Dinner will start soon, and the presentation will begin after the salad course." He smacked my ass as I went into the bathroom. "Don't make me come after you."

I laughed indignantly and then cooed, "Yes, Daddy." I ran the last couple of steps to a stall. I wouldn't put it past him to walk in here and throw me over his knee.

Alex and I stopped at the bar for another drink, and while we waited, he pointed out several stuffy-looking people who were the bigwigs among the New York elite. He felt it was important I knew a few bits of trivia about each so I wouldn't feel uncomfortable if I met them.

And speaking of uncomfortable, Alex suddenly yanked me in front of him, presumably not so much for intimacy—more like for a shield. I felt his breath at my ear and heard his molars grinding again. "Here comes my dad, say as little as possible for your safety." *My safety?*

His father wore a tux almost as well as Alex. He was a real silver fox with broad shoulders and flawless skin. He carried a crystal highball filled with amber liquid and a diamond pinky ring that screamed the 1980s.

"Son. I'm thrilled you could make it," his dad said drolly.

Alex smirked. "Like I had a choice."

Come now, Alex. We are your family. We stand together—always. The board needs to see us united and strong. I built this foundation. I'm not about to hand it off to some nimrod to run into the ground." His monologue sounded passionate, but Alex's expression said otherwise.

Alex scrubbed his face and then pulled me to his side. "About that, Dad. For my participation in tonight's charade, I'm asking for a $50,000 donation to the middle school I've been hired to consult for. I'll tell you more about it later—just plan to cut the check next week."

What? "Alex." I tugged at his pocket.

"Fine," his dad grunted, taking a sip of his cocktail.

Alex gave me a pointed look—apparently, I was supposed to stay quiet.

"Father, Maxim, this is my date—and girlfriend, Trudie." He grinned.

"A pleasure, dear. How long have you known Alex?" He was probing, and I couldn't blame him. I was still reeling from Alex's declaration of me being his girlfriend. *When did that happen?*

I gave him the most genuine smile I could muster. "We met this summer in San Francisco. We found each other on a sunset cruise, and, well, the rest is history." I grabbed Alex's elbow and looked up into his adoring face. I had romanticized our meeting for his father's sake, but he liked my answer, and his eyes beamed.

Even his dad seemed pleased. "Isn't that lovely? I hope you two will be very happy." He nodded his head and then gave Alex a stern look. "Ten minutes after the salad is served, meet me to the left of the stage. Be prepared to field some questions as well."

Maxim was done playing the interested father and walked off quickly to meet his wife at their table. Bell tones sounded, and everyone found their seats.

The table was exquisite. Gold-filigree porcelain dishes sat on white organza linens with gold gossamer threading that made florets in the material. It almost looked like a work of art, and I was afraid if anything fell off my plate, it would be ruined.

I took advantage of the empty seat next to me to set down my purse. Alex sat to my left and pulled my chair closer to his, forcing me to move my whole place setting. My annoyed look must have irritated him because he grabbed my knee and opened my legs wider. *Didn't he get enough of me upstairs?*

The people we sat with weren't the oldest—one couple claimed to be longtime friends of Alex's parents, though he didn't seem to recognize them. There were a couple who had flown in from Toronto and someone who had worked in some government position in the city. It started to make more sense why we were sitting with these people and not Alex's sisters. After a few strategic questions, Alex was able to flush out their reasons for attending the gala: they were potential donors and more than likely, Alex's father wanted them babysat.

Fake smiles and polite manners were the evening's fare, and so far, I'd managed to hold my own. When the salad course arrived, Alex stood to take his place with his family like clockwork.

"I'll be back soon. Keep being your fabulous self." He kissed my cheek and left.

I wanted to call him my man, but then again, we weren't anywhere near that point. Even though he introduced me as his girlfriend to his father, I knew it had been just a pretense. But I loved watching him up there. He looked beautiful and formidable, standing next to his sisters. His mother was coiffed to the nines, and God knew how much that gown she was wearing cost. My rental dress was awesome, but I had only paid for a piece of it, not the whole thing. I doubted I could ever fit in with this kind of wealth. It felt foreign and uncomfortable. I'd much prefer a backyard barbecue.

The presentation began, and since much of what was being said wasn't relevant to me, I spent my time people-watching and gauging the dynamics between Alex and each of his family members. They had this facade worked out perfectly. A parent would speak, and the children would radiate love and appreciation for such terrific and honorable parents while chewing on the insides of their cheeks. Didn't anyone else see how canned this all was?

Maxim stepped forward and introduced himself as the founder and president of the Foundation for Educational Excellence. He recited the mission statement and all sorts of mildly interesting factoids that should have put everyone asleep, except these were elite members of society, and yawning would be gauche. Giant checks were presented to the educational organizations the foundation supported, and thunderous applause rang throughout the ballroom.

The chair next to me moved, and I looked up to see a tall, slender woman with raven-black hair wearing a white sheath gown with a slit that traveled a little too high for modesty.

"Is this seat taken?" she purred.

"Ah, no. Please." I picked up my purse and motioned for her to take a seat.

"Thank you," she replied in a haughty tone. I watched as she surveyed the other couples at the table. She smiled and nodded her head, not seeming to recognize anyone. Next, she turned and gave me the once-over.

"Hmm," she murmured, "I don't think we've met." She avoided making direct eye contact with me, making it clear I wasn't worth her time, but good manners required her to be polite.

I looked up at the stage and saw Alex clenching his fists and staring at our table. His smile faded as his olive skin paled to white. What was wrong? I hadn't been paying attention to what was being said for the past few minutes, so I couldn't piece things together. Maxim was wrapping up, and I hoped Alex could get back to the table quickly. I didn't like the vibe this woman was giving off.

Above all else, I, too, was polite. I was representing us as a couple, and so far, I was 3-0 with his family. Putting my best foot forward, I replied to her inquiry.

"Hello. I'm Trudie, a friend of Alex Pierce." The disturbing smile she gave me sent chills down my back. She reeked of toxicity, and I didn't want to sit here any longer.

"Really?" she snarled. I didn't like her tone.

Turning in my seat to face this bitchy woman, I gave her a hard look myself.

"And you are?" I asked, challenging her unsettling comment.

"Sheila Lancaster. Alex's fiancée," she declared.

"I think you mean ex-fiancée," I retorted. "You broke up three years ago."

"Did Alex say that?" she asked and then chuckled. "And you believed him? We were on a break."

"Three years isn't a break."

"Call it what you will. You will never fit into his family. He and I share a long and deep past that you'd need a lifetime to understand. He is still mine." She bared her teeth like a feral cat, and I couldn't stand to sit there for one more minute. She was right about one thing, though—I didn't fit in with these pretentious people. It was time to leave.

I stood up as regally as possible, looked over at Alex again, and walked out of the room as quickly as possible. I saw him dash off the stage out of the corner of my eye, but I wasn't waiting for him or his lies. I needed to find a door out of this nightmare.

"Please call me a cab immediately. It's urgent," I implored the doorman.

Five seconds later, I was sliding into a yellow cab and saw Alex rushing out the Waldorf's sliding glass doors and running down the stairs, anger staining his face.

"Drive!" I barked at the cab driver.

I wasn't sticking around to have a conversation with Alex. He'd lied to me. He told me his engagement was over, but clearly, what he hadn't told me was that she wasn't out of his life. I wanted to believe every word he said. He promised to tell me about her, but even a simple explanation would have sufficed. Devastation rolled over my body, making me numb. He may not have been my father, but he sure acted like him—making promises he would never keep.

"Take me to the airport," I begged the driver.

I had to get away. Being with Alex was too much of a long shot, and after that evening, my nervous system couldn't handle another day with him. We were over.

The End... For Now

Wait! The conclusion to this story is in
Book #3 of the Perfect Series, Making Perfect Sense.

Thank you for reading *The Perfect Lessons*.
I hope you enjoyed reading it as much as I enjoyed writing it.

If you loved it, please consider leaving me a review on Amazon. It would mean the world to me!

https://www.amazon.com/review/create-review/?channel=glance
-detail&ie=UTF8&asin=B0BSWQV74S

ABOUT THE AUTHOR

Tʜᴇ sᴀssʏ Bᴇᴛʜ Gᴇʟᴍᴀɴ is a professional pianist and vocalist who loves being a steamy romance author. Authentic, resilient, loyal, and spiritual, she's not afraid to learn, fail, speak her mind, or try new things. She loves writing romances, especially romances that make her readers grow and appreciate their strengths and weaknesses. She loves her devoted husband, children, lattes, yoga, and every dog on the planet. Learn more at www.BethGelman.com.

YOUR OPINION MATTERS TO ME!

I would love to hear what you thought about

The Perfect Lessons at:

Amazon.com/dp/B0B3W4YMRF

GoodReads.com, Bookbub.com, and Barnesandnoble.com

You can also follow me on:

Facebook: Beth Gelman's Insatiable Readers

Instagram: BethGelmanWrites

Sign up for my Newsletter at BethGelmanWrites@gmail.com for fun, freebies, and more!

ACKNOWLEDGEMENTS

Please give a round of applause to the following instrumental people who make up my village:

Always to Daryl—my man behind the curtain who makes all I do possible. You complete me.

To Pam, Hillary, and my editor, Megan – Thank God you have magical eyes to catch every grammar mistake and every timeline mishap and generally make my work the best it can be. You're the best. (I like the smile emoji the best.)

To the many writing platforms that continue to educate me –The Self-Publishing Formula, RSJ Convention, 20Booksto50K, Wandering Words Media, Written Words Media, and Kindlepreneur.com.

To Kim Sakwa—who continues to offer her support and insights into writing and marketing.

To Shira— for the Rest and Return area in her classroom. Brilliant!

To Nora—who reminds me to stand up every hour to let her out and stretch.

To Everyone else—thank you from the bottom of my heart for letting me talk about the writing process, encouraging me, lifting my spirits, and cheering me on to the finish line.

SNEEK PEAK: Making Perfect Sense

Book #3 The Conclusion of The Perfect Lessons

CHAPTER 1 – TRUDIE

"Thank you for coming over so soon, *cariño*. I'm sorry this couldn't wait." My mom hugged me and pressed my hair down after I removed my knit cap. It was the beginning of October, and mornings were already dipping into the fifties.

"I'm not going to lie, Mom. When you called about Dad, I almost told you to tell him to go to hell. Why does his health need to concern me? He never cared about my health or anyone's health in this family. Besides, where has he been for the past fifteen years? Calculating weather damage that giant conglomerates create with pollution and chemical spills?"

I didn't expect any answers to the questions I fired at my mother. She was as affected as we all were. My daddy issues weren't the typical abuse stuff you hear on podcasts and *Dateline*-type shows. Mine were of the neglected genre of abuses. The "all promises and no follow-through" kind. Hello today, goodbye in ten minutes.

After thousands of dollars of therapy, I'd discovered that leaving wasn't the biggest problem I had to deal with, it was the reentry into our family unit that caused all my issues.

"What am I expected to do now? And where are my brothers? Aren't they part of this 'happy family' equation?"

My shoes were off, and I marched into the kitchen, looking for coffee during my tirade. My mom fell in tow, letting me have my rant. She'd learned that the only way to get me to listen was to let me have diarrhea of the mouth first.

I dumped several large dollops of my favorite chemical creamer into a giant mug that I'd bought off Etsy for my mom on Mother's Day when I was fifteen. It said, "Happy Mother's Day, Mom. Keep That Shit Up!" Best mug ever. It was a toss-up between that and "I'd walk through fire for you, Mom. Well, not fire. That would be dangerous. But a super humid room. Okay, not too humid, because you know ... my hair." Those Etsy sayings get me every time.

"Cariño, sweetheart, listen to me. You have to do some things in life, and this is one of them. Your father needs all of us to help him. He has cancer. From asbestos. From all those buildings he had to go into that were filled with toxic smoke and materials. He has no one else to help him, and I hoped, prayed even, that you'd find it in your heart to ease his suffering by spending what little time he has left with him. Think of it as an opportunity to put your mind at rest and give a stubborn old man some peace. Please, Mija, he needs you. I need my children to find peace with their father. He had his finer moments and his charms."

I hated it when she turned on the puppy dog eyes and pleading hands. It was my kryptonite. I flopped onto one of the kitchen chairs, my eyes closed in frustration. I hated having to be the one that always had to travel the high road. Why did I have to abide by a higher moral compass than everyone else? It exhausted me. I fell forward over the table, rubbing my eyes with the heels of my hands, grappling with my feelings and the reality of what happened to me as a child vs. what it meant to me as an adult. I guess my therapy was working.

"Fine. I'll take the fucking high road—again!" I screamed my anger and helplessness into the universe. I suppose I could have walked away from this situation. But even if I had, it would have haunted me like the rest of the crap inflicted on my life. I was tired of carrying these emotions. Tired of thinking my rightness was the most essential thing to me. It wasn't. I needed to put this down. I was enough. I wouldn't be the one left with regret when he died. No way!

My mom and I didn't say anything else. She came to her knees in front of me and grabbed my hands as if we were both in prayer. Our foreheads touched, and we drew energy from each other to find homeostasis. I was doing this as much for her as for myself. Whatever my father thought would happen from our meeting, he was going to have to be the bigger person to have a breakthrough.

I spent the rest of the afternoon helping my mom organize her new library, a.k.a. my old bedroom. I dropped several books on her counter every month, so by then, she needed the Dewey decimal system for her collection. We also moved her knitting materials into the room, along with a comfortable chair that was collecting clothes in her bedroom and a reading light extracted from the basement. Now that she had her indoor she-shed setup, I yawned and dragged myself to the front door to leave.

"Hey, Mom! I'm going now." I pulled on my coat and stuffed my hat in my pocket. She came running over to give me a hug and a sack full of her Mexican wedding cookies. My favorite. "You're the best." I kissed her and mumbled, a cookie in my mouth, "Text me where to find him."

"Thank you, baby. You're a class act." Her sweet smile got me right where it counted.

I mumbled under my breath as I walked down the front steps, "All the praise in the world isn't going to make this any better for me." let out a huge sigh after I started my car. This Sunday Funday hadn't been fun at all. Neither would the rest of my Sundays as long as he was alive.

It was seven o'clock when I realized I still had my phone off. I didn't want to hear from or look at Alex ever again. I didn't care that I sounded like a petulant teenager. That's how I felt. I had all the bad feels: anger, frustration, betrayal, and mostly embarrassment. I burrowed my butt into a nest made of blankets and a scarf. I wrapped my head and barricaded myself before turning on the phone, then waited for all the beeps and pings to stop. Most of them were from Alex.

Where are you?

Why won't you pick up?

What did she say to you?

These were all good questions—I was still deciding whether to respond to any of them. Then his tone changed. Dr. Alexander Pierce, the king of psychology and my personal sex education teacher, was now threatening me.

You need to speak with me... NOW!

Ooh. Shouty. Not answering that one.

Damn it, Trudie. You're going to feel stupid when you hear the whole story.

Will I?

And my not-so-favorite: *"You're acting like a child. Grow a pair and call me."*

Then there was the frustrated father's text. That one made me a little moist.

Ugh! I was too tired to deal with this. It had been almost twenty-four hours since I ran away from that lying sack of shit, Dr. Alexander Pierce. All I wanted to do was rewind time to the trip I took to California this past summer. I had wanted an adventure. One that included a hot sexy guy with great lips, knowing hands, and a dick that knew how to please me. No more vanilla sex. That's all I wanted. And, of course, the real reason I had traveled was my psychology conference. Suddenly, I wondered what Jared, the hot guy I met on the plane, was up to. He checked all the boxes—minus the dick—which I didn't have the opportunity to test drive. *Hmm.*

I needed to get ahead preparing for this week and went to my tiny kitchen to pack lunch for tomorrow and start some laundry.

Girl's gotta have clean panties. Realization hit that I had left my luggage in New York and should probably figure out how to get it back when the banging on my front door startled me. *Crap!* I was pretty sure I knew who it was, but I wasn't sure I wanted to answer the door. What if he broke up with me? Were we even together? He was always intimidating me and leaving me confused. Was Alex my peer? Or client? A teacher or mentor? My lover or my boyfriend? I was so confused.

Shucking all the self-doubt from my mind, I walked to the door, opened it, then walked away. I knew he'd barge in and scream at me about how childish it was of me to run away and that I should have trusted him to explain everything. He might be right about that, though it still didn't excuse what he did. He hid a very important piece of his past from me. He knew there was a high probability I'd run into his ex at the foundation gala his family hosted, yet he had said nothing.

There weren't too many places to hide in my tiny apartment, so I returned to the spot that brought me the most comfort—my couch nest. I waited for Alex to begin, but he didn't. I tilted my chin up, looked over my shoulder toward the front door, and found it empty. The only thing in my doorway was my luggage and my purse. My heart stopped. I knew in that instant not only had I hurt him terribly, but I'd also hurt myself irrevocably as well.

Click on the below link to finish Trudie and Alex's epic love story:

www.amazon.com/dp/B0BSFX6JX7